Ornam

5

1940 – 1960

Chris Fogg is a creative producer, writer, director and dramaturg, who has written and directed for the theatre for many years, as well as collaborating artistically with choreographers and contemporary dance companies.

Ornaments of Grace is a chronicle of ten novels. *Return* is the fifth in the sequence.

He has previously written more than thirty works for the stage as well as four collections of poems, stories and essays. These are: *Special Relationships, Northern Songs, Painting by Numbers* and *Dawn Chorus* (with woodcut illustrations by Chris Waters), all published by Mudlark Press.

Several of Chris's poems have appeared in International Psychoanalysis (IP), a US online journal, as well as *in Climate of Opinion*, a selection of verse in response to the work of Sigmund Freud edited by Irene Willis, published by IP in 2017.

Ornaments of Grace

(or *Unhistoric Acts*)

5

Tulip

Vol. 4: Return

by

Chris Fogg

flax**books**

First published 2020
© Chris Fogg 2020

Chris Fogg has asserted his rights under Copyright Designs & Patents Act 1988 to be identified as the author of this book

ISBN Number: 9781699782675

Cover and design by: Kama Glover

Cover Image: The Proclamation Regarding Weights & Measures, one of the Manchester Murals by Ford Madox Brown, reprinted by kind permission of Manchester Libraries, Information & Archives.

This book is sold subject to the condition that it shall not, by way of trade or otherwise be lent, resold, hired out, or otherwise circulated without the publisher's prior consent in any form of binding or cover other than that in which it is published and without a similar condition, including this condition, being imposed upon the subsequent purchaser.

Printed in Poland by Amazon

Although some of the people featured in this book are real, and several of the events depicted actually happened, *Ornaments of Grace* remains a work of fiction.

For Amanda and Tim

dedicated to the memory

of my parents and grandparents

Ornaments of Grace (or *Unhistoric Acts*) is a sequence of ten novels set in Manchester between 1760 and 2020 Collectively they tell the story of a city in four elements.

Return is the fifth book in the sequence.

The full list of titles is:

1. Pomona (Water)

2. Tulip (Earth)
    Vol 1: Enclave
    Vol 2: Nymphs & Shepherds
    Vol 3: The Spindle Tree
    Vol 4: Return

3. Laurel (Air)
    Vol 1: Kettle
    Vol 2: Victor
    Vol 3: Victrix
    Vol 4: Scuttle

4. Moth (Fire)

Each book can be read independently or as part of the sequence.

"It's always too soon to go home. And it's always too soon to calculate effect... Cause-and-effect assumes that history marches forward, but history is not an army. It is a crab scuttling sideways, a drip of soft water wearing away stone, an earthquake breaking centuries of tension."

Rebecca Solnit: Hope in the Dark
(Untold Histories, Wild Possibilities)

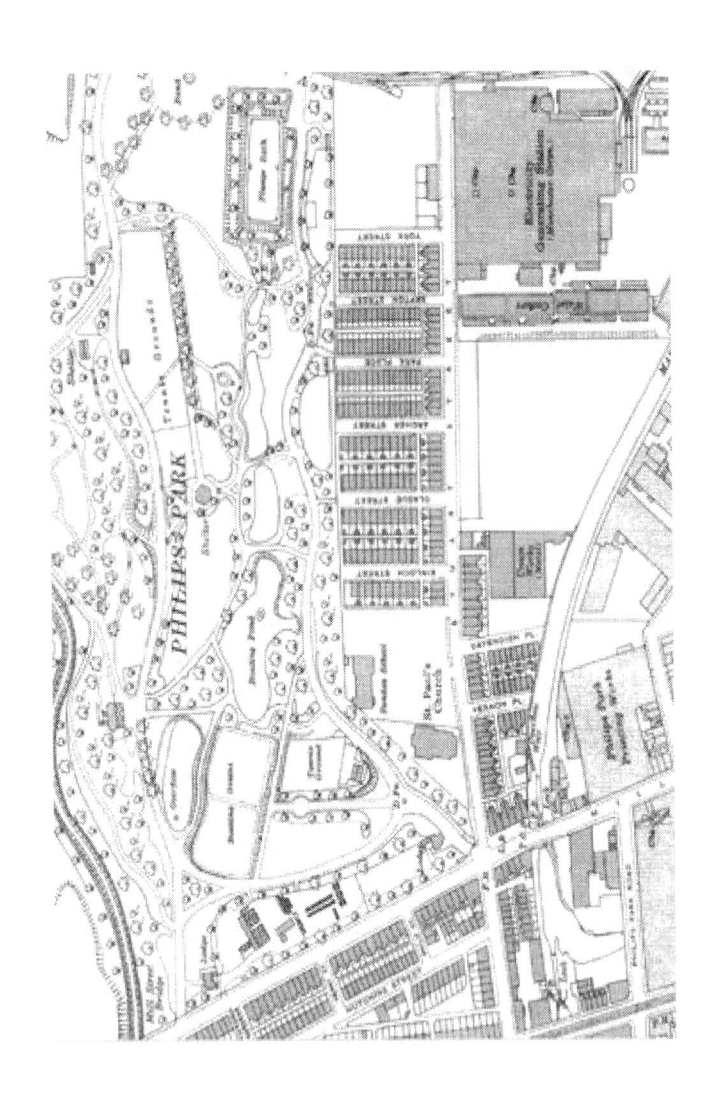

Philips Park

Contents

ONE

Three Christmases

Chapter 1:	Christmas 1940	17
Chapter 2:	Christmas 1944	130
Chapter 3:	Christmas 1948	188

TWO

On The Shoulders of Giants

Chapter 4:	March 1953	318
Chapter 5:	October 1953	368

THREE

The Photograph

Chapter 6:	8th May 1960	379

Map	10
Dramatis Personae	459
Acknowledgements	468
Biography	471

Ornaments of Grace

"Wisdom is the principal thing. Therefore get wisdom and within all thy getting get understanding. Exalt her and she shall promote thee. She shall bring thee to honour when thou dost embrace her. She shall give to thine head an ornament of grace. A crown of glory shall she deliver to thee."

Proverbs: 4, verses 7 – 9

written around the domed ceiling of the Great Hall Reading Room
Central Reference Library, St Peter's Square, Manchester

"Fecisti patriam diversis de gentibus unam…"
"From differing peoples you have made one homeland…"

Rutilius Claudius Namatianus:
De Redito Suo, verse 63

"To be hopeful in bad times is not just foolishly romantic. It is based on the fact that human history is a history not only of cruelty, but also of compassion, sacrifice, courage, kindness. What we choose to emphasise in this complex history will determine our lives. If we see only the worst, it destroys our capacity to do something. If we remember those times and places—and there are so many—where people have behaved magnificently, this gives us the energy to act, and at least the possibility of sending this spinning top of a world in a different direction. And if we do act, in however small a way, we don't have to wait for some grand utopian future. The future is an infinite succession of presents, and to live now as we think human beings should live, in defiance of all that is bad around us, is itself a marvellous victory."

Howard Zinn: A Power Governments Cannot Suppress

Tulip (iv)

*"What triumph crowds the rich divan today
With turbaned heads of every hue and race,
Bowing before that veiled and awful face,
Like tulip beds of different shape and dyes
Bending beneath th'invisible west wind's sighs…"*

Thomas Moore: Lalla Rookh

Earth (iv)

"Show me heaven's pathways, the stars, the sun's many lapses, the moon's many labours; whence come tremblings of the earth…"

Virgil: Georgics, Book 2

"I must essay a path whereby I, too, may rise from earth and fly victorious…"

Virgil, Georgics: Book 3

ONE

Three Christmases

1

Christmas 1940

"This is Germany calling, Germany calling, direct from the Reichssender Station, Hamburg. This is Germany calling. Do you English really believe you can defeat the superior German forces? Haw, haw! This afternoon the pasty-faced housewives of Manchester, who never see the light of day because of the thick, polluted smog created by her antiquated industries, have been scurrying through the city's grimy streets like rats in a sewer to purchase scrawny chickens for their Christmas dinner tables. But you will not be eating them any time soon, ladies, for these chickens are going to be cooked by the flames from the devastation and ruin heaped upon you by the Mighty Luftwaffe tonight – yes, tonight, do you hear? – after which you will be begging your weak and powerless government to seek surrender from our most merciful Führer for the greater glory of the undefeatable Third Reich. Heil, Hitler! This is Germany calling, Germany calling. Haw, haw…"

Francis tuned away from the braying William Joyce, replacing him with the deep, reassuring warmth of Alvar Lidell.

"Good evening. This is the BBC Home Service, Sunday 22nd December 1940. It is now time for the nightly nine o'clock news, with me, Alvar Lidell, reading

it. We are just receiving reports of a series of major air attacks in the North-West, concentrating on the cities of Manchester and Salford, including the neighbouring towns of Stretford, Hulme and Stockport, with particularly heavy bombing on the factories of Trafford Park and the Royal Pomona Docks. All church services have been cancelled and people are advised to remain in their shelters until the all-clear sounds."

Eight hours later, just before five in the morning, an exhausted Jabez cycled back to Philips Park from Piccadilly where, for the past twelve hours, he had been manning the pumps.

At the outbreak of the War he had enrolled as a volunteer fire fighter and now, after the months of nerve-shredding waiting, his training had been put unsparingly to the test. It had been more than twenty-two years since he had last encountered the sights and sounds of warfare, during the final weeks of the last war, when he had witnessed its dying throes on the plains of Northern Italy. In his first few months back, he'd been nightly disturbed by dreams of those horses he had set free while cannon fire resounded around the Dolomites. Gradually those nightmares had subsided, but tonight they had returned with a ferocity even greater, for this had been no dream. Some of the things he had seen and heard would, he knew, stay with him a long time, probably for ever – buildings engulfed in flames and crashing to the earth, railway viaducts collapsing like packs of cards, the ground heaving and convulsing as yet more bombs fell, the panicked screams of people trapped beneath mountains of masonry and glass, the dismembered bits of bodies he stumbled over as they tried to keep the fires under control. While it was happening, they had all been simply too busy with their various much practised drills and routines to take in the full horror of it all. Now, as he cycled home, he could feel his body trembling with the aftershock so violently that he found it hard to keep control of his bicycle as he rode through the dark, unlit streets in the blackout, trying to avoid the pits and pot holes as showers of ash still rained down. His ears rang from the pounding of the bombs despite the raid having ended more than an hour ago, and in that ringing he heard the terrified whinny of a horse trapped in a bricked up builder's yard desperately trying to kick its way out as the smoke and flames engulfed it.

When Jabez finally reached the cobbles of Mill Street, he was forced to climb down from his bicycle, which unsurprisingly had a puncture, and wheel it alongside the railings by the park's edge, feeling his way in the near impenetrable dark at the fag end of what had been a seemingly endless night. His feet hurt. More precisely, the big toe on his left foot was throbbing so strongly that Jabez wondered if perhaps he'd broken it. He had no recollection how or when.

His mind played over the events he had witnessed while he counted them off, one by one, as he ran his hand along each railing in turn…

The first of the incendiary bombs had landed in Albert Square just before seven o'clock, opposite the Princess Street corner from the Town Hall.

A building on Clarence Street was set ablaze, and that

was when he was first called out, with instructions to carry the station's hand pump from their local muster point, right across the city if need be.

A few minutes later a second incendiary struck the corner of Bridgewater Street and Chepstow Street, landing directly on the roof of an air-raid shelter, but local street wardens were able to deal with this before it caught fire.

He could see flames leaping out of the top of the Royal Exchange building. High explosives had destroyed more than half the floor.

The Victoria Buildings near Manchester Cathedral were now alight.

The gas main at Hailwood's Creamery in St Mary's Gate was gushing fire.

Jabez had to make his way round this firestorm as more crew were diverted to the Victoria Buildings. When he eventually got there, two incendiaries had been put out, but a third, roaring out of an awkward corner of the roof, was proving unreachable. Part of the buildings had collapsed into Deansgate, the debris blocking their way from Blackfriars Street, where the *Manchester School of Modern Painters* once stood with it first floor gallery, now reduced to rubble, towards Victoria Bridge, which was nothing but a heaped tangle of collapsed overhead tram wires and smashed concrete, forcing them to make a wide detour along Chapel Street, back over the River Irwell across the New Bailey Bridge, which was threatening to collapse beneath them with every step, before passing through a curtain of fire as they fought their way back up Deansgate from the south.

While climbing one of the eighty-five foot turntable ladders, Jabez was showered by more falling rubble as the Victoria Buildings were struck by a second high explosive bomb, including a large coping stone, which glanced off his left foot.

At the far end of Deansgate a third high explosive bomb, falling on the corner of Great Jackson Street with the City Road, effectively trapped the fire crews, with each end of Deansgate now closed off by mountains of debris.

The blast blew out all telephone lines and cut the electricity supplies. The city was thrown back into primeval darkness, as the earth quaked under the hail of falling bombs, the people's faces licked by the lurid red glow of flames...

*

Bron feels the ground shift beneath her, a distant drumming of marching feet and horses' hooves coming up through the earth. She's wide awake. She's always slept lightly but after she saw the lynx she knew she had to stay alert, on her toes, ready to warn the others. It was an omen. Something was coming. Something big. She doesn't know what and she doesn't know when. All she knows is that, as surely as the moon waxes and wanes each month, come it will. She's kept watch through the dark of each night since.

Pard stirs a few feet away, the boy she was carrying the night the big cat disappeared. That was a dozen years ago. He's grown lean and tall in that time. Tries to arm wrestle Cuinn, who lets him beat him sometimes. Is already better with a bow. But not with a sword. There's been another child since. Wem. A sister for Cora. The two of them lie curled together by the fire. Dru lies beached beside her. His breathing sounds laboured. As it does most nights. His body's grown thicker round the waist. He's not the soldier or the hunter he once was. But still as strong as a bear. And just as bad-tempered if crossed or disturbed. As anyone bold enough, or fool enough, to try to challenge him quickly finds out. When he and Cuinn butt heads, which they do from time to time, Dru will cuff him aside.

But not for much longer, Bron thinks.

She worries that he won't be strong enough when the time comes. Which she knows it will. Maybe tonight. She feels the earth give another shift and shake. Feels the rumble of thunder from below. It's getting closer.

The air trembles. She wraps a blanket round her like a cloak. One she stitched herself from cow hides and horse hair, it forms a second skin, helps her pass through the camp unseen, unheard. Shadow of a shadow.

She walks barefoot on the hard, crisp ground till she reaches the palisade. There's more of them here now. Perhaps a hundred, scratching out a life in the confluence of the three rivers. More than scratching, she would say. They raise pigs, keep cows, catch fish. The trees in the valley bear enough fruit and nuts for all. They hunt deer and the occasional boar. More people come each month. The settlement grows. Manceinion, they call it now. No one uses the Roman words any more. Mona, they say, instead of luna. Sonne, instead of sol. Waeter, instead of aqua. Eorthe, instead of terra.

Everyone who comes here must appear before Dru. It is he whose word is law. But he lets in all comers. He sets them tests, in strength, in cunning, in husbandry, but nobody fails. Dru finds something in everyone that they can do that no one else can. Cuinn quarrels with him over this sometimes. He worries someone might take the leadership from him, which he expects to inherit when Dru dies. Or becomes too weak. But Dru tells him over and over. Make each arrival feel they're valued, with their own special role and task to suit their skills. That way they stay loyal. Bron knows that Dru worries Cuinn will not make a good leader when his time comes. He's a brave warrior, he tells her, but not always a wise one.

Bron hears a twig crack behind her. She presses herself against the dark, sharpened stakes of the palisade. But it's only Cora. Can't you sleep, either, she says? Cora shakes her head. It's the baby, she says, he frets. She pulls back a corner of her blanket to reveal the scrawny child suckling at her breast. Cora has seen fourteen winters. She's strong. She'll bear many children. Eä, her man, is a Settanti, from the south-west. Dru has taken him under his wing.

The air continues to tremble. The stars overhead flicker. The sky suddenly twists into a new shape. As if it is trying to turn itself inside out. Like when Bron will skin a rabbit. Then it reverts to how it was. Bron and Cora look at each other. This is something neither has seen before. Should we wake Dru, whispers Cora, or Eä? Cora shakes her head. And tell them what?

It happens again. The whole sky is dancing now. A

shimmer of green. Like fish. Dace and barbel leaping from the Irk to the Erewell. The stars are liquid fire.

Yes, says Bron urgently. Sound the alarm. Wake them all.

She feels the thunder from the earth growing stronger, can hear the marching feet, running now, and the horses' hooves galloping.

Cora lifts a stick to beat the metal shield hung above the palisade, whose sound will rouse the sleepers. She strikes it once, twice, but before she can manage a third an arrow flies through her throat.

Bron grabs the baby from her breast, snatches up the stick and beats it hard against the shield before diving back inside the palisade.

This is what the palisade was built for. A fortress to protect, from which they can defend. Now, everyone is up and running to their posts. Dru has drilled them many times in case there is an attack. They will be safe.

But arrows are raining down on them from all sides. Their tips carry flames. So as they blaze across the night sky they appear as part of the dancing lights and leaping fish above. Fish with teeth that tear and bite. Tongues that burn and swallow whole.

There is rising fear and panic in the camp as the fire storm rages all around and catches hold, setting roofs and buildings alight. No longer a fortress. A tomb.

We are besieged by dragons, they cry. Flying serpents.

No, cries Cuinn. I know these arrows. Picts. From the North.

A great roar of rage goes up from the camp. Swords are beaten against shields.

Hold firm, cries Dru. Stand fast. Do not yield.

But the flaming arrows keep on coming. The sky itself, it seems, is attacking them. Dru has fought many enemies in the past. But never before ones he cannot see. He thrashes about him blindly. But still they do not come.

When the Picts eventually do arrive, vaulting over the palisades as if they were boarding a fleet of ships at sea, the thunder from the earth erupts at last. They swarm all over the camp, like locusts, intent on razing it to the ground. But once inside, on terrain less familiar to them than it is to the camp dwellers, those who've come to call Manceinion their home, the fight becomes more equal. Dru has built the village like a maze, with blind alleys and dead ends, into which they lure the Picts and slaughter them.

But they are hampered by the falling buildings, the straw roofs ablaze and crashing all about them. Soon it becomes impossible to know which way to go. The whole village becomes a dead end, with both sides hacking the other to try and fight their way out...

By dawn the fighting's over. Very few are left alive. On either side. They wade knee deep among the gore. Heads and limbs and broken bodies litter the ground. A few fires still smoulder and burn. Black smoke rises thick and acrid. The smell of dead and rotting corpses. Blood and shit leaching into the three rivers.

Bron, still clutching Cora's baby, searches through the bodies, looking for Dru, for Cuinn, for Pard, for Wem. She finds Wem first. Naked, shivering, unable to speak, but still whole. Pard too has survived. But he has a deep gash along one arm, another, less deep, across his chest. His face is swollen and bleeding, one eye closed. She hands Cora's still silent baby to Wem while she patches Pard. Stay with him, she says to Wem, while I look for the others.

She finds Cuinn's shield before Cuinn himself. The one he made twelve winters ago, on which he painted the sign of a bee. Bee. This had become their emblem. Scratched on walls and flown on rooftops. But this was the first. Now it lies at her feet in the dirt, broken, rent in two, a diagonal slash across the bee itself. She holds the pieces up and tries to fit them back together. It's as she lifts them she sees Cuinn, whose body had been hidden underneath. His face is strangely calm, his eyes still open, but seeing nothing. Bron forces herself to look down upon the ruin of her son. She kneels beside him, closes his eyes. There'll be chance to mourn him later. Now she must find Dru.

She doesn't have long to wait. A voice calls her from another burnt out street. Dru has been found. He's alive, but trapped beneath a fallen roof beam. She goes to him. Men are trying to haul the roof beam clear with ropes, but carefully, in case they bring another crashing down upon them.

His eyes clear when he sees her. She knows he hasn't long left. I want you, he says, to take over from me. You were here before any of us. She tries to quieten him. But he's insistent.

She waits by his side while a pale sun slowly climbs the sky and the smoke starts to clear. A few surviving

Picts are rounded up and brought towards her.

Still Bron waits. The whole camp has gathered near her, waiting for Dru to die. Each in turn comes to him, placing the palm of their hand against their forehead and then gently touching his as a mark of honour and respect. When the sun reaches the top of the sky, his last breath finally leaves him.

Bron touches her own head against his, then slowly stands.

Some of the villagers begin talking about leaving, moving on, finding somewhere else. Others even go as far as to suggest they should abandon the camp altogether. They look towards Bron.

No, she says. We stay. Those of you who want to go, leave if you must. But where will you go? This is good land. We have fresh water. Stay. We've had setbacks before. We'll have them again. But this is Manceinion. This is our home.

What shall we do with these, someone asks, pointing to the surviving Picts. Bron walks towards them, unties the ropes that bind them. Let them stay too. That's what Dru would have said. Everyone's welcome here.

On the opposite side of the square, Cora's baby starts to skrike. She's hungry, says Wem. I'm too young. And I'm too old, smiles Bron. I'll do it, says one of the Picts, a warrior woman who'd survived the fighting. She points to her chest. Moire, she says. Bron nods. Wem hands the baby over to the woman, who puts it to her breast. Eä moves to stand by Moire's side. The crying stops.

Over the next few days the villagers begin to repair and rebuild the palisade. They bury the bodies in a mound outside the camp. Cuinn and Bron are given their own separate chamber. The broken shield is placed across them before the chamber is covered with earth.

*

Eventually Jabez found the gate into the Park, unlocked it and made his way the last few yards to The Lodge, where he could see Mary peering through a crack in the curtains. As soon as she saw him, she rushed to open the front door and flung her arms around him.

"I'm all right," he said. "Just bone tired, that's all."

"Shall I heat up some water for a bath?"

He shook his head. "I know I could do with one, but I need to sleep first."

She nodded and took hold of his hand. "Come on," she said, and she led him up the stairs, which he could barely climb, thinking only there'd probably be more of the same later that night. Just as he was crawling under the sheets, another air raid siren sounded. Groaning, he heaved himself back up, as Mary went to wake the children, only for the all clear to sound immediately afterwards. A merciful false alarm and a temporary reprieve at least.

Manchester Evening News

Monday 23rd December 1940

Bombs Shower on City: People Trapped in Wreckage

MANCHESTER BLITZ

Fires Rage Till Noon

City Prepares For Second Night Of Bombing

Just three days before Christmas Manchester was last night the target of one of the fiercest bombardments yet visited upon Great Britain by enemy aircraft. Many iconic buildings were hit, hundreds of shops and factories destroyed, as well as thousands of homes right across the Manchester conurbation, with Salford, Stockport, Swinton and Stretford, Eccles, Monton, Pendleton and Hulme all suffering extensive damage.

It is understood that 270 aircraft took part in last night's raid. They dropped 233 high explosives and 1,032 canisters of incendiary bombs. The incendiaries sparked around 1,300 fires. Reports say that some German bombers heading from the east failed to penetrate the barrage from the ack-ack guns and so turned north, attacking Manchester and Salford from the north west. But the most daring pilots rode the storm straight to their targets, using the River Irwell as a navigation guide.

Fire crews have been working all night but are still fighting fires with great determination. As workers flocked to the city centre this morning, they saw our courageous fire fighters playing their hoses over the roof of the Royal Exchange, where flames flickered persistently. The good news is that by midday every fire in the city was under control. Around 400 extra appliances were brought in to Manchester overnight – a force of

3,400 extra men – with some crew members returning to the scene of last night's battles to try to uncover equipment buried beneath fallen debris in case it is needed tonight.

Extra Constables have also been drafted in to the city this morning, but police chiefs say they have no concerns about law and order for members of the public are conducting themselves remarkably well. An official report says rescue workers in Salford have worked 'magnificently' overnight. They have been assisted by dozens of young people who formed a Corps of Messengers to deliver hundreds of urgent missives and help put out small fires.

Tales of Heroism and Hope Emerge

Keep smiling through . . . despite losing his home to the bombs, this blitz survivor emerges from his shelter to give the thumbs up

11-year-old Richie Catch, who had been buried under the ruins of a friend's home in Great Clowes Street, has been pulled into the daylight. Rescuers spent hours trying to free his head and shoulders. One rescuer was heard saying: "By Jove, I could go for a pint!" The boy replied: "Aye, so could I!" Richie's mother, the popular Manchester Songbird, Miss Chamomile Catch, who carried on singing last night right through the Blitz at *The Queen's Hotel* in Piccadilly, which miraculously survived unscathed, wept tears of relief and joy as she was reunited with her son after his terrible ordeal, when he was duly rewarded with his pint – of ginger beer!

In Nell Lane, Withington, a group of men with a hand pump set out to tackle a blaze. They ended up fighting another fire and then another, and eventually worked their way to the other side of Manchester to Cheetham Hill Road. They fought a dozen different fires in the process, carrying their 10cwt pump all the way.

Meanwhile, 70 parents and their children have gathered for a Christmas party at the Midland Hotel. It will go ahead as scheduled in spite of the bombing as the hotel has completely escaped damage in the attack. Said Organiser Mrs Annie Wright, pictured here with her daughter and assistant, Lily, "There's nothing Herr Hitler can do to prevent the people of Manchester from celebrating Christmas."

Miraculous Escape for Manchester Cathedral

Manchester Cathedral suffered a direct hit. A bomb fell on its north east corner at 6 in the morning, the last to be dropped. Dr Garfield Williams, the Dean of Manchester, said: "The noise of the fires was so terrific that we didn't hear anything. The sensation was just like being in an earthquake."

The blast at Manchester Cathedral lifted the lead roof and lowered it back down – miraculously in place. But every window has been smashed. Chairs, carpets, furnishings have been swept into the air and have dropped in heaps everywhere.

Dr Garfield Williams added: "The high altar is just a heap of rubbish 10 feet high. The two organs are scattered about in little bits. Showers of sparks still sweep across the place, but the old cathedral just refuses to burn."

Civil defence teleprinters at Manchester Town Hall may once again this evening be whirring into life with the news that everyone is dreading:

AIR RAID WARNING RED. AIR RAID WARNING RED. AIR RAID WARNING RED.

As Manchester braces itself for another possible attack tonight, let us leave the final words to Dr Garfield Williams:
"Manchester will rebuild her city. She will rebuild her shops and warehouses, her churches and cinemas. She will rebuild her hospitals, she will rebuild her schools. She will make wide roads and open spaces, and bus stations and railway stations, and she will build thousands of new homes for her citizens to dwell in."

*

Jabez was back on duty the following afternoon, part of the emergency deployment of additional fire crew brought in by the Area Team Co-ordinator to help with the retrieval of equipment buried beneath the debris of the previous night's bombing.

By early evening, as once again incendiary bombs began to fall on the city, he was moved to Bridge Street, which had been blocked by the collapse of a building at the corner of Gartside Street, where he was joined by local police and members of the public in trying to snuff out fresh fires before they took hold.

Gun crews on the outskirts of Manchester flung up a curtain of steel around the city to try and intercept the German planes before they could inflict further damage.

Among them, experiencing his first action since joining up with the Royal Engineers some six months before, Private Paul Lockhart was busy erecting extra defences for the over-stretched anti-aircraft detachments. Enemy aircraft appeared at first to be panicking in the face of this sudden barrage and began dropping their bombs early, on the south side of the city, in Stretford and Trafford Park.

Delphine, visiting her former colleagues from *The Manchester School for the Deaf* for Christmas, observed how, even though they could not hear, they could feel the shattering salvoes of the ack-ack guns vibrating right through them, along with the intermittent shift in tone of the bombers' engines as they swooped and dived overhead.

She followed the trail of the guns' projectiles as they arced across the night sky, zoning in upon their targets. But still, several of the planes got through. She saw pillars of flame rising up from the incendiaries dropped behind Stretford Town Hall.

Less than six miles away to the north-east Victor was working a night shift in the deepest seam at Bradford

Colliery. He too could feel the earth shake with the vibration of the bombs now falling across the city for the second night in succession. Even half a mile below the surface, the ground shook and coal dust showered the men's helmets. His son, Joe, was working the same shift. Victor saw a look of anxiety whiten his grimy face and winked. "Don't worry, son," he said. "We're well shored up down here. This mine's withstood far worse rumbles than anything Jerry can throw at us. Isn't that right, lads?"

The other men nodded grimly, hacking away at the coal face with their hand-held picks.

Fire bombs were raining down right across the city. As well as the heavy bombardment in the south, the east of the city was now under attack, with Stockport, Davenport, the Heatons, Reddish and Offerton all suffering direct hits. Following a huge bomb blast in Clopton Street, Hulme, which killed fourteen people attending a wedding party at *The Manley Arms* pub, Paul was sent as part of a small attachment of Engineers to assist with further rescue operations. The bomb had also destroyed much of the nearby *Beehive* pub, where Paul pulled out a man who kept repeating over and over what had happened.

"I were just enjoyin' a quiet drink when t' siren went off. There were only three of us in t' pub, plus the landlady, an' we all left together. Not the landlady. She stayed behind. I don't know what happened to her. We was running down Ward Street to t' public shelter in th' Alexandra Brewery when t' bombs began to fall. *T' Beehive* were hit just a couple o' minutes after we come out. Hulme Town Hall were hit, *Radnor Cinema* were hit. It were only recently opened, by George Formby a few weeks back. I were there. No more lamp posts to lean on now. Or windows to clean. Did you find the landlady at *T' Beehive*, lad?"

Paul didn't. But he did recover an old couple who'd been in bed when the bomb fell. They slithered down through the collapsing bricks and slates, still on the mattress, like some fairground helter skelter ride, till they came to rest at the bottom of the crater, where Paul found them, shocked but miraculously unharmed.

Back in the centre Jabez was still pouring water on burning buildings from the previous night's raid when the *Luftwaffe* broke through the anti-aircraft's defences and once more began to heap destruction across the city.

All Saint's Church in Oxford Road took a direct hit and was damaged beyond all repair. Just around the corner St Augustine's Church in York Street was also wrecked by a huge bomb that landed on the roof above the nave. The clergy house and the church school were destroyed. Four priests at St Augustine's Church spent the night fighting incendiary bombs which were showered on the district surrounding the church. They helped rescue people trapped in the wreckage of their homes, shepherded them to safety and gave absolution to the dying. One priest was killed and two others wounded. The church was a gaunt ruin.

Further along Oxford Road *The Manchester Royal*

Infirmary was temporarily put out of action by a heavy blast.

Six staff, including the Medical Superintendent and the Matron, a Miss Iris McMaster, were killed. Local grammar school boys joined the rest of the staff to work in stretcher parties to help evacuate as many of the eight hundred patients as they could. Several of those too ill to be moved were saved by the wire glass protecting the windows. Surgeons continued to perform emergency operations on the never ending stream of casualties arriving through the night by candlelight and Tilley lamps. Their work was further hampered when the hospital took the full force of a second huge incendiary bomb. Two nurses were killed when an upper floor collapsed, the resulting debris trapping one of the surgeons, Dr Charles Trevelyan, behind a wall more than two feet thick. Rescue teams, fighting fires breaking out on the remaining wards, aided by some of the injured patients, tunnelled their way through to clear a passage to Charles. After several hours they eventually reached him, where he was pinned beneath a heavy door. Anxious not to release a further cascade of tumbling masonry, they delicately manoeuvred this from him, pulling him to safety just before the ceiling caved in completely. Despite his injuries Charles insisted on resuming his duties immediately, pausing only briefly for a mug of strong, sweet tea made for him by one of the grammar school boys.

In Gorton, in Englefield Road, a whole row of terraced

houses collapsed like falling dominoes.

As soon as War was declared, Winifred, remembering her various roles in the previous war, immediately wanted to be of more practical use this time around. She volunteered as an ARP Ambulance Attendant. It was her job to give first aid to casualties, search for survivors and recover bodies. She arrived on her bicycle in Englefield Road shortly after the last house had fallen. There was a temporary lull in the raid and the sudden silence was strangely other worldly. A shower of brick and cement dust settled on everything – her helmet, her hands, even her eyelashes. If it had not been so eerily quiet she would probably not have heard those first faint cries coming from the end house, a woman's voice calling weakly for help.

Winifred located her, trapped in what remained of her kitchen. Close by, a fire was breaking through the fallen masonry. If help did not arrive soon, it might spread and there would be no possibility of pulling the woman out alive.

"What's your name?" she called out.

"Martha," came the weak reply.

"Good. My name's Winifred, and I'm here to try and help you. Can you move at all?"

"My fingers and toes, but nothing else."

"That's good," called back Winifred. She edged her way closer to where the voice was coming from, where there was a tiny gap, through which she could just make out, several feet below, a hand. "Can you move those fingers for me now please, Martha?"

The fingers on the hand twitched.

Good, thought Winifred. At least I know where she is. The problem was how to reach her. The way the house had crumpled meant that the only possible way of retrieving her would be through the roof, against which she was now leaning.

"Martha? I'm going to go and fetch some help for you."

"Please don't leave me."

"I'll have to. I can't get you out by myself. It's going to take some proper lifting gear. So I'm going to let the right people know to send an ambulance and a rescue team. But I'll be back soon. I promise. Try to stay awake if you can."

She leapt back on her bicycle and pedalled as fast as she could, navigating the rubble and the pot holes, until she reached the ARP's headquarters about half a mile away on Hyde Road, where she reported the situation and then returned to Englefield Road. She'd been gone less than half an hour.

"Martha?" she called.

No reply.

"Martha?" More urgently. "Martha?"

Eventually Winifred could faintly hear a feeble reply. She was fading fast. If the rescue team were to have any chance of reaching Martha and bringing her out alive, Winifred knew she would have to try and get to her first and apply any necessary first aid as a holding operation till more specialist medical help arrived. In order to fetch Martha out, Winifred could see that it would be necessary to bore a hole through the roof and create a space wide enough for them to get at least two people and a stretcher down. But, by removing a couple of slates, it might just be possible, she thought, for her to worm her way through and reach Martha herself.

Gingerly lifting first one slate, then a second, she squeezed her shoulders through the narrow gap and inched her way down, careful not to disturb any masonry, or splinter the fragile joists and beams that jutted out at improbable angles, lest the entire structure collapsed further. Progress was agonisingly slow as she snaked her way down towards Martha, sometimes having to bend her body in the opposite direction to avoid a delicately balanced coping stone or ridge tile. The whole edifice reminded Winifred of a human skeleton whose bones had been shattered, but whose shape and frame could still just be discerned despite several missing pieces.

Half an hour later she reached Martha. There was a small pocket of air which made breathing possible, if difficult. She could still see light up above at the surface from where she had come, the red, glowing sky illumined from the fires burning around the city. But it was a fire much closer to them that she quickly saw represented the most immediate danger. It was beyond the narrow chamber she and Martha occupied, but it was infernally hot and she could see that the flames were getting inexorably closer.

She turned her attention to Martha. She was lying under a heap of rubble, comprising a mixture of bricks, plaster and glass, with a section of wall across her back. Winifred quickly ascertained that, although parts of what were covering Martha were too heavy for her to lift, her spine appeared not to be broken, since she had feeling in her arms and legs, which she was able to move, albeit in a severely restricted way. From what Winifred could tell, Martha's left wrist and lower right leg appeared to be broken, but there were no bones protruding from the skin, or worse – sights which had become more familiar to her in the last twenty-four hours than Winifred would have thought possible. Delicately she started to remove the lighter pieces of masonry from Martha's body, taking immense care not to set off a potentially fatal avalanche by doing so.

A few minutes later the ambulance arrived and Winifred shouted up to alert them of their position, apprising them of the situation as she saw it. She was becoming increasingly concerned by the spread of the fire close by. The rescue team followed on close behind. They quickly confirmed what Winifred had first thought, that the only viable route down to them was through the roof, and they immediately began to drill a hole just wide enough to clear a pathway for them to carry Martha back, once they had succeeded in removing as much of the rubble from her body as they could without causing a further landslide. At the same time, though, this action would clear a route for the flames of the fire to reach them even quicker. Two boys out in the street were sent off to Hyde Road to try and summon up a hand pump, while in the meantime one of the ambulancemen managed to drag free from the rubble further up the street a large piece of asbestos, which they successfully wedged as a guard between the fire and the airlock where Winifred and Martha lay waiting. This would hold, they hoped, long enough to enable the men worming their way down from the roof to make it through and then lift Martha back to safety, a process they still had to carry out with painful slowness.

"How long?" called Winifred back up.

"An hour," came the reply, "maybe more, maybe less."

Martha, hearing that, began to whimper.

"Hush now," said Winifred, gently stroking her fingers. "Let's tell each other stories to help pass the time. You start."

"I don't know what to say."

"Tell me about yourself. Are you married?"

"I was."

"Oh, I'm sorry."

"Don't be, I'm not."

"Divorced then?"

"Separated. We only got married cos we 'ad to. We was far too young. During the last war, it were."

Winifred had a sudden sense of foreboding. Her senses were, if it were possible, on an even higher alert now.

"Martha," she said, "what's your married name?"

Martha's tone too now began to change. "Who wants to know?"

"Oh," said Winifred, thinking fast, "for the records, you know? You'll be wanting re-housing when you're back on your feet, won't you? The Corporation'll be making a list."

"Yeah, I suppose," said Martha, accepting the logic of this. "Collins."

The inside of Winifred's chest was pounding. So this

was Victor's Martha.

"Will you," she began, somewhat tentatively, "be wanting us to contact your husband for you? To let him know you're safe and where you are?"

"I shouldn't bother," said Martha, "but I'd be grateful if you could let my son know. His name's…"

"Joe. I know."

There. It was out now. She'd said it.

Martha's eyes narrowed further. "How…?"

And then Winifred saw the understanding slowly dawn across her face. Even in this dark space, buried in the earth beneath a ton of rubble, their eyes had accustomed sufficiently to see each other's faces.

"You're… her," she said.

"Winifred. Yes."

"I've wondered about you. Often. I'd think – we might catch t' same bus, or shop at t' same market, or pass each other in t' street, never knowing. I used to wonder what it was 'e saw in you that he didn't find wi' me no more, what had you got that I hadn't? P'raps you was prettier 'n me, but I see now that you're not. No offence."

"None taken."

"But never in a million years did I ever imagine summat like this. What are the odds, eh?"

A sudden shower of dust fell upon them, followed by a fierce hail of bricks as up above the rescue team extracted more debris in their painstakingly slow descent towards them. Instinctively Winifred threw herself forward, covering Martha's body with her own, her ARP tin helmet taking the full force of the rubble.

"Are you all right?" called a voice from above when

everything had settled and was still again.

Winifred eased herself up from Martha and looked at her. She nodded, shaking with fear.

"Yes," shouted Winifred back. "I'm not sure we could withstand another blow like that, though. How much further to go have you got?"

"Not far," the man replied. "But we can't hurry any faster. You see what happens if we do. Just be patient."

"I don't want to die," whispered Martha.

"You won't," said Winifred, looking her firmly in the eye. "I'll not let you."

The flames were beginning to burn through the asbestos fire guard, which was starting to glow a deep red. Winifred placed herself between it and Martha. They're going to have to be quick, she thought.

The minutes crawled by.

In the pause, while they continued to wait, Martha asked in a quiet voice, "Is he good to you? Victor?"

"Yes," said Winifred, "mostly. He's no saint, mind."

"No," said Martha, coughing in the dust. "He never was. But he doesn't..." She paused, as if seeking the right word, "... stray?"

"No," she said quickly. "He doesn't."

"How would you know if he did?"

"Oh, I think we women can tell, don't you?"

Martha looked at Winifred and nodded.

"He's always been..." Now it was Winifred's turn to choose her words carefully, "... appreciative of me."

It was quieter now. No bombs had fallen for nearly an hour. All they could hear was the slow, painful removal of the rubble to clear a way wide enough for the rescue workers to reach them, a single brick at a time, with further pauses in between as the men debated which one they might move next so that the whole precariously balanced edifice would not crumble beneath them. It was like that child's game of 'Pick Up Sticks', in which every decision might result in calamity. Winifred could hear the audible sighs of tension and relief as the men edged nearer, brick by brick by brick.

"Joe's always liked you," said Martha.

"I'm glad. He's a lovely boy."

"That used to make me so jealous."

"Yes. I expect it would. But *you're* his mother, not me."

"He's down t' pit tonight, working a late shift."

"So's Victor."

"D'you think they'll be all right?"

"I reckon it's safer down there than it is up here tonight."

Martha tried to laugh, but it quickly turned into a cough once more, which made her wince. "I think I might've cracked a few ribs," she just about managed to say in between the coughing.

"They'll check you over properly as soon as they get you out of here," said Winifred, craning her neck to see if they were any nearer yet.

"Ay," said Martha, "but when will that be?"

"Just about now," said a voice immediately above them, as a hand wriggled through to the space where the two women lay. Winifred immediately grabbed it.

"Thank goodness," she said. "Any longer and I think you could've served us both up for Christmas dinner instead of a turkey."

"Please don't make me laugh again," winced Martha.

Having painstakingly cleared the way down, the way back up was much quicker, for a safe pathway had been laid. There was no room for a stretcher once the two men had made it through, nor for Winifred, so she crawled her way lightly towards the upper air, while the two men removed the heavier pieces of masonry from around Martha's body before carrying her back to the surface between them, where Winifred was waiting for her. A great cheer went up from the crowd who had gathered round while the rescue operation had been taking place and Martha managed a weak smile.

"It's this woman you should be cheering, not me," she said, indicating Winifred, then beckoned her over. "Thank you," she croaked. "I…"

"Don't say anything more," said Winifred. "You must be exhausted."

"I want you to know," said Martha, and she laid a hand upon Winifred's arm. "I want you to know that as soon as I'm mended, I'll give Victor his divorce."

As the ambulance pulled away, weaving its precarious way between the craters and collapsed buildings, the sirens sounded the all clear. The teleprinters in the Town Hall once again whirred into life with the joyous message, "RAIDERS PASSED. RAIDERS PASSED. RAIDERS PASSED."

It was just after midnight. Christmas Eve, 1940.

Against the skeletal silhouette of Manchester

Cathedral a congregation of more than five hundred people, each carrying a lighted candle, softly began to sing.

> "*It came upon the midnight clear*
> *That glorious song of old*
> *From angels bending near the earth*
> *To touch their harps of gold*
> *Peace on the earth, good will to men*
> *From heaven's all gracious King*
> *The world in solemn stillness lay*
> *To hear the angels sing…*"

A few stars were starting to show through the smoke and clouds as Winifred cycled home along Hyde Road back towards Denton. A wind was picking up from the north-east. Sparks and embers from the still burning buildings were carried up into the air, where they danced and swirled above her.

> "*Still through the cloven skies they come*
> *With peaceful wings unfurled*
> *And still their heavenly music floats*
> *O'er all the weary world*
> *And man, at war with man, hears not*
> *The love song which they bring*
> *O hush the noise, ye men of strife*
> *And hear the angels sing…*"

By the time she reached Denton, the streets were empty. She paused outside the shop, wondering if Francis might still be awake and whether she might call on him. Victor wouldn't be home for a few hours yet, and she didn't feel like being alone. She couldn't wait to tell him the news about Martha.

She knocked lightly on Francis's door, but there was no answer. Either he was fast asleep, or he was busy working on some new idea in his studio at the back and hadn't heard her. The latter probably. She didn't think he ever slept. She was worried about him lately. Since George had been called up and gone away who knew where – "It's top secret, classified, sorry, don't even know myself," he'd said with a grin – Francis had withdrawn into himself, like a snail pulling in its horns. She had invited him to join Victor and her for Christmas dinner, but he'd declined. "I'll be all right," he'd said. "I'd rather be on my own anyway. I'm poor company these days." So she hadn't pushed it.

She waited another minute and then got back on her bicycle to pedal the last quarter of a mile home. It was as if the giant pair of spectacles that hung above the shop watched her cycle away, receding until she was just a dot, before she disappeared indoors. The great lidless eyes lifted their gaze back towards the city, where the sparks and embers that had been dancing in the night sky above Winifred's head on her journey home from Gorton had now joined together to form a vast, swirling red inferno, pulsing over Piccadilly, fanning outwards in a great arc. A sharp wind was picking up. Manchester was ablaze again.

*

"This is the nine o'clock news for the BBC Home Service on Christmas Eve, 1940 with me, Alvar Lidell, reading it.

"After two consecutive nights of the fiercest bombing, Manchester has suffered further damage today caused by a strong north-easterly wind, which whipped the flames still burning from the previous night's raid, into a deadly firestorm. It swept through the blast-shattered factories and warehouses that had until then escaped destruction. A wall of fire encircled Piccadilly. Portland Street, Mosley Street, Parker Street and Aytoun Street were impassable. Fuelled by the wind, the fire spread to Princess Street, Miller Street and Victoria Bridge. The Shambles was a smoking ruin. So that by midday more than half the city was consumed.

"In a desperate attempt to contain the blaze, a unit of Royal Engineers was sent in to blow up selected buildings to halt the path of the encroaching flames. The rumble of their blasting operations reverberated for many miles around and was even felt underground by miners working in the Lancashire coalfields. At its height the conflagration was greater and more widespread than any in England since the Great Fire of London in 1666. But eventually the fires began to fall back.

"The final death toll is thought to be in the region of seven hundred and seventy people who have lost their lives over the last two nights around Manchester, with forty still not accounted for. Two thousand three hundred and sixty-five people have been wounded and upwards of

thirty thousand are temporarily without homes.

"His Majesty King George VI, whose father had a long and deep association with the city, has sent his heartfelt sympathies to all, praising the emergency services and all citizens for their courage and fortitude. His prayers, as indeed are everyone's, are with the people of Manchester this Christmas. Goodnight."

Winifred turned off the wireless and sat alone in the kitchen. Everything had changed. Even the tea she was drinking, made with a teaspoon of damp, powdered milk, tasted good as she stirred in the white lumps. If there was one thing the last war had taught her, it was to savour that taste of unexpected honey as if it might be the last.

She looked at the clock on the wall. Half-past nine. Victor would be home by ten.

When Victor put his key into the lock and opened the front door, the house was strangely quiet. Usually the radio would be on and Winifred would be listening to one of the dance bands broadcast from *The Savoy*. But tonight he was greeted by silence. Perhaps she wasn't yet home herself, he wondered, if it had been another long day on her rounds.

He closed the door behind him, checked the blackout curtain was in place, and was just about to switch on the hall light, when he noticed a faint glow emanating from a point half way up the stairs. It was a candle. Intrigued he made his way towards it. At the stair's bend he turned to see another, glowing on the landing. His eye was then led to a third candle on the small table outside the tiny bathroom they'd had installed a couple of years ago. Victor stood outside the door, listening. He could make out a faint glow creeping out from under it. He could hear water very gently lapping the side of the bath. And he thought he could hear the quietest of giggles.

He turned the handle and slowly opened the door. Around the bath were several more candles and in the water, waiting for him with her arms outstretched, was Winifred, a wide smile spreading across her face.

"Merry Christmas," she said, and giggled again.

Victor noticed a bottle of sherry beside her on the shelf and a now empty glass that had once been full.

"Merry Christmas to you," he said, grinning.

"Come here," she said. "I've got something to tell you."

"Have you now?" he said, his grin becoming broader.

"Yes," she said, "but I've got to whisper it."

Victor bent down towards her. Winifred wrapped her soapy arms around him and pulled him close. Then, murmuring softly into his ear, she said, "I met Martha." Victor's instinct was immediately to pull away, but Winifred held him near. "I rescued her," she said. "I saved her life. And…"

"And?" said Victor warily.

"She's going to give you a divorce."

Victor opened his mouth as if to speak, but no words came out, so he shut it again. Then he opened it once more, but still he could say nothing, so once again he closed it.

"Well don't just stand there like a goldfish," laughed Winifred. "What are you going to do about it?"

"I suppose," he said, with that twinkle in his eye that could only mean one thing, "I should make an honest woman of you."

"But not too honest," she laughed. "Not yet any road."

It took Victor less than ten seconds to join her in the bath.

Later, when they had finished, and both lay there, not minding the water getting colder, he turned to her and said, "Winifred Holt, will you put this poor fool beside you out of his misery and do him the honour of marrying him?"

"I don't see any fool," she said, kissing him, "but I will marry you…"

Fourteen miles across the city, in the two-roomed flat they lived in on Silk Street, still standing where many of its neighbours were not, including the one across the way, at the junction with Great Clowes Street, from which Richie had been pulled out the day before, requesting a pint of beer, Cam crept into the smaller of the two rooms to see if he was awake, just as Christmas Eve tipped over into Christmas Day.

"*Joyeux Noel*," she whispered. Richie was still half asleep and he drowsily rubbed his eyes.

"Is it Christmas already?" he said.

"*Oui, mon petit chat.*"

"Why do you call me that?" he asked, his head still

muddled from dreams of falling bombs and ack-ack guns, searchlights and newspaper cameras flashing in his face.

"*Regarde*," she said, putting her finger to his lips. From behind her back, with her other hand, she pulled out a row of dancing cats, cut from a newspaper. "*Pour toi,*" she said, "*un cadeau.*"

Richie shook his head. "I don't understand."

"*Tu es mon petit chat. Tu retombes toujours sur tes pattes.* A cat has nine lives, *mon cheri. Mais tu en as perdu une.* You have lost one. Make sure you don't lose another," and she hung the row of nine dancing cats above his head, one of which was hanging upside down.

Richie nodded. "*Oui, Maman.* I'll be careful," crossing his fingers as he did so, thinking, I still have many more.

*

The Pathé Newsreel cockerel crows. The jaunty martial fanfare gives way to the more sombre, mournful sound of the Ancoats Excelsior Perseverance Brass Band playing 'How Sweet The Name Of Jesu Sounds' beneath a montage of devastated, smoking streets, over which the film's title is superimposed:

MANCHESTER DEFIANT!

Voice Over:

For the last three nights Manchester has suffered one of the fiercest and most concentrated aerial bombardments of the War so far. More than thirty acres of land within a mile of Albert Square now lie in ruins following two night's of bombing. One hundred and fifty roads in nearby Salford are blocked by debris and unexploded bombs.

While the following text is spoken, an image for each place mentioned is shown.

Famous buildings that have been badly damaged include the Free Trade Hall, Victoria Bridge and Cross Street Unitarian Chapel. Smithfield Market was completely destroyed.

Chetham's Hospital and the Manchester Cathedral have suffered grievously.

Hidden in George Street in the city centre is this fine old eighteenth century house that is a relic of bygone Manchester. It is the headquarters of the Manchester Literary and Philosophical Society. The much loved Lit & Phil, as it is affectionately known. A fire has torn through it. It has even destroyed the apparatus that was used by John Dalton while forming his atomic theory. Also destroyed is a piece of scientific equipment once used by Sir Isaac Newton.

The John Rylands library has had most of its windows blown out, but its unparalleled collection of rare books, including the Gutenberg Bible and the Kelmscott Chaucer, complete with its Burne Jones woodcut illustrations, remains intact.

The Corn Exchange and St Ann's Church reeled under the blows, but stood defiant.

As the music continues to swell, there is a further montage of images showing the emergency services helping people who have lost their homes, dressing wounds, offering cups of tea, bomb-damaged shops and cafés determinedly putting up signs saying 'Open' and 'Business as Usual'.

Voice Over:

Also standing defiant are the people of Manchester, who refuse to bow their heads, but who are already getting on with the work of putting the city back on its feet. 'Make Do and Mend' is the motto of the day.

A second title appears on the screen over the scene at Lancashire County Cricket Ground.

BOMBS STOP PLAY!

Voice Over:

Following a direct hit on the cricket square at Old Trafford, there is now a huge crater in the middle of the pitch. The bomb almost landed on the crease! Much to the consternation of Head Groundsman Peter Marron, seen here scratching his head. It's going to take a fair bit of work to get this repaired and ready in time for next season's Roses Match, but don't worry – he'll do it.

The music shifts to the dance tune, 'They Can't

Black Out The Moon', sung by Chamomile Catch, which underscores the next section.

*"I see you smiling in the cigarette glow
Though the picture fades too soon
But I see all I want to know
They can't black out the moon..."*

Voice Over:

Despite what Lord Haw-Haw and his like might have to say to the contrary, Manchester, just like the rest of Great Britain, is not, and never will be, defeated. The rebuilding of the city has already begun.

Here's the lovely Giulia Lockhart, Manchester's original Miss Ice Creams, more recently a costume assistant in the newly opened film studios on Dickenson Road, from where Giulia was plucked to play a beauty queen and the object of Sandy Powell's desire in *Lytham Lovelies*, in which she appears on a railway poster, before, in Sandy's imagination, she steps down out of the frame wearing nothing but a sunny smile and a beach ball. Here she is, visiting workers on Christmas Eve in Trafford Park's Metro-Vickers factory where, despite being hit during last night's raid, their non-stop, round-the-clock production to assemble the latest Avro Lancaster bombers, powered by the legendary Rolls-Royce Merlin engines, continues unabated. These magnificent flying machines will soon be ready to take to the skies and carry the fight back to the enemy. Twenty-five yards long, with a wingspan of more than thirty-five, and a flying range of two and a half thousand miles at a cruising speed of nearly three hundred and fifty miles per hour, their cockpits will carry a crew of seven. These workers here, though, seem much more interested in Miss Lockhart's vital statistics. And who can blame them? With her picture on the fuselage, there's bound to be a rush of new recruits wanting to be part of those seven man crews!

A picture of Giulia, wearing a swimsuit, looking over her shoulder and winking, is displayed on the side of the prototype Lancaster.

The film now shifts to a close-up of an air raid shelter standing proud, surrounded by a sea of rubble.

Voice Over:

As the song says, 'They Can't Black Out The Moon', and in the end love really does conquer all. Two babies have been born here during the Blitz. A little girl was born in an Anderson Shelter in Fallowfield, while a boy was delivered in the beer cellar of a Patricroft hotel, where the mother, taking refuge from the falling bombs, was rescued by ARP Warden Mrs Esther Ward, who, having been a VAD during the last war, was able to use her nursing skills to ensure the baby was born safely. In both cases mothers and babies are doing well, we understand. We say, "Congratulations and Welcome to the World." We don't know whether names have yet been chosen, but how about Victor and Victoria?

The iris of the camera narrows to a close-up of a

smiling Esther waving to the camera, next to the mother holding her baby, gradually diminishing to black, before re-opening to show again the rebuilding work taking place in the centre of the city.

Voice Over:

And so we say to the citizens of Queen Cotton and King Coal, three cheers and a Merry Christmas. Temporarily down, but never out, Manchester Can Take It!

*

No church bells rang that Christmas morning.

The wind had died. The fires were out. A grey pall hung over the city, a ghostly plume of smoke and mist and low cloud. Petals of ash fell in a silent shower like grimy snowflakes.

There were no trains running anywhere, no trams, no trolley buses. Telephone lines were down, and, since so many of the roads were still blocked with fallen debris, there was virtually no traffic, save the occasional ambulance or rattling bicycle wobbling precariously between the ruined outcrops.

Annie Wright had been walking for nearly an hour. She stepped out into Lapwing Lane as soon as the first pale webs of light began to show. She needed to check on the Printing Works and on Portugal Street, on whether they had survived the bombing. There was no other way than to walk the six miles from Didsbury to Ancoats. If she set off early, she told Lily, there was every chance she'd make it back before darkness fell. They could have their Christmas dinner at night. Luckily Evelyn and Pearl had arrived a few days ago, before the first of the bombs began to fall, otherwise there was no knowing how they would have got there.

If circumstances had been different, she would probably have visited Hubert's grave this Christmas morning, as she did every year, and it had crossed her mind whether to go there anyway, but she had decided against it. It was too much of a detour. The chances were that she would have to make several diversions in any case to avoid where the roads were now blocked or impassable. This also meant that she wouldn't be able to pass their old house on St Werburgh's Road in Manley Park, which she liked to do from time to time, to see what changes the new owners might have made.

She didn't like being out of doors in the blackout. It frightened her. Frequently she'd get disoriented and lose her way. Hubert would have hated it. She was glad he was not alive to have experienced these last three nights of bombs and fires. He would not have been able to withstand it. Of that she was certain. Relatively little damage had been visited upon Didsbury, although a bomb had fallen near Withington Station, close to Fog Lane Park, blowing out the glass of several houses.

Now, though, as she reached the edge of Rusholme, the full force of the attack quickly became evident. A tented city of temporary shelters had been set up in Platt Fields and the WRVS were already busy serving food from the hastily erected field kitchens. Through the coils of smoke and mist in the chill iron dawn she began to make out bent grey figures stooping low over the broken ground of the streets bordering the park. Wrapped in scarves and overcoats, covering their mouths to keep from breathing in the noxious fumes that vented from the gaping holes and craters, they picked their way through the rubble trying to salvage what they could from what had once been their homes. Like the crows that flocked about them they poked and rummaged with stiff fingers for anything shiny catching their eye. Some carried pots and pans looped on string tied around their waists, whose dull forsaken clanging reminded Annie of the bells rung by lepers. Others pushed prams precariously over heaped piles of masonry, loaded with their last few pitiful possessions – a chair, a tin bath, a chest of drawers stuffed with clothes and blankets, knives and forks wrapped in scraps of cloth, a cracked, framed photograph, a Christmas tree.

Annie wondered whether these represented all that remained of what this family once owned, or whether some desperate, anguished, hurried choices had had to be made. She suspected the latter. What would she keep, she asked herself, if this had been her instead of them? People first. Possessions didn't matter. Or did they? She'd spent more than half her life creating a series of homes for herself, Hubert and George, and now Lily, filled with beautiful things, just to prove to herself that she mattered, that she amounted to something, had risen from such humble beginnings to a position where what she said and what she did counted, had influence, made a difference. But since Hubert had died, six and a half years ago, she'd begun to question those choices she'd made, so consciously and with such certainty, more and more.

"Do we really need this?" Lily would say, holding up a brass candlestick or a china ornament, when people came calling, asking for contributions to charity auctions or fund raising bazaars, and frequently she had heard herself reply, "No. Let them have it. And this too. How many glass vases do we actually use?"

And now, surveying this misery all around her, this desperate scrabbling for any last vestige of something to remind them of who they once were and might yet be again, she was filled with what felt close to shame.

A pale, thin child, with dark circles under her eyes, her face devoid of all expression like an abandoned doll, clutched a spinning top tightly in her fingers. As Annie drew nearer, the child held it out towards her like an offering, then gestured with her other hand mechanically towards her mouth, as if to indicate she would give anything, even her most precious toy, for something to eat. Annie reached inside her pocket. Lily had thoughtfully made her a sandwich for her journey with a slice of corned beef, which Annie now held out towards the starving child. She looked at it for a long time, as if she scarcely believed what she was seeing. Gingerly, in case it might explode in front of her, she took it, sniffed it, then raised it to her cracked lips, scabbed with cold sores, and suspiciously nibbled a corner of it. For the briefest of milliseconds a flicker of light registered in her dead doll's eyes, then slammed shut again as she took herself away to perch on a doorstep where there was no longer a door to wolf it down.

Annie lingered a moment to watch her.

"Say thank you to the kind lady," said the child's worn out mother.

Solemnly the child wiped her hands on her threadbare skirt, which she'd long outgrown and which revealed bare knees and legs encrusted with dirt and plaster dust, and walked gravely towards Annie, holding out her spinning top to her.

Annie bent down so that her own face was level with the child's. "The sandwich was a gift," she said. "I don't want anything in return. But I do like your spinning top," she said. "Can you show me how it works?"

The child frowned, looked back over her shoulder towards her mother, who nodded. The child then squatted on a patch of bare earth between the piles of shattered bricks and proceeded to pump the top's handle firmly up and down, up and down, faster and faster, until finally it was steady enough to spin. The swirls of colour that were painted around it blurred into a single white light. It began to emit an eerie, high-pitched whine, which filled the air. A few yards farther off, a man, clambering over a smashed and slithering wall, suddenly started to shout in panic, covering his ears. "It's another attack," he screamed, over and over.

The child's mother roughly snatched up the top so that the whine ceased at once and the man was able to be calmed. She took hold of her daughter's hand and marched her back towards their loaded pram, which she tried to push before it toppled, back in the direction of Platt Fields and the field kitchens. The child gave Annie a last hard stare before her crow's eyes lit upon a pair of outsized ladies shoes, which she straight away slipped on her feet, tottering on their broken heels after her harassed mother.

A rat nosed its way from a crack between the stacked cards of fallen concrete slabs, its whiskers twitching, scenting the chill air before deciding which way to go next. After a few moments of patient deliberation it headed hard right towards a row of still standing burnt out hulks of houses. It was followed smartly by a second younger, smaller rat skittering in the freezing plaster dust. Annie watched them skilfully navigate their way between the rusting grids, which had been roughly thrown up by the earth's recent convulsions, then scale a vertical door jamb before scuttling across the floorless rotting joists like stoic tightrope walkers. Lessons in survival, thought Annie. She was reminded of her first ever visit to the house in Portugal Street, with Hubert just before they were married, when a different pair of rats had emerged from the alleyway alongside to inspect the new arrivals. She'd shuddered then. Now she barely shrugged. She'd done more than survived. She'd thrived. And to do that she'd learned to adapt. As she would have to again.

Her circuitous walk through Manchester's burnt and bombed streets now forced her to leave Oxford Road behind. Up ahead the road was still closed following the attacks on the Infirmary. It meant too that she would not now pass through Victoria Park to check on how their first house after Portugal Street at Hirstwood on Daisy Bank Road was coping with the aftermath of the Blitz. Instead she skirted up Dickenson Road, passing the still intact Methodist Chapel which now housed *The Mancunian Film Company* studios, where Claudia's

Giulia now worked – Claudia, whom Annie would call on first before checking on the Printing Works. From Dickenson Road she crossed into Stanley Grove, turning left into Redgate Lane, which promptly petered out into the now unrecognisable wasteland behind *Belle Vue Exhibition Hall*, whose huge plate glass windows and roof had been completely blown out. For several hundred yards Annie walked on the shattered fragments of broken glass, which crunched underfoot, like frayed and jangling nerve endings. She had to clamber over a scree of sliding rubble at the far end of Hunter's Lane, which forced her onto quite unfamiliar terrain, the warren of back streets between Kirkmanshulme and Gorton Lanes, both of which were impassable, Malpas Street, Corby Street, Pomfret Street, Brinksop Square, Ellenbrook Court, Textile Street, all of which were deserted, smouldering ruins, reminding her of when she was a girl, living on Corelli Street in the Tripe Colony where, as children, they would race each other up and down the slag heaps and coal tips, which would skid beneath them as they tried to climb them, throwing up great clouds of black dust.

On a whim she decided she'd see if her old childhood street was still standing. Flung out of this maze like a regurgitated owl pellet, Annie emerged at the back of *The Clayton Arms*, not open for business this Christmas Day, nor looking likely to reopen any time soon. She found herself on the more recognisable territory of Grey Mare Lane, edging past Bradford Pit where, behind the wire fence, she could see and hear the creaking of the cables in the overhead winding gear, still in full operation today. A torn scrap of paper flapped against the fence in a sudden, sharp gust of wind as Annie walked past. "*The Road to Victory Runs through the Mines*," it read, with a painted scene of mines, mills and factories all belching smoke behind. "*Light Consumes Coal. Save Light, Save Coal. Don't Waste It. Save Fuel for Battle.*" Annie shivered, remembering how, after dark, she would take her younger brother and sister out with her to pilfer what few sticks of coal they could carry between them to take back home to Corelli Street for the rare treat of a fire.

She was almost there now. Grey Mare Lane gave way to Forge Lane, along the edge of Philips Park, locked up for Christmas Day, which in turn became Hulme Hall Lane. Just before she reached the chapel where she and Hubert had married, she turned off down Lord North Street from where she plunged into the Tripe Colony. Even after a gap of so many years, and even though many of the streets had suffered severe bomb damage, she could have walked these streets blindfolded. Her feet soon brought her to the house in Corelli Street where she'd been born. It was still intact, just, but partially boarded up, as were several of its neighbours.

"*Keep Out*," a notice warned. "*Danger. Subsidence. Roof and Walls May Collapse.*"

She didn't linger. She had no ties here any more, save those that were in the past. Her parents had died a long while ago, her father of black lung, her mother of exhaustion. Her brother was in the army somewhere and her sister had married and moved to Sheffield years before. At first, after she got married, Annie had visited them regularly, but when she moved to Daisy Bank Road, these visits grew less. Her father accused her of "putting on airs", and perhaps he was right, but her mother was different. She was proud of her. "You're just jealous," she told her husband, "cos she's made summat of 'erself." He nodded, emptied the ash from his pipe into the grate, and said, "Ay lass, 'appen you're right…" Once Annie had tried to give them some money, but they'd been deeply offended and Annie was mortified. "We'll not be wanting any charity, young lady," was their damning response.

The wind she'd felt by the pit was picking up again, and she realised she needed to hurry if she were to see Claudia, check on the Printing Works and still be home before dark. She quickened her pace as best she could along the blocked streets and pavements. She picked her way towards Oldham Road, where she turned left towards Ancoats. The Italian Quarter had suffered some damage, but not uniformly so. Several streets had whole rows of houses which appeared to have had their roofs and upper floors lopped off, like razed, scorched earth after crop fires, charred and blackened with upright sections of still standing walls poking up like sharp, broken stubble, while others remained almost untouched. Portugal Street was one such. A quick first glance showed Annie that both the Printing Works and their old house opposite, where George had lived most of the time for the past six years before he was called up, rose up from the surrounding rubble like beacons. She could feel some of the tension in her shoulders ebb away as she looked up and down the street where she had been happy for so many years.

Since Hubert had died and she had handed over all the running of the Printing Works to George, she had rarely visited it, and so its appearance now, surrounded by so much ruin all around, seemed almost as though she were seeing it fresh, resonant with both memory and hope.

Relieved, she promised herself she would return to look at it more carefully after she had visited Claudia. She had her keys with her and would venture within both the Works and the house, neither of which she had stepped inside for more than five years, and try to see them new minted. That they had somehow endured the worst that the *Luftwaffe* could throw at them felt almost miraculous, but it was a fragile survival that required more assiduous nurturing, especially now that George was no longer living there, and she vowed to attend to this in the New Year. She craned her neck further around the corner from where Oldham Road intersected with Portugal Street and saw too that the spindle tree was still very much standing. It was in its winter coat now, of course, leafless and spiny, its skeletal frame sprinkled with a patina of brick dust. The sight of it filled Annie with the same excitement it had always done from when she had first lived there and, with Claudia's encouragement, she had begun making those series of collagraphs, depicting it in all seasons and all weathers and all moods. On the first anniversary of Hubert's death, George had surprised her with an album of photographs he had taken of it, every day for twelve months, capturing in the minutest of details each tiny nuance of change during that period. It was something she looked at often back in the house on Lapwing Lane late at night.

She turned off down Bengal Street, hurried along Naval and then Gun Street before turning onto Radium

Street, where she hoped to find Claudia in, or if not, a neighbour, who might give Annie news of her. She knocked on the door and waited.

Claudia lit a candle for her brother Matteo in the side chapel of St Alban's Church on Fawcett Street, as she had done every day since he was sent overseas. The precise whereabouts of his ship she did not know, for obvious reasons, but for the moment he was alive and, in these uncertain times, that was all that mattered. Soon she might have to start lighting one for Paul also, but for now he was yet to be posted, although she supposed that that would only be a matter of time, now that he had completed his training. She would see him later, at Harriet's parents, Mary and Jabez, where he spent every spare moment, who had kindly invited her to share Christmas Day with them, later in the afternoon. She thought she would light Matteo's candle first, therefore, before returning back home to collect the few small gifts she had assembled for Harriet, for Toby and for Gracie, whose undauntable spirit never failed to impress her. For Mary and Jabez she would take some fresh pasta she had made earlier that morning. From what she knew of them from Harriet, she thought they'd be game to give it a try.

Claudia watched the smoke from the candle rise in a blue column up towards the vault, carrying her prayers and hopes for a safe passage for Matteo with it. She smiled as she watched it ascend. Anyone watching her would take her for a traditional Italian *contadina*, dressed all in black, with a shawl over her head, which is what she supposed she had become. It gave her little amusement to speculate on exactly how such a transformation had come about. She looked now how she remembered her mother had used to look back when she, Claudia, was a girl, and quarrelling with her about staying on at Grammar School and then going on to work in the science laboratories at the University. Do we all become our mothers, she wondered? She laughed mirthlessly. The prospect of Giulia ever kneeling here in St Alban's Church lighting a candle for her brother seemed impossibly remote, despite her occasional displays of humility recently, though no more remote than it would have appeared for Claudia to be there now when she had been Giulia's age.

She thought back to the conversation she had had with Miss Leslie, her former teacher and mentor, when she had so unexpectedly run into her that Tulip Sunday in Philips Park eleven years ago. They had been reminiscing about the work they had shared as part of Professor Rutherford's team trying to split the atom. As the scientific knowledge increased, enabling them to be able to see smaller and smaller particles right inside the atom, Miss Leslie had asked Claudia a question that she had been pondering more and more in recent years. "Where's the room for God?" If we keep squeezing him further and further, she argued, will there eventually come a point when He disappears altogether? At the time, Claudia had been astonished that so rational a scientist as Miss Leslie should even be asking the question at all and had dismissed all notion of God from her thoughts, especially after her experience of losing Marco in the final few days of the last war. How could a revered, merciful God countenance such random cruelty? But now, in the grip of another war a mere twenty years after the end of the so-called war to end all wars, she no longer felt so sure – of anything. The certainties of her youth she had shed with the years, so that they now appeared as evanescent as the smoke rising up from the candle in front of her, decreasing with distance.

Once, when she had been a student at the university, one of their lecturers asked them if they felt it was possible to weigh accurately something as insubstantial as smoke. None of them could come up with a satisfactory idea. She mentioned this later to Marco, who listened with a broad smile on his face, before then proposing his own rather elegant solution.

"What you should do," he explained, taking out a cigarette as he spoke, "is to weigh one before you light it, like this. Then you should stay very still while you smoke it, making sure that every single piece of ash is carefully tapped onto a dish, where you place the butt of the cigarette once you've finished smoking it. Then you weigh the ash and the butt. The difference between that and the weight before you smoked it is the weight of the smoke. *Ecco*," he said, stubbing out his own cigarette, looking very pleased with himself.

There was no doubting its neatness, and she tried it out on her lecturer the following week. All of the students were similarly impressed, but the lecturer merely smiled.

"That is a poet's proposal, not a scientist's," he said. "When a cigarette burns, it takes some mass out of the air. It oxidises. Mostly what a cigarette burns is carbon, so that the act of smoking creates carbon dioxide, which is added both to the smoke and the ash, which therefore negates your solution, for the weight you have calculated for the smoke actually contains the weight of these additional gases."

Eighteen months ago, just before Mr Chamberlain made his announcement that he had "received no such undertaking" and that "consequently we are now at war with Germany", Giovanni had died – peacefully one warm summer's night in his sleep. Afterwards, not able to afford a burial plot, she and her brother had decided they should cremate his body. When Father Fracassi handed them the urn containing *Nonno's* ashes, it barely seemed credible that such a man should weigh so little.

They were then faced with the problem of what should be done with them. Should they keep them? Or scatter them? For a while they kept them, but every time one of them caught sight of the urn, on the hearth in the front room opposite the chair where he had spent so much of his final years, which now lay empty, it upset them, and so they decided they must scatter them. But where? It was Paul who came up with the idea.

"Remember that old story he liked to tell?" he said.

"About the kite?" said Claudia.

Everyone smiled. *Nonno* had told that story so many times they could relate it word for word.

"What about it?" asked Matteo.

"Well," continued Paul, "what if we make a kite just like the one *Nonno* did as a boy and tie a long tail to it, made up of a series of small cut-out birds, like the wren in his story, and fill each of them with some of the ashes.

But we don't seal them up, so that once the kite is up in the air, his ashes will scatter randomly from the sky, landing just where they will."

The others looked at him in silence, trying to picture it. It was Giulia who spoke first. "That's so gross," she said. "Imagine if you were just walking along, minding your own business, and then bits of *Nonno* fell on you out of the sky? It'd give you nightmares for weeks."

But Paul was undeterred. "We'd fly the kite somewhere out in the open, away from people."

"Where?" asked Claudia, warming to the idea.

"How about Philips Park? He used to like it there, especially when the tulips were out. We could go there really early, before the park was open – I could get Harriet's Dad to let us in – and then we could go to the Amphitheatre in the centre, which is like a bowl, and fly the kite from there."

Paul looked at them, smiling already at the thought of it.

"Paulie," said Matteo, clapping him on the back, "*è un grande suggerimento.*"

The following Sunday, which happened to be *Nonno's* birthday, they all assembled at Philips Park just as it was getting light. Jabez unlocked the gates and let them in. He led them to the Amphitheatre, where Harriet joined them. She had grown very fond of *Nonno* in her weekly visits to Radium Street. There was just the right amount of wind. Paul had built the kite using *Nonno's* description of the one he'd built himself as a small boy as his guide. Now, he lay it down reverently on the top of the nearby slope, carefully arranging each of the small birds in the tail, which now contained between them all of *Nonno's* ashes. Once he was satisfied, he walked slowly down the slope away from it, unwinding the string from the reel, which he held tightly between his hands. Gradually he increased his speed until soon he had burst into a run. The kite took off from the slope and climbed into the sky. Paul played out the string until the kite had reached its full height. Then he pulled down on either side of the reel, so that the kite began to dance. As it did so, the ashes began to shake from each of the paper birds and rained down onto the central bed of the park, which Jabez had recently dug out, now that the tulips had finished. It was a comforting thought to think that *Nonno's* ashes would help the next year's crop of flowers to grow. As they merged with the air, they formed a series of miniature clouds, tiny parachutes, some of which descended gracefully to the ground, while others rose ever higher, up into the stratosphere, like smoke from a candle.

Eventually no more ashes fell. Slowly Paul reeled in the kite until it landed safely beside them.

"What shall we do with the kite?" asked Giulia.

"Keep it," said Paul at once. "Then fly it each year on his birthday."

Harriet beamed and linked her arm through his. The others nodded.

And Paul had been as good as his word, managing to arrange a day's leave from his training in Sheffield, to return in midsummer to fly it as promised. No ashes this time, just the kite, dancing in the sky.

Harriet had asked afterwards if she might fly it next year, if Paul had been posted overseas, and Claudia had blessed her goodness.

Now, in the side chapel of St Alban's, the candle she had lit for Matteo had burned itself out. Claudia watched the last of the smoke coil towards the vault before it dissipated and merged with that of the other candles now burning this Christmas Day.

Returning from the church, the black shawl still covering her head, Claudia rounded the corner of Radium Street to see a figure sitting on her doorstep. It took her a moment to recognise that it was Annie, who stood up when she saw her and waved. She too was dressed in black, more soberly than had been her custom some years back, and she also had a scarf tied around her head, from beneath which Claudia could see hair escaping that was now streaked with grey, as was her own. We are both fifty now, she thought. How can that be? What had happened to the two girls who roved the Italian street markets on Saturday mornings nearly thirty years ago? They were like two pencil drawings that had become smudged but were still just about recognisable – though not for much longer, thought Claudia wryly. Those pencil marks would eventually fade away completely, leaving nothing but a faint imprint on the page, only visible from close up.

The two women embraced warmly outside Claudia's front door.

"I wanted to make sure you were all right," said Annie first. "The phone lines are all down, there was no one I could ask."

"How did you get here?"

"I walked. How else?"

"You must be frozen. Come inside. I've some soup from last night I can warm up for you."

Annie followed her inside. She had never, she realised, been inside Claudia's home before. They had always met at some point in between. She took in the meagre furnishings, the lack of unnecessary ornamentation, the scrubbed floors. It was scrupulously clean.

"I don't know how you manage it," marvelled Annie, "with all the dust and soot from the factories, and especially now with all the bombs."

Claudia smiled thinly. "We've been lucky," she said. "We've escaped the worst of it here. Though we could feel the heat of the flames fanning out from Piccadilly yesterday. We were advised to evacuate. But I'm not going anywhere." She handed Annie a bowl of soup with the end of a crust, which Annie accepted gratefully and finished in no time. "You clearly needed that," smiled Claudia.

"Thank you. It was delicious. I set off early, just as it was starting to get light. I've been walking non-stop ever since, often over broken ground."

Claudia didn't need to be told. She could see evidence of her friend's journey in the layers of dust which had settled on her hair, shoulders, shoes.

Annie traced Claudia's gaze. "I must look a fright," she said.

"A very welcome one." They both laughed.

"How's Matteo?" asked Annie after a pause. "Any news?"

Claudia shook her head. "Not for some weeks. The whereabouts of his ship are classified."

Annie nodded.

"Still," Claudia continued brightly, "no news is good news."

"Yes. And you?"

"I have my job at the library."

" 'Assistant in Charge of the Young People's Reading Rooms', I seem to recall."

Claudia laughed.

"Most impressive."

"In sole charge now."

"Even better."

"My superior was called up. But I don't get his salary," she added ruefully. "Still the same – 94 shillings per week. But I'm not complaining. After the last few years of looking after Giovanni, when all I could do was take in sewing, it feels like a small fortune."

Annie nodded. "And the children?"

"Ah, well…" Claudia smiled. "Giulia has her head in the clouds as always, while Paul has his feet on the ground."

Annie shook her head in wonder. "Chalk and cheese," she said, then paused. "When you have only one, it's difficult to imagine what it must be like with two…"

"But you have Lily now."

"Yes," said Annie, brightening, "I do, and I bless the day that fate unspooled her towards me."

"Like Ariadne."

"Yes."

The two women sat silently for a while in the back

kitchen, each remembering the thread of years which bound them.

"I have to be going," said Claudia at last. "I'm expected at Harriet's parents this afternoon. Giulia and Paul are already there."

"Yes," said Annie, "and I too need to be heading back before it gets dark. I want to check in on The Works and the house first as well."

"I'll walk along with you," said Claudia, picking up her shawl once more and wrapping it around her head. "It's on my way."

They stepped outside, back into the damp iron chill of the day, and began walking, their feet in step, along the cracked pavements of Radium Street, before turning into Naval Street.

"Do you think they'll get engaged," asked Annie, "Harriet and Paul?"

Claudia smiled. "I'm certain of it," she said. "But they're not in the same hurry as we were."

"Maybe the War will change all that?"

"*Si*," said Claudia thoughtfully, "*è possibile*."

Just as they reached the corner of Gun Street with Poland Street, Claudia stopped. "I'm sorry," she said. "I've just realised I've forgotten the presents I'd got ready for Toby and Gracie. I'll have to go back. You go on, Annie – we're nearly at Portugal Street already. Let's get together again when things get back to normal."

"Yes," said Annie. "You must visit us in Lapwing Lane. You're welcome any time."

They held each other briefly close, then turned in opposite directions.

Claudia had just reached the turning back into Radium Street again when a sudden flash lit up the whole sky, followed a fraction of a second later by an enormous explosion, the force of which flung her across the street. The earth buckled beneath her. A hail storm of broken glass rained down all around. She lay face down on the ground, covering her head with her arms, as the shattered shards continued to fall in endless slow motion. With her ears temporarily deafened by the blast, the sound they made was like distant, far off, tinkling bells.

When the shower of glass finally stopped, and her senses roared back to her, she got to her feet, checked to see if she was injured – apart from a thousand tiny paper cuts along her hands and arms she was unhurt – and instinctively ran back in the direction of the explosion.

She reached Portugal Street within seconds. Already there were people there – air raid wardens, police constables, ambulancemen – all trying to keep people away, but Claudia dodged between them.

Portugal Street was no longer there.

What had once been a short row of terraced houses was now an unrecognisable pile of bricks and slates, cobbles and concrete, smoking and smouldering before her. In the far corner, where once had stood the Printing Works, was now a flattened heap, from which she could feel the heat of the molten printing presses.

Her ears were still ringing, but among all the shouting she heard the words, "Unexploded landmine... Someone must have stepped on it..."

Of Annie there was not a sign.

Claudia looked about her in a daze. Needle tracks of

blood from the slivers of glass cuts on her body were now beginning to flow. Someone sat her down on a fallen coping stone, wrapped her in a blanket, and handed her a cup of tea. "You'll be all right, love," they said. "Someone'll be along to take care of you soon…"

Claudia drank the sweet, strong tea instinctively. She looked down. Poking out from beneath a smashed ridge tile was a shoe. Annie's shoe. Claudia picked it up and cradled it like a doll. Attached to it was a snag of burnt cotton.

Around her volunteers had interrupted their Christmas dinners to come and help put out the small fires that were still threatening to take hold. A hosepipe was trained upon the charred embers of all that was left of the spindle tree, a black stump jutting through a nest of smashed paving slabs, its roots still intact somewhere out of sight.

Smoke rose in a thick, twisting column up to where it mingled with the low grey cloud. Claudia watched it climb, just as she had watched the smoke from her candle in St Alban's Church less than an hour before. "We're all of us carbon," she thought bitterly. "Smoke and ash." The radioactive half life of carbon, she recalled from her times working with Professor Rutherford, the time when she and Annie had first met and become friends, was five thousand, seven hundred and thirty years. And then another five thousand, seven hundred and thirty years for the remaining half to decay, and so on, until the amount left was so infinitesimally small that it was invisible, not only to the naked eye, but to the most powerful of microscopes, smaller and smaller, but never disappearing entirely, always another half life surviving, on and on, mingling with the air, incalculable, like the weight of smoke, ultimately unknowable, but still a sufficient space left, if not for God, then for memory.

The spindle tree root would throw out new fibres, deep within the earth, beneath the concrete, even if its leaves never again saw the light of day, and wait, surviving in Annie's collagraphs which, at that very moment, Lily was dusting back in Lapwing Lane.

Later that night, in the lounge of *The Queen's Hotel*, which, having had to close its doors on Christmas Eve while the Great Fire of Piccadilly had leaped and licked for miles around, had reopened. Cam sang to the faithful, who gathered like midnight mass, hungry for hope.

"It's a lovely day tomorrow
Tomorrow is a lovely day
Come and feast your tear dimmed eyes
On tomorrow's clear blue skies…"

In Lapwing Lane, Lily, Evelyn and Pearl waited with growing anxiety. Just after midnight, there came a knock on the door. Lily opened it to see a young constable standing on the step, looking as though the last few days had aged him too many years. He'd seen sights that nobody should see, yet it was still duties such as these which pained him the most.

"Is this the home of Mrs Annie Wright?" he asked, removing his helmet.

"Yes," replied a pale-looking Lily. "It is."

The constable could see past the young woman into the hall where a much older woman was leaning against the banister rail of the stairway, being supported by a second young woman.

"Then I'm afraid to say that I have some very bad news for you."

Lily nodded. "You'd best come in," she said, pulling the front door fully back.

The constable stepped across the threshold, wiped his muddy feet on the mat as the young woman closed the door behind him.

"If today your heart is weary
If every little thing looks gray
Just forget your troubles and learn to say
Tomorrow is a lovely day…"

*

A month later a thick blanket of snow lay across much of Salford and Manchester. Lack of electrical power and water shortages meant that schools had not yet gone back after Christmas, with utilities and reserves being first diverted to the factories in Trafford Park where, despite the Blitz, aircraft and weapons production remained at full strength as the country continued to mobilize, to be ready to take the fight back to the enemy. Manchester had been bloodied and bowed by the Christmas bombing, but not beaten. Metro-Vicks would build more than a thousand Lancasters by the end of the War, working from meticulous designs produced by people like Jaz, Esther's husband, who since the turn of the year had been frequently working a double shift. The raids had continued, but sporadically, with less intensity, while the *Luftwaffe* switched its attention to Portsmouth and Plymouth, Swansea and Southampton.

The snow had brought a lull, to Salford especially, covering streets and houses, fields and factories alike, in a unifying white, so that it resembled more a scene from a Christmas Card than a city under siege. Sound, as so often happens with snow, was deadened, creating a world of silence and serenity, which was as beguiling as it was misleading.

On Friday 31st January 1941, as the late afternoon light began to drain from the sky, the last few stragglers of children were defying their frozen fingers for one final bout of snowball throwing and a last sledge ride down the long, steep slope of Buile Hill Park.

Among them stood eleven year old Richie Catch, a navy woollen balaclava on his head, knitted by his mother in one of her occasional burst of domesticity. "*Mon chevalier en armure brillante*," she had cooed as she cast off the final stitches and held it out in front of her. "*Richard, Coeur du Lion*." Richie had pretended to be embarrassed and squirmed as she hugged him to her, but on this late Friday afternoon he was secretly glad of it, in spite of the relentless teasing by the other kids when they first saw it. Now they regarded him enviously, shivering with their blue lips, pink ears and raw, red knees. He sucked and chewed on the wool of the balaclava in front of his face like it was an iced lolly.

"Are you coming out again after tea?" called Mack, the oldest of them and self-styled leader of the gang. Mack's elder brother, Jim, was an RAF Pilot, and had assumed god-like status. Mack, just by virtue of being his brother, had, by natural osmosis, acquired at least a veneer of this.

"Depends if there's an air raid," said Ian, his bouncy red hair dusted with snow.

"Or if our mam'll let him," said Maisie, his younger sister, who stuffed a snowball down the back of his neck. The two of them ran squealing down the slope.

Richie and Mack each had a sledge and were trudging up to the top of Buile Hill for one last ride.

"Last one down's a cissy," yelled Mack, launching himself forward, lying prone on his stomach.

Richie watched him race away from him before sitting astride his bigger, but slower sledge, kicking his heels into the packed ice to try and work up some speed. Although Mack was faster, he had no way of controlling his direction, so when he started to veer off to the right, there was nothing he could do about it, while Richie, the tortoise to Mack's hare, slowly made up ground, gradually gathering speed, until he drew level with, then passed him. Furious, Mack threw himself to his right, forcing his sledge back on track. Below them the bottom of the slope loomed, where it pooled out into a wide collecting bowl, like the bottom of a fairground helter skelter ride. Just before this bowl was an elevated, overhanging shelf, formed by several inches of hard-packed snow which had fallen on what was a brick retaining wall, now completely covered. The boys always tried to make for this because, if they timed their arrival right, it would give them sufficient lift to clear the collecting bowl and land on another down slope, which would then take them all the way down to the park gates right at the bottom. Both were now heading straight for this overhang, which was only wide enough to take one sledge at a time. They raced beside each other, nip and tuck, till, at the very last moment, Mack leant further across to his left and deliberately nudged Richie's elbow, which tipped him off balance, so that he missed the shelf and landed with a hard thud in the centre of the bowl. Whooping like a cockerel, Mack soared above Richie's head, but just failed to make the down slope, swerving to a stop with a spectacular spray of thrown up snow from the sledge's edge, much of which landed on top of Richie, who lay in a heap, his old sledge broken and in pieces all around him.

Mack, Ian, Maisie and the other kids all roared with laughter, pelting Richie with further taunts and snowballs.

"Look at tha' sledge, it's a reet dog's dinner…"

"I'd brek it up for firewood, if I were thee…"

"It's fit for nowt else…"

"Throw it on t' scrap heap…"

"Same as thee…"

"Tha's nowt but rubbish tha'self…"

They all knew about his unusual home life, which they never tired of reminding him of.

"Where's tha' dad, eh…?"

"Din't tha' know, 'e 'an't got one…"

"What 'appened to 'im then…?"

"Tom, Tom the Piper's Son
Learnt to play when he was young
But the only song that he could play
Was 'Over the Hills and Far Away'…"

"I 'ear your mam does it under t' arches for a penny…"

Richie picked up the iron runner from his broken sledge and began to whirl it in a wide circle, howling as he ran towards them. He didn't care how much damage he might do if he hit any of them. He wanted to, in fact, but his rage was so wild, so uncontrolled that he swung wildly without aim or purpose, and they easily dodged him. They ran off down the slope. By the time they reached the park gates they had already forgotten him and were taunting Ian about his sticking out ears instead.

"I reckon," said Maisie, "if tha' flapped 'em 'ard enough, tha' could tek off from t' top of th' hill an' fly all by tha'self."

"Ay," said Mack, joining in with relish, "then if we tied 'im down wi' string, 'e could be our very own barrage balloon."

"'Is face alone'd be enough to scare off t' Jerries…"

They swooped down the hill, through the gates, and spilled out into the main road, around the corner and out of sight, their voices becoming lost in the raucous racket of rooks roosting in the winter sycamores as darkness fell. The moon rose in the sky like a shiny coin, towards which individual birds made final, daring raids before settling in the branches, cawing insults to one another.

Richie trudged home, dragging the broken sledge

behind him. Home. He was never sure about this, for he had two – the flat on Silk Street which he shared with his mother, and the shack alongside his *Grandpère's* Smithy, where he spent most of his time, and where he was headed now.

He kicked the snow from off his shoes against the wall outside before scraping off what was left on the soles along an upturned horse shoe hammered into the earth for the purpose by his *Grandpère*. Catch was standing by the old cast iron gas cooker in the far corner of the single long room, which ran the length of the shack, frying bacon. He didn't look up as Richie tumbled in through the front door, knowing it would be him.

"You're late," he said, without turning round.

"Sorry," mumbled Richie, hanging his sodden gloves and balaclava over the guard in front of the fire, which his *Grandpère* kept lit throughout the year, whatever the weather. Tonight Richie was glad of it. He peeled off his stiff, frozen socks, hung them up beside the gloves and balaclava, and pushed his feet up to the guard as close as he dared.

"Careful," said Catch, still not turning round. "It doesn't do to put too much heat straight on to too much cold."

"I know," said Richie, more sullenly than he intended, withdrawing his feet a few inches.

The change in tone caused Catch to look round. "What's up wi' you, young 'un?" he said, depositing the plate of bacon on the table, mopping up the fat from the pan with a slice of dried bread, which he then lay alongside on the plate. "Eat," he said. "That'll put hairs on your chest."

Richie got up and sat at the table. The smell and sizzle mollified his mood. The dog, which up until then had been lying comatose under the table, twitched his nose and moved alongside Richie, looking up at him in pitiful hope.

"Away with you, Quilt," said Catch. "You've been fed already." Quilt, tail between his legs, slunk away towards the threadbare rag rug in front of the fire. All of Catch's dogs were called Quilt. This was the fifth one he'd had, all of them black and tan, all of them mongrels. It was Clem who'd named the first one, and that was fine with Catch. He'd seen no reason to name the others any different, especially now, since Clem had gone.

Richie followed his *Grandpère's* gaze, towards another horse shoe, which leant against the wall, on the mantel above the fireplace. He knew he was thinking about his *Grandmère*, who'd died when Richie was only four. He had vague memories of her still, like the way she used to wield the heavy hammer above her head as if it was no more than a feather before bringing it crashing down upon the anvil, she and *Grandpère* working together in a steady rhythm, as old and easy as the ticking of a clock. If he was playing outside in the yard, Richie would always be able to tell which of them was striking the anvil by the different sound each of them made. Clink, clank. Tick, tock.

She had kept chickens, which would scratch and scrabble about the yard. He had another faint picture in his mind of holding her hand, creeping softly up to the coop and reaching inside to see if there were any eggs, and how she would allow him to carry them one by one cupped in his own tiny palms. How one morning they woke up to find feathers bloody and scattered behind the forge, where a fox had laid waste to the entire flock one hot summer's night when somebody – mentioning no names, but a hard stare in Catch's direction – must have forgotten to lock up the shed. There'd be no repeating that mistake, she said, and a few months later he remembered her ears prick up at the sound of a scurry outside, her picking up her shot gun that lay propped up in a corner of the one long downstairs room in the shack, then storming into the yard like a hurricane and blasting that poor fox to Kingdom come.

But in truth those memories were fading now. He could no longer rightly recall what she looked like, save a face with eyes that shone in the dark, a skin the colour of roasted chestnuts, and a mouth with horse shoe nails clamped between its lips which, when she'd spit these out to hammer home the shoe sweet and sure into the horn of the horse's hoof, would sing like warm honey. "Your *Grandmère*," Richie's mother would say, "she was the real singer, not me…"

Catch's gaze was still fixed upon the single horse shoe propped up on the mantel. He caught Richie's eye watching him.

"There used to be three," he said, coughing. "I made one for each of us. By rights I should've made you one."

Richie didn't like to ask him why he hadn't.

"But then your *Grandmère* got sick, and it just didn't seem right."

Richie accepted this.

"What happened to the other two?" he asked.

"One was buried with your *Grandmère* when she died. The other... your *Maman* has got it somewhere. She took it with her when she moved out."

"Oh," said Richie, realising, "yes. It's in a tin she keeps on her dressing table with all her brushes and pins. She never said you'd made it."

"Did you ask her?"

"No, I didn't."

"I reckon she'd've told you if you had."

Richie finished his bacon, wiping his plate clean with the last of the bread. "Thanks, *Grandpère*," he said.

Catch nodded and cleared it away. "So what's been eating you?"

Richie said nothing.

"I know there's something. The way you stomped across the yard, then kicked the snow from off your boots like you was trying to shake some chain from round your ankle."

Richie opened his mouth to speak, then closed it again. How did his *Grandpère* always know when something wasn't quite right?

"Tell me when you're ready," said Catch, opening the back door, letting in a sharp blast of cold air. "I'll be in the forge."

Richie mooched around, looking for something to do, but he couldn't rid his ears of the taunts thrown at him by Mack and Maisie, the one about his missing father. He'd once asked his mother about him, about why it was they never saw him, had never seen him in his case, and she only smiled, a dark, cat-like smile that spoke of things he didn't understand. She opened a drawer near the bottom of her dressing table and pulled out a small metal tin. Then she rooted among her rings and necklaces in her crocodile skin jewellery box.

"Is it a real crocodile?" he'd breathlessly wondered when he was much younger. "*Non, cheri*," she'd said, distractedly holding up a pair of ear rings she'd found that she'd evidently forgotten she'd had, "it's pretend," and she'd laughed in that way she had that sounded like bells tinkling far off, water running over rocks.

"What's the point of it then?" he'd asked, genuinely puzzled.

"It was your *Grandmère's*," she'd answered. "She gave it to me when I started to make my own way as a singer. In the country where she was born they have real crocodiles – alligators – that she would see sometimes, basking in the mud on the banks of a swamp, or lying half submerged under the water. They would remain still like that for hours at a time, so that you might almost forget that they were there. That's when they were at their most dangerous. They just bided their time till you wandered a little too close. They'd open their huge mouths, almost as if they were yawning, then – bang! They'd snap tight shut and never let go till they'd swallowed you whole."

When she told this story, Cam would clamp her elbows together, hinging her arms stiffly, capturing Richie in their grip, so that he squealed and giggled in equal measure, as she pretended to gobble him up.

"I still don't understand," he said, after he'd recovered, and Cam was holding up a different pair of ear rings, which she hung from Richie's ears, sitting behind him, looking at both their reflections in the mirror.

"See," she would say, "how the light catches them…"

Then she put them down upon the dresser, her thoughts far away once more. She picked up the open jewellery box. "It reminded her of home," she said, "and the lucky escape she'd had," and she snapped the box shut.

In her hand she was holding a key. She inserted it into the metal tin, which opened stiffly. Inside were assorted treasures – a horse shoe, a bird's feather, a dried chamomile flower, a few loose photographs. She looked swiftly through these, occasionally stopping to linger over one, which she would pass across to Richie – a camp by a river with three tepee-like tents made from branches, an old man sitting alone at the water's edge, another man skinning moles, a couple cooking fish over an open fire, and his *Grandmère* and *Grandpère* when they were younger looking directly at the camera, *Grandmère* leaning on her shotgun, *Grandpère* with his hammer slung over his shoulder; his *Grandmère* and *Grandpère* again, a bit older now, standing outside the forge in Buile Hill, with his mother as a little girl drawing something with a stick in the dirt at their feet, her hair starred with chamomile flowers; and then a handsome man in a sharp suit, a pork pie hat on his head, a trumpet dangling loosely from his fingers. Richie brought this last photograph right up close to his own face, poring over every detail of it. Something about the eyes, looking out from under their wide, hooded lids, a ghost of a smile, wreathed in cigarette smoke, held him.

"Is this…?" he began, but could not finish the

sentence.

"Your Papa?" said Cam, taking the snap from him, shaking her head with a lazy smile. "*Oui, vraiment.* It sure is." She looked back at Richie. "I know what you're thinking. You're wondering how come he ain't around no more. Let's just say he wasn't the kind of man cut out to be a father. Don't ask me where he is, cos I don't know. I woke up one morning and he was gone. Like a swallow looking to return to Africa…*Une petite hirondelle*…"

Her eyes took on that far away look that Richie had seen before but had not known the reason for. She drifted over to the record player on its low table in the corner of the room. She selected a disc from the small pile next to it, took it carefully from its sleeve, dusted it on the hem of her skirt, then placed it on the turntable. Through the warm hiss of crackles a muted trumpet cut through the night, its notes full of loss and a yearning for home. "Man," she said, lying back on the moth-eaten chaise longue, "he could sure blow that horn…"

Richie tried to shut out those long drawn out notes and phrases. Five nights a week his mother sang at *The Queen's Hotel* in Manchester. Even on Christmas Day she'd sung there. So Richie spent most of his time here at his *Grandpère's*. A Granny Reardun, the kids had called him. That was when his *Grandmère* was still alive, but somehow the taunt had stuck. He reached for his socks from the fire guard. They steamed. Not completely dry, but no longer stiff with snow or ice. He pulled them back on his feet, tied on his boots which, though battered and old, were water proof and did not leak, for which he was grateful, especially on days like these. He threw open the back door and stood for a moment on the step, feeling the cold air hitting his face, shrugging off those awkward memories of the past, flinging him right back to the present, the here and now. Quilt looked up from beneath the table, wondering whether to join Richie and venture outside for one last walk, but then thought better of it, and lay his head back down between his paws. Richie stepped outside, slamming the door behind him. He strode quickly across the yard, into the forge, where he could see his *Grandpère* bent over some task, his face and torso lit from the red glow of the fire, holding something with a pair of tongs in his left hand, which he turned for the hammer in his right hand to strike. Turning, striking, turning, striking. Hammer and tong, hammer and tong. The soothing, changeless rhythm of it began to quieten Richie. He patiently waited. He stood and watched and waited. Until his *Grandpère* had finished.

Catch, satisfied that the job was complete, plunged the iron into the cooling trough, where it sizzled, and held it there till the smoke stopped rising and the hissing ceased.

"Here," he said, extending the tongs towards Richie. "Hold out your hand."

Richie looked up at him with a frown.

"Don't worry," he said. "It's quite cool."

Richie held out his hand and Catch deposited into it a freshly wrought horse shoe. Richie closed his fingers around it and held it up close to inspect. "For me?" he whispered.

"Ay lad," said Catch, taking off his apron and hanging up the tongs, "I thought it were about time."

"Thank you."

Catch ruffled the boy's hair.

"Now," he said, "I suppose you've come to tell me what all the bother's been about…"

"It's the sledge," he said. "It's rubbish."

Catch smiled. "Is it now? Let's have a look at it then."

Richie brought it over and Catch examined it respectfully. The one thing Richie could never accuse his *Grandpère* of was treating him like a kid. He ran his finger over the rim of the iron runner, spat on it, then flicked the saliva away with his thumb. He grunted, then turned back to Richie.

"These are not too bad," he said. "There's no rust in 'em. But they're shaped wrong." He laid them on top of his work bench, while he bent to pick up what remained of the wooden-slatted sledge, which had splintered, cracked and broken in several places. He clicked his tongue. "You're right," he said. "This *is* rubbish."

"I told you," said Richie hotly.

"It's not the wood's fault," said Catch quietly. "Where did you find it?"

Richie paused, his face reddening despite the cold. "It was lying in a corner over there," he said, pointing to where all kinds of what, to the untrained eye, looked like things which had seen better days, or been thrown away for firewood. But Catch never threw anything away. It wasn't in his nature. He'd always find a use for it, whatever it was, maybe not now, maybe not for several years, but one day, eventually, he'd rummage through the pile, pluck something up from the chaotic heap, and declare with one of his rare smiles that perhaps its time had come.

"I seem to recollect your mother making this when she was about the same age you are now." He chuckled at the memory, which then turned into a cough.

Richie bit his tongue, wanting to say no wonder it was rubbish, what would a girl know about building sledges, but then he remembered his *Grandmère*, who'd shown him how to arm wrestle when he was only five, and told him that the trick was not just in how strong you were, but in timing. "You've got to take 'em by surprise," she'd said. "Watch," and she'd challenged his *Grandpère* to a contest, who immediately pushed her arm down to the side. "Best of three," she'd added. Then, before his *Grandpère* was ready, she'd caught him off guard and levelled the score. For the decider the two of them looked each other in the eye, smiling. Richie remembered how she'd kept fooling his *Grandpère* into thinking she was about to push, then ease off, so that he was never quite sure just when to press the trigger and apply all of his strength. While he was trying to puzzle this out, she'd quickly thrust his arm down, almost, but not quite, to the table's top. Catch would then put everything he had into trying to push her arm back up, inch by inch, until both arms were almost vertical again. "Is that the best you can do?" she'd say, and he'd laugh, relax again for a split second, at which point – wham – down she would press again, rapping the knuckles on the back of his hand onto the table.

His *Grandpère* would wipe his brow and shake his head. "You watch this one," he'd say. "She don't play fair. Never has, never will."

"That's right, honey child. Play to win."

"But never cheat," added Catch, looking at Clem with fierce pride.

It was, surprisingly, Clem who'd backed down first and returned to tousle Richie's hair. "No. You have to be able to look yourself in the eye and know you're being true. That's what I admire so much about your *Maman*."

Richie hadn't understood what she'd meant by that at the time, but he was beginning to, he thought. "Do unto others," his mother had said to him, when she was putting away the photograph of his father back into its tin. "He'd have been like a bird in a cage if I'd made him stay, which he would have if I'd asked him to, if I'd told him about you."

"Then let's not keep him locked away in your drawer any more."

Cam nodded, leant the photograph against the mirror, and began to sing.

"I wish I were a little swallow
And I had wings, and I could fly
I'd fly back home to one who loves me
And try to pass my troubles by

But I am not a little swallow
I have no wings, neither can I fly
I'll lie down here and sleep till morning
And let my troubles pass me by…"

Richie was brought back to the present by the sound of his *Grandpère* rummaging through the pile of misshapen lengths of wood.

"The thing about your mother is," he said, "she was always in a tearing hurry. Still is." He smiled, holding up the broken sledge. "Not a bad effort, though, for a nine year old."

Richie's eyes widened.

"Ay lad, that's right. She were younger 'n you when she built this. Could you do any better?" He tossed the sledge back to him. Richie, cradling the separate pieces of wood in his arms, knew that he couldn't.

"Could you show me?"

Catch thought for a moment.

"I'll tell you what," he said, then paused while another bout of coughing wracked him. "I'm thinking you'll be wanting to get back out there tonight for another go. Am I right?"

Richie nodded.

"I don't blame you. The snow might all be gone tomorrow, and you never know when there'll be this much again."

"Strike while the iron's hot," said Richie, grinning.

His *Grandpère* smiled back. "Cheeky," he said, cuffing his ears lightly. "I'll knock you one up quickly then," he continued, "so you can try it out tonight. And if it suits, if it fits you, then tomorrow I'll show you how to make one yourself. In the meantime, you go back inside and wash up. Deal?"

"Deal," said Richie, and they shook hands solemnly. "Thanks, *Grandpère*."

"Don't thank me yet. Wait till you've tried it first."

Richie lingered by the forge door. "What do you mean – if it fits me? You make it sound like something to wear."

"The sledge and the rider must move as one," said Catch. "Like a second skin. I remember my own grandfather telling me that about the first horse I tried to ride. I kept falling off. Nothing to do with the horse, nothing to do with me. We just didn't fit right, that's what he said. Off you go now. Get those dishes washed, and take Quilt out one last time."

Richie looked up as he stepped outside. It was completely dark now. The stars shone bright and clear, arching across the sky. He could make out the Plough, the *Pleiades*, Orion's belt. One thing about the blackout, it was great for seeing the stars. His *Grandpère* had different names for them from the ones Richie was taught at school. The Fox. The Serpent. The Council of Chiefs. The Star That Does Not Walk.

"It's a bomber's moon," he called out over his shoulder. A hunter's moon, his *Grandpère* would call it. "Is it true, do you think, the German pilots use the Ship Canal as a sighter?"

There was no reply from Catch, just the sound of sawing wood, hammer and nail, an anvil's ring, the breeze rattling the three iron egrets hanging in the eaves of the forge, as if preparing to take flight.

He went back inside the ramshackle, old cottage to wash the dishes, placing the horse shoe Catch had made for him on the mantel above the hearth next to his *Grandpère's*. Under the table, Quilt opened one eye briefly, then closed it again.

An hour later Richie was standing at the top of Buile Hill, the new sledge tucked under his arm, looking down the slope which stretched away from him. There'd been a fresh snowfall since he was there in the late afternoon, and the hill lay pristine and untouched before him, blue in the moonlight.

Richie placed the sledge reverently upon the printless snow in front of him. He'd deliberately climbed the hill around the outside edge of it, so as not to leave a single footprint to impede his first run. The newly sanded and ground runners caressed the snow beneath them. As he lay face down upon the wooden base, he felt it mould to his shape. A pair of handles, carved from ash, curved up on either side of him, like the prow of a ship, simple, clean, uncluttered lines, whose rounded ends he could clasp each hand around effortlessly. "These will help you steer," his *Grandpère* had said. "Just the slightest extra pressure should be enough. Any more and you'll topple sideways."

He steadied himself, set his eyes first upon the overhanging wall of packed snow three quarters of the way down which, if he timed his arrival there correctly, would propel him just far enough to clear the upturned bowl in the centre of the park, catch the second downward slope to take him clear through the first set of iron gates, which marked the entrance to the bowling green through the other side, where he would come naturally and, he hoped, gracefully, to a stop.

He kicked back with his feet and felt the sledge begin to move beneath him. Gradually it started to pick up speed. The iron runners cut through the snow easily, like paring cheese, without gathering any of the snow to them, which might have slowed his progress. It took the leap at the overhang effortlessly. Richie felt the wind in his face, the air pinning back his ears, and for those few seconds it seemed as though he were actually flying. When the sledge hit the ground again, its base held him comfortably, but he over-compensated with the steering and it flung him to the side, rolling down the slope another twenty yards by himself until he managed to bring himself to a stop.

Cross with himself, he dusted off the snow from his coat and trousers, picked up the sledge and made his way once more back to the top of the hill. The second time he managed to stay aboard for longer, the third time longer still. He was beginning to understand just how much – or little – pressure he needed to exert to allow the sledge to run, unencumbered and free. It needed his weight upon it for it to acquire the necessary speed, but then just the slightest shift to the left or right, the gentlest of easing, was all that was required for the sledge to adjust its course to the line sought and aimed for by Richie. After half a dozen runs, it was taking the overhang in its stride, responding to every nuance and adjustment Richie asked of it – a pulling up of his weight from the front of the sledge just before take off saw him gain extra height and distance, the merest suggestion of a lean to the left just before it landed would already be altering its course to allow Richie to steer his way dead centre between the iron gates, enabling him to complete a three-sixty turn at the bottom, by digging his heels in the snow as he reached the bowling green. Seen from above, these spectacular spins resembled the whorls of fossils, delicate ice patterns tracking each landing, a skater's drawing, like rock art, proof that he was making his own marks on the land, for some future archaeologist to uncover in years to come and speculate as to their meaning. But they would never understand the true joy in their making, the pure, unadulterated pleasure of creation for its own sake.

After his eleventh run, one for each year of his life, the siren went for an air raid. Richie knew he should go back, join Catch and Quilt in the crude iron shelter his *Grandpère* had constructed at the back of the forge, but something held him there. With the Ship Canal glittering beneath the huge bomber's moon, the German pilots would be able to fly their *Junkers* and their *Messerschmitts* directly to their targets in Trafford Park. He'd be as safe here as back in the shelter, from where he wouldn't be able to see a thing.

As if to confirm what he was thinking, at that moment he became aware of the now familiar heavy drone of the German bombers. All of them at school had become expert in identifying whether the unseen aircraft above the clouds were British or German just by sound alone. Tonight, though, there would be no need to put such powers to the test. Almost as soon as he had heard the drone, he saw the dark silhouetted shapes of the planes ranging in attack formation above him in the frost-clear sky.

Instantaneously the searchlights mounted on concrete bunkers in nearby Urmston and Irlam picked them out too. Caught in the powerful cross beams the pilots tried to alter their course or trajectory, but they didn't possess the manoeuvrability of fighter planes, so they just hovered there like sitting ducks for the ack-ack guns, which immediately opened fire. It was like watching a war film at *The Rex* on Chapel Street, where Richie went sometimes on Saturday mornings. Planes exploded in mid air or, having been hit, nose-dived towards the Irwell in a spiralling, smoking whine, slowly sinking in its muddy ooze beneath its thin plate of ice, or crash landing in the boggy meadows alongside. Some of the pilots evidently made it through this cordon of steel and light, for he saw explosions blossom like flowers over Trafford Park.

Suddenly, a much louder crack split the sky above his head. He looked up and saw a *Messerschmitt* moving in and out of the twin searchlight beams, which hunted it down, flitting from light to shadow in some hypnotic *danse macabre*. The plane had been hit, but not fatally. Richie could see the smoke funnelling from its tail. He imagined the pilot desperately trying to wrestle back control of the joystick, the dials on the altimeter and fuel gauge rapidly revolving like pinwheels. Another burst of gunfire smashed a wing, sending the plane into a final, terminal tail spin. But at that moment the pilot ejected himself from the cockpit. For a split second he was caught as he fell by the searchlight's beam, then lost again, as it shifted its gaze towards another target, but not before Richie had seen the parachute open, a dandelion clock floating earthwards like thistledown.

Richie counted. One o'clock, two o'clock, three o'clock...

And there he was, picked out briefly by the bomber's moon as he dropped towards the park. Richie strained his eyes to keep track of him silently falling.

Four o'clock, five o'clock, six o'clock...

Richie could see exactly where he was headed. Dropping his sledge at the point where he started each run, he raced towards the opposite side of the park, past the frozen pond, on which he could see a family of perplexed ducks huddled against the stiff, ice-encrusted reeds at what would normally be the pond's edge, around the side of the great sandpit, in which huge diggers were temporarily stuck fast, extinct dinosaurs which would come back to life with the thaw to excavate the sand to try and meet the inexhaustible demand for sandbags everywhere now, the stacked mountains he and Mack would race each other to climb, round the craters in the bombed out streets, towards the line of trees behind the Big House – willow and pine, beech and alder – where the pilot's parachute was inexorably falling.

Seven o'clock, eight o'clock, nine o'clock...

Richie reached the trees just as the parachute did. He heard a ripping and screaming as the pilot fell through the upper branches of the tallest pine, before hanging there, suspended, caught in a tangle of harness and lines, the white silk canopy of the chute extending out and away from him, like an angel's wings.

Ten o'clock, eleven o'clock, twelve o'clock...

The all clear sounded.

Richie looked up, catching his breath. The pilot looked down, groaning and creaking in the wind.

They stared at each other a long time.

Eventually Richie cupped his hands to his mouth and called up.

"Hello?" No answer. "Are you alive?"

A dry cough and a mirthless laugh.

"*Ja. Ich bin am Leben.* I'm alive."

Richie's eyes widened. "You speak English."

Another feeble laugh. "*Ja. Ich spreche Englisch.*"

"Are you hurt?"

"*Ja.* Very much, I think."

Richie surveyed the tree. He reckoned he could probably climb up to reach the pilot, but what would he do once he got there? He wasn't strong enough to carry him down again. Perhaps he might be able to untangle the mass of lines so that the pilot could then climb down himself. That is, if he was able to climb down. Perhaps his injuries would prevent him. But if he did, then he might get away. Or he might take him as a hostage to bargain his own way to freedom. Unless he, Richie, managed to capture the pilot first and make him his prisoner. Then he'd be a hero. He'd be in all the papers. He might even feature in one of those newsreels down at *The Rex*. That'd be one in the eye for Mack. For the moment, though, neither of them did anything.

Suddenly, there was a loud creaking in the branches above and the pilot began to slide further towards the ground. In a great rush of splintering wood and flapping silk he fell, only for the chute to become caught up in another unstable knot of branches, so that the pilot now dangled just a few feet above Richie's head.

When the shower of cones and twigs and needles had finally ceased, a precarious stillness settled on them once again. The pilot was moaning louder, in obvious pain and distress. Richie could see matted clots of blood which had soaked through his uniform from the region of his right foot and lower leg. If he did fall right to the ground, he wasn't going to be running off anywhere any time soon.

"Wie heisst du?" said the pilot, his voice rasping in his throat.

Richie, not understanding, said nothing. The rattling of the pilot's chest frightened him.

"What's your name?" repeated the pilot.

Richie wondered whether to tell him or not. You weren't supposed to consort with the enemy – that's what had been drummed into them at school. But if you had to, only give them your name, rank and number.

"Richie," he said, then added, "what's yours?"

The pilot smiled thinly. "Roland."

Roland? That didn't sound German. He'd been expecting a Hans or a Fritz. There was a Roland in Richie's class at school.

"How old are you, Richie?"

Age wasn't a part of the name, rank and number routine, but Richie didn't see what harm could come of telling him. "Eleven," he said.

"You're very brave."

Richie could feel his cheeks redden. Was this some kind of enemy trap? Was Roland trying to lull him into a false sense of security, lure him with flattery, then pounce when his defences were down? Richie didn't think so. Richie didn't think of Roland as any kind of enemy. He didn't look that different from Mack's brother, Jim. Both wore blue-grey uniforms. Maybe Roland's was a bit darker, that's all.

"What are you doing out in the middle of a raid?

Shouldn't you be sheltering somewhere?"

"I was sledging," said Richie simply.

"Ah yes, I see. A very good night for sledging. I apologise for interrupting you." He paused. Richie could see the look of pain cross his face.

"Do you...?" he began. "Do you want me to go and get help? Or... do you want me to try and cut you down? I could reach you if I climbed."

"And do you have a knife?"

No. But I thought you might..."

Roland tried to laugh but winced instead.

"I think," he said, "you should try to cut me down. I'm not sure I could survive another fall to the ground. But it might just be possible, if you're careful, to cut the lines one at a time, so that I am lowered little by little."

Richie shinned up the tree in a trice, climbing to a branch just above Roland, which would take his weight, and from where he could reach up to cut through the parachute in such a way as might allow Roland to descend in slow stages. But first he would need a knife.

"The inside pocket of my flying jacket," said Roland. "I'd pass it to you myself, except that my arms are too tangled, and I fear that if I tried to reach it, I might bring both of us crashing to the ground."

Richie didn't hesitate. Hanging almost upside down, his knees hooked round the branch of the tree, with one arm wrapped around the trunk, he inched the fingers of his other hand slowly towards the pilot's flying jacket. He carefully slipped them inside and at once could feel a patch of sticky blood which was still slowly oozing from between cracked ribs. Their faces were now extremely close to one another. Richie could feel Roland's hot breath mingle with his own. He worked his fingers agonisingly slowly, deeper inside the jacket, until at last the tip of one of them brushed against the handle of the knife. Barely gripping it between his first and second fingers he gently eased it out towards him. Just as he had almost pulled it clear, it caught on the teeth of the zip and he dropped it. Instinctively Roland thrust out his hand, caught it and held it towards Richie. Their eyes met just as the first few snowflakes of another shower began to fall. Richie no longer saw an enemy pilot. Instead he saw someone who simply needed his help. He saw hope and he saw trust, and he knew that these were being mirrored back.

He nodded, took the knife and, with the help of his other arm wrapped around the tree trunk, he manoeuvred himself back into an upright position, from where he began to cut through the first of the lines. The harness dropped a couple of feet, then held. He cut a second line. The harness dropped another foot. But when he cut through a third line, the harness was released completely, something Richie had not anticipated, and Roland began to fall. Richie desperately tried to pull back on the parachute silk, but it slipped through his fingers. He made one last lunge and lost his balance, so that the two of them tumbled the remaining ten feet or so to the earth below. Fortunately, the snow cushioned their landing. Richie had a sense of being held in the parachute as he fell, protecting him like a pair of outstretched wings, an egret flying across the moon. When he hit the ground, he was enveloped in a world of white.

The fall had knocked the breath out of him, but otherwise he was unhurt. As he recovered his bearings, he heard, after a few moments, Roland moaning several feet away. From the sound of him, he had not been so lucky. Richie managed to crawl his way out of the parachute, back into the night air of the park, where he could see Roland still struggling with his harness. A patch of fresh blood had stained the snow.

"I'm sorry," said Richie. "You were too heavy for me."

"*Nein*," gasped Roland. "You made the fall a lot less bad than it would otherwise have been."

Beneath the bomber's moon, which had once again emerged from behind the small cloud that had briefly covered it while the last snow flurry fell, Richie could begin to see just how badly injured Roland was. As well as the injury to his ribs, one arm looked as though it might be broken, but it was the foot which was causing him the greatest pain. Roland saw Richie looking at it.

"*Ja*," he said, "it looks bad, I think."

Somehow the last fall had wrenched off his boot, and Richie had to turn away from the black and swollen mass he briefly caught a glimpse of.

"I need to get help," he said. He dragged the parachute towards Roland and covered him with it.

"*Ja*," said Roland again, speaking less fluently now. "*Danke*." His teeth were chattering. "*Das wird mich warm halten…*"

Richie raced away past the trees towards the drive which led away from Buile Hill House to the park's main entrance onto Eccles Old Road. The stone piers on either side of the imposing iron gateposts were capped with snow. Someone had stuck pieces of coal in for eyes and a twig for a nose, with a tin helmet balanced on each, so that they resembled a pair of rather comical Home Guards. Richie, reaching the road, wildly looked in both directions, desperately hoping that some actual members might be at hand, whom he could call on for help, but there were none. Not knowing which direction to take he headed for the junction with Weaste Lane. Rounding the corner was an ARP Warden on her bicycle. Tucked beneath her helmet was a scarf of white muslin, which flowed behind her, like an Arabian princess.

"Help!" he shouted.

She stopped at once.

"What is it?"

"A German pilot," he said, pointing back to the park. "Over by the trees. Badly injured. Lost a lot of blood."

"Show me."

Immediately Richie turned tail and ran back the way he had come. The woman followed him as best she could, but her bicycle became bogged down in the snow, which was deeper in the park than it was on the roads. She flung it down, threw her first aid bag over her shoulder and ran hard after Richie.

"You did well to fetch me," she said as soon as they arrived. Roland had slipped out of consciousness and she had to revive him by gently slapping the side of his face. "Good," she said briskly as his eyes fluttered back open. "My name's Esther. What's yours?"

"R-Roland," he stammered.

"Well, Roland, Richie here tells me you speak

excellent English, so I'm going to explain to you what I'm going to do. First of all, I'm going to clean and dress that foot of yours. I'm afraid it's going to hurt, but you can shout all you want, there's no one to hear you except me and Richie, and we don't mind, do we, Richie?"

"No, Miss."

She quickly took out lint and bandages, disinfectant and a pair of scissors. While she was laying everything out ready, she spoke to Richie in a low voice so that Roland couldn't hear. "This is going to be quite unpleasant," she warned, "so if you'd rather not stay, I'd quite understand."

"No, Miss. I want to help if I can."

"Good boy. Talk to him while I attend to his foot. Keep him distracted."

"Very good, Miss."

Richie briefly glanced down as Esther cut away Roland's sock and briefly caught sight of the pulped mess that was Roland's foot. Suppressing the urge to throw up, he quickly turned away and started to speak to Roland, the first things that came into his head.

"How come you know so much English?"

"We learn it in school, but my grandfather, he spent a lot of time here as a boy, so he taught me too."

"Did he fight in the last War?"

"No. But my father did." He gasped suddenly as Esther began to clean around the wound. "Did yours?"

"No," said Richie. "My *Grandpère's* a blacksmith. He had to make shoes for the horses. He reckons he made thousands and thousands of them. What did your father do in the War?"

"He was a soldier. In the trenches. One time, at Christmas, they held a truce. They met with the English Tommies in the middle of No Man's Land."

"My brother was one of those English Tommies," said Esther, as she finished bandaging Roland's foot. "Perhaps not one of those your father met, for it happened in lots of places, didn't it? He wrote to me about it. He said he didn't know why he was fighting men who were just like him."

"*Ja*. That is what my father said also."

"No Christmas truce this time, eh?"

"Perhaps it is taking place now, a few days late," said Roland, coughing and wincing at the same time.

"Perhaps," said Esther briskly. "Let's tackle those ribs of your next, shall we?"

"*Ja. Danke.* You are most kind."

Esther slipped her arms inside his flying jacket and began wrapping another bandage as tightly as she could around Roland's chest. "Richie," she said, "can you go back towards the trees and find me as straight a branch as you can? About eighteen inches long and the thickness of a cricket stump."

"Yes, Miss," and he ran off at once.

"What is this place?" asked Roland.

"It's a park," said Esther. "With swings and roundabouts for the children, and tennis courts and bowling greens, gardens of flowers, and avenues of trees."

"Did someone used to live here? Before it was a park?"

"Yes. Sir Thomas Bayley Potter. The first Mayor of

Manchester. He built a big house here, which still stands today. Over there, behind the trees. You can't see it from here. Not far from where you fell."

"Who lives there now?"

"Nobody. It's more like a museum these days, a reminder of how Manchester used to be once upon a time. A famous novelist came here, about thirty years ago, all the way from America, just for a visit. But she liked it so much, she kept coming back. She wrote a book about it."

"What's it called?"

"*The Secret Garden*. It's a children's book. The sort of children's book you like more as you get older, for you understand it better."

"What's it about?"

"Oh, lots of things. Childhood. Greed. Selfishness. The realisation that true happiness only comes through doing things for others, not for oneself... Some children find a neglected garden, overgrown with weeds and completely forgotten. One of the children is sick. She's also rich and spoilt. But the other children take her to the garden anyway, and together they begin to clear away the nettles and brambles. Flowers start to grow there again, and the little girl not only gets her health back, she gets wisdom too... And it all takes place here," she added, sweeping her arm to include the whole of the park.

"It sounds like a nice place."

"It is. Not a place to be dropping bombs on."

"*Nein. Es tut mir leid.* I'm sorry."

"Yes. I know you are. But it makes me so angry. I thought after the last War we'd never again have to see young boys' lives wasted like this. And for what? The vanity of old men."

"The *Führer* is not old."

"He's older than you. And he's not out here bleeding to death on a freezing winter's night, is he?"

Roland was very quiet. "Is that what's happening to me?" he said at last. "Bleeding to death?"

"I hope not, Roland. But you had lost a lot of blood before I got here, and if Richie hadn't rescued you, you'd probably be dead already."

Roland tried to take this in. He looked suddenly even younger to Esther.

"How old are you?" she said. "I bet you're not even twenty-one yet, are you?"

Roland shook his head. "Next month," he croaked. His mouth felt very dry.

"You're still only a boy," she said bitterly. "What would you be doing now?"

"*Ich verstehe nicht.*"

"I mean, if there wasn't a war?"

"Mathematics," he said, and his face lit up briefly.

Esther smiled. "I always struggled with that in school."

"Numbers cannot lie," he said. "There's a purity in them that I find so…" He searched for the right word. "Comforting. There's an order and a logic to them, and yet…"

"Yes?"

"They can still surprise you."

Esther put her hand upon his brow. Although he was still shivering, it was hot to her touch. "Here," she said. "Drink this," and she pulled out a hip flask of whisky from her warden's coat pocket. "It won't quench your thirst, but it might keep you warm."

"*Danke*." He lifted the flask to his lips, but his hand was shaking too much for him to be able to manage. Esther held it for him and gently tipped a few drops into his mouth. His shaking began to calm a little.

"Richie?" called Esther. "Have you found me that branch yet?"

"Will this do, Miss?" he said, running back.

"Perfect," she said. "Now, Richie, are you going to help me make a splint for Roland's broken arm?"

"I don't know how, Miss."

"Don't worry. I'll teach you. And while I do, I'll tell you both a story. I was first shown how to do this by an American Indian. I'd fallen into a manhole…"

"How did you do that, Miss?"

"I was riding my bicycle and not looking where I was going – that's how."

"Was he really an American Indian, Miss?"

"He was. But I like to think of him as my knight in shining armour, for he came to my rescue just when I needed him."

"What happened?"

"It was my leg that was broken, not my arm, and there were no branches nearby like the one you've found for us, Richie, but believe it or not, poking out of the ground in the trench where I'd fallen, was a human bone…"

"Ugh! I don't believe you!"

"It's as true as I'm sitting here now in the snow."

"And did he…?"

"He did. He used the bone for a splint, just like we're

using this branch for Roland. It was better than a branch actually, because a bone is much stronger, but this branch will do very nicely. There. All done. Now – Richie, if you could just hold Roland's splinted arm steady while I put it in a sling, we'll have done all we can for now."

"*Danke.*"

"What's it like?" asked Richie suddenly, his voice barely more than a whisper.

"What?" said Roland.

"Up there," said Richie, and he pointed towards the sky, "when you're flying?"

Roland thought a while. "It's the best feeling in the world," he said at last. "There's nothing else like it. When you look down onto the earth, it all looks so..." He searched for the right word. "... tidy, so ordered, the villages and towns, like toys."

"Yes," said Richie, imagining.

"But there's so much more. From high up you can see what there was before there were any towns, before there were any roads, ancient marks upon the land, hill forts, burial mounds, contours of old strip fields, hedges and forests, animal tracks and crossing points. Then, when you fly even higher, above the clouds, you don't look down any more, you look up. The sky is always blue above the clouds, so many different shades of it, right through to black the higher up you go, except for when it's night time, and there's nothing between you and the planets, the stars arching over you seem so close you could almost touch them, like a bridge to..." His voice trailed away as he became lost in the memories of these night flights.

"Where?" asked Richie, desperate to know.

"Sometimes..." whispered Roland, "sometimes... I think I see angels."

Richie was entranced. He remembered how, when he first saw Roland hanging from the lines of his parachute from the branches of the pine tree, he thought he was looking at an angel.

Esther, tucking the white muslin scarf that had been Rosie's out of sight under her helmet, inwardly scoffed. She'd no time for these flights of fancy. Angels of death would have been more accurate. "Take no notice of him," she said to Richie. "He's becoming delirious."

Roland shivered. Esther helped him to drink a little more whisky. "What will happen to me?" he said at last.

"Technically, when I hand you over to the Home Guard, which I'm obliged to do, you'll become an official prisoner of war. But because of the seriousness of your injuries, I shall insist that they take you to a camp where there's a hospital. Probably the one in Gorton, on Melland Road. That's close to where I used to live," she added.

"Is it far?" asked Roland.

"Just over seven miles. About half an hour in an ambulance. That's if we can rustle one up. Our first job now is to get you down to the road, which is easier said than done. Richie and I might just about be able to support you between us, if you put an arm around each of our shoulders, but then you'd have to hop. You mustn't put weight on that injured foot of yours on any account."

"I could try," he said, but even the thought of it made him blanch.

"I've got a better idea," said Richie. "We could pull him on my sledge."

"That might work," said Esther. "Have you got it with you?"

"It's just over there," he said, pointing, then he ran off to fetch it.

"Right," she said, when he'd brought it back. "Come on, Roland. Can you drag yourself onto it? That's it. Easy does it."

They set off slowly down the slope beyond the trees, where bits of Roland's parachute still hung in shreds and tatters like afterbirth. To prevent it going too fast and risk losing control of it, they traversed the hill in a series of slow zig-zags.

"This is a very fine sledge," Roland managed to say admiringly.

"I know," said Richie proudly. "My *Grandpère* made it."

Just before they reached the bottom, Esther picked up her abandoned bicycle and set off at a lick along Eccles Old Road, while Richie tried to make Roland comfortable. She was back in less than five minutes followed by a couple of members of the Home Guard, who formally placed Roland under arrest. One of them gave Richie a mint imperial, which he surreptitiously handed to Roland. Esther had brought a flask of tea with her, which she insisted Roland should drink. Less than a quarter of an hour later an ambulance arrived and Roland was transferred carefully from the sledge to a stretcher, then lifted aboard. Just as they were closing the doors he called out, "Thank you, Richie. You saved my life." Then he was gone.

"The hero of the hour, eh my lad?" said one of the Home Guard men, tousling his hair.

"Though if you'd left him to die," said the other, "that'd've been one less Jerry for us to worry about."

"We'll have no more remarks like that if you please, Corporal."

"Sorry, sir."

"Ever heard of the Geneva Convention?"

"Yes, sir."

"If we're to win this War, we're going to have to take a leaf out of young Richie's book here."

"Sir?"

" *'If a clod be washed away by the sea'*," he quoted.

" *'Europe is the less, as well as if a promontory were'*," continued Esther, carrying on from the Home Guard officer.

" *'As well as if a manor of thy friends or of thine own were'*…"

" *'Any man's death diminishes me'*…"

" *'Because I am involved in mankind'*…"

" *'And therefore never send to know for whom the bell tolls'*," added Esther, before they completed the poem together.

" *'It tolls for thee'*."

"Yes, sir," said the Corporal.

Esther and the Home Guard officer regarded each other solemnly.

"What are his chances?" he said.

"Oh, he'll live," said Esther grimly, before adding in a lower voice, so that Richie might not hear, "but I'm not sure they'll be able to save his foot."

The Home Guard Officer nodded, then turned back to Richie. "What's your name, young fellow?"

"Richie, sir. Richard Catch."

"Well then, Richard Catch, I'll make sure you're mentioned in dispatches. That was a good night's work. Now – best be off back home. There'll be people wondering where you've got to."

"Yes, sir. Thank you, sir."

Esther and Richie watched the two Home Guard men cycle away.

"He's right. Off you go. But have a swig of this tea before you do. You look like you need warming up a bit."

Richie swigged from the flask.

"Drink some more when you get home. Water'll do. You've had quite a night of it, and you might feel a bit of shock later." She gripped his wrists. "The Officer was right, Richie. You really have been a hero."

"No, Miss. It were just lucky that I were there."

"Lucky for Roland, certainly."

"I'll never see him again, will I, Miss?"

"No, Richie. Probably not. But you'll remember this night for the rest of your life."

"I already have."

"Oh," she said suddenly. "Look."

She pointed back towards the sky, which was glimmering with a ghostly green light.

"What is it?" whispered Richie. The entire sky seemed to buckle and fold.

"I do believe it's the Northern Lights," said Esther, her eyes widening in wonder. "They're normally only seen in the Arctic."

"Near the North Pole?"

"Yes, that's right." She realised she was whispering, holding her breath in awe at the other worldly spectacle of dancing lights.

All around people were coming out of their houses to look at it, their faces uplifted and caught in their refracted glow.

"It's like being in church," said Richie. "The whole sky's like one giant stained glass window."

"Except this one's constantly shifting and changing," answered Esther. "Like waves in the sea."

"I wouldn't like to be a boat in that sea, Miss. But I wish I could fly in a plane and get a closer look at it."

For nearly an hour or more the people of Salford stood spellbound in awe, each individual iris in their eyes reflecting the sky's iridescent shimmer, until finally it flickered one last time, then faded. A silence fell on the city. People drifted back to their homes. Esther placed her hand on the top of Richie's head before cycling away into the blackout dark of the streets.

The bomber's moon shone down brightly on the park once more, bathing it in a silver monochrome. A frost was hardening the surface of the most recent snowfall, which glistened and sparkled, crunching deliciously beneath Richie's feet as he cut through it on his way back to his *Grandpère's* forge.

He reached the top of the slope from which he had made those eleven runs earlier in the evening. That all seemed a lifetime ago now, so much had happened since, and he reflected on some of the things Roland had said about what it felt like to be a pilot and fly so high that it was almost like touching the stars. The hero of the hour. That's what the officer had called him. He didn't feel like a hero. Just lucky. Lucky to have been in the right place at the right time. He wondered what his *Maman* would make of it when he told her. She'd probably tell him he'd lost another of his cat's nine lives. A lucky escape, she'd call it, and maybe that was true. Everything about this night had been lucky. Especially that sighting of the Northern Lights, when time had seemed to stop. Perhaps it all came down to the horse shoe his *Grandpère* had fashioned for him earlier. Heavens, he thought. *Grandpère*. He must be wondering where on earth I've got to.

He decided he'd make one last ride down the slope. For one thing it'd be quicker, and for another, he wanted to. He positioned the sledge in the centre of the summit of the hill, ran it up and down before him, to test that the runners were smooth and clean, then prepared himself for launch. The recent snowfall and the beginnings of the frost should, if anything, he thought, enable him to go even quicker than before. He was all alone in the park, king of the hill. He looked up at the sky. The Milky Way arched bright and clear above and all around him. The stars did indeed resemble a bridge, but to where? Just then the beams of two searchlights, one from Urmston and one from Irlam, intersected directly over his head as the air defences went through their final drill for the night. He thought he heard his *Grandpère's* hammer strike the anvil, ringing clear as a bell across the sky, signalling for him to begin. He lay face forward on the sledge, kicked the hard, packed earth beneath him and began. The sledge ran fast and true, the runners carving through just the topmost layer of the snow, so that his speed picked up, rather than diminished. He aimed it like an arrow for the centre of the overhang. He could feel the sledge holding its line – wood and iron, earth and sky – and he was caught between. His ears began to hum with the speed of his descent, the rush of air flying past him, so that when he reached the overhang's lip it was as though someone else's hands held him gently there, hovering on its edge, before catapulting him into the void, arcing through time. He heard the sound of ancestral voices singing to him, calling to him, from a land he'd never seen across the ocean, in a deep, rumbling explosion issuing from below the ground, a collision of two bodies sinking in Chat Moss, bare feet pounding the water's edge, a skewbald mare galloping out of a wood, his mother's voice crooning a Cajun lullaby, embers and sparks dancing above his *Grandpère's* forge, an egret flying across the moon, caught in the searchlights' cross beam.

When he landed, he hardly felt a thing. The sledge carried him as lightly as a feather, floating like thistledown, a dandelion clock, blowing him all the way home.

Ten o'clock, eleven o'clock, twelve o'clock...

"*It came upon the midnight clear*
That glorious song of old
From angels bending near the earth
To touch their harps of gold..."

Richie knew something was wrong the second he opened the door. It was too quiet. The fire in the grate had gone out – which never happened, not even in summer. Quilt did not pad towards him as he usually did, to greet him with a cursory sniff or lick. Instead he lay, not moving, by the chair where Catch was sleeping.

Richie crept towards him. He didn't want to wake him, he was a notoriously light sleeper, but part of him hoped he would, so that he could recount to him his adventures – seeing the *Messerschmitt* tail-spinning out of the sky, the pilot ejecting, the parachute landing in the tree, his rescue of Roland, his running to fetch Esther, the angel of mercy, the things that Roland had said about what it was like to be a pilot, something Richie might like to be himself one day, seeing the Northern Lights, but mostly about the sledge and how true it had run.

But he didn't wake. Richie sat beside him with Quilt and waited. Quilt began to whimper, and Richie realised that his *Grandpère* wasn't breathing. He put his hand on his brow, like he remembered seeing Esther do with Roland. It was clammy and cold. He picked up his *Grandpère's* wrist, like he'd seen people do in the pictures. He didn't know what it was he was supposed to feel, but he felt nothing. Nothing at all. He put his head to his *Grandpère's* chest to see if he might be able to hear a heartbeat, however faint. But again there was nothing. He understood. He pulled Quilt towards him and buried his face in the dog's fur.

Afterwards Richie was never quite able to recall precisely

the sequence of events that followed.

He stayed with his head buried in Quilt's fur a long time.

Some time later he snatched up the horse shoe Catch had made for him that night, which was propped up on the mantel over the hearth next to his own, looped a lead through Quilt's collar and ran.

He ran the two miles from the forge to Cam's flat on Silk Street, with Quilt running beside him.

His *Maman* was not yet back from *The Queen's Hotel*, so he sat outside on the stone steps and cried.

He woke up some time later in his own bed. It was day time outside. Light was showing through the beaded curtain hung up at the window. There were sheets and blankets and an eiderdown on top of him. Placed on his chest was a red hot onion poultice wrapped in a cloth. He fell asleep again...

When he woke the next time, it was night. He felt less hot. His *Maman* must have been sitting close by and heard the bedclothes rustle, for now she was by his side, holding his hand, wiping the sweat from his forehead with a cool flannel, removing some strands of hair that lay plastered there...

Maman is drawing back the beaded curtains. A low winter sun is slanting across the floorboards next to his bed, making squared patterns of light. She helps him to sit up, propped up by pillows. She feeds him warm soup with a spoon. He thinks it is perhaps the best thing he has ever tasted...

Maman is singing. Quietly in the next room. She probably thinks he cannot hear her. Otherwise she wouldn't be singing it. It's a sad song, the first one she can remember her mother teaching her.

> "*J'ai passé devant ta porte*
> *J'ai crié 'bye bye' à la belle*
> *Y'a personne qui m'a pas répondu*
> *Oh-Yé-Yaille mon cœur fais mal...*
>
> *Quand j'ai été cogné à la porte*
> *Quand ils ont rouvert la porte*
> *Moi j'ai vue des chandelles allumés*
> *Tout l'tour de ton cercueil...*"

I passed before your door. I called out 'Bye, bye, Beautiful', but no one answered me. *Oh yé-yaille*, how my heart hurts...

When I looked carefully, I saw lighted candles all around the coffin. *Oh yé-yaille,* how my heart hurts...

When Richie was finally better, the snow had melted. Not a trace of it remained, almost as if it had never been. Like a dream.

Catch was buried with his horse shoe and the hanging sculpture of the three cast iron egrets flying across a metal moon. Cam closed and locked up the forge, declaring that she'd deal with it later, but that for now she'd rather leave it as it was. Quilt came to live with them. He was Richie's dog now, and he never let him out of his sight. When Richie returned to school, Quilt would walk with him there in the morning, then wait outside the gates till lunch time, when Richie would come out to give something he'd saved for him from his school dinner.

Back at home, Richie propped up his horse shoe next to his mother's in the larger of the two rooms in their ground floor flat, the one which served as living room, kitchen and Cam's bedroom, while the paper dancing cats were strung from the ceiling in his own box room of a bedroom. Three of the cats' heads had been snipped off.

*

Six months later, on the second anniversary of Giovanni's death, Claudia, Giulia, Harriet and Paul gathered by the Central Amphitheatre in Philips Park to fly the kite in memory of the old man's life. With no ashes to scatter it was a less solemn occasion and more a day of celebration. They each took turns to hold onto the reel and control the kite as it tried to climb the wind.

Paul, after several weeks of extra specialist training up in Catterick, had just learned that the recently formed X Corps of The Royal Engineers, of which he was a part, had been assigned to their first overseas posting, in support of the Eighth Army in North Africa. To Harriet and the rest of them, that conjured up two words – 'Rommel' and 'desert' – neither of which anyone cared to utter. They were the unspoken elephants in the room.

But they all of them managed to banish such thoughts watching the kite dancing in the summer skies above them. When it came to Harriet's turn, the engagement ring upon her finger glinted in the sunlight. It had been Claudia's before, a plain ring with a modest single stone set in its centre.

"Are you really sure you wouldn't rather still be wearing this yourself?" Harriet had asked her the day after Paul had falteringly offered it to her.

"Quite sure," she had said. "It looks beautiful on you, and in any case my fingers have swollen far too much for me to be able to wear it nowadays. It's far better being worn than mouldering away in a drawer, and it will mean so much to Paul to know you're wearing it while he's away."

Harriet nodded.

"Hey," said Paul, "taking the reel back from her. "Watch what you're doing. You nearly crashed the kite."

"Sorry," she said. "I was miles away." Quite literally, she thought, looping her arm through his, as he successfully steered the kite high above the trees once more…

… where it might just have been visible through the giant spectacles above Francis's shop five and a half miles away to the south-east.

Taped to the glass of the shop door was a hastily hand written notice which read, 'Closed for One Hour', with a cartoon of a pair of lucky horse shoes underneath it. Further down Market Street, waiting outside Denton Town Hall, stood a nervous Victor Collins, uncomfortable in a suit and tie, a flower in his button hole, smoking the last but one cigarette in his packet of Woodbines. Standing beside him, looking equally flustered and red in the face, stood his son, Joe.

"Look," said Joe, stubbing out his own cigarette with evident relief, "there she is."

"About bloody time," said Victor under his breath.

Winifred, scuttling towards them both on high heels, carrying a bouquet of flowers and struggling to keep her hat in place, said breathlessly, "I heard that, Victor. It's a bride's prerogative to be late."

"That's as mebbe," said Victor, "but not when we've only got an 'alf hour slot booked in our lunch break. Where's Francis?" he said, wheeling round.

"He'll be here, don't worry," said Winifred. "Here, Joe, hold these for me, will you, love," handing him the bouquet, "while I make sure my face is on straight."

She flipped open her compact and re-applied her lipstick, just finishing as Francis hurried round the corner, carrying a camera and tripod under his arm.

The four of them scurried up the steps and made their way up the sweeping marble staircase to the first floor, where the registrar's office was situated. They arrived just as the large railway clock on the landing chimed the half hour. The registrar, checking the time against his own fob watch, was waiting to greet them.

"Mr Collins?" he said, pushing his glasses up from the bridge of his nose, over which a pair of large bushy eyebrows rose merrily.

"That's right," said Victor, awkwardly straightening his tie.

"Miss Holt?"

"Not for much longer," joked Winifred.

"No, indeed," said the registrar, his eyebrows practically performing somersaults as he spoke. "Follow me if you please," and he led the way into the chamber set aside for conducting the ceremony. There was a highly polished mahogany desk at one end, behind which on the wall was a mounted shield bearing Denton's coat of arms, featuring red, black and silver horizontal bars, with three silver *cinquefoils* above and, curiously, a beaver mounted on top.

"What's he for?" said Winifred, pointing.

"Ah," said the registrar, his eyebrows shooting upwards like an owl, "no one's ever asked that before. I believe it represents the hat and fur trade."

"Very interesting, I'm sure," said Winifred, holding back a giggle. "Well, I've got a hat but no fur. I trust that won't prevent you from marrying us?"

"By no means," replied the registrar, hastily looking down to make sure he had all the necessary paperwork on his desk. Really, he had never met anyone quite like this not-so-young bride-to-be before. He wondered if perhaps she had been drinking. He looked up, smiling towards Francis and Joe. "You, I take it, are the two witnesses required by law?"

Joe mumbled that he was, while Francis beamed, saying, "I have a triple role. As well as being a witness, I shall be giving the bride away, and I am also the official photographer."

Winifred gave him a sly kick on the ankle. He was being outrageously camp.

Victor was peering at the coat of arms on the wall. "What does it say beneath the coat of arms?" he asked.

"Oh," said the registrar, once again feeling thrown off guard. He pushed up his glasses and read, " *'Persevere'*."

"Ay," said Victor, "that's what I thought." And that about sums it up for both of us, he thought but didn't say, turning towards Winifred. She's had a hell of a lot to put up with, the way I go off the rails from time to time, but she's stuck by me, through thick and thin. And that's what I intend to do by her from now on, he said to himself. She looked beautiful, standing there smiling back at him, in her charcoal grey suit and matching hat, which he knew she'd had to scrimp and save to afford. He took her hand. "Come on, lass," he said. "Let's get married."

Seizing this opportunity, the registrar began at once to recite the familiar text of the ceremony, until he reached the part which was his favourite, where, whatever the mood might have been beforehand, it suddenly became serious, and the couple would look at him, listening to every syllable. And so it was now. This strange pair gave him their complete and undivided attention as he spoke.

"Do you each solemnly declare that you know not of any lawful impediment why you may not be joined together in matrimony? To have and to hold, from this day forward, for better or worse, for richer or poorer, in sickness and health, for as long as you both shall live? "

"I do solemnly declare…"

"I do solemnly declare…"

Afterwards, standing on the steps in front of the Town Hall, when Francis had finished taking the photographs, Victor lit another cigarette.

"Right," he said, "back to work."

2

Christmas 1944

It was just before six in the evening. Claudia was putting on her coat and scarf, about to leave the house for her work at the library in Ancoats, when the telegram arrived.

The postman touched the rim of his cap as he delivered it, then stepped back a few yards to allow a respectful distance between him and the anxious-looking lady on the step. He had delivered far too many of these in the past few years. They invariably contained bad news, and the recipient, nearly always a woman, sometimes needed him to linger a moment, so that she might thank him stoically before retreating behind the closed door to howl her grief. He always waited just in case they might need him, not that he could have done anything. On this occasion, however, the response was different. Yes, there were tears in the woman's eyes, but then she rushed towards him, flung her arms around his neck and kissed him on the cheek.

"Look," she exclaimed. "He's coming home," and she thrust the telegram in front of him. "Read it for me please," she said. "Just in case I'm dreaming this."

He took it from her and read aloud.

POST OFFICE
TELEGRAM

Date: Thurs 21st Dec 1944
To: Claudia Lockhart
From: Matteo Campanella

Message:

SHIP DOCKS LIVERPOOL TOMORROW STOP
WILL ARRIVE ON SAT IN TIME FOR WEDDING
STOP MATTEO

"*Grazie*," she said, before running down the street without even fastening her coat, hugging the telegram to her chest.

*

Five years earlier.

"This is the BBC Home Service on Wednesday 4th September 1939. Here is the news read by me, Alvar Lidell. Following yesterday's announcement by the Prime Minister Mr Chamberlain that this country is now in a state of war with Germany, an estimated 70,000 British resident Germans and Austrians will become classified as enemy aliens with immediate effect. The Home Office is now in the process of setting up 120 official Internment Tribunals across the country to determine which of three categories these aliens will fall into – Category A: to be interned; Category B: to be exempt from internment but subject to restrictions imposed by a Special Order, and Category C: to be exempt from both internment and

restrictions. All male aliens over the age of 16 are required to register their details with their local police in accordance with the 1914 Aliens Registration Act..."

"Here is the news read by me Alvar Lidell for Tuesday 4th June 1940. Following the surrender by France to invading German forces and the subsequent withdrawal of British troops from Dunkirk, the Prime Minister Mr Churchill has ordered a further purge of resident enemy aliens here in Britain, including thousands of Category C refugees claiming to be fleeing persecution from Nazi oppression in Germany, as well as several females, for immediate internment..."

"The BBC has just learned that the Italian Generalissimo Benito Mussolini, the self-styled 'Il Duce', has formally signed a treaty allying his country with Germany, at the same time declaring war on Britain. This is the nine o'clock news for Monday 10th June 1940 read by me, Alvar Lidell..."

Memorandum from Prime Minister's Office: Midnight, Mon 10th June 1940

Collar the lot...   *Winston S. Churchill*

Daily Mail

Friday 14th June 1940

KEEP BRITAIN SAFE FROM ALIEN PERIL

We stand squarely behind our Prime Minister's bulldog stance to round up all foreign aliens and intern every last one of them. "It's the only way to keep Britain safe from enemy spies and fifth columnists," says British Union of Fascists Party Leader, Oswald Mosley, and we agree. No matter if they're German, Austrian or Italian. No matter how long they claim to have lived in this country. No matter if they say they're only fleeing Nazi persecution. We echo Mr Churchill's call to "Collar the lot!" It's the only way to be sure we do not harbour traitors in our midst. We say, "Better Safe Than Sorry," and we urge all our readers to Keep their Eyes and Ears Open and Alert for this potential Stranger Danger.

Isle of Man Examiner

Saturday 15th June 1940

Internment of Aliens Demanded

KEYS TAKE ACTION

There is only one place for the enemy alien while the War lasts. That place is behind barbed wire.

This opinion was expressed with the strongest possible emphasis by the Manx Government in the House of Keys yesterday, when it was unanimously decided to ask His Excellency the

Lieutenant-Governor if all enemy aliens in the Island had been interned, voluntary or otherwise, and if not, why not?

The House also expressed the unanimous view that the people of the Isle of Man were ready and willing once more to do their bit for Great Britain's national security by housing the mainland's internees as they had done in the last war.

Extract from Hansard: Tuesday 18th June 1940

Parliamentary Debate on Proposals for Internment and Deportation of Enemy Aliens

Right Honourable Colonel Victor Cazalet, MP:
"In the febrile atmosphere that has permeated the national debate in the past fortnight I believe we are in danger of losing sight of the facts in the face of overheated, hysterical opinion, the flames of which are being fanned by certain sections of the press, whose intentions and sympathies have been revealed as being all too transparent.

"Let us focus, therefore, Mr Speaker, on these facts and examine them closely. Already there are more than 30,000 internees being held behind barbed wire on race tracks, in tented cities, derelict factory warehouses and

other makeshift facilities across England, including a large camp on the Isle of Man, where preparations are so incomplete that men – and women – are being forced to huddle in cowsheds. Conditions in these camps are appalling. Foreign aliens, a significant majority of whom are refugees who have come to this country for sanctuary from our enemy's atrocities, are forced to sleep in overcrowded tents without mattresses. Men and women have been sent to different camps, so that husbands and wives have been cruelly separated. Internees are refused the right to read newspapers, write or receive letters, or listen to the radio. These are people who have committed no crime, nor, in the vast majority of cases, is there any justification for us considering them as anything but loyal supporters of Great Britain and her allies. Their sole misfortune is to have been born in a country with whom we are now currently at War, even though they have expressed no sympathies for the causes of these countries of their birth. Yet they must now suffer the indignity of being held without charge where there are insufficient toilets and frequently no access to running water. Some camps, such as the one at Warth Mills in Bury, less than a dozen miles to the north of Manchester, are overrun with rats. If we were to house prisoners of war in these camps, instead of enemy aliens, we would be in breach of the Geneva Convention on Human Rights.

"As an Englishman, I am ashamed by this situation. As a government I believe we should be setting an example to our citizens and to the world by behaving decently, honourably and compassionately, as well as

legally, fairly and prudently.

"Meanwhile employers are sacking all foreign workers regardless of the country of their origin, some local authorities are evicting aliens from council properties, despite their having lived in these dwellings for more than a generation, many of them with children having been born in this country, and there are examples of the Home Guard rejecting applications from men of alien origin, including one example of turning down an English soldier who had been awarded the Victoria Cross for his actions in the First World War on account of his foreign parentage.

"This is a ludicrous situation and we need a swift return of cooler heads. Why, if we were to take these current policies to their logical conclusion, we should have to intern His Majesty King George VI and his family, whose father was forced to change their name from Saxe-Coburg to Windsor on account of anti-German feeling!

"Frankly, I shall not feel happy, either as an Englishman or as a supporter of this Government, until this bespattered page of our history has been cleaned up and rewritten."

The Right Honourable Member for Chippenham sat down to a mixture of boos and cheers in equal measure. (Volume 624: Ref. Co.42748/18.06.40)

MALE ENEMY ALIEN – APPLICATION FOR EXEMPTION FROM INTERNMENT

Surname: CAMPANELLA
Forenames: MATTEO
Alias: None
Date of Birth: 15th Sep 1888
Place of Birth: CAMPANIA, ITALY
Nationality: BRITISH
Police Registration No: 697368
Home Office Reference: N/A

Address:
36, COTTON STREET, ANCOATS, MANCHESTER
Normal Occupation: TILE MAKER
Name of Employer: STEFANUTTI & SONS

Case for Appeal Against Internment: APPLICANT LESS THAN ONE YEAR OLD ON ARRIVAL IN THIS COUNTRY. HAS LIVED IN ENGLAND ALL HIS LIFE. SERVED WITH DISTINCTION IN THE FIRST WORLD WAR AS A GUNNER IN THE MANCHESTER REGIMENT.

Decision: EXEMPTION DENIED.

Reason for Decision: Applicant falls into Category B as laid down by Emergency Amendment to 1914 Aliens Registration Act.

Regional Advisory Committee: No 5, MANCHESTER
Signature: *D. G. Seex* (Chairman)
Date: 27th June 1940

"This is the BBC Home Service. Here is the nine o'clock news for Sunday 30th June 1940, read by me, Alvar Lidell. Following intense debate in recent weeks, the Government has decided, in response to offers of support from several of our Commonwealth Allies, to ship overseas more than seven and a half thousand enemy aliens currently being held as internees in camps around the country. Tomorrow and the day after, His Majesty's Ships The Ettrick, The Sobieski, The Duchess of York, The Dunera and The Arandora Star will set sail from Liverpool to Canada, where the internees will be held for the duration of the war..."

Claudia turned off the radio and flung it across the kitchen. The inside of her head was a hornet's nest, as it had been for weeks, ever since Churchill had issued his command to 'collar the lot'. She was furious and distraught in equal measure. She'd been to the police, to the Corporation, to her local MP – a Mr John Jagger, who expressed his sympathy but confessed his hands were tied.

She used her recent access to the City Libraries' Archives to track down the Special Correspondent who had compiled an in-depth report for *The Manchester Evening Chronicle* entitled *How Refugees Help Lancashire*, praising the immediate impact of new arrivals to the county who, in escaping persecution under Hitler, had been welcomed in Manchester with open arms and given assistance in setting up all manner of new businesses, creating hundreds of new jobs in the process, but he could do nothing.

"The paper's agenda has changed in recent weeks, especially since Italy joined the War," he said. "It has to reflect the views of its readers," and he shook his head sadly.

"What about *my* views?" said Claudia. "I'm a reader too."

The reporter spread his hands. "But you're a minority."

"That's exactly why you should be supporting us."

"I agree. But we're at War now. Different rules apply. I'm sorry."

In desperation she turned to the *Italian Mutual Aid Society* – the *Italiano di Mutuo Soccorso Vittorio e Garibaldi* – the *Italian Catholic Society*, and finally to Father Fracassi himself one Sunday after Mass.

"Is there nothing to be done?" she said.

"*Niente*." He was busily taking off his vestments and wiping clean the communion cup.

"*Per favore*," she begged, "there must be something."

"Claudia, if there was something, don't you think I'd have done it by now?"

"But it's so unfair. Matteo has lived in Manchester since he was just a few months old. He would have been born here, except Mamma wasn't able to travel in the final weeks of her pregnancy."

"I know, Claudia, it's ridiculous."

"And what about his War Record? Doesn't that count for anything?"

"It should. But it doesn't."

"He was a hero. He was mentioned in dispatches. He's

proved he's loyal to King and Country."

"That was the last war. Italy and Britain were allies then."

"But he fought for the British Army, not the Italian."

"I know, Claudia. I'm not trying to defend the situation, I'm just explaining it."

"Are there no exceptions?"

"No, Claudia. They're rounding up all the Category C's now too. Even me."

"You, Father?"

"*Si*, Claudia. Me."

"But you're a priest, Father. They can't take priests – surely?"

"No exceptions, Claudia."

Claudia was incredulous. A heavy silence hung between them, a thurible without benediction.

"The only dispensation I've been granted is that I have been allowed to stay here until the last possible moment, rather than being detained in a camp first."

"When do you go?" she said at last. All the fight seemed to have gone out of her, like a punctured balloon.

"The day after tomorrow I have to be at the quayside at Liverpool Docks."

"The same as Matteo."

"You've heard from him?"

"They were allowed to send one letter, once their fate had been decided. He sails on the *Arandora Star* for Canada…"

"As do I…"

"… where he'll remain for however long the War lasts."

"And then he'll come home."

"That rather depends on the outcome of the war, don't you think? And right now it doesn't look too good for us."

"You must have faith." He patted her gently on the shoulder. Claudia exploded.

"Faith?" She tutted derisively. "In what? Human nature? God's infinite mercy?"

"You could do worse."

"Where is God," she said, impotently stretching her arms out wide, "in all of this?"

"Christ died on the Cross to redeem our sins and save our souls."

"Oh – and is that what you are doing now, Father, you and Matteo and the rest of our friends and neighbours who are being shipped off to the other side of the world, sacrificing yourselves for the safety and well being of the rest of us?"

"You're angry, Claudia, I understand that, and when we're angry, we say things that later we come to regret."

"But…"

"God moves in mysterious ways. The nature of His plan is often hidden from us."

"And do you truly believe that part of His plan requires us all to lie down like lambs for the slaughter?"

Father Fracassi spread out his hands. "*Che sarà sarà*."

Claudia roared in anguish, hitting the sides of her head with her fists. "How can you be so accepting of such an injustice?"

"Did not the Good Lord teach us to turn the other cheek…?"

Claudia fell silent. She could never be so passive, but she recognised that her rage was achieving nothing either. One person cannot move a mountain by herself, she thought, yet somehow she had to try. She couldn't just let her brother slip away without doing everything she could to prevent it.

Father Fracassi came and sat by her side. As if reading her thoughts, he said gently, "You have nothing to reproach yourself with. You have done all that you possibly could. But sometimes we have to realise that we're…"

"Powerless?" said Claudia bitterly.

"I was going to say 'not alone'."

Claudia shook her head.

"Jesus tells us we become powerful through prayer. *'Truly I say unto you, whoever says to the mountain, "Be taken up and thrown into the sea," and does not doubt in his heart, but believes that what he says will come to pass, it will be done to him. Therefore I tell you, whatever you ask in prayer, believe that you have received it, and it will be yours'.*"

"I'm done with prayer, Father."

"How can you be so certain?"

"Because these people who take you and my brother away from us now do so in God's name too. They invoke His name, 'with God on our side', they say. 'Onward, Christian Soldiers', they sing. God can't be on the side of both. Either He's on the side of right, or He's nowhere."

Father Fracassi paused. "What does Matteo say?" he said after a while.

"Oh," said Claudia smiling, "much the same as you.

'Be patient, don't worry, I'll be back before you know it'…"

"He's always been a good boy."

"And that's my point, Father. Matteo is a good man. So are you. So are most people. We're taught not to complain, to accept the cards that are dealt to us. Even when his wife died last year from diphtheria…"

"*Ah si, l'angelo che strangola.* The strangling angel…"

Claudia shook her head incredulously. "That's what I'm saying. Even then, he quietly accepted it. Even though it could have been prevented."

"There's one thing that gives radiance to everything…"

"And what's that?" she said witheringly.

"… the idea of something around the corner."

"Who said that? It doesn't sound like you, Father."

"G.K. Chesterton."

"This is no Father Brown story, though, is it?"

"Pity. I've always been partial to those. Perhaps they'll have a copy on the *Arandora Star*. It's a cruise ship, after all." He smiled. "I once read that Chesterton and Shaw, who were great friends you know, made a silent home movie of themselves playing at cowboys."

"Who do you think might have won?"

"I'm not sure. They were both rather quick on the draw, and I don't suppose either of them enjoyed playing dead. I rather think it might have been honours even." He extended his hand towards Claudia. Standing, she held it in her own and shook it. She felt not so much calmed, as emptied.

"You know," she said, "in my job at the library, I run the evening classes for those wanting to learn new skills, mostly to improve their reading. I come across all types, but the one thing they have in common is a desire to make a better life for themselves and their families. Isn't that what we all want in the end? Many of them are not from here originally. Like us they've come from other countries – France, Holland, Germany; Poland, Russia and Italy, like *we* have, Father, or our families have – and Manchester has extended them a hand of welcome, of friendship, like you have just done for me, and I say to them all, rather like you do, Father, 'Have faith', but unlike you I mean in themselves, that we all have inside of us something that makes us who we are, and that we need to hold on to it, feed it, water it, watch it grow, till it's strong enough to manage by itself. We all of us jostle against one another in the crowded streets, like molecules randomly bumping into each other. Sometimes these collisions cause some of us to join together, to form new particles, hybrids, that are stronger than the sum of our parts. I believe this, Father, it's my catechism if you will, so that when something like this forced internment happens, which so crudely tries to separate what has been forming naturally over many generations, it's like a rupture in the fabric of the universe, like when you split the atom – the resulting force it unleashes is so powerful it could threaten to destroy us all. That's why we must learn to harness it, for the benefit of all."

She paused, fastening up her coat and tying back on her scarf.

"What will you do now?" asked Father Fracassi.

"I'm going home to make supper for Paul and Harriet, then going out to work."

"First the meal, then the moral."

"Something like that."

"That was a good thing you did for Paul."

"What?"

"Changing his name."

"Mine and Giulia's too."

"*Si.*"

"I was being pragmatic, that's all."

"And it's worked. At least he's not at risk of being rounded up."

"He was born here, so he wouldn't have been anyway, at least not yet. But he's still the same person. Changing his name hasn't changed him."

"Hasn't it?"

"No. But meeting Harriet has. That's what I was saying."

"Random collisions."

"I suppose you would argue that it wasn't random?"

The Father spread his hands. "We're all part of God's plan."

"Good night, Father." She was too exhausted to argue any more. She walked out of St Alban's Church. It was still light. The market stalls were selling the last of their wares before packing up for the evening. She recognised several people, nodded to some and spoke briefly to others, as she made her way back along Poland Street, into Naval Street, Bengali Street, and finally to Radium Street, where Paul and Harriet would be waiting. Knowing Harriet, she would already have started preparing the food, chopping and slicing the onions, while Paul rolled out the flour for the pasta. She could picture them, standing side by side, laughing and talking together. It was their last night before Paul headed off to Sheffield to begin his training. They would probably have preferred to spend it alone, but knowing that Matteo was to be shipped out to Canada the following day, they had chosen to stay with Claudia instead. She didn't know how she felt about Paul joining up. It had been his decision entirely. He had skills, he said, as a plate layer that he thought the Army might need. And so it had proved. The Royal Engineers had snapped him up. Private Paul Lockhart. At the time it had seemed like a justification of her decision to Anglicise their names, especially when the anti-Italian protests began to grow, like the underground rumbling they would sometimes feel rising up from the deep seams of Bradford Pit, which spread their network of tunnels far below, vibrating the earth beneath their feet. While they were still in the middle of what the newspapers were calling the phoney war, she didn't think too much about the possible dangers that might be waiting – just around the corner, as Father Fracassi might have said – but since Dunkirk everything had changed. Paul was off tomorrow for training, after which it would only be a matter of time before he was posted to who knew where. Harriet appeared quite sanguine about the prospect – "I'd rather he didn't go, obviously, but I understand why he feels he must." – but Claudia's thoughts turned inevitably to Marco, whose slow, confident, infectious smile Paul had inherited. Marco had always been at ease with himself, with who he was, as was Paul, and so, too, Matteo. Only she, it seemed, railed against the tide whose waters she could not turn back. Harriet said that when the children who she taught at school asked her why there was a War, she told them that they were fighting to try and protect people from being cruelly and unjustly persecuted, so that the world might be a better place for when they, the children, grew up. She wasn't especially religious herself, but the school was, and so she would read to them from the Sermon on the Mount. "For the meek shall inherit the earth…" But shall we, wondered Claudia? Tonight it did not seem so.

She walked head down back through Ancoats' busy streets. As she turned into Radium Street she was suddenly alone. She heard her shoes clatter on the cobbled pavement beneath her feet, offering proof of her existence. I am walking, she said to herself, upon these stones. The echo of my footsteps bears witness to my passing. She remembered a lecture from Miss Leslie in one of her 6th form science classes.

"A chemical bond is a lasting attraction between atoms. It enables the formation of new compounds. Since opposites attract through a simple electromagnetic force, the negatively charged electrons which orbit around the nucleus are attracted to the positively charged protons contained inside the nucleus. This attraction constitutes the chemical bond. The strength of the bond depends entirely upon the sharing of electrons between the different participating atoms. Hydrogen and Oxygen are perfectly fine elements in themselves, but only when the two combine do we get water."

A fine rain began to fall as Claudia ran the final

hundred yards towards her house, where Harriet and Paul would be waiting.

Manchester Evening Chronicle

Tuesday 2nd July 1940

SS ARANDORA STAR SINKS IN MID ATLANTIC

More Than 800 Lives Lost

In the early hours of this morning the *SS Arandora Star*, a British passenger ship of the Blue Star Line, was torpedoed by German submarine U-47 and sank some 70 miles west of Ireland in the deep Atlantic swell with the loss of 805 lives.

The ship was *en route* for St John's, Newfoundland. On board were 712 Italians, 438 Germans and 374 British seamen and soldiers, who were escorting the Italians and Germans to Canada, where they were to be interned for the duration of the war.

The *Arandora Star* was part of a convoy of ships sailing across the Atlantic, including the *Ettrick*, the *Sobieski* and the *Duchess of York*. None of these other ships was hit and all have safely reached their destinations.

The ship was struck by a single torpedo on the starboard side, flooding her engine room. Her turbines, main and emergency generators were all immediately out of action, and so the whole ship was plunged into darkness. Chief Officer Frederick Brown gave the ship's position to a radio officer, who at once transmitted a distress signal. This was picked up by Malin Head at

07.05 hours and subsequently retransmitted to Land's End and to Portpatrick.

The Arandora Star carried 14 lifeboats and 90 life rafts. The destruction wrought by the torpedo meant that the crew were only able to launch 10 lifeboats and just over half of the rafts. Some were quickly overloaded by prisoners descending the side ladders. One was so swamped it sank shortly after being launched. Meanwhile many of the Italians were too confused and frightened in the darkness and refused to leave the ship, so that some lifeboats left less than half full.

The ship then listed further to starboard. At 07.15 hours Captain Moulton instructed his senior officers to "walk over the side" and into the rising water, leaving behind many of the Italians still too afraid to leave the ship. Five minutes later, at 07.20 hours, the ship rolled over, raised her bow and sank.

Of the 805 lives lost, 12 were officers, including Captain Moulton, 42 were ship's crew, 37 were military guards. The remaining 715 were internees.

One of those who did survive, Sergeant Norman Price, described the scene. "I could see hundreds of men clinging to the ship, like ants. Then the ship went up at one end and simply slid down, taking the men with her. Many injured themselves jumping or diving into the water, others by landing on fallen wreckage and debris near the sinking ship."

At 09.30 hours an RAF Coastal Command Sunderland Flying Boat circled the scene, dropping first aid kits, food, cigarettes and a message that help was coming. That help arrived three and a half hours later, at 13.00 hours, in the shape of the Canadian C-class destroyer *HMCS St Laurent*, which rescued 865 survivors, of whom 568 were detainees. The injured were taken to Mearnskirk Hospital near Glasgow, while those deemed fit enough to continue were returned to Liverpool, where they were immediately transferred to the *SS Dunera* bound for Australia.

The Government, while lamenting the loss of life, remains unrepentant. In a brief statement the Duke of Devonshire defended its position. "The national tribunals, which have been in session throughout the land since March, have determined that there are some 73,000 enemy aliens resident in Great Britain. If we are to intern them all, which we have to consider as a contingency, there simply isn't the room within these shores. When the Dominions volunteered their assistance to accommodate an initial selection of 7,500 detainees, it seemed a sensible way to husband our resources and get rid of useless mouths to feed and so forth."

Here at *The Evening Chronicle*, we have long championed the benefits and advantages to the Manchester economy brought to us by our German and Italian friends and neighbours now living and working here among us. We say to the Duke of Devonshire, therefore, and to Mr Churchill too, "Enough is enough. End internment now. Close the camps."

Of the 73,000 so-called enemy aliens referred to by the Duke, only 569 have been classified as Class A, representing any kind of threat to our national security. We say, "Bring the rest back home to their families where they belong, and where they can contribute to the war effort along with everyone else."

As soon as she saw the newspaper, Claudia rushed to St Alban's, where scores of people had gathered, waiting for further news. None came. Signor Francesco Testa, an Italian teacher at St Michael's School, took it upon himself to contact the Ministry of Shipping directly, requesting the release of the names of those who had survived and those who had perished as soon as possible. John Jagger MP repeatedly asked Ronald Moss, the newly appointed Minister responsible for Information, in the House of Commons, but neither received an answer. It took an intervention by Bishop Henry Marshall of Salford for the government finally to relent and publish the names.

During that agonising time Claudia had taken part each day in the vigil the families of those waiting had vowed to maintain until their demands for information were met. Finally, after three weeks, Bishop Marshall, John Jagger and Signor Testa appeared together outside St Alban's. They had only one list, they explained. It contained the names of those who were known definitely to have survived. The whereabouts of these survivors, however, was less certain. They fell into three distinct categories. Some had been treated in hospital in Glasgow for their injuries. Of these some had been discharged and already reassigned to camps in this country, but for the moment it was unclear who had gone where. They had a letter 'C' after their names, while those still in hospital receiving treatment had a letter 'H' after theirs. They would be transferred to a camp as soon as they were well enough. Some had been deemed fit enough to be transferred immediately after they had been rescued from the Arandora Star. These were currently *en route* for Australia and so had a letter 'A' after their names.

"I regret to say," concluded the Bishop, "that anyone whose name does not appear on this list can be assumed to be missing, presumed drowned. The only person I have any more precise information about is Father Fracassi. He did not survive, I'm afraid."

A huge gasp arose from the waiting crowd.

"Several eye witnesses from among the ship's crew members who did survive testified to his extraordinary courage. He chose to stay on board with those of his countrymen who were too frightened to leave the ship, giving them what comfort and succour he could."

There was no undignified scramble to read the names once they'd been posted on the church door. Instead the men, women and children formed a silent, orderly queue, awaiting their turn with stoic patience. The cries of relief which greeted the recognition of a loved one's name on the list contrasted keenly with the sobbing which came with the realisation that a name being sought was not in fact there, and what that absence signified.

Dusk had fallen on the square. A few of the crowd left once they'd learned the fate of their loved ones, but most stayed, wanting to add or receive comfort from the rest of the community, bound together in this simple act of climbing the steps and running their finger down the list of names, until they found, or did not find, the one they were seeking. Someone started to sing *Ave Maria,* falteringly at first, but one by one it was taken up by everyone, its fragile notes fluttering in the night air like a moth, fragile but determined, the Manchester moth, that celebrated variant of the white peppered moth, which had singlehandedly proved Darwin's theory of evolution, by adapting to survive, changing its colour from white to black, the better to be camouflaged against the city's soot-darkened mills and so avoid the unwanted attentions of predatory birds.

By the time it was Claudia's turn, it was too dark for her to read the names. Signor Testa held a candle up to the list, then turned his face away respectfully, so that Claudia might look at it alone.

Her eyes lighted upon Matteo's name almost immediately. Her lips and hands trembled with relief. There was a letter 'A' after his name. Australia, then. The other side of the world. As far away as it was possible to be. But alive.

She approached Mr Jagger.

"Those who are destined for Australia," she said, "do we know whereabouts?"

Jagger shook his head. "We don't even know if they've landed there yet. In all probability they haven't. They'll be somewhere in the Southern Ocean by now, I should think."

Claudia tried to picture this, but her imagination failed her.

Jagger saw her face go pale and hurried to assist her down the church steps.

"*Grazie*," she said.

"Who is it you've been waiting on?"

"My brother."

Jagger nodded solemnly. "A terrible business. The government's behaved disgracefully over this. But now they've been shamed by the Bishop here into finally releasing some news, I'm confident we'll hear more soon. In your case, Mrs…?"

"Lockhart."

"Mrs Lockhart… I'd say that no news is most definitely good news."

Claudia looked up. "Why?"

"If the *Dunera* – the ship that's carrying your brother – had met with any form of mishap, we'd have heard for sure. The fact that we haven't means that it's still ploughing the seas somewhere."

"Yes, I see. Thank you, Mr Jagger."

She stepped back into the square. The singing swelled around her. Instinctively she found herself joining in.

"*Ave Maria*
Mater Dei
Ora pro nobis peccatoribus
Ora pro nobis
Nunc et in hora nobis
Et in hora mortis nostrae
Ave Maria…"

And so Claudia began dressing in black, lighting candles with a scarf on her head, every day from that point onwards, first for Matteo and then for Paul. The sinking of the *Arandora Star* shifted public opinion from a trickle to a flood of protest, clamouring for the return of all detainees from the camps both in Britain and what the Duke of Devonshire referred to as the Dominions. There was growing cross-party support in the House for a decisive end to internment, with the likes of John Jagger and Victor Cazalet finding themselves unlikely bedfellows.

The release of one thousand six hundred and eighty-seven Category 'C' and 'B' enemy aliens was authorised in August 1940, and by October almost five thousand Germans, Austrians and Italians had been released following the publication of the Under-Secretary of the Home Office, Osbert Peake's White Paper, *Civilian Internees of Enemy Nationality*. The Paper identified categories of persons who could be eligible for release, which amounted to more than ninety-five percent of all those initially rounded up. By December eight thousand internees had been released, leaving some nineteen thousand still interned in camps in Canada and Australia. Here the process of release would take longer. But by March 1941, twelve and a half thousand of these had been freed, rising to over seventeen and a half thousand in August, and by 1942 fewer than two thousand remained interned, mainly in Australia, where the last batch of less than five hundred was finally sanctioned for return to Britain in the dying weeks of 1944. Matteo was among this final cohort.

Four and a half years after Claudia first read his name among the list of survivors on the steps of St Alban's, four and a half years of writing, petitioning, protesting, campaigning, marching in rallies, speaking at public meetings, four and a half years later and two and a half miles across the city she sat inside a different church, St Jerome's, on the edge of Philips Park, for the marriage of Paul to Harriet, at which Matteo was to officiate as best man, still clutching the telegram she had received the day before tightly in her hand.

*

"There's one thing that gives radiance to everything..."

Claudia, sitting in St Jerome's Church waiting for Harriet to arrive, recalled these words by Chesterton first spoken to her by Father Fracassi the night before the *SS Arandora Star* had set sail, and smiled, not because she had come to accept the implication that this was as a result of everyone being wrapped up in some grand divine plan, but because of her wonderment at the sheer resilience of the human heart. It breaks, but it mends.

She remembered Miss Leslie explaining its biology. "Not only is the heart an incredibly strong organ," she said, "a muscle powerful enough to pump blood continuously around our entire bodies, it also has its own independent, highly complex nervous system, responsible for much of our identity. In addition it exerts an electromagnetic energy field that can be measured up to ten feet away, which can change the brain waves of people around us."

Now, watching Matteo joking with Paul, who kept nervously glancing over his shoulder to see if Harriet was here yet, she gazed in wonder at the two of them, sitting side by side once more after so much uncertainty. She felt happier than she would have thought possible, even while acknowledging that she wished Marco could have been sitting alongside her, sharing this moment with her. Even then it was not diminished.

"Most animals," Miss Leslie had explained, "experience around one billion heart beats during their lifetime, whereas humans will receive more than twice that many." Claudia smiled again. Plenty more beats left yet.

Outside, the air was crisp and invigorating, the sky a dazzling blue. It was eleven o'clock on the morning of Saturday 23rd December. The church had been decorated with branches of holly for Christmas. Harriet linked her arm through her father's and beamed at him.

"Ready?" he asked.

"Ready," she said.

"Wait," called a muffled voice from below. "You're not ready *yet*."

Emerging from behind the two of them sprang Giulia, her mouth full of pins, a needle and cotton in her hands. "You trod on your hem walking up from The Lodge. I'll only be a moment."

"Leave it, Giulia," said Harriet, still smiling. "It won't matter."

Giulia looked dumbfounded. If it had not been for the pins wedged between her lips, she would have rattled off a string of expletives in both English and Italian. Instead she merely contented herself with an incredulous groan, before disappearing round the back again, where she furiously continued to sew up the hem.

"Best do what she says, Harriet," chirped another voice cheerfully. It was Gracie, casually tossing her posy of flowers from one hand to the other. "We mustn't upset the artist while she's creating! Shh! Genius at work!"

"*Grazie,* Gracie," Giulia managed to spit between the pins and stitches. "*Eco, finito. Bella*, eh Gracie?"

"*Si, Giulia,*" mimicked Gracie, "*molto bella…*"

Giulia laughed.

When she'd first encountered Gracie, when Gracie was a rambunctious three year old, she'd been quite intimidated by her. She simply never stopped. Like a mechanical toy which, once wound up by the key in her back, kept moving from the moment she woke up at dawn until sleep finally overtook her at night, all the while accompanying everything she did with a ceaseless running commentary of questions and challenges, her favourite words being "No" and "Why?" Nothing, least of all her polio, was going to prevent her from doing whatever it was that she set her mind to. Over the years the intimidation Giulia first felt was replaced by admiration, and she no longer even noticed Gracie's calliper, which was exactly what Gracie hoped from everyone. "See *me*," she'd chant, "not my *leg*."

And so when the subject of what Gracie should wear as a bridesmaid for her sister's wedding arose, Giulia was not in the least surprised by her answer.

"Nothing long," she said. "For one thing we can't afford the material. For another, *'Waste not, want not'*.

That's our school motto. We save everything," she added, counting each item off on her fingers. "Paper, food, rags and bones, tin foil, metal, boxes, paper – wait, I already said that, didn't I?"

"Whoa, Sailor, slow down!"

"I bet that's what you say to all the boys, isn't it?"

"Only the sailors," said Giulia with a wink. Gracie laughed.

"We have all these slogans at school," she said breathlessly, her voice now speaking at a mile a minute, rising an octave with each new thought. "I like to make up new ones. '*Save the Wheat! Help the Fleet!*' Or, '*Salvage Scrap to Blast the Jap!*' I've got loads more where they came from…"

"It's OK. I get it. Nothing long. But…"

"But what?"

"Well…"

"I know what you're going to say."

"You do?"

"Uh-huh."

"What?"

"No. You've got to say it."

Giulia paused. "Well… I was going to say…"

"Aren't I worried about people seeing my calliper?"

Giulia lowered her head. "Yes, I was. I'm sorry."

"Don't be. I'm not. The way I see it is that everyone already knows I wear it, so why bother to hide it. That way we get to save material too and donate it to the War effort. Anyway, I like my calliper, I want people to see it. Without it I couldn't do half the things I do now."

"Like what?"

"Like ride my bike, or kick a football, or climb trees."

"What about at school?"

"It's the same. Some things I can do well, some things I can't. Like everyone else. Nobody's good at everything. Unless you're Penny Wilkinson – she's in my class and she's a proper genius. She's top in every subject and she's also a fast runner."

"But can she dance?"

"I don't know. I expect she can."

"I bet she can't dance as well as you."

"You've never seen her."

"But I've seen *you*."

"When?"

"Every time the radio comes on. Like this." Giulia switched it on. A dance band was playing from *The Savoy*. Immediately Giulia started to jive. Gracie laughed with sheer physical pleasure. It was the kind of sound that filled the room with joy, as if a whole flutter of sparrows had burst through the window, all cheeping and chirruping at once, and the more Giulia jived, the more Gracie giggled. She rolled on her back like a beetle, kicking her good leg in the air.

"This is all too square for me," said Giulia and she retuned the radio to the American Forces Network. Betty Hutton was part way through singing *Murder, He Says*.

"Oh," cried Gracie. "I love this," and at once she launched into her own quirky dance, filled with explosive, syncopated rhythms, singing along to the words as she did.

"He says, chick chick, you torture me
Zoom, are we livin'?
I'm thinkin' of leavin' him flat
He says, dig dig the jumps
The old ticker is givin'
Well you can't talk plainer than that…"

Now it was Giulia's turn to laugh. Encouraged by her response, Gracie continued with ever more outrageous gestures and poses, growling just like Betty Hutton herself.

"He says Murder, he says
Every time we kiss
He says Murder, he says
Keep it up like this
And that Murder, he says
In that impossible tone
Will bring nobody's murder but his own…"

The band finished playing, and Gracie and Giulia fell in a heap on the floor.

"That's just given me an idea," said Giulia, and she raced upstairs. She came straight back down carrying a pile of film magazines.

"Waste not, want not," warned Gracie, wagging her finger towards her. Giulia whacked her playfully on the top of her head with one.

"This is not waste," she declared, sitting herself next to Gracie on the floor. "This is essential reading matter. Strictly educational."

"Oh really?"

"Yes really." She flicked open one of the magazines at random.

"What are we looking for?" asked Gracie.

"Pictures of Betty Hutton," said Giulia.

"What for?"

"To get an idea of what your bridesmaid's dress might look like, that's what for. Now, you take this pile, and I'll take the other, and if either of us sees anything we like, we show it to each other. Deal?"

"Deal," said Gracie, spitting into the palm of her hand and offering it to shake one of Giulia's.

"Eugh! No, thank you. Not till you've wiped it first."

Gracie grinned.

They passed several companionable minutes in silence looking for exactly the right picture, laughing at some, groaning at others. Suddenly, Gracie squealed with delight.

"This one," she shouted, pointing to a poster image of *The Perils of Pauline*, a Paramount picture starring Betty Hutton and John Lund. The photograph showed Betty in a navy dress with a white collar swinging like Tarzan from a rope. "I'd like to look like that," said Gracie.

Giulia considered it for a moment, looking at the page from several angles, as if working out how it might be made. "Perfect," she said, "on one condition."

"What?"

"You don't swing from a rope wearing it…"

"Aw…"

"… until *after* the wedding. Agreed?"

"Agreed," cried an excited Gracie. "When do we

start?"

"We?" said Giulia, raising one eyebrow.

"I want to help," said Gracie determinedly.

"All right," said Giulia, hastily thinking on her feet. "How about you design something to decorate your calliper?"

Gracie's eyes widened.

"Well," continued Giulia, "you said you didn't want to hide it. Let's make it a feature."

"Yes!" said Gracie and she instantly ran to find some scrap paper and crayons to begin working out some possible designs.

Now, standing outside St Jerome's Church beneath a crisp winter sky, Giulia regarded both her creations – Harriet in fairy tale white in a dress made from salvaged parachute silk, and Gracie in a navy blue sailor dress with a white collar – with satisfaction. Gracie had painstakingly cut out tiny circles of coloured paper (from several of Giulia's magazines, "Waste not, want not, remember,") and meticulously glued them onto pieces of cardboard, which she had shaped to fit exactly the leather straps and fastenings of her calliper, over which she'd then sprinkled glitter, so that from a distance it looked bejewelled. ("It's going to be the very devil to get off afterwards," her mother had said. "I'll manage," Gracie had replied, beaming benignly). Then she'd painted the iron braces on either side with navy blue paint to match her dress and put white string in her boots for laces to match the collar. "I'm going to have to start calling you

Pauline from now on," Giulia had said. Gracie had grinned. For the final fitting Giulia took Gracie with her to the dressmaking workshop at the back of the *Mancunian Film Studios* on Dickenson Road. When she emerged from behind a curtain for Giulia to see, the rest of the wardrobe mistresses and assistants all applauded.

"Right," said Jabez finally, turning back to Harriet, "are we ready now?"

Harriet looked over her shoulder to check with Giulia, who nodded decisively.

"Yes," said Harriet, once again linking her arm through her father's, "I'm ready."

"Come on then. Best not keep that young man of yours waiting any longer. He'll think you've changed your mind."

"Never," she said, as together they stepped through the church doors into the nave. The organist struck up the familiar *Wedding March* from *Lohengrin*. The small congregation of family and friends rose to their feet, eagerly glancing back for their first view of the bride. Mary was already in tears and a much relieved Paul exhaled a deep breath. Gracie walked behind her sister, carrying her posy of flowers, while Giulia brought up the rear, making sure that all was as it should be.

"I, Paul, take thee, Harriet…"

"I, Harriet, take thee, Paul…"

"Let these rings be to Harriet and Paul a symbol of unending love and faithfulness…"

Gracie stepped forward and held out the two rings, which she had been carrying in a special pocket in the front of her sailor dress up until that moment…

"I now proclaim you man and wife…"

The reception was held back at The Lodge in Philips Park for just the immediate family – Harriet and Paul, Jabez and Mary, Toby and Gracie, Claudia, Giulia and Matteo. Jabez and Toby had set up the drop leaf table to its full extent in the sitting room, which was festooned with paper Christmas decorations made by Harriet and Gracie. Paul was outside, doing something secret which he said was a surprise for later, while Claudia and Giulia helped Mary with the lunch.

"Is that turkey?" asked Claudia in amazement.

Mary laughed. "Fat chance. But it's the next best thing. Mutton, which I got the butcher to bone, stuffed with all the trimmings, or at least the pretence of them. Mostly sausage and swede."

"It smells wonderful. You've gone to so much trouble."

"I've been saving on the rations for weeks, and we're lucky living where we do. Jabez has turned over all the flower beds in the park for vegetables. I got the recipe from the wireless – *The Kitchen Front*."

Giulia immediately began to mimic the posh voice of the radio recipes.

"Under the War Office Scheme a girl can learn to become the perfect wife at a Local Corporation Training Scheme – not the old way, with poor hubby as a sort of human guinea pig for early experiments, but under the guide of an expert, who can always help when things get a bit… er – sticky. What's this? 'Add a quart of cream?'

Can't be right. Better try, 'Mix the ingredients thoroughly': powdered eggs, swede and marrow as substitutes for fruit, margarine instead of butter. How's that pie doing? Mm, smells good. There's one husband at least who, when he gets home, won't need to whistle, 'Ma, I miss your apple pie!' "

Mary and Giulia laughed companionably together. Claudia watched in wonderment. This was a side to her daughter she hadn't known existed.

Lunch was a relaxed, enjoyable affair, with much appreciation of the delicious food, the warm fire, fuelled by a great deal of laughter and the happiness of the occasion, Paul home on leave for the wedding, Matteo back from Australia.

The mutton turkey was followed by eggless Christmas pudding, in which Harriet found the sixpence. They drank wine, brought by Claudia, even Gracie, who was allowed a thimble full of it and who declared it delicious, but then wrinkled her nose and said perhaps she might prefer to suck on a beetroot instead.

When everyone had finished, it was time for the speeches. First up was Matteo.

"I am not much of a speaker. I thought maybe my ship docks late and I arrive after the speeches. Better for everyone. But here I am, and happy to be so. Sometimes I wonder if I ever make it back home, but my sister says I have to, and we all do what she says, *si*? If we know what's good for us. I feel I am partly to blame – *scusa*, responsible – for bringing Paul and Harriet together. Years ago, when you were just a *bambino*, Paulie, you used to help me with the rag and bone cart. *Ti ricordi? Si*.

Con Bombola. Ah, everyone remembers Bombola, such a good, patient old horse. You and I, Paulie, we help Mary and Jabez to move here, all your belongings piled high on the back of the cart, which Bombola pull in the pouring Manchester rain. We sing songs all the way, and after we unload everything, the sun came out, and Bombola gives rides to all the children. That is when you and Harriet first meet, *non è vero*? And the sun, it shine today also. I wish you both *Buona Fortuna*, or as we say in Campania, *Bocca al Lupo*. Good luck. Paul and Harriet…"

He raised his glass and everyone joined in the toast. There were further sighing reminiscences about Bombola and a rousing chorus of *Take Me Back to Manchester When It's Raining*. Next up was Jabez.

"Thank you, Matteo. Or perhaps that should be '*Grazie*'." Good humoured laughter greeted his pronunciation. "It were a happy day indeed that first brought Paul to Philips Park, and I'm proud to welcome you into our family. I knew your father well, Paul, 'e were a good pal of mine in the last war, and I hope, Claudia, you'll not mind me mentioning Marco on a day like this, but it only seems right that 'e should be with us here today, if only in spirit. I wish that you'd 'ad the chance to get to know 'im too, Paul. He'd've been so proud of you and what you've done. I know you'll do right by our Harriet, and that she'll do right by you. I believe, as father of the bride, it falls on me to ask you all to join wi' me in drinking a toast to the beautiful bride. I'm sure you'll all agree that she looks as pretty as a picture. Harriet, if you and Paul are 'alf as 'appy as me and your mother 'ave been, then you won't do so bad.

The beautiful bride."

More applause followed. Jabez gave Mary a kiss, who was wiping her eyes on a tea cloth. "You daft ha'porth," she said, playfully flicking him with it, while Harriet looked on, beaming. Finally, it was Paul's turn.

"Thank you, Mr Chadwick," he said, then turned to Harriet. "We'll do our best, won't we, love?" Harriet squeezed his hand. "As it happens," he carried on, "I too have been thinking about my father. I never knew him, it's true, I never even saw him, but he wrote me a letter, just before he died. Mamma gave it to me when I was twelve. It didn't say a lot. I reckon he didn't have much time for writing in the trenches. I can understand that, it was the same for me in the desert. But what he did say I'd like to share with you all today." Giulia leaned forward in her seat, Claudia looked down at her hands folded in her lap, while Paul continued. "He said, 'Make sure you look after your *Mamma*...' Well, I've tried my best with that, but it feels more like she's always looked after me, for which I'm eternally grateful, and then he said, 'I hope when it comes time for you to find yourself a wife, you meet someone just as beautiful, just as loving, just as loyal...' Well, I think I've struck lucky on all three counts, don't you?" He bent down to kiss Harriet and everyone applauded. Even Gracie, who normally would have screwed up her face in disgust, or covered her eyes with embarrassment. "I'd like to take this opportunity of thanking Mr and Mrs Chadwick for always making me feel so welcome here, for all the work that you've done into making today so memorable, and for offering Harriet and me a room to stay in, till the War's over and we get chance to sort something out for ourselves. *Grazie*. Finally, it's customary for the groom to thank the bridesmaids for carrying out all their various duties, which I'm sure you'll all agree they did to perfection, and to give them a small token of appreciation. So for Giulia, I got you this." From the pocket on the inside of his jacket he produced an envelope, which was passed along the table until it reached Giulia.

"What is it?"

"I could say that it was a signed photo of an army pal of mine, which would be true, but which probably wouldn't interest you."

Frowning but intrigued Giulia opened the envelope and withdrew a photograph, just like Paul had said. She turned it over. A look of disbelief passed across her face before she began squealing and jumping up and down. "Look, everyone," she cried, "it's Audie Murphy."

Claudia, Mary and Harriet all crowded round to see. Paul, Matteo, Toby and Jabez looked at one another in bewilderment. "Apparently he's quite famous," shrugged Paul, with a mischievous grin spreading across his face.

"How did you get hold of this?" said Giulia, eyeing her brother suspiciously. "Is he really a pal of yours?"

"Not exactly a pal, but we did serve in the same unit for a while during the Sicily landings. We got to talking and I told him that you were probably a fan."

"Probably!" She flung her arms around him. "Now you really are a hero," she laughed.

Disentangling himself from his sister, he now turned his attention towards Gracie. "For your present," he said seriously, "you have to close your eyes first."

Gracie duly obliged, while the rest of her wriggled with unconcealed excitement..

"Now," he said, standing behind her, "I have to guide you outside…"

"Outside?" she whispered, barely able to contain herself.

"That's right. Toby – will you open the door please?"

Toby jumped up and opened the front door, letting in a blast of cold air. The others shivered and complained.

"Don't worry, it's not for long. Just a few more steps, Gracie. Now – open your eyes."

When she did, she found she was standing outside the front door of The Lodge. The sun had dipped below the Avenue of the Black Poplars. It took her a few moments to notice what had changed. Then she let out a huge shriek of delight. Hanging from the old pear tree standing a few feet away from the house was a rope. Gracie did not need a second invitation. With a whoop and a roar she galloped towards it. Then, with a single leap, she grasped it in her hands and began to swing around the tree.

"Look, Giulia," she cried, "guess who I am."

She was every inch the poster image of Betty Hutton in *The Perils of Pauline*. Taking one hand off the rope, she hollered like an American Indian. The action swung her off balance, so that she almost collided into the trunk of the tree but, using her good leg, she kicked away from it just in time and resumed her war cry.

Claudia, watching from the doorway, whispered to Mary, "How do you let her do such things? I'd be running to catch her all the time."

"I know," said Mary, shaking her head. "That's

exactly what I feel like doing too. But Gracie would hate it. She's not to be molly-coddled. She'll fall in a minute, she's bound to, but watch – she'll just..."

" *'Pick herself up'*," interrupted Harriet and Giulia, singing in unison, " *'dust herself down...'* "

Now everyone joined in. " *'And start all over again'!*"

Endings and beginnings, thought Claudia, as she and Matteo made their way back to Radium Street later that evening. This was the first chance they had had to be just the two of them since Matteo had arrived back from Australia, and now a kind of shyness held them, each pursuing their own thoughts, as they walked through the blackout-dark streets of Holt Town and Miles Platting towards Ancoats.

It was Matteo who broke the silence first.

"I'm sorry for being so quiet."

"That's all right. I'm not saying much myself, am I?"

"Things happen so quickly. Two months ago I still have no release papers. You write and write. Without you

I am still there for sure. Then, one night they wake me up. Come, they say. We leave now. Is all arranged. Next thing I know we are on a train to Sydney, where a ship is waiting. Is it true, I ask? Are we really going home? There are less than a hundred of us, the last ones to leave Hay Camp. Sometimes I think I stay there always. There are some who do. After their release. They say, where else can I go? No one is waiting for me in England. But I have you, Claudia, and the memory of Constanzia. Just before she die, she says she wish she had children. We had each other, I say. Is enough. I need to come home, I think, to be close to her. And to you. That is what keep me going. When the *Arandora Star* sink, I try to get people to leave the ship, but they are too frightened. In the end I jump. The water is so cold. I try to swim but soon my arms grow heavy. Then someone haul me into a lifeboat. Just in time. We wait there, float, for hours. I fall asleep. When I wake they take me aboard another big ship. They give us soup and a blanket. Then they lock us up in the hold. The ship heaves and rolls. Many people are sick. Fifty-five days they keep us there. The smell is… I can't find words. I think I die. When we land and go ashore, we have to shield our eyes, the light is so bright. We are in Sydney Harbour. They put us on trains, they take us to the camps. 'The Dunera Boys', they call us. I go to Hay. All Italians are put in Camp 6. More of a prison than a camp. To keep secrets from the guards we decide to speak only Italian. That is why my English so poor now. After six months we leave Hay. They need more space for Japanese prisoners. We go to Orange. A small town a hundred and fifty miles to the west, in the mountains. Many years ago they find gold there. A large camp was built. They put us there. There are names and initials carved on the walls. Maps with crosses showing where only fool's gold is found. More relaxed in Orange. We are not locked up all day. Some of us ask if we can work. At first they say no. Only prisoners can work. If internees work, we have to pay you, but they have no money. Then they have an idea. They pay us in tokens, which we can use only in the camp shop – look, I show you. I work in market gardens, growing food for the war effort. I save my tokens to buy stamps to send you letters. Then they start releasing us. A few at a time. When release papers come through. Some decide to stay in Australia. England has turned her back on us, they say. They like the weather. Hot like Italy. Some even join the Australian Army. But many, like me, we just want to go home, wherever that is. London, Northampton, Liverpool. A few, like me, Manchester. Giancarlo, Filippo, Franco. You remember Franco? One of the Stefanuttis. Finally they tell me I can leave. They put me on a train. Back to Sydney. Then on a ship. We stay on deck this time. No more lock up down below. I watch Australia disappear. Then I stare at the horizon for six weeks. When we reach the Bay of Biscay a convoy of battleships escorts us. To protect us from U-boats. We don't want torpedo a second time. Then we see Liverpool. The liver birds looking out to sea from the Pier Head. They are chained down. I ask one of the sailors what it means. He tells me one is female, one is male. The female looks out to sea, waiting for the men to return. The male looks to the city, watching over their families. But why the chains, I ask?

He says legend tells how they arrive from far away, when the River Mersey flooded. When they come, the river waters fall back. The birds bring good luck, they bring prosperity. So they chain them down, so they won't fly away, in case the river floods again. I like this story. It makes me hope I am welcome again now I come home…"

"Very welcome," said Claudia, putting her arm around her brother's waist.

They continued to walk in silence. She knew he would never speak of this again, but that he needed to, just once, to exorcise it. He wrapped his own arm around her shoulder. Together they marched in step quickly through the empty streets, their feet echoing on the pavements, as if reclaiming a homeland.

After they had made love, Harriet held Paul tightly in her arms, feeling the rhythm of his breathing rise and fall as sleep took him. She lay awake as the minutes passed by, adjusting her body to his as he nestled closer to her. She had never felt happier. She was sure she would never succumb to sleep herself – she was far too excited still, the events of the day replaying themselves in her mind, like a ball of wool she could constantly unspool and then wind back in again – but eventually she must have, for some hours later, she awoke with a start. She was cold. She reached out a hand towards where she expected Paul to be, but the space beside her was empty. She opened her eyes. The sky was just beginning to lighten, a smudge of grey seeping through the black. Paul was sitting on the recessed window sill, his back to the alcove wall, looking through the open window, smoking a cigarette. The red glow of it, as he inhaled, intensified, like a tiny blood blister would show more strongly when the skin was squeezed, or the last ember of coal would spark into flame when riddled and poked. She let her eyes accustom to the light. His face lay in shadow, the expression in his eyes clouded and distant. Slowly, so as not to startle him, she got out of bed, put on her dressing gown, for her skin was already starting to goose-pimple, and lightly crept towards him. At first he appeared not to notice her, but then she saw his head turn, as he stubbed out the remains of his cigarette.

"Sorry," he said. "Did I wake you?"

"I wondered where you were."

"Only here."

"You seemed miles away."

"I suppose I was."

"What is it?"

He shook his head. "Nothing."

"Paul," she said, taking his hand gently in her own, "let's not start our married life by keeping things from one another."

He breathed deeply and looked back out of the window.

"I keep thinking," he said, "about the others."

"Others?"

"In my unit." He eased the position of his back against the wall and rubbed his hip. "I should get back to them." Harriet watched him closely.

"Does it hurt?" she asked.

"It aches a bit in the cold, that's all."

"Come back to bed."

He shook his head again.

"Then at least keep warm." She fetched a blanket and placed it around his shoulders. "Do you want to tell me what happened?"

He looked at her sharply.

"I think it might help if you did. Don't think you have to spare my feelings. I'm strong enough to hear it. Whatever it is."

Paul looked down. Neither of them spoke for a long time. Harriet could sense him working out whether he should. From the other side of the park she heard the winding gear of the pit head at Bradford Colliery whirring into life, hauling up the men from one shift back to the surface, carrying the next one down. She waited.

"I've never felt Italian," he said at last. "Not really. I know I can speak the language and I grew up with all of *Nonno's* memories of the old country, but that always felt like something from a story book. Real life was here. In Manchester. With you."

He paused. He was not by nature a talker, and the effort of saying even this much seemed to have exhausted him. Harriet waited patiently. She knew him, probably better than he knew himself, and understood that there was more to come. Paul looked back through the window again. The smudge of grey had become a wider band across the sky, like someone had dipped a paint brush into a tin of water colours and allowed the tiniest splash of colour to spread very slowly.

"In Africa I didn't see much actual fighting. Our job

was to repair and customise the tanks for operations in desert conditions, so we were always some miles behind the front lines. The first thing people think about when you say the word 'desert' to them is the heat, and yes, it is hot, but so long as you've got water, you can get used to that. What nobody tells you about beforehand is the wind. It's always there. It whips up the sand, which gets into everything – your eyes, your nose, your throat. It seems to form a film all over you, like a second skin. What's even worse, at least for us sappers, is that it gets into every single component and engine part of the jeeps and the tanks. We spent all of our time trying to keep 'em free of it, but it was like painting t' Trafford Park Road Bridge. No sooner had you finished than you had to start again."

He paused to light another cigarette. His hands, Harriet noticed, were shaking slightly as he tried to strike the match.

"The other thing you notice," he said, "is the way the desert keeps changing – literally, right before your eyes. A stretch of dunes that was there yesterday will shift and be gone tomorrow. So you never quite knew where you were. You couldn't be sure either that your compass was working correctly, the sand got into that too. Who knew if north really was where it said it was. At night I used to try and get a fix on true north so I could imagine where you might be and face myself in that direction. It were better at night, for at least you could trust the stars. By 'eck, Harriet, I wish you could've seen them stars down there. So clear and sharp, like you could reach up and touch them. I suppose it's a bit like that here, now there's a blackout..."

Harriet nodded.

"Over the next few months, as our lads began to start pushing Rommel back, we began to move further and further east. That's what the compass said, and what the stars confirmed, but you'd never 'ave known it from t' desert. It's no respecter of countries or borders, which are all just made up straight lines on a map. You could've been anywhere. Or nowhere. It were just the desert, and it felt like the only world there was. Covered in sand you couldn't tell us or the enemy apart. We all looked the same. After t' second Battle of El Alamein, when t' tide started to turn in our favour, we began taking prisoners – whole truckloads of 'em, all crammed in tight wi' their hands on top o' their 'eads. Quite a few of 'em were Italian. I could hear 'em talking, wishing they could go home, but I didn't let on that I could understand 'em. I didn't want to risk being thought one of 'em, I suppose..."

He was quiet a long time after he'd said that. Harriet understood how compromised he must have felt.

"But damn it, I thought, my father fought in the last war, why shouldn't I in this?" He flicked the ash from his cigarette out of the open window. "We were laid up in Egypt for a few weeks – Alexandria – waiting on orders. I knew what they'd be before they came. And I were right. Invasion of Sicily. Then everything changed. Operation Husky. We landed near Cassibile, just south of Syracuse. We were much closer to t' fighting this time, and I saw things I wish I 'adn't... After we'd took Syracuse, we headed further north to try and capture the ports of

Catania and Augusta. Which we did. But then there was a counter attack by enemy tanks. It were a close run thing, but luck was on our side, and we managed to make it through. The Yanks had it much tougher. They were having to fight on t' slopes of Mount Etna, before pushing on to Palermo, where they had to fight off Panzer divisions. We met up at t' Straits of Messina, but by then, most of the enemy had retreated to t' mainland. It had taken just six weeks to get from one side o' th' island to t'other. We thought it were all over, but it had barely got started…"

Outside the window a blackbird began to sing. Harriet picked it out in the growing light on top of the pear tree, where yesterday Gracie had been swinging round on the rope tied up there by Paul. How long ago that now seemed. She looked across to Paul, whose eyes, she now saw, were far away, lost somewhere in the toe of Italy. To bring him back she needed to let him tell his story to its conclusion, however hard he was trying not to.

"Five hundred of us in X Corps were reassigned to the 5th Army, under Lieutenant-General McCreery. We made land at Salerno. We thought it'd be easy. After Sicily Mussolini were kicked out. Those who replaced him tried to make peace with the Allies, so we thought it'd be like a stroll in t' park. Nobody told us just how many Germans there'd be there, and that many of the Italians still wanted to carry on fighting. We 'ad to make a detour. While the navy shelled the port, we cut inland, only about five miles or so, fighting our way across the Sorrento Peninsula, till we came out on top of a hill overlooking the whole Plain of Naples stretching out before us. At first I thought nothing of it, but then it dawned on me. This were Campania. Where our family's from. Where *Nonno* flew his kites. What was I doing here, fighting against folk who might've been cousins?"

He looked directly at Harriet. She took his face in her hands and brought him close to her.

"Shh…" she whispered. "Shh…"

She continued to hold him while he finished his story.

"It were September. The sun beat down strongly. We made our way down th' hill towards fields of wheat. There weren't a breath of wind. The wheat were so dry it could hardly stand. It lolled to one side, like a dog's tongue panting. We could see a way in to the east of Salerno down a back road, just t' other side o' t' field. A big field it were, mind, mebbe a mile wide. General McCreery ordered us to march in a straight line right through t' centre. The wheat were as tall as us, it'd give us protection, he said. An' it did. For a bit. We'd not got half way across, though, when suddenly we was ambushed. Or at least, that's what we thought. Fifty yards to our left about a hundred Italian soldiers leapt up out o' t' field and started firing at us. Then, fifty yards to our right, another hundred Italians leapt up and started firing at us too. Only they weren't. It took us a while to realise what were going on. One lot were Partisans, wanting to join the Allies. T' others were Blackshirts, still loyal to Mussolini. They were firing at each other. Many of 'em weren't dressed like soldiers. Just farmers and peasants. Former neighbours, who probably helped each other farm this field in t' days before t' War, gathering in t' wheat together. Now they were killing one another, an' not just wi' guns, but knives, even their bare hands. It were like if City an' United fans started shooting at each other, but much, much worse. These men – an' women too – knew each other. They probably went to school wi' each other, sat next to each other in church, helped each other's families wi' t' harvest. Now, they were killing one other, right up close, seeing themselves reflected back in the eyes of another. The General ordered us to look after ourselves as we saw fit. I must've killed half a dozen, Harriet, from both sides. And all I could think of was not so long ago this might've been *Nonno*, or Maurizio, my mother's father. Instead it were me. And for the first time in my life, I felt Italian. And here I was, killing other Italians, in the same valley where my family first came from. It were the same as if I'd turned on my pals in the unit. We all of us live under t' same sun, don't we? So what are we doing trying to kill one other…?"

Paul was silent for a while, remembering the slaughter, the wheat fields cut down and flattened by the dead and dying bodies, the gold of the corn stippled with red. There'd be no harvest gathered in that year.

Harriet wanted to cry. But she knew she mustn't. She gripped Paul even tighter as he took a deep breath and prepared to carry on.

"A week later the General said we were being reassigned to new units, as replacements for battle casualties further up the line. Some of the men refused. 'What about us?' they said. 'We've had losses too – thousands, if you count the Desert Campaign.' It were almost a mutiny. The General did his best to try and persuade them to obey their orders, but nearly half refused."

"Why didn't you?" asked Harriet. "I wouldn't have blamed you."

"They were court martialled. Imprisoned. Some might yet face execution."

"Oh."

"I just kept my head down. It were a real slog. A hard grind. We was held up for months on end. A mixture of heavy defences, difficult terrain, terrible weather. Until finally we made it to Monte Cassino earlier this year. And – well... you know the rest."

"Yes."

She remembered the dread she experienced when she received his letter – "I've been bashed about a bit" – then the relief when she saw Paul as he stepped from the boat train at London Road.

The sky was almost light now. She looked at the scars on his back, where the burns on his skin were starting to fade. They would never disappear altogether, but already they were less red and angry than when she'd first seen them a few weeks ago, less puckered and livid. She moved her hand down his chest and round towards his hip. Instinctively he flinched and gripped her wrist to prevent her from going further, then relaxed and let her explore the hole which was gradually healing there with her fingers, followed by her lips, which tenderly kissed around the wound. She would know every inch of him.

Some time later she said, "Will you have to go back?"

"I don't know," he said. "I shouldn't think so."

"Good. You're home now."

"There's always plenty for an engineer to do back at

base, fixing and repairing things."

Harriet pulled him close. "Let's make a start then, shall we? Come back to bed."

A pale winter sun dispersed the cloud, its light falling on the two of them like a drawing by Klimt. *Lovers* or *Couple in Bed.*

*

The next morning Claudia stepped out of her house with fresh purpose. A renewed sense of vigour quickened her pace as she made her way across the city centre towards Central Station behind *The Midland Hotel.*

It was Christmas Eve, a little after 7am. She was preparing to catch the train to Withington & West Didsbury, from where she would walk the one and a half miles to Southern Cemetery to pay her respects to Annie, something she now did every year at Christmas. There was a more direct bus route, which would have taken her right outside the cemetery gates, but since the air raids this was no longer always passable, whereas remarkably the railway had suffered little bomb damage, and in any case Claudia was relishing the prospect of a brisk walk on what was promising to be a bright Sunday morning.

Matteo had decided he would look up his old Stefanutti pals, while Giulia had said she would make a start on the preparations for their Christmas dinner tomorrow, leaving Claudia free to make this annual pilgrimage. She missed Annie more than she could say. Although in later years, after Annie had moved away, they saw less of each other, whenever they did, they quickly fell back into their former comfortable way with one another. She could say things to her that she could say to no one else, and so she was looking forward to telling her some good news for a change – Matteo's return, Paul and Harriet's wedding. Although she knew that Annie was not there in the cemetery – not a trace of her body was recovered after she had stepped on the unexploded mine in Portugal Street four years before – she nevertheless derived much solace from speaking aloud the thoughts she carried around in her head from one year's end to the next.

When she arrived at the grave, it was, as always, immaculately kept, with no weeds and a vase of fresh flowers. She imagined that Lily must tend to it regularly for it to remain in such pristine condition, although a little bit of weathering had begun to affect the headstone, with signs of yellow lichen fringing the grey limestone. She stood looking down at it for several minutes and then thought, "Why am I doing this? Who am I carrying out this ritual for? Not for Annie, that's for sure. This focus on the past is not healthy, this harping on about the dead is becoming morbid. We should look forward, not back," she told herself. "I should devote my attention to the living instead."

She immediately turned on her heels and decided she would go directly to Lapwing Lane and call on Lily. She would arrive at around nine o'clock. She was sure she would not be too early. She would invite her to join her, Matteo and Giulia for part of Christmas day tomorrow. She began to sing *La Donna è Mobile* from *Rigoletto*, its brisk march matching her stride, the words too chiming with this seemingly sudden change of heart in her. *Qual piumo al vento*. Like a feather in the wind. She thought back to the time when Marco had first sung these words to her, in Philips Park, when Billy Grimshaw, 'The Gramophone King', had played his recordings of the Great Caruso, and how she had teased him. She smiled.

As she approached Fog Lane Park she became conscious of a high pitched hum vibrating in the air. At first she thought it must be the wind quivering in the overhead telegraph wires, but it was too loud for that. She stopped singing, paused in her walking, and looked up.

The humming grew in intensity.

The air shimmered and crackled.

Mesmerised she scanned the skies for what it might mean.

Then, as abruptly as it had started, it stopped.

The silence which followed was deafening, like a nerve tightening and stretching. Her whole body tensed with the anticipation of the nerve finally snapping.

Time slowed almost to a standstill.

In the final single second each of the hundred billion neurons buried in her brain fired at least two hundred times, connecting to another thousand simultaneously.

She could feel every separate heartbeat deep inside her, a *rallentando* timpani roll, as each individual blood corpuscle flowed through and around her in an intricate map of veins and arteries.

Five hundred skin cells flaked and floated away from her in the same nanosecond.

She felt herself diminish and expand concurrently, a single sub-atomic particle touching the limitless reach of space.

Vapourised.

For ever and ever. World without end. Amen.

In the final moment, before consciousness left her completely, she thought she heard another sound. A child's voice singing very far away. It was Giulia. Practising her audition piece to join the choir of nymphs and shepherds fifteen years before. The notes flowed down to Claudia, becoming louder and clearer, until, just when she thought she might hold them in her hand, they too evaporated and were gone.

"God be in my head, and in my understanding;
God be in mine eyes, and in my looking;
God be in my mouth, and in my speaking;
God be in my heart, and in my thinking;
God be at mine end, and at my departing…"

*

Manchester Evening News

Wednesday 27th December 1944

DOODLEBUGS RAIN DOWN ON MANCHESTER

Germans Launch V1 Christmas Eve Attack

No Known Casualties

On the morning of Christmas Eve 45 Doodlebugs were launched off the Yorkshire coast from beneath Heinkel bombers patrolling the skies above the North Sea.

The V1 Flying Bombs were all aimed at Manchester, but most missed their target, landing harmlessly in largely unpopulated areas, some as far away as Durham, Chester and Northampton. 14 fell straight into the North Sea. A sure sign that Jerry's getting desperate.

Only one missile made it within the Civil Defence Area for Manchester, and that was in Didsbury, between Fletcher Moss and Fog Lane Park. Windows are reported to have been blown out in buildings up to a mile away, with observers adding that mini-after shocks were experienced that appeared to temporarily suck the oxygen out of the air.

There are no known casualties.

3

Christmas 1948

Trompe l'oeuil.

    George leaves. Francis listens. Lily looks.
    George paints. Francis panics. Lily plots.
    George tricks. Francis transmits. Lily triumphs.

    Obfuscation. Sleight of hand. Trick of the light.
    Camouflage. Subterfuge. Decoy.
    Doctored negative. Echo chamber. Cracked mirror.

    What the eye thinks it sees.
    Ripples in a pond. Radio signals spooling outwards.
    This is Manchester calling, Manchester calling.

    A grid, a dial, a chart.
    Veins and arteries, tunnels and vapour trails.
    The home, the city, the world.

Lily in the rabbit hole.

For six months after she learns the news of Annie's death, she barely goes out. George returns, fleetingly, for the funeral. The house is yours, he says, to do with what you will, then he leaves again.

The bombing stops. Evelyn and Pearl return to Bignor Street. Lily moves in to what was Annie's bedroom. She sits at the dressing table. The three-sided mirror shows endless reflections. On and on, more and more of them, tumbling down the rabbit hole, Lily through the Looking Glass, the pool of tears.

Pearl comes to visit. This won't do, she says, picking up unopened mail from the mat. I'll deal with it later, says Lily. When was the last time you went out, asks Pearl? Or cooked a proper meal, or last had a wash? Lily flaps her hand. Soon, she says, turning back to the mirror.

Pearl comes every week. She runs Lily a bath. She washes and combs her hair. She dries her with a towel in front of the fire. She helps her get dressed. She feeds her soup.

The next week she finds her ration book. She looks in the cupboards and makes a list. She puts each of Lily's arms through a sleeve of her coat. She ties a scarf upon her head. She opens the front door. They step outside. Lily shields her eyes from the brightness.

Pearl suggests they clean and tidy the house.

No, says Lily, I'll do that. She fills a bucket with hot water. She scrubs every inch of the house. Inside and out. When she's finished, she looks around. Then starts again.

Pearl holds up an envelope. You need to open this, she says. I will, says Lily. But not now. When, says Pearl? When I'm ready. You're ready now.

Enlistment Notice, it reads. Manchester Posting Section, Sunlight House, Quay Street. Registration Number PWS 6622.

Lily wants to screw it up and throw it on the fire. Pearl prevents her just in time. She smoothes out the creases on the kitchen table. Sit, she tells Lily. Read it.

> Dear Miss Wright, *it says.* In accordance with the National Service Act you are called upon to offer your service to the country along with all single women and childless widows between the ages of twenty and thirty in this time of war. You must report to your Local Posting Section to arrange your assignment. If you do not respond within twenty-eight days you will be posted where this office feels you will be most needed. Failure to comply could lead to imprisonment.

Pearl looks at the date at the top of the letter. You've got two days left, she says.

I'll go tomorrow, says Lily.

You'll go today, says Pearl, marching her upstairs to change.

Half an hour later they are walking down Lapwing Lane to West Didsbury & Withington Station from where they catch the train for Manchester Central.

The journey takes just twenty minutes. But in that short space of time Lily passes from one world into another. She's not listened to the news since Christmas. She has no idea of the devastation visited upon the city. Didsbury's been spared for the most part. The sound of bombs falling in the distance, that's all it's amounted to, and she has shut her ears to those. Now, as the train travels over an elevated section of track near Cornbrook, she sees for the first time the full extent of the damage wreaked by the air raids of the past six months. The train crosses the iron bridge slowly. Through its bars Lily sees the disconsolate straggle of survivors picking their way through the rubble below, an army of rats scavenging for scraps and leftovers. The sight of it is a slap in the face.

She turns to Pearl. Thank you, she says.

What for?

Rescuing me.

From Central Station it is only a five minute walk to Sunlight House. On the way Pearl tells Lily she's lucky. Lily nods.

I'll tell you why, says Pearl. I got one of these letters. I thought it didn't apply to me, so I ignored it. But I was wrong. It applies to all of us. I missed the deadline, so I had no say in what I did. They sent me to Crossley's in Levenshulme. Making engine parts. It's noisy, dirty, tiring work. After the first week I ached in muscles I didn't know I had. I thought I'd go mad with all the clamour and din. But you get used to it. I reckon a body can get used to most things given time.

Lily looks up sharply at this. A long buried memory stirs uneasily.

So now I just get on with it. Six days a week. In the evenings I look after Mrs Evelyn. And on my day off I come and see you. The time passes quite quickly. The other girls are all right. We go dancing sometimes on a Saturday. You might want to come with us?

Lily shakes her head. I don't like dancing, she says, with a shudder.

Pearl ignores this. You'll be all right with me, she says. I'll show you the ropes. We'll get round, you'll see.

By now they are standing outside Sunlight House.

First, says Pearl, you've got to get your call up sorted.

Don't just let them fob you off with anything. Ask 'em what's on offer. Then choose what you think you'd like the sound of. In you go. I'll wait here.

Fifteen minutes later Lily is back outside.

By 'eck, says Pearl, that were quick.

I'm a plotter, says Lily, with a grin.

What's that when it's at home?

I don't really know. But I'm about to find out. I start tomorrow.

Well at least you're smiling – that's summat…

Lily is a plotter.

She goes on a short course to the Air Crew Dispatch Centre in Heaton Park. In the distance she thinks she sees George, but she's not sure. From there she's sent to the Control Command Centre in an underground bunker beneath Manchester Town Hall. The Ops Room, they call it.

She stands with other girls around a big table. The table is a map. It shows the whole area covered by the local fighter group. All along the coasts are radar stations, which track incoming enemy war planes. These are transmitted by relays to each of the regional headquarters. Lily hears the information on the headphones she wears. Unidentified aircraft approaching, a voice says, followed by a map reference. She then has to push out a little model of a plane on a stand onto the big map to show where it's coming from. She has to keep plotting it, as it gets nearer and nearer. Eventually, the voice will confirm if it's 'friendly' or 'unfriendly'.

She has to be quick. The information comes thick and fast. The planes are identified by numbers and letters. Alpha Charlie 6257. She has to plot this on the map. If she misses it first time, she has to wait till the voice says it again. Which it might not. Then she's in trouble.

Above and behind the Ops Room table are the officers of Fighter Command. They look down on the plotters like gods from Olympus, watching the models of planes moving across the map like toys. Once they are sure it's an enemy plane, they contact the nearest squadron and alert them for action.

Sometimes the planes get through. A loud explosion will sound above. The electric lights will flicker off and on several times. Lily dives under the table with the other plotters. Plaster dust showers on them from the ceiling. When it's over, they stand up, brush the dust from their uniforms, check that everyone's all right, then carry on. Lily is asked if she might make them all a cup of tea.

She doesn't like working underground. She never knows whether it's night or day. When her shift ends, she steps out into Albert Square and breathes as deeply as her lungs will permit her. She might share a cigarette with one of the other girls. She's started smoking again. For the first time since she left Globe Lane.

She never knows what time it will be when she finishes, so she's taken to riding into Manchester on George's DOT RS. He's told her she can. He taught her how to ride it not long after she first came to live at Lapwing Lane. She likes it best when it's dark. She rides as fast as she dare, not switching on the headlights because of the blackout. She remembers the night George

193

rescued her from Angel Meadow. It's a long fucking way to Didsbury, she'd said. And it is if you have to walk it on an empty stomach, when you've not eaten since God knows when and the insides of your legs are bleeding and bruised. But now she can do it in less than half an hour. She weaves in and out of the mountains of rubble, speeding through the skeletal streets, till she reaches home.

Some nights, if the timing works, she does go dancing with Pearl.

The Levenshulme Palais. Manchester's *Ballroom de Luxe*. With *The New Palais Dance Orchestra* led by Bill Edge. Admission two shillings, but free if she wears her ATS Uniform.

It's not as bad as she fears. Pearl keeps an eye on her. There's safety in numbers.

There's no shortage of men asking her to dance. They go for girls in uniform, winks Pearl. Maybe next time I can borrow yours, she quips, we're about the same size. Lily smiles weakly. That's not a bad idea, she thinks.

But though she's always in demand, she's rarely asked to dance again by the same man twice. Not much of a talker, they report back to their pals. Holds herself stiff. This suits Lily just fine. She only goes to keep Pearl company. She perfects an awkward way of dancing, of stepping on a feller's shoes, of shrugging as if to say, I know, I'm hopeless, aren't I? And pretty soon it becomes a self-fulfilling prophecy. The boys lose interest. She doesn't mind. She stands at the side. She listens to the band. She steps outside for a cigarette.

There she bumps into Lamarr. He's wearing a uniform

too. He's a G.I. Stationed at Broom Lane. Say, can I bum a cigarette, he says? Lily likes his accent, the way he drawls his words. He points to Pearl dancing a lively jive inside. Is she your friend, Lamarr asks, only I thought I seen you come in with her? Yes, says Lily, she's my friend. Her name's Pearl. So this is the game. Pearl, Lamarr whistles? That's a mighty pretty name. Might you introduce us? Lily smiles. Why sure, she says, in her best American accent. She's always been a good mimic. Lamarr smiles and stubs out his cigarette. Lead the way, lady, he laughs.

Pearl and Lamarr hit it off right away. Pretty soon they're clearing the floor with their jitterbug and lindy hop. Pearl catches Lily's eyes over Lamarr's shoulder. She makes a perfect circle with her thumb and forefinger and mouths 'He's gorgeous' towards her.

After that Lily doesn't go to any more dances. She knows that Pearl would want to try and pair her off with one of Lamarr's buddies. She's not interested in that and besides, she doesn't want to cramp their style. On her nights off she goes instead to the pictures. *The Trocadero* in Didsbury, *The Scala* in Withington. She laughs with Bob Hope, Bing Crosby and Dorothy Lamour in *Road to Zanzibar*, and thinks Pearl would look good in a sarong. She cries with Greer Garson and Walter Pidgeon in *Blossoms in the Dust*, a true story about a woman who takes it upon herself to find good homes for orphans but runs into prurient opposition from those who think that illegitimate children should be shunned, which gives Lily an idea, plants a tiny seed for when the War is over, if it ever does end. Right now that possibility seems like a distant dream. And she shies away from *A Woman's Face* with Joan Crawford as the disfigured heroine of the title. It's a little too close to home. She hardly thinks about the strawberry mark now, barely registers it when she looks at herself in the mirror, but sometimes she's brought up short by the thoughtless remarks of strangers.

But mostly she goes home after work. Sometimes she takes longer rides on the DOT RS. If it wasn't for petrol rationing, she'd do this more often.

She decides to quit being a plotter. She's finding the long hours underground more and more of a strain. It's like being in a tomb, she tells her supervisor, or a mole for ever burrowing in the earth. When she comes up for air, the light hurts her eyes. The supervisor is sympathetic. He's seen this pattern before. It's not for everyone, he says. But you've done well. I'll recommend you for something else. What do you have in mind, she asks? I notice you ride a motor cycle, he says, rubbing his chin…

Lily's a dispatch rider.

She's still based at the Town Hall, where she reports each day for duty. They send her right across the city delivering messages. Packages, letters, instructions. Blueprints rolled up in cardboard tubes. Statistics, dockets, invoices. Lists. The numbers of displaced families requiring temporary re-housing. The names of casualties ward by ward. Where there's a surfeit. Where there's a shortage. Orders for supplies. Requests for the relocation of resources. Permissions granted, permissions refused.

She rides to Ringway for updates on the readiness of aircraft after repairs. Then to Barton with requests to extend the range of their radar. To Urmston to check on the gun emplacements. To Stockport to arrange an inspection of the largest public air raid shelter ever built in Britain. It holds more than six thousand people. When Lily arrives, apart from the warden to whom she must deliver the message, it is completely deserted. Their voices echo in the vaulted red sandstone tunnels. They are so large Lily could ride her DOT RS right into their heart. She looks around and shivers even though it is midday in summer. People have scratched their initials on the walls, as if to prove to future generations that once they were there, they were alive to leave their marks upon the land, remember us.

She rides from hospital to hospital. The Infirmary, Salford Royal, Prestwich. Crumpsall, Pendlebury, Stretford. Are there enough blankets? Are there enough bandages? Do they need more nurses, doctors, blood?

She rides to Pomona Docks to check on the food convoys. She rides to the railway stations to ensure preparations have been made for the latest arrival of prisoners. From North Africa, from Sicily, from Greece.

She gets to know the city like a second skin. She knows every street in every district. She learns the short cuts, which roads are impassable, which squares no go zones. Where there are sink holes, land mines, unexploded bombs.

She can ride Manchester blindfold. Day or night, it makes no difference. When the bombs are falling, when the streets are quiet. She sees the moon shine between roofless, windowless buildings. She watches the sun rise over Audenshaw Reservoirs. Herons rise from the water out of the mist. She looks and she remembers.

Once she gets an order to ride out to Dukinfield. To a WRVS Centre where they are teaching first aid. Among the volunteers she spots Mrs Baines, teaching young women to make a sling. The years have not been kind to her. It's been a long time since they were both at Globe Lane. Lily studies her across the hall. Mrs Baines looks up. She stares directly at Lily but doesn't recognise her. Lily steers clear, just in case. She delivers her message to the WRVS Nurse conducting the course, then leaves.

Lily has a dream.

She is walking in a maze. Instead of hedges, high walls surround her. They remind her of the air raid tunnels in Stockport. Every inch of them is covered with initials scrawled and scratched out. These are not survivors, but memorials to those that perished.

Lily must reach the centre. She knows that something is waiting for her, something she must rescue and retrieve, then help to carry back outside. She is unwinding a ball of wool behind her so she won't get lost. But the more she twists and turns, the more the wool gets snagged on shards of rock, splinters of stone. It unspools behind her like memories she can't quite grasp. If the thread snaps, she knows she'll never get out. Slowly she makes her way to the centre, inch by inch, as if she is waiting in a queue for some unspecified, unrationed item.

Others have been here before her. She sees their bleached bones poking through the earth.

When she finally makes it, she is surprised, disappointed almost. Instead of the giant or beast or monster she has imagined dwelling there in the centre, she spies someone small, kneeling down, facing away from her. The figure appears to be scrabbling in the dirt. It turns around.

Before Lily can make out the face, she wakes up...

Lily is an ack-ack girl.

Her ATS Supervisor calls her into his office. You've been a dispatch rider for quite some time now, haven't you, Lily, he says? Yes sir, she replies, almost eighteen months. Fancy a change, he asks? Depends what it is, sir. The supervisor smiles. I'll get straight to the point then, he says. We've a shortage of operators for the Anti-Aircraft Guns at Melland. An ack-ack girl, says Lily? She blushes. Apologies for interrupting, sir. That's all right, Lily. An ack-ack girl, yes. Think you're up to it? If you think I am, sir. The supervisor hands her an envelope. That's the spirit. Report tomorrow for training.

The gun emplacement at Melland is sited on the playing fields near Mount Road between Levenshulme and Gorton. Not far from the Prisoner of War Camp. Lily has delivered messages to both before, so she knows where it is.

Another ATS girl – Caroline – is waiting for her. She explains what's involved. There are three main roles, she says. Spotters, Rangers and Predictors. Spotters use binoculars to scan the skies to try and find enemy planes. Rangers calculate the distance a shell from the gun would have to travel to hit the target. Predictors work out the length of the fuse needed to make sure the shell explodes at the right height. Only the men operate the guns. Got that, she says? Lily nods. Here, adds Caroline, thrusting a pair of binoculars towards Lily. Start as a Spotter. Oh – and you'll need these, your most important piece of kit. She hands over a pair of cotton wool buds. Lily frowns, puzzled. Ear protectors, says Caroline with a grin. It can get quite noisy.

It's 1943. There are fewer raids these days. The Germans are targeting other cities. Occasionally planes will empty their undropped bombs on Manchester on their way back from a sortie elsewhere, and sometimes there'll be a full scale attack. But rarely. Many of the ack-ack girls have been reassigned to other duties but they still need a skeleton crew, explains Caroline on a quiet night. Most of their time is spent waiting. Lily trains her binoculars on the skies but hardly ever spots anything.

When she does, though, all hell breaks loose. The noise from the guns is like nothing she's ever heard. Ack-ack doesn't cover it. They boom. They pound. They resonate deep within her. The earth shakes beneath her. Her body trembles and quakes. The cotton wool proves its worth over and over again. They have to shout to make each other heard above the cannons' roar and thunder.

One time Lily forgets to put the cotton wool in. The deafness stays with her for days. She feels like she is living under water…

Lily is a camp whore.

Midsummer's Eve, 1944. Lily's ears are still ringing. She's not able to ride the DOT RS for a few days. As well as deafness she experiences a temporary loss of balance. Labyrinthitis. She decides to walk the three and a half miles to Lapwing Lane. It's nine o'clock in the evening, but with the long light nights she should still be back before it gets dark

The walk takes her past Melland Camp. Both Italian and German prisoners are kept here, though they are kept separate from each other and don't mix. In the German section there are still prisoners loitering outside, taking advantage of what is a warm June evening. Some are standing in groups, talking and smoking. Some are doing press ups, trying to maintain fitness. Some are working still in the allotments. Lily knows from her time as a dispatch rider that the prisoners must grow their own provisions. Anything in excess can be dispersed among the local population. Lily was shocked to discover that a prisoner's rations are greater than a civilian's. These men are better fed than she is.

If she were on her motor bike she would not have passed this way, but there's a short cut when walking, across the playing fields where the Camp is housed, around its perimeter fence, which is several feet high, topped with barbed wire. There are guards patrolling with Alsatian dogs. So far as she knows, there have been no successful escape attempts from here, though elsewhere in the country that is not the case.

She reaches a kink in the fence. This is the farthest point from Mount Road. It's the most out-of-the-way corner of the Camp. Beyond the bend Lily sees a line of girls. Each of them is talking to a prisoner. They swap cigarettes in exchange for certain favours, those few which are possible between the wire mesh of the fence.

One of the women approaches Lily. She appears to be in charge of the others. New here, are you, she says? You'll have to wait your turn. But don't worry, love. There are always more soldiers than girls. A siren sounds. The prisoners at once head back towards the barracks on the far side of the Camp. Oh, says the woman, you're just too late. Try again tomorrow night, only come a bit earlier. If any of the other girls ask you questions, just tell them you've spoken to Mags. That's me. She looks Lily critically up and down. And don't wear your uniform tomorrow, okay?

Lily says nothing. The other girls eye her warily. But Lily knows how to behave in this kind of company. A sort of muscle memory kicks in. She offers some of them a cigarette. They relax around her, then walk on.

Lily looks back through the fence into the Camp. The men are all lining up for their final inspection before being confined to their barracks for the night. But something catches her attention in the corner of her eye. Over where the allotments are she sees a prisoner who appears to be bent over a trug of vegetables. He scrabbles for something in the dirt. He is turned away from her, so she can't see his face. She wonders why he doesn't join the others. Then she understands. Two of his fellow inmates are sent across to him. They each take one of his arms and help him to his feet. There's something wrong with one of them, she notices. He limps painfully. There's something about him that strikes her as familiar.

Lily returns to the camp several times in the next fortnight. She goes in the day time, so as not to be confused with the girls who visit by night. She seeks out the man with the limp. He's easy to spot. He's always to be found in the allotment. Usually alone. Kneeling as he weeds around the onions or fetches up the carrots.

He's too far away to see clearly. Once, while he is checking the broad beans, which appear to be about ready to fall down unless they are tied up soon, he turns in her direction. The sun is behind him, so she still can't see his face, but she shields her eyes and waves tentatively. Surprised, he raises his hand and waves back. Then, a whistle is blown. He is needed elsewhere. The same two prisoners who helped him before hoist him to his feet. He hobbles away.

The next day she arrives early. A full hour before her shift at the gun emplacement is due to begin. She waits by the fence. She scans the Camp for sight of him. When she sees him, she calls out a hello and waves, more forcibly this time. He sees her, looks around and then makes his way towards her. What is it, he asks? Oh, she says, surprised, you speak English. *Ja*. He looks faintly amused, as if well used to this response. Lily delves into the satchel she wears over her shoulder and pulls out a ball of string. Here, she says, passing it through the wire mesh of the fence. For the beans, and she points towards the allotment where the plants are almost keeling over. A boyish smile lights up his face. *Danke*, he says, and he takes the ball of string from Lily's outstretched fingers. He looks furtively all around him. We're not supposed to fraternise with the locals, he says, though it happens all the time. People are very kind. But you must try and be a little more discreet. Lily blushes. I'm sorry, she says. I don't mean to get you into trouble. I'll be more careful next time. He looks her straight in the eye. Next time?

Lily feels her mouth go dry.

He turns. He walks towards the patch of beans. Lily, in her confusion, has kept hold of one end of the ball of string. It unspools from her fingers as he moves further away, until it tugs on the fence, causing him to halt. He looks back. The string is taut between them. Now she remembers why he has seemed so familiar. He's the figure from her dream. The man from the centre of the maze, where he's been waiting for her to come and find him.

She lets the end of the string fall to the floor. He quickly reels it in. She watches him begin to tie back the beans as she checks her watch and realises she is going to have to run if she is to make it to her shift on time.

She's a Predictor now, calculating the length of fuse required so that the shell will explode at the correct trajectory...

Lily is a binary girl.

Lily attends the Camp every day. Whether she's working or not. On her days off she doesn't wear her ATS Uniform but a floral patterned dress. She and the prisoner interlock fingers through the fence. The other women, who live nearby on Mount Road, see her as they pass by on their way to Levenshulme Market. They look at her knowingly, tut and mutter to each other when they think they're out of earshot. Camp whore, they say, and spit.

What's your name, she asks?

Roland.

Where are you from?

Koblenz.

What happened to you?

I'm a pilot. I was shot down.

Oh. Is that how...? She looks down at his foot.

Ja. I was lucky.

Lucky?

A boy with a sledge rescued me. He climbed a tree and cut me loose. He fetched help. A nurse with a white scarf. She saved my foot. It was crushed. I think they would have cut it off if she had not done what she did.

Yes, I see. Lucky.

Lucky they send me here. Lucky I meet you.

Lily looks down.

What did you do? Before you were a pilot?

Mathematics. Look.

He begins to draw with a stick in the dirt. A series of circles and straight lines. Ones and zeros.

What is it, she asks?

The future.

She squats low on her haunches to gain a closer look. I don't understand, she says.

Instead of ten digits, imagine just two, he says. Zero and one. His eyes shine in adoration for the sheer elegance and simplicity of it.

It looks like one of those games you might play as a

child, she says. Find your way from here to there following only the ones…

… or zeros, yes.

A labyrinth.

Technically, a maze.

What's the difference?

A labyrinth has only a single, non-branching path leading to the centre, then back out again, with only one entry and exit point. With a maze there are many paths, many directions, many possible entrances and exits.

But also dead ends.

The two of them regard each other through the wire of the fence.

Think of it this way, he says. One equals on, zero equals off.

Like a switch.

Like a switch, *ja*.

Lily nods. Roland continues.

I want to build a machine that can perform calculations much faster than humans can, using this binary code.

Binary?

Two. On, off. One, zero.

And unlock the most complicated mazes?

Ja.

Lily is entranced. Tell me more, she says. Paint me a picture of how it might work.

Roland pauses. Do you know what a pianola is, he says?

Yes, says Lily. A piano that plays by itself.

Roland smiles. It looks like a piano that is playing all

by itself, but what makes it able to do that?

A piece of paper, she says, with a perforated pattern on it.

Genau! Exactly. The pattern uses binary codes to translate the musical notes into a series of on/off instructions, which tell the piano which keys to play.

And you want to write new codes which will do even more complicated things?

Solve many difficult problems, *ja*.

She looks at him closely. But will it stop this War, she wants to say? Will it tear down this fence between us? Instead she says: Where will it all lead?

Codes have to be programmed, he says. By humans. And humans are flawed. But numbers – they can't lie. They have rules and laws. They can be trusted.

But can they surprise?

Now it is Roland's turn to look closely at Lily. Have you ever studied a snowflake really close up, he asks?

She shakes her head. As a child, she says, I used to like to try and catch them with my tongue, but they always melted before I could see them.

They have the most perfect crystalline structure, yet each one is different from every other, unique.

She nods.

A pianola, he continues, can reproduce Beethoven, but it cannot compose Beethoven.

Not yet...

Not ever, I don't think. But this calculating machine I while away my time in here imagining may help future generations to do things we haven't even dreamed of.

Lily is reminded of Hubert's dream about the power of

learning to unlock potential, to create a more even playing field. She hears Jenny's voice singing in the great domed Reading Room of Central Library the day that it opened. Wisdom is the principal thing, she says, more to herself.

I know this, says Roland, we read it in school. She shall bring thee to honour when thou dost embrace her...

Their eyes fuse together.

Ornaments of Grace.

I'm a binary girl, says Lily. Sometimes I'm happy, sometimes I'm sad. One minute I'm up, the next I'm down. Sometimes I know why, but often I have no idea. I only know that whatever mood I might be in at any given moment, it's not going to last for ever. It changes. With time. But I can't just flip from one to the other at the turn of a switch. I'm more complicated than that.

He looks at her. *Ja*, he thinks. Like a maze. A maze I'd like to get lost in.

At the convent where I grew up, she says, there was a doll. It was a baby. When you lay her down she closed her eyes. When you picked her up, her eyes would open. Always. Just like that. Open, closed. Open, closed. Then one day it broke. You could never tell after that when her eyes would open and when they would shut. Often they would stay shut for days, weeks even. Then, you'd pass it one day and notice that her eyes had opened while you weren't looking at it. I liked it better like that. I used to wonder what it was that triggered her eyes to open, what she hoped to see, then what it was she saw that forced her to snap them shut again.

Purely random.

I know. But my imagination liked to make up stories. Was it purely random that I forgot to put cotton wool in my ears and went deaf from the ack-ack guns, so that I had to abandon my motor bike and walk home past the Camp one night? And was it purely random that my eye was drawn to fall on you?

He shrugs.

Probably, she smiles. But is it random that I keep coming back?

Choice. I hope.

They look at each other a long time. To each the other's face seems haloed in light, a light that goes out when they are away from one another. Like the flick of a switch. On, off. On, off. On...

The year turns.

1944.

Lamarr embarks for the D-Day landings. Pearl doesn't see him again for more than a year. In Manchester the mood lightens. There's cautious optimism that an end to the War is in sight. The Home Guard is stood down. Prisoners from Melland Camp are allowed, under supervision, to leave its confines. It's not uncommon to see small groups of them carrying out tasks in and around the city.

The air raids have all but ceased. Lily's days as an ack-ack girl seem numbered. Then, on Christmas Eve, the V1 attack is launched. In London more than three hundred and sixty ack-ack girls lose their lives to the flying bombs. Although there are no known casualties within the overall Civil Defence Area for Manchester, there are twenty-seven fatalities in Oldham, another seven in Tottington near Bury, and one in Worsley, a six year old child who, when his body is found, is lying prostrate and doll-like, covered in plaster dust from falling masonry almost a mile away from where the bomb fell, he has his eyes wide open.

*

Three and a half years earlier. May 1940.

Winifred was on the point of locking up the shop on Market Street in Denton, as she did most evenings, when a frantic and distraught Francis bolted in from outside. He flipped the sign to closed, pulled down the blind and flung the evening edition of *The Chronicle* down on the counter for Winifred to see.

'Collar the Lot!' the headline screamed.

Francis was panicking. He paced up and down the shop as Winifred quickly scanned the article.

"I can't face internment again," he said. "It'll kill me."

"Who said anything about internment?"

"There," he yelled, pointing at the newspaper. "Our beloved Prime Minister, that's who!"

"But if I'm understanding this right, they're only taking people who weren't born here."

"But I wasn't, that's the point. That's what did for me last time. I was two when my parents first came here. I'm forty-two now, so I'm not past the upper age limit of sixty either."

"Calm down, Francis," said Winifred. "Let's think this

through. Who actually knows you were born in Germany? You've changed your name since the last war. You couldn't get a more English-sounding name than 'Hall'."

"I got a whole set of new certificates at the same time too."

"There you are then. What does it say on your passport? You only renewed that a few years back, didn't you, when you needed to go to Sweden to set up that contract with Hasselbad's of Gothenburg?"

"Victor Foto, yes," said Francis, beginning to see a chink of hope. He went into the back office, where Winifred could hear him rummaging through his desk drawers. "Here," he proclaimed, triumphantly waving his passport over his head.

"Now," said Winifred, "let's see what it says."

She flicked it open. "There," she said, pointing to the bottom of the front page.

'National Status: British by Birth'."

"Are you sure?" he said, snatching it from her.

"Read it for yourself," she said. "It's there in black and white."

Francis read it aloud three times just to make sure. Then he lifted Winifred by the waist and swung her round and round the shop, before a new doubt surfaced.

"What if they check? What if they go back to Somerset House and can't find the original birth certificate?"

"First of all, they won't. For a start they'd have to come round here in the first place, and why would they? Apart from me, who knows you weren't born here?"

"Er... George and... Delphine, Charles's friend...

Nobody else, I think."

"There you are then."

"Yes, I suppose."

"And even if they did come round, all you'd have to do is show them your passport. End of story."

Francis breathed an enormous sigh of relief. The anxiety, followed by the euphoria, then the nagging uncertainty, and now this final reassurance from Winifred, had cumulatively exhausted him. He sat down on a chair and wept.

Winifred looked down on him with a mixture of affection and compassion. She was extremely fond of Francis. He was not only her employer of more than ten years, but her friend. She waited quietly until his heaving shoulders had begun to subside, then said, "Shall I put the kettle on?"

Francis nodded. "Thank you. I don't know what I'd do without you."

"Dissolve into a great big puddle, I shouldn't wonder."

"Yes. Probably," he smiled.

While they were drinking their tea, he turned to Winifred and said, "Just to be on the safe side, I think I should volunteer."

Winifred spluttered into her tea cup. "Excuse me, Francis, but what as? You're hardly fighting material, are you?"

"No, of course not, and with my eyesight the way it is I'd fail every medical."

"What as then?"

"Propaganda," he said.

Winifred looked up. "Now that's an idea," she said.

"I've got my contacts still at the BBC," said Francis, warming to the idea.

"You could be Manchester's answer to Lord Haw-Haw," said Winifred, pouring them both a second cup.

Sunday 24th October 1943

Some martial music begins playing. Over it a German-sounding voice begins to speak.

"Here is Radio Aspidistra, bringing you the Soldiers' Radio Calais, broadcasting on 363 metres, 410 metres and 492 metres in the medium wave band and, not forgetting our comrades in the U-boat service, we are linking up with Radio Atlantic on 38.7 and 40.3 metres on the short wave band to bring news, music and greetings to all members of our brave fighting services wherever you may be. We shall bring you some important news in a moment, but to begin with, here is some dance music..."

The martial music is replaced by a lively dance band.

Up in the control room of the makeshift studios of *Radio Aspidistra* in Crowborough in East Sussex, on the edge of Ashdown Forest, close to the Weald, Sefton Delmer sat back and breathed an enormous sigh of relief. It had been a long and arduous road to make it this far for the former *Daily Express* journalist who, returning from a visit to Germany, had conceived the plan for what he liked to refer to as his 'intrusions' into the living rooms of the ordinary German people. Unlike the seditious broadcasts of Lord Haw-Haw, which the vast majority of the British listening public scoffed at with derision, and which the BBC had tried to ape with similar propaganda items of their own, Sefton Delmer had proposed a series of more covert 'black' operations, principally through the creation of *ersatz* radio channels, which could be transmitted directly into German homes, and which people would mistake for genuine *Reichstag* programmes. The news items they contained, however, although appearing to carry the weight of official state authority, would in fact be false, bogus, fake, and, it was hoped, serve to undermine German morale more subliminally and effectively than the smug, preening, self-aggrandising mockery of Lord Haw-Haw, Axis Sal, Tokyo Rose and their ilk.

Delmer's first attempt, *Soldiers' Calais Radio*, featured the creation of a fictional General of the old patriotic Prussian school, known simply as *Der Chef*, The Chief, who crustily attacked what he perceived to be the weakness and corruption of the German High Command. He was never openly critical of *Der Führer* – that would have aroused suspicion. Instead he was scathingly contemptuous of what he referred to as 'the party rabble', who had seized the Fatherland in the *Führer's* name. Listeners tuning in across Germany gained the impression that they were somehow eavesdropping on a clandestine German military transmitter broadcasting angry diatribes from a dissatisfied, loyal officer no longer able to contain his opinions. One of his more colourful tirades was saved for Rudolf Hess's unexplained solo visit to Scotland, allegedly to sue independently for peace.

"Hess packs himself a white flag," lambasted Der Chef, *"and flies off to throw himself – and us – on the mercy of that flat-footed bastard of a drunken, old cigar-smoking Jew, Churchill..."*

The German public, when stumbling across such uncontrolled outbursts, made the assumption that they were intended for other soldiers – *Soldiers' Calais Radio* – and so would be more accustomed to such profanities. It had to appear honest, for the Fatherland's military personnel would not be so easily fooled as the wider public. Therefore it struck a chord with German listeners everywhere as the voice of the 'Good Soldier'. It became the third most popular radio station in Germany, so that *Der Chef's* more tempered broadcasts carried more weight as a consequence.

"The five hundred British terror bombers, which attacked Hamburg last night, causing widespread damage to the Docks, and killing two hundred and thirty-one expectant mothers in the Maternity

Hospital, paid dearly for their atrocity. Five of them – yes, five – were shot down by our brave Luftwaffe fighter pilots…"

This was broadcast more surreptitiously on short wave. By themselves short wave radio signals could not be transmitted far, but, by reflecting them from a layer of electrically charged atoms in the ionosphere, they could be reflected back to the earth at great distances, beyond the horizon. In this way the signal could be bounced from one transmitter to another until they reached Germany. This was where Francis came in. He was part of a team of engineers in secret positions around the country deployed in hopping *Der Chef's* rantings across Europe in a thrilling cat and mouse race to remain one step ahead of the German trackers trying to jam whatever frequency Sefton Delmer's broadcasts might be occupying at any given time.

So successful were they in evading discovery they even fooled some of their allies, notably the Americans, whose own Head of the COI (Coordination of Information), William J. Donovan, sent a confidential dossier to President Roosevelt informing him of a dissident Prussian General, calling himself *Der Chef*, who appeared to have gone rogue and whose explicit criticisms of the Reich suggested the whole party machine in Germany was on the point of collapse. Given that this was back in 1941, when the Americans had still not entered the war, the British Government, while privately delighted at the success of Delmer's first foray into what everyone now breezily described as 'intrusions', was concerned that, by not informing the Americans of what they were doing and even hoodwinking their own Secret Service, they might have offended their allies and risked the possibility of them thinking their military presence in Europe was not in fact necessary. Accordingly Churchill sent David Bowes-Lyon, the Queen's younger brother, on a special mission to meet with President Roosevelt personally and delicately explain to him that his COI had been mistaken in their assessment of *Der Chef*, who was in fact an invention of Sefton Delmer and portrayed by Peter Seckelman, a German exile and would-be actor. Roosevelt, far from being offended, was delighted and roared with laughter. Unfortunately, the President had liked the joke so much he shared it with colleagues, and so *Der Chef's* identity was deemed to be compromised, necessitating him to be not so quietly put out to grass. For two and a half years he had continued to defy the *Gestapo* and burn up the ether with his sulphurous broadcasts.

> *"Our brave soldiers have another enemy to contend with – the scurrilous, conniving pimps of the corrupt party crowd who are delaying the supply of warm clothing to our brave soldiers at the Front, where our courageous sons are dying in their thousands, not from Bolshevik bullets, but at the hands of these despicable spies sitting at home in soft jobs, feathering their own foul-smelling nests far from danger and..."*

Der Chef is urgently interrupted by one of his own anxious adjutants.

"Sir, sir, there are men outside – Gestapo. You must flee!"
"Let the poxy, filth-infested vermin in. Let them see what a true patriot of the Fatherland looks like!"

A sudden burst of gunfire. Der Chef is treacherously killed.

Undeterred, Sefton Delmer's next 'intrusion' featured the creation of *Radio Atlantic*, another short wave broadcast targeting the crew of German U-boats. Churchill was especially keen on this. He felt that because the submarines were cut off from the German mainland, the men on board were more likely to believe what was broadcast if it sounded genuine. To help the show sound even more authentic, the band of the British Royal Marines recorded real German military music. The show spread rumours such as German prisoners of war earning large wages by working in America, in the hope that this might encourage more of the men to surrender or desert.

Radio Atlantic had several things going for it. A former U-boat radio operator who had escaped to England was persuaded to contribute to the scripts, by giving his former comrades at sea tips on how to delay sailings or operations without getting caught. Delmer managed to obtain a working German News Service tele-typewriter, which had somehow been 'left behind' in London in 1939, and which enabled his team to tune into it easily and receive genuine up-to-the-minute news and information direct from Berlin, which they could then feed in 'live' to their own *Radio Atlantic* broadcasts, thereby providing even more authenticity. They interspersed these news items with prohibited music, such as American jazz and the banned Marlene Dietrich, both of which made the station extremely popular with its audience of submariners thousands of miles from home.

But the jewel in *Radio Atlantic's* crown was the introduction of 'Vicky', the Sailor's Sweetheart, a hitherto out of work actress, Bryony Pritchard, who introduced each show in a sultry, syrupy voice, which made her something of a heart throb, so that the seductively subversive messages she relayed became all the more potent for their teasing, sexy playfulness.

"And now," she drooled, *"a Brahms Lullaby for Captain Mole's U-boat, in the hope that it will help preserve the peace aboard in case the Captain has discovered that the man who has been sleeping with his wife is his own 1st officer..."*

Radio Atlantic continued to widen the crack in the morale of Hitler's U-boat men, and Vicky was its mouthpiece. By the spring of 1944 this crack had become a yawning fissure. Vicky's voice continued to drip through the airwaves like honey.

"Radio Atlantic," she purred, *"sends its heartiest congratulations – and a special kiss from me – to the 7th Flotilla football team for their well-earned 4-1 win over the 3rd Flotilla. Top scorer was Torpedo Officer Hans Braun who, judging by his last report, is better*

at shooting penalties than he is at firing torpedoes..."

Finally, Delmer and his team had access to multiple short wave transmitters, including some that were mobile, so that the Germans would continually get different fixes on their source and were always just one step behind as they tried to prevent *Radio Atlantic* from reaching the U-boats. This was where Francis really came into his own, demonstrating his electronic agility. He could hop all over the wave band, hotly pursued by the hue and shriek of German jamming stations vainly trying to drown him. Francis could change wave lengths in a fraction of a second, a task normally requiring several hours by those with less expertise. So effective was he in evading detection that, according to a secret report issued by Goebbels, the German Ministry of Information was frustrated to learn that all their efforts to interrupt the broadcasts were mistaken by the U-boat crews to be bodged attempts by the *British* to jam the frequencies and prevent them from listening to their favourite programme.

"And now," whispered Vicky in her husky, breathless voice, *"a special request for Captain Wolfgang Weiner and his crew, who left Lorient yesterday on a top secret mission..."* She then proceeded to play a dance band version of Who's Afraid of the Big Bad Wolf?

But for all the success of *Soldiers' Calais Radio* and *Radio Atlantic*, Delmer aspired to more. He would not be satisfied until he had penetrated every single German household without fear of being suspected. To do that he would need access to a medium wave transmitter far more powerful than any currently in possession of the BBC.

Brigadier Gambier Perry KCMG, Head of the British Naval Intelligence Communications Branch, visited the United States to see what he could find by way of broadcasting equipment. He returned extremely pleased with himself.

"Well, gentlemen," he informed a meeting of representatives from Whitehall, the BBC and *Radio Atlantic*, "I have purchased a transmitter. It was on offer from the Radio Corporation of America. HMG put in a bid, and now it's ours. We thought it might be useful for these 'intrusions' of yours, Delmer, to help your potent mixture of genuine and false news reach a much wider audience."

"But how?" said a sceptical BBC boffin. "We just don't have the capacity. We've tried, believe me."

"This is not one of your fifteen kilowatt squawk boxes, gentlemen. It's nearly..." and here he paused for maximum effect, taking a sip of water. "... three quarters of a million watts."

A stunned silence fell on the room.

"A raiding dreadnought of the ether," continued the Brigadier, "penetrating every occupied corner of Europe, firing massive electronic broadsides at the enemy and blasting Dr Goebbel's ear drums. We're calling it *'Aspidistra'*."

" *'The biggest aspidistra in the world'*," they all sang with spontaneous glee.

It was so large, in fact, it needed its own water supply

to cool the transmission valves. Soon the whole team was singing along to Gracie Fields.

"We 'ad to get it watered by the local fire brigade
So they put the water rates up half a crown
The roots block up the drains
All along the country lanes
And they come up half a mile outside the town…"

Radio Aspidistra was the chance Delmer had been waiting for, the chance at last to realise his ambition of reaching into every German household.

"It shot up like a rocket till it nearly reached the sky
It's the biggest aspidistra in the world…"

Sunday 24th October 1943.

Some martial music starts playing. Over it a German voice begins to speak.

"Here is Radio Aspidistra, bringing you the Soldiers' Radio Calais, broadcasting on 363 metres, 410 metres and 492 metres in the medium wave band and, not forgetting our comrades in the U-boat service, we are linking up with Radio Atlantic on 38.7 and 40.3 metres on the short wave band to bring news, music and greetings to all members of our brave fighting services wherever you may be. We shall bring you some important news in a moment, but to begin with,

here is some dance music…"

The martial music is replaced by a lively dance band…

Radio Aspidistra was an exotic plant. Its perfume, wafting across Germany and seeping into the minds of its unconscious, unsuspecting listeners, was to prove deadly.

"A reassuring message for fathers has been received from the Administrative Headquarters of the Children's Evacuation Department. Thanks to the magnificent efforts of the Reich's Medical Service, children's deaths due to the diphtheria epidemic have dropped from a weekly average of five hundred and forty-eight to only three hundred and seventy-two. Despite the acute shortage of doctors and medical supplies, it is hoped to hold this figure during the next few weeks. And now, some more music…"

Radio Aspidistra's subtle poison seeped into the German consciousness like an incipient Trojan horse, welcomed by its listeners everywhere, who could not get enough of its mix of news and music.

"*The dogs all come around for miles*
A lovely sight to see
They sniff around for hours and hours
And wag their tails with glee…"

Himmler's Security Department meanwhile would wring their hands in impotent fury as they were unable to find a way of catching up with Francis as he zig-zagged from beacon to beacon, bouncing off the ionosphere.

> *"They all begin miaowing when the buds begin to sprout*
> *From the biggest aspidistra in the world…"*

At the start of 1945, as the Allies slowly began to tighten their net around Germany from all sides, a final intrusion was required from *Radio Aspidistra*. On this occasion, however, it would not be Delmer writing the scripts, but Churchill, and for Francis, it was the biggest challenge of all. His job was to 'intrude' into the live broadcasts from *Radios Berlin, Hamburg, Frankfurt, Cologne* and *Munich* exactly two hundredths of a second after each began transmitting, seamlessly substituting their programme output with *Radio Aspidistra's* own.

Martial music is playing.

The studio announcer in Crowborough calmly counts down the seconds before the live broadcast commences.

"Ready to go in ten, everybody. Stand by. Good luck. Fade music and… Go."

> *"This is Radio Berlin… In a few minutes this station is going off the air. Here is an urgent bulletin. Thousands of enemy terror bombers are approaching the city. Intelligence reports say that Berlin is to be*

completely destroyed. Everyone must leave the city. Do not use the air raid shelters when you hear the siren. Repeat – do not use the shelters. Leave whatever you are doing. Employees working on public utilities are hereby authorised to leave their posts. You must flee. You must flee or be killed."

The sound of aircraft approaching is now heard, followed by a distant siren. These continue beneath the announcer as he continues.

"Special transport facilities are being provided at fire stations, ambulance stations and anti-aircraft gun battlements. If you cannot reach these points, you must leave by any means possible..."

The sound of sirens increases, mixed in with shooting on the streets. The announcement fades.

Francis switches transmission to each of the other radio stations in turn, which relay variations on the same message.

"This is Radio Frankfurt..."

"This is Radio Hamburg..."

"This is Radio Cologne..."

"This is Radio Munich..."

"... you must flee. Flee. The whole city is being burnt to the ground..."

Francis then flicks back to Berlin for a new message, with a different announcer's voice.

"This is Radio Berlin. This is Radio Berlin. The enemy is broadcasting counterfeit instructions on our frequencies. Don't be misled by them. Stay where you are."

Beneath his words the sounds of a street battle outside are growing louder, adding to the confusion. The 1st Announcer returns to the air waves.

"This is Radio Berlin. The enemy is trying to transmit fake information, instructing you to stay where you are, but the city is being destroyed. You must flee..."

An extremely loud explosion is heard.

Francis pulls the plug on all transmissions. The final broadcast by *Radio Aspidistra*.

It was over.

Francis emerged from his studio bunker in the cellar of his shop blinking in the early evening light. He felt as if he'd lived most of the last four years underground, like a mole, which he probably had. Making his way up the stairs he was momentarily disorientated. It took him several moments to realise where he was. Outside he could hear church bells ringing, for the first time since the War had begun, and he could see a steady stream of people walking past the window outside, waving flags, linking arms and dancing. Yes, of course. He remembered now. It was V.E. Night.

In the shop he found Victor. Another surprise. Victor rarely ventured this far, preferring to loiter outside if he happened to be meeting Winifred.

"Evening, Francis," he said amiably.

"Hello, yes. Is everything all right, only...?"

Victor smiled, spreading his hands expansively. "I'm just waiting for Win. She's cashing up."

"Ah, yes. I don't know what I'd do without her. I hired her as my *Passepartout*. Now she's become my *Chef du Guerre*."

"She knows you're grateful, Francis. Don't worry."

"Yes. But even so..." He took off his spectacles and vigorously cleaned them with a rather grubby handkerchief he produced from the top pocket of his jacket. He looked quite blind without them, which of course he was, almost reptilian. "Now that the War's over, perhaps we should consider a rise...?"

"I'm sure she'd appreciate that, Francis."

Francis nodded, replacing his spectacles and blinking rapidly once more.

"What's up, Francis? You don't seem quite yourself."

"I'm not. I can't seem to find my bearings."

"You're overwrought, that's what it is. You've been working down there for years on end. It's not natural, hiding yourself away in the dark like that. Why don't you join Win and me for a bit of a drink and a celebration tonight? It's going to be a night to remember. After all, you don't win a war every day, do you?"

"I suppose not. Maybe. We'll see."

Victor grinned. He came over towards Francis and pulled out a chair for him. "In my experience, Francis, 'we'll see' usually means 'no'."

Francis sat down obligingly. "Yes. No. The truth is, I don't feel much like celebrating. If I'm honest."

"And it's always best to be honest, Francis, especially with ourselves. Why don't you tell your Uncle Vic all about it?"

Victor sat down next to Francis. He'd clearly begun celebrating already. Francis could smell the beer on his breath now that he was closer to him. He knew about Victor's drinking. He'd found Winifred upset about it on more than one occasion. "The trouble is, Francis," she'd say, "once Victor starts, he doesn't know when to call it a night. One drink leads to several, and that usually leads to trouble." But not recently. Since they'd been married, there'd been no mention of such lapses. Perhaps that particular itch had been well and truly scratched. He certainly seemed affable enough now as he playfully punched Francis on the arm, as if he were one of his work mates from the mine.

"Can I ask you a question, Victor?" he said.

Victor leant back. "Ask away. Anything you like."

Francis paused, as if deliberating with himself whether to give voice to the feelings that were so evidently troubling him. In the end he decided to risk it.

"Is winning everything?"

"That all depends," said Victor.

"On what? Tell me. You understand about these things more than me."

"I'm not sure I follow you," said Victor, beginning to regret his invitation for Francis to open up.

"When you boxed, did it matter how you won? Or was it only important that you did win?"

"I liked to win – sure. I wouldn't be human if I didn't. But if you're implying that I'd've bent the rules if I had to, just to make sure I won...?"

"No, no, no," said Francis hastily. "I didn't mean that. I'm sorry. I put it clumsily."

"It 'appens," said Victor. "Everyone knows that. Vaseline smeared on a glove to make an opponent's eyes flare up. Bets placed on which round a fight will end. But I never had owt to do with any o' that. My fights were all over so quick it'd've made no difference any road. Blink and you missed 'em." He laughed and lit a cigarette. He offered one to Francis, who declined.

"What about when you lost?" he asked, somewhat diffidently.

Victor inhaled deeply. "I only lost the once," he said. "And you were there to see that."

Francis winced at the memory of it, the brutal, bone crushing pummelling that Victor had been forced to endure, round after round, with Winifred praying that he'd throw in the towel, but of course Victor was not a man to do that.

"There were nothing bent about that fight," said Victor simply. "I'd've given my eye teeth to have won, but he were simply better than me, that's the truth of it. I gave it my best shot but he just swotted me aside like I was some kind of troublesome gnat." Victor had fallen deep into reminiscence. "Leonard 'Len' Benker Johnson," he said with a warm smile. "The best boxer I ever saw. He could've tied one arm behind his back and he'd still 'ave knocked me from here to Kingdom come. Sheer class. And a real gentleman. Although I got beat – and I reckon I lost every single round – I still say that it were the best fight I ever fought. I really took it to 'im, an' 'e recognised that, so 'e didn't try to humiliate me, 'e treated me wi' th' utmost respect, from t' first bell to t' last, and I appreciate that, right to this day. So, Francis, in answer to your question, winning isn't everything. Not always. I lost that night fair and square, but now, when I look back on it, I feel like I won."

"Yes. I see."

"What's this all about, Francis?"

"Suppose," he said at last, "just suppose, that you'd been in a fight, and you discovered that the man you were up against was cheating, using dirty tricks to try and make sure you lost. What would you have done? Would you have stuck to the rules? Even though you knew that would probably mean you lost? Or would you have fought back like for like and come up with some tricks of your own?"

"Dirty for dirty?"

"Yes."

"That's a tricky one, Francis. What you're asking is, does the end justify the means?"

"Yes, I suppose I am. Hypothetically speaking."

"Hypothetically speaking?"

"Yes."

"Sometimes, Francis, you just have to do what it takes. If someone threatened Win," he said, leaning in close and whispering, "I wouldn't be sticking to no Queensberry Rules, know what I mean?"

Francis replied that he thought that he did.

"For the greater good, Francis. That's what counts in the end."

"Yes, but who decides what constitutes that greater good?"

"You just know, Francis, you just know."

"And what if your opponent thinks he's fighting for the greater good too?"

"All's fair in love and war."

"But is it?"

"I think that's what tonight's celebrations are all about, don't you? Listen…"

Outside, the bells were still ringing. A band had started playing and the crowd were singing and dancing in the street.

"Run, rabbit, run, rabbit, run, run, run
Don't give the farmer his fun, fun, fun
He'll get by without his rabbit pie…"

Winifred, roused by the singing, had finished cashing up and crept towards them, in time with the music, joining in with the last line as she mimed pointing a gun.

"So run, rabbit, run, rabbit, run, run, run…"

"What's up wi' you two?" she asked. "You've got a face like a wet weekend. Anyone'd think we'd just lost the War, not won it." She turned without waiting for an answer to Victor. "Are we dancin'?" she asked.

"Are you askin'?" he grinned.

"I'm askin'," she said.

"Then I'm dancin'," he said, and arm in arm they sashayed towards the shop door and out into the thronging street, leaving Francis all alone, which was exactly how he wanted it.

He made his way upstairs to his living quarters above the shop. On the kitchen table Winifred, with typical unasked for generosity, had put by a plate of corned beef sandwiches for him, but he didn't feel much like eating. He was still troubled, despite Victor's reassurances. For the past four years he had lived on the addictive buzz of adrenalin, caught up in the euphoria of the electronic dance he had employed to keep one step ahead of the German jamming and tracking devices. Now that it was all over at last, he had come down with a rush and landed with a sickening thud. All he could think about were the hundreds, possibly thousands, of deaths his technical wizardry might inadvertently have caused.

"Collateral damage," Sefton Delmer would have countered. "You didn't drop any bombs, or pull any triggers yourself, did you, Francis? Here – have a drink. Don't worry about it."

But he did worry about it. He found that he could not console himself with Victor's words about all being fair in love and war. Who first said that, he wondered? Probably Shakespeare. No – that was *'All's Well That*

Ends Well', but this hadn't ended well, not as far as Francis was concerned. Victor was a pragmatist, whereas he had always been an idealist. A dreamer, George would say. Francis wondered where George was tonight. Enjoying V.E. Night somewhere, he hoped. George was always better at compartmentalising life than he was.

He continued to let his thoughts drift. The hours slipped by. His corned beef sandwich remained untouched. He became aware that all was quiet outside. *Our revels now are ended.* Shakespeare again. Then it came to him who had first spoken of love and war in the same breath. It was Don Quixote. Francis smiled thinly. Yes, that summed up his efforts perfectly. Tilting at windmills – that's what he'd been doing, and now he was paying for his hubris. He remembered his long walk home from Liverpool more than a quarter of a century before, after the end of the last war, when he'd at last been released from his internment on the Isle of Man, how he'd decided to follow the route of the telegraph poles marching across the land, to let them be his guide and, by and large, they'd served him well.

At the time he'd been struck by the promise of speed and change they offered, the ability to send a message the two hundred miles from Manchester to Edinburgh in less than fifteen minutes, while it was taking him more than three days to walk the thirty-five miles to Manchester from Liverpool. The whole world seemed to be opening up before him, the future his to inherit. In the twenty-five years that had passed since then a global network of communications had spread its tentacles across the city, right from his own home, reaching out not just across the country, but crossing continents, deep into outer space. Now he could bounce radio waves across Europe in less than two hundredths of a second. Wasn't this precisely what he'd been dreaming of as he made that first walk? He tried to persuade himself that the uses others made of such discoveries were not his responsibility, and yet he'd colluded with them, hadn't he?

Round and round in circles these thoughts buzzed, until his brain felt like a hornet's nest. Exhausted, he stood up and went to the window of his sitting room, which looked out over Denton's Market Street. The window was on a level with the giant pair of spectacles which had first drawn him to purchase this shop. If he leaned out and craned his neck to the right, he could see right through them directly into the night sky. As he looked, he thought he caught sight of the tail end of a meteor before it burnt out on entry into the atmosphere, then smiled. No. It was probably just a final firework from the end of the V.E. Night celebrations. He picked up the old Dollond three-draw terrestrial, achromatic, refractor brass telescope, which he had found when he first took possession of the shop, which had been left behind by the Kaufmans, and which was now permanently on the window ledge in the sitting room. He looked through it and, to his surprise, he realised that his first thought had been right all along. It *was* a meteor, a whole shower of them, tumbling out of the Aries constellation. Where had they come from, he wondered? A comet? An asteroid? Did they follow an orbit which, if the equipment was powerful enough, he might one day discover and track for himself?

After what must have been almost an hour of scanning the skies, he sat down again. He felt suddenly hungry and wolfed down the corned beef sandwich Winifred had earlier put by for him. Turning his gaze upwards to the stars, observing the various celestial events that nightly occurred, always made him feel better. It put things in a clearer perspective, reminding him just how small he was, how insignificant when set against the vast distances of space, and yet nevertheless he mattered. He was alive, bearing witness.

He resolved to try and find a way in which his three great passions – radio, photography and astronomy – could be synthesised, brought together in such a way as to give his future a purpose again. George was right. He was a dreamer. Now it was time to start dreaming again.

He put on his hat and coat, skipped down the stairs, opened the front door onto the now silent street. Standing directly beneath the giant pair of spectacles, staring out into unseen distances beyond the horizon, he set off in the direction of the city, following the line of the overhead telephone cable, first one foot, then the other, with increasing pace and purpose.

Meanwhile, six miles away at *The Queen's Hotel*, Cam sang her last song of what had been an emotional night.

"When the lights go on again all over the world
And the boys are home again all over the world
And rain or snow is all that may fall from the skies above
A kiss won't mean 'goodbye' but 'hello' to love

When the lights go on again all over the world
And the ships will sail again all over the world
Then we'll have time for things like wedding rings
and free hearts will sing
When the lights go on again all over the world..."

*

George decided he would volunteer at the start of 1940.

"I'll only be called up anyway at some point this year, I might as well get it over with sooner rather than later," he said. "You know how I hate uncertainty."

Inevitably this made for a somewhat tense and awkward Christmas. His mother was stoical. "I can hardly complain," she thought privately, "after the way I insisted Hubert join up in the last war."

In the lounge bar of *The Queen's* Francis was inconsolable. "I shall lose you," he wept. "I'll never see you again." Winifred poured him another gin and tonic and told him not to be so melodramatic.

Only Lily was truly understanding. "George is merely being realistic," she announced over the Christmas dinner. "He'll have to go some day, it may as well be now. And who knows? By volunteering he might get a say in what he does."

The others looked at her pityingly, narrowing their eyes. "I think he's being brave," said Evelyn. "Your grandfather would have been so proud," while Pearl batted her eyelashes and sighed.

"I like a man in uniform," she purred admiringly. Evelyn regarded her sharply.

"Someone's been having too much sherry." The others laughed.

"Well," said Annie, "what's the harm? It's Christmas, after all."

Afterwards, when they were sitting by the fire, listening to the wireless, Lily came and sat next to George, who was staring into the flames. "Penny for them," she said.

"Sorry," he replied. "I was miles away."

"I could see."

"Keep an eye out for my mother, won't you?"

"Two when I can spare them."

George smiled. "Thank you."

"What's going to happen about the Printing Works?" asked Lily a few moments later.

"That's all taken care of," he said. "Mr Hibbert's going to take over for the interim. He's been there for years, knows the place inside out. He's too old to be called up himself, so there'll be no further disruption before I'm back again."

If, they both thought, though neither of them said.

"I'll keep popping in from time to time," said Lily, then added mischievously, "make sure they're all doing what they're meant to."

"Really?" said George, raising an eyebrow.

"On one condition…" She was trying to suppress a smile as she spoke.

"Oh yes?"

"You let me have the use of your DOT RS while you're away."

"And why should I do that?"

"Because," she said, then leaned in closer to him, so that she whispered the rest, "it's a long fucking way from Didsbury."

George laughed. "It's a deal." They shook hands. "Mind you, I shall want weekly reports, *i*'s dotted and *t*'s crossed."

"You shall have them."

George let a few more moments pass before he spoke next. "It seems a lifetime ago since that night I found you."

"It is," said Lily simply, looking at George directly. "I don't know what I'd have done if you hadn't come by when you did. I'd be dead now, as like as not..."

"Don't think about it," said George, standing up.

"I don't," said Lily. "It was you who brought it up."

"Yes. I'm sorry."

"So," said Lily, also standing up, "are you going to let me ride your motor bike while you're away or not?"

"I don't see how I could stop you," said George.

"Thanks," said Lily. She looked at him and smiled. "Good luck for when you go."

He reported for duty early in March at the RAF Training Station at Heaton Park. The centre was meant to be secret, but everyone knew about it. George, having inherited colour blindness from his father, knew that becoming a pilot was not a viable option, and so, in his initial interview, he had mentioned his experience with tuning the speedway bikes for high level performance at Belle Vue. He saw how this piqued the curiosity of the

Recruiting Sergeant and so he was not surprised when he was trained to work on different aircraft engines, which he did quite uneventfully for several months. Then, shortly after the Christmas Blitz of 1940, he was summoned to his C/O, Squadron Leader Captain Peter Rowley.

"At ease," said the Captain. "Please accept my condolences for the loss of your mother."

"Thank you, sir."

"Good to have you back with us."

"Work helps, sir."

"Indeed. Now – I'll get straight to the point, Wright. It's been brought to my attention that you were an art student in Civvy Street, at *The Mechanics' Institute* in Salford. Is that correct?"

"Yes, sir," replied George, somewhat nonplussed.

"I also see that you've had some success with several photographic exhibitions?"

"Yes, sir."

"And that in addition you ran the family printing business for more than five years?"

"Yes, sir."

"I won't deny, Wright, that I don't know the first thing about any of that, especially all this modern rubbish that tries to pass itself off as Art, and I don't generally care much for artists. Queer lot, if you ask me. Still, you strike me as being a down to earth sort of chap. You ride a motor cycle, I understand?"

"Yes, sir."

"What make?"

"A DOT RS, sir."

"Hmm. More of a Norton man myself. What made you go for a DOT?"

"They're made right here in Manchester, sir."

"Yes, I see... Anyway, much as I'd like to discuss with you the various pros and cons of a DOT versus a Norton, I'm afraid we do have rather more pressing matters. There's a War on, I understand."

"Yes, sir."

"And my superiors have made it crystal clear to me that an important piece in the jigsaw if we're to win it is deception."

"Sir?"

"That's right. I don't like the idea any more than you do, Wright. There's nothing I'd like better than to take a squadron up into the clouds with me right this minute and meet the *Luftwaffe* head on, and may the best aeroplane win."

"Sir."

"The trouble is the *Luftwaffe* have by far and away the best aeroplanes. For now. And more of them. But we'll catch them up soon, I know we will. In the meantime, we've got to make them think we're better prepared than we actually are. We can't have a repetition of the hammering we took at Christmas, can we? Deception, you see?"

"Yes, sir," said George, not really seeing at all.

"So it's imperative that when Jerry starts sending his bombers over here to Manchester again, which is only a matter of time by the way, he does not do any further damage to our factories in Trafford Park, in Salford, or further north in Lancashire. There must be no slowing down of production if we're to be ready to face him in the field, on the sea, or in the air. Do you understand?"

"Yes, sir. Nothing must halt or slow down production here at home."

"Exactly. And that's where your artistic skills come into play."

"Sir?"

"The boffins at the Ministry of Defence have come up with a plan to utilise artists and craftsmen to create a number of decoys."

"Decoys, sir?"

"Yes, Wright. Dummy airfields, fake factories, camouflaged vehicles and buildings, all designed to fool the enemy into thinking they're dropping their bombs onto our key military and industrial targets, when in actual fact they'll be falling harmlessly into the countryside on to these decoys, while our real airfields and factories remain safe."

"Like a stage set, sir?" said George, beginning to understand and warming to the idea.

"Precisely so, Wright. In fact the MOD have requisitioned the Dickenson Road Film Studios to be at our disposal to construct anything we might need by way of these 'stage sets', as you call them. We're to create a sort of 'Manchester on the Moors', which is where we want to lure the *Luftwaffe* and keep them away from the real thing."

"Manchester on the Moors... I like the sound of that, sir."

"Good. I'm yet to be convinced, but as I said, I don't know a damn thing about Art. Ever heard of a chap called

Penrose?"

"*Roland* Penrose?"

Captain Rowley consulted the paper in front of him. "Yes, that's the one."

"Yes, sir. He's a renowned surrealist."

"What the devil's that?"

"It's a style in modern Art, sir, which depicts things in a highly realistic way, yet what it depicts is not real at all."

"See what I mean? They can't be trusted, these damned fellows."

"With respect, sir, I'd suggest that these surrealists, painters like Roland Penrose – and Julian Trevelyan…"

"Yes, he's on the list too."

"… are exactly the type needed to design and produce these decoys."

"Excellent. I'm glad you think so, for I'm sending you on a training course, where you'll meet with this Penrose and Trevelyan, to learn all about it. Then I want you to come back here and head up our own team of Decoy Artists here in Manchester. Understood?"

"Yes, sir."

"Well don't sound so pleased about it. If any German bombs land on real military or industrial targets here in Manchester, I'll hold you personally responsible. Now – what are you waiting for?"

The training course was in Surrey, in Farnham Castle, where the *camoufleurs*, as they were now all dubbed, resided as well as studied. In addition to Roland Penrose and Julian Trevelyan, there were the two Hughs – Catt and Casson – the film maker Geoffrey Barkas and the stage magician Jasper Maskelyne. Catt was a zoologist whose specialism was the way different animals had evolved to remain concealed – tigers and zebras, for example, whose stripes enabled them almost literally to disappear when hidden among grasses or in dappled sunlight. Trevelyan had just returned from a fact-finding trip to North Africa, where he had witnessed at first hand the complete unsuitability as he saw it of the British Army's current camouflage kit, which was fine for jungle combat but totally inadequate for the desert, where it could easily be spotted. Together with Catt he set about redesigning the uniforms for the soldiers currently serving in Tobruk, while Barkas laid out his plans for constructing an entire dummy army, complete with inflatable tanks and mannequin soldiers, with which they planned to occupy the attention of Rommel's forces, while the real British army would circle round from behind and attack them unawares. Meanwhile Maskelyne kept them all entertained with devices he had invented to aid British soldiers should they ever find themselves in enemy hands, such as hiding weapons inside cricket bats, saw-blades inside combs and small maps disguised on playing cards. He was less successful when attempting to demonstrate his claim that he could make pill boxes, airfields, even whole cities, "disappear before your very eyes". George viewed it all with enjoyable scepticism.

Penrose was the epicentre of it all, a cauldron of ceaseless, restless energy, constantly challenging them to come up with ever more daring ideas. The bolder, the better, he would say. He was very much in awe of Trevelyan, whom they all looked up to, for he had already established himself as a major figure. The leading British Surrealist of the day, he had shown work alongside Miro, Kokoschka and Picasso. Casson too, like Trevelyan, was still only in his early thirties and something of a *wunderkind*. He had published seminal works on modernism and architecture. His credo was unapologetically iconoclastic. "Don't be reverential," he'd say, "tear things down, break the rules. If something doesn't work, rip it up and start again. There's no such thing as failure, only bad art." George smiled as he listened to that, wondering how Squadron Leader Rowley might have reacted had he heard it.

The atmosphere was intense, febrile and fiercely competitive. Penrose spent much of his time painting the naked body of his American girl friend, Lee Miller, in order to prove the superiority of his camouflage painting skills. "If I can conceal *her* charms," he professed, "then hiding a factory will be child's play."

Several weeks later, after he'd returned to Heaton Park, George smiled at his recollection of stumbling over Miss Miller, whom he'd mistaken for a grassy mound. When he'd blushingly apologised, she'd just laughed and said, "Say, you don't happen to have a blanket in that haversack of yours, do you? I'm freezing my ass off out here…"

Drawing on his schoolboy memories of stories of Sir Walter Raleigh, he took off his coat and laid it over her.

"Why thank you, kind sir. My knight in shining armour. It's comforting to know that gallantry is not dead after all. I'm for ever in your debt." She stretched out a languid arm so that he might help her to her feet, and they walked together back towards the house. "Could I bum a cigarette?" she said. "I – er... don't appear to have one about my person," she added coyly.

George duly obliged. Miss Miller drew deeply and appreciatively on it.

"Is there anything else I can get you, Miss?" asked George.

"Lee," she said. "Enough of the 'Miss' already."

"Well...?"

"Right now I could do with a bath and try to get all this paint off me that Roland's been applying so assiduously all afternoon."

"Of course."

"You know how pernickety he can get when it comes to details. Care to join me?"

George's eyebrows shot up.

"What's the matter? Cat got your tongue?"

George said nothing.

"I guess he has. Well?"

George turned away.

"I don't usually have to ask twice."

George smiled despite himself.

"That's better." She slipped his arm around her waist inside the coat.

George withdrew it. "Actually," he said, "I'd rather not."

Now it was the turn of Lee's eyebrows to rise. "Half the men in Europe would give anything to be standing in your shoes right now."

"Then I guess I must be one of the other half."

"Oh," said Lee, the penny dropping. "You ride a different bus. Well, that's OK. I shan't tell. At least come up and scrub my back for me."

George hesitated. He looked towards the French windows at the back of the Castle where Penrose, Trevelyan, Catt and Casson were already ensconced with their whisky and sodas.

Lee caught the direction of his gaze. "Don't worry about them," she said, taking his arm. "They're there for the duration."

Penrose was sitting at the piano. He started to sing and play very loudly. The others joined in raucously.

"Oh the Grand Old Duke of York
He had ten thousand men
He marched them up to the top of the hill
And he marched them down again…"

"Penrose and I have a very open relationship. I'm sure he half expects you to make a pass at me. He'd be rather disappointed if you didn't." George shot her an awkward glance. "Relax," she added with a smile. "Your secret's safe with me."

"And when they were up, they were up
And when they were down, they were down
And when they were only half way up
They were neither up nor down…"

"Fix me a drink, will you?" said Lee as they reached

her private bedroom. "I'll call you when it's safe to come in." She let George's air force coat slip to the floor and retreated into the adjoining bathroom, from where George could hear the sound of running water.

"Yoo hoo," called Lee after a few minutes. "Come on in, the water's lovely."

George opened the door. The bathroom was filled with steam. Lee was lying in the bath, strategically covered with soap suds and bubbles. She stretched out a foot, its toe nails painted in neon red, and adroitly turned off each tap. George handed her the drink he'd got ready, a martini with an olive, which she sipped provocatively.

"Well," she said, "isn't this cosy? You, me; me, you…?"

George smiled and shook his head.

"No?" she said. "I can't tempt you? Are you sure?"

"I'm sure."

"Oh well, you can't blame a girl for trying."

She put down her drink on the rim of the bath and sat up. The water tipped and sloshed around her. She leant forward, holding up a sponge towards George. "Could you do the honours?"

George perched on the side and began to scrub Lee's back, who rolled and twisted her shoulders, purring with pleasure.

"I hear you're a photographer," she said, out of the blue.

"Yes. At least, I was. Before all this started."

"Me too."

"Really? You're a photographer?"

"You sound surprised."

"No. I didn't know, that's all."

"Oh, there's lots of things about me that people don't know."

"I imagine so."

"Will you go back to it, presuming you make it through?"

"Yes. But I'll also get a job that pays the bills."

"Sensible boy. What kind of job?"

"I'm not sure. I used to be a printer, but our works got blown up last Christmas. I was thinking of trying something else."

"Like what?"

"I've still not decided. What about you?"

"Me neither. I used to be a model."

"I'm not surprised."

"But that's not for the future. I started doing fashion shoots in Paris. With Man Ray. I started playing around with solarisation. Are you familiar with that, George?"

"It's where you reverse the tones in the negative, so that what was originally dark now appears light, and vice versa."

"Clever boy. Ten out of ten."

"I've never used it myself."

"You should try it."

"And they say the camera never lies."

"I think the truth's over-rated," she said, sliding back into the water, submerging herself completely for a while. "Towel please," she said, when she re-emerged, holding out her hand. Her eyes were closed. George handed her a large, luxuriant, soft white towel. She wiped the soap from her face, then stood up, wrapping the towel around her as she stepped out onto the mat.

"You know as well as I do, George, just how an image can be manipulated in the dark room. You think you've taken one picture, only to discover that in fact you've taken a different one altogether."

"That happens, yes."

"More often than we'd care to admit, I'd wager, and that's where the craft comes in, the artist's eye, deciding on what's the best choice to make."

"I try to remain honest if I can, Miss."

Lee eyed him shrewdly. "Really? What was your first exhibition?"

"A series of portraits of different types of workers – coal miners, foundrymen, dockers, welders, mill girls, typists, car mechanics…"

"Butchers, bakers, candlestick makers?"

"Something like that, yes."

"The worker as hero of the people?"

George knew when he was being mocked. "Naïve, I know, but it was my first exhibition, I was only twenty-one."

"That's not what I meant," said Lily, brushing her hair. "I've not seen them, I know, but they sound uncannily like the kind of images the *Führer* might appreciate…"

"I hope not, Miss."

"… or Stalin – one can hardly tell the difference these days."

"In the gaze perhaps, Miss."

"Perhaps, and do let's cut out this 'Miss' business. I'm not your school teacher – though that might have some interesting possibilities."

"Sorry. It's the Air Force. Deference becomes a habit."

"I hate deference. What comes of being an American, I guess. You Brits are just crippled by it. Even the boys downstairs…"

The 'boys', as she referred to them – Penrose, Trevelyan, Casson and Catt – were still singing loudly below. They'd moved on from nursery rhymes to Gilbert & Sullivan. George could make out Penrose's voice.

"As some day it may happen that a victim must be found
I've got a little list — I've got a little list
Of society offenders who might well be underground
And who never would be missed — who never would be missed..."

"Poor Penrose," crooned Lee, "trying to impress the big boys. Pass me my lipstick, would you, George? I feel more naked without this than I do without clothes. It's all artifice," she continued, expertly applying her make up. "I don't mean this," she said, indicating her reflection, "that's Art – but the whole shebang. This course, the War, everything. Did you notice how they called it the 'phoney' war at first? There's nothing phoney about *Blitzkrieg*, is there? You know that better than anyone. But still we treat it like it's some kind of game, hiding away here in this fairy tale castle, calling ourselves *camoufleurs* for fuck's sake…"

"It might make a difference."

"You think?"

"Worth trying anyway."

"Then we'll have to try harder than we've been doing so far. All Penrose wants to do is take my clothes off and paint me green all over to match the grass, like that's going to help us win the War. When I argue with him, he just says, 'It's your patriotic duty. Lie down and think of England'. I say, 'If you just want to get up close and personal with your paint brush in my tits, you can do that any time. Just don't pretend it's all part of some war effort'. He just laughs and says I'll never be a true surrealist. Well you know what, Penrose?" she shouted, aiming her voice down towards the room below where the boys were still singing. "I don't want to be."

She slipped out of the towel that she was still wrapped in and replaced it with a Japanese silk kimono. She walked over to her wardrobe, opened it, riffled through various dresses hanging on rails, pulled one out and held it in front of her. "What do you think?" she said, walking around a bemused George. It was a leopard print dress.

"The perfect outfit for a *camoufleur*," he said.

"Are you teasing me?"

"I wouldn't dare."

"Then why are you smiling?"

"I was just thinking how much Francis would like it."

"Francis?"

"My friend."

"Oh? Would he?" She wove her way between the furniture to where George was sitting and dragged him to his feet. She stood behind him, mischievously holding the dress in front of him. "On him or on you?"

George gently pushed the dress aside. "On him."

She tapped the side of her nose with her finger and winked. "It's OK. Mum's the word."

"Why are you so hard on the surrealists?" he asked, trying to shift the subject away from himself. "I'd have thought you'd like their…"

"What? Their arrogance?"

"I'd prefer to call it self-confidence."

"OK."

"No, I was going to say irreverence, their disregard for authority."

"Yes, that is attractive, I suppose. I found it quite intoxicating at first, its 'anything goes' approach, its 'fuck you' attitude, its wit. But after a time, even that becomes sort of predictable. I mean – how many bowler-hatted men with apples in front of their faces can a girl take?"

"Or clouds…?"

"Or fish." They laughed. "But in the end it's in danger of disappearing up its own ass, unless…"

"Unless…?"

"It can find itself a manifesto."

"I thought it had. André Breton?"

" 'The main goal of surrealism'," quoted Lee, standing with one arm raised in the air and the other crossing her chest, its hand placed upon her heart, " 'is to free one's mind from the past and everyday reality…' "

" '… to arrive at truths one has never known'," chimed George, joining in with her.

"Someone's been to Art School," teased Lee, wagging her finger at him.

"So what's wrong with it?"

"Nothing. It's just that I think, with very few exceptions, nobody's really delivered. Where are the images that surrealist artists have produced that have indelibly imprinted themselves onto the public consciousness that will be remembered long after all of us have gone? You can count them on the fingers of one hand. Giraffes burning in a desert... Clocks melting... A woman literally tearing herself apart, her old gnarled fist ripping at a young voluptuous breast..."

"Dali."

"If there's been a better depiction of a civil war I've yet to see it." She was quiet for a few moments. Then she went back to her wardrobe, picked out another hanger and shimmied into a simple black dress. "Do me up at the back, will you, George?" After he had finished, she turned to face him. "I just want to take photographs of things that matter," she said, "instead of all this artifice and sleight of hand."

"I'm with you there," said George.

He did not see Lee again until the final night of the course.

Following the usual frugally rationed evening meal, which now always resulted in indulgent reminiscences for the kind of food they used routinely to take for granted before the War, Penrose decided that some after dinner entertainment was needed, "to boost morale". This involved everyone doing their various party pieces. George, thankful for Chapel Bazaars and family Christmases past, gave them his rendition of Stanley

Holloway's *Three Ha'pence a Foot*, whose gallows humour and self delusion struck just the right note of gentle mockery.

> *"It rained and it rained for a fortnight*
> *It flooded the whole countryside*
> *It rained and it still kept on raining*
> *Till th' Irwell were fifty foot wide…"*

In spite of the overwhelming evidence of impending doom and disaster, Sam, the protagonist, refuses to budge when it comes to lowering his prices for Noah to build him an ark to escape the rising flood water, and is prepared to drown rather than swallow his pride or his principles, hoping instead for a miracle.

> *"They stared at each other in silence*
> *'Til ark were alongside all but*
> *Then Noah said what price yon maple*
> *Sam answered three ha'pence a foot*
>
> *Said Noah you'd best take my offer*
> *Tis the last time I'll be hereabouts*
> *And if water comes half an inch higher*
> *I'll happen get maple for nowt*
>
> *Three ha'pence a foot it'll cost you*
> *And as for me, Sam says, don't fret*
> *Sky's took a turn since this morning*
> *I think it'll brighten up yet…"*

Everyone stamped their feet and roared their approval at the exposure of Sam's pompous and ridiculous posturing, a wry, sly two fingers to the spivs, jobsworths and paper pushers all at the same time. George sat down relieved to have got through it, while others took their turn.

Casson delivered a lecture on the future of British architecture and how Jerry might be doing them all a favour in the long run by carving a clean slate, a blank canvas, on which they might begin to build their Brave New World. He drew diagrams on a blackboard, like cartoons from a comic, wielding his chalk like a ray gun, the Skylon, the Dome of Discovery, the Shot Tower. Maskelyne entertained them with his magic tricks, Catt did a series of rather startling animal impressions, Trevelyan played the spoons, and then Lee made her dramatic appearance.

She was wearing a man's lounge suit, complete with kid gloves and a felt trilby hat. In the breast pocket of her jacket she sported a bright red silk handkerchief. Penrose sat at the piano and, at a wordless signal from Lee, he started to play. It was a slow, witty version of Cole Porter's *My Heart Belongs to Daddy*.

Without a word Lee began. Just as it appeared she might sing, instead she sneezed. She took out the red silk handkerchief to blow her nose and then, in the confusion, it disappeared. It was a sleight of hand Jasper Maskelyne would have been proud of. Lee looked under her hat. It wasn't there, so she tossed the hat towards a rack in the corner of the room, where it unerringly landed. She then checked each of the pockets of her jacket in turn. It was not there either, so this too was cast aside. It soon became apparent to the disbelieving male audience that Lee had embarked upon an elaborate striptease. Next to go was the waistcoat, in which the handkerchief was still nowhere to be found. Then the gloves, teasingly one finger at a time, until finally being pulled off by her teeth, and then the tie, which she looped like a noose around Penrose's neck, while he continued to play the piano, a cigarette drooping from the corner of his mouth. After pulling down, one at a time, each of the braces that held up her trousers, Lee searched in vain in the pockets. No luck. Shrugging, she kicked off both her shoes before proceeding to slide her trousers slowly down, folding them with deliberate neatness before hanging them over the back of a chair. Shaking her head, she 'reluctantly' began to unbutton her shirt, while staring out 'innocently' towards her audience, as if to ask, where will this all lead? Once the shirt had been discarded, she looked down helplessly at her stockinged legs. Clearly the red, silk handkerchief was not in either of those, but she removed them even so, unrolling each one down over her knees with delicious slowness before draping them separately around the necks of two of the men sitting on the front row. Having unhooked and cast aside the suspender belt, she was left in just her bra and pants. She looked down at her breasts, flicked a corner of each cup as if in the hope the handkerchief might be concealed in one of them. Uncertain, she slipped the straps off her shoulders before unclipping the bra at the back. Twirling it above her head, she flung it high into the air with seemingly reckless abandon. All that now remained was the pair of very small silk pants, virginal white. Swaying her hips slowly from side to side, she gradually lowered them past her hips, letting them fall about her knees and down to the floor, before daintily stepping out of them and flicking them casually to the side with one pointed foot. Now completely naked, she feigned coyness and surprise, covering her breasts with one arm, placing the hand from her other neatly over the shaved triangle of pubic hair. The red, silk handkerchief was still nowhere in evidence. She looked at her audience once again with a puzzled expression – where can it be? Then, as if a light bulb had just gone off in her mind, she raised the finger of the hand that had been across her breasts and tapped the side of her temple with it. Perhaps there was still one place she had not looked? Placing both arms across her chest, she looked down, then back out towards the audience. Slowly she proceeded to walk the fingers of one hand down her stomach, below her belly, till they reached the narrow crack between the top of her legs. Surely not, her eyes seemed to say? Oh, really? Do you think so? Let's see, shall we? She delicately licked the tips of the first and second fingers of her left hand, then hesitantly began to explore. Inevitably, a corner of the red silk handkerchief began to be visible. Gently she teased it out until, with a final flourish, she removed it entirely, a broad smile of relief on her face greeting the rapturous applause from her hugely appreciative audience. She brandished it before her face like a veil before exiting the room.

"*Trompe l'oeuil*, gentlemen," she proclaimed as she returned for a final bow.

The next morning was grey and cloudy. George stepped out of the Castle's imposing front door and was just making his way across the gravelled courtyard when a voice regaled him from behind. It was Lee.

"Leaving us so soon?"

"My train goes in half an hour."

"Back to Manchester?"

By a circuitous route, yes."

Lee pulled a face. "Poor you. Why don't you let me give you a ride? I'm going to Manchester myself today as it happens."

"Well… thank you, but I have my ticket already."

"Oh do," she said, linking her arm through his, "it'll be much more fun. For both of us. The train's bound to be filthy dirty, it'll be packed to the gills, you'll never get a seat, you'll have to stand all the way, and Lord knows what time you'll eventually make it back. Whereas with me," she gestured towards the expanse of flat, open grass behind the Castle, where a Tiger Moth bi-plane stood waiting, "you'll be there by lunch time."

George looked at Lee with disbelief. He hadn't registered her flying coat and trousers. "Is there no end to your talents?"

"I hope not, honey." She walked on ahead of George with bold confident strides. An engineer was waiting by the plane. He handed Lee a leather attaché case, which she tossed back to George. "Hold this for me, will you, darling?" she said, then climbed up easily into the front of the craft. The engineer, noting George's RAF Uniform, gave an unobtrusive salute.

"Need a hand with the prop?" said George as he

reached him.

"No thank you, sir. I think we should be all right. You climb in behind Miss Miller."

George did as he was bid, and Lee tossed him a pair of goggles and flying cap over her shoulder, which George duly put on. "What's in the case?" he asked.

"That's for me to know and you to keep *shtum* about," she said with a grin. "Just something I've been asked to deliver to your Squadron Leader as a matter of fact."

"You could have just left them with me, saved yourself the trouble."

"I don't think so, buddie. Above your pay grade. Anyway, aren't you glad you came?"

All further talk was cut short by the propellers, after a brief stutter, exploding into life. Lee turned her attention fully to the matter of take off. With a thumbs up to the engineer, then another to George, she taxied along the grass, quickly picking up speed, lifting into the air just before they ran out of field. She banked to the east, circling the Castle, before turning north for Manchester, the whole of Surrey stretched out below them, its neat fields spread out like Stevenson's *Land of Counterpane*.

They climbed steadily and soon became enveloped in thick cloud, the Tiger Moth shaking and rattling but somehow holding together. Despite having worked on aeroplanes for more than a year, apart from one or two brief circuits above Heaton Park to check whether an engine was performing as it should, George had not flown properly before. He was sorry he could not see more. The cloud was, if anything, getting thicker and Lee signalled that they would have to descend and fly lower. She pushed down on the joystick until they were flying through the wisps and rags of the cloud's base. Thin, wet tendrils clung to George's face and hands. Below them was little better. A mist lay over the Home Counties. They could see little or nothing for the next half hour. George was becoming increasingly anxious. This was not flying weather. But Lee seemed untroubled.

"Don't worry," she shouted over the noise of the engines, "I've flown this trip hundreds of times. I could do it blindfold."

"I'd rather you didn't," George mouthed back.

If anything the fog thickened the further north they flew. Lee pursued a low trajectory, following the line of pylons, which strode like giants through the belly of England. Like harbingers of the future they marched relentlessly, their steel arms holding up the power lines on which the country now depended. George was reminded of the story Francis had told him of his long walk back from Liverpool to Manchester, following the telegraph wires, just as Lee now skilfully navigated her way towards a destination that lay hidden from them almost until it was upon them, by flying as close to the pylons as she dared. George reflected ruefully that no camouflage or decoy he might construct could ever hope to match a Manchester fog for hiding the city from enemy aircraft. Unlike Lee, who kept a close watch on all the instruments and gauges in her cockpit, as well as communicating by radio with various airfields at regular intervals, George felt completely cocooned. He had no idea at any time where he was. He had expected England to spread herself before him like a map, a body whose contours he would recognise and watch as they unfolded. But the more he looked, the more disorientated he became. It was like trying to find again something which he once knew every inch of, the spindle tree on Portugal Street, whose daily changes he had documented throughout an entire year, but which now lay buried beneath smoke and ruin. Even the negatives were lost.

With a cruising speed of sixty-nine miles per hour, it should have taken the Tiger Moth just three and a half hours to cover the distance between Farnham and Manchester, but it was closer to five by the time they sighted Heaton Park. A red warning flag flew from the top of the control tower, fluttering defiantly like a red silk handkerchief that had temporarily gone missing.

As soon as they had touched down and jumped out of the cockpit, Lee was immediately business-like. Before George got a chance to thank her or praise her on her aviation skills, she was striding ahead of him. When they reached the Squadron Leader's hut, she turned coolly to George, requesting the attaché case. "Wait here," she said, as he handed it over. "Captain Rowley will call you when we're done."

She left him standing there on the wooden verandah, while she headed inside. George had a brief impression of Lee and Rowley shaking hands before the door was closed.

A quarter of an hour later the door opened again and Rowley summoned him in. Lee was nowhere to be seen. Evidently she had left by a different door. Rowley made no reference to her whatsoever, demanding instead a full report on the Farnham training course from George, with recommendations, to be on his desk by 0800 hours the next morning.

"Sir," said George, saluting then leaving by the same door through which he had entered.

The fog was beginning to lift. But there was no sign of Lee. It was as if she had vanished with the mist. George never saw her again. Occasionally he heard her name whispered. Some said she was a spy for the Russians, some for the Americans, others for the British, while some even suggested she spied for all three. But nothing was ever proved.

He next came across her in 1945, just as the war was ending. He was drinking coffee in the NCO's mess, flicking through the newspaper. In it were the most appalling and sickening pictures of the liberation of the German concentration camps – Auschwitz, Buchenwald, Dachau. They were the most powerful and remarkable photographs George had ever seen. The by-line beneath them showed the name of the photographer – Lee Miller.

George recalled her words to him on his last day at Farnham. "I want to take pictures that matter."

The week after his return from Farnham. he was sitting in the front of a different aeroplane, an Avro Anson reconnaissance craft, circling over Trafford Park, Pomona Docks, key installations in Salford and Manchester, then Barton and Ringway Aerodromes, taking photographs from above, trying to replicate the way an enemy bomber might see them, to serve as templates for the decoys he would then commission from the Dickenson Road Film

Studios. He must remember to tell Francis about the action of the camera they were using – a Fairchild F8 focal plane high altitude day time surveillance model, fitted with a Schneider Xenar 240mm lens. The Anson carried five of them: one mounted obliquely in the fuselage, plus two pairs hung below the undercarriage in split-verticals, all with different focal lengths to give stereoscopic coverage of each target and its surrounding area. In addition, George himself operated a fifth from the specially adapted nose cone of the aircraft. The weather could not have been more different from the day he'd flown with Lee. It was crystalline, perfect for seeing. Once in the air George could see not just the whole of Manchester spread out below, but all the way to the Cumberland Fells in the north, the Pennines to the east, and the mountains of Wales to the south.

From the information garnered from the hundreds of images accumulated by the five cameras on board, George was able to present his technical drawings and designs to the set builders at Dickenson Road in sufficient detail for them to construct full scale mock-ups, replicas of several warehouses and factories within the heart of Trafford Park, which housed vital and sensitive operations that High Command were especially keen should avoid being hit by future enemy raids. Under George's supervision, these were then erected at various sites around Manchester – at Carrington Moss to the south-west, Buckton Castle near Stalybridge to the east, and a ring across the West Pennine Moors near Burnley, Haslingden, Accrington and Oswaldtwistle to the north. At each of these George gathered his team of camouflage painters to create the various decoy sites. Once completed, they were cordoned off and placed under a twenty-four hour guard. When an air raid siren sounded, they could spring into action within seconds. Individual light bulbs were remotely operated to switch on and off, mimicking the sparks from a hundred welders' torches flickering through the slatted plywood used to build the mock-ups. On Carrington Moss they created a large starfish site, planting scores of metal baskets packed with highly flammable material to create a sunburst of spreading fire, each triggered by nearby pill boxes, to simulate a city burning at night, as if it had already been hit by enemy attacks, in the hope of luring the *Luftwaffe* away from their intended targets.

How successful these decoys were remained a matter of dispute. The ring of sites to the north, dubbed Manchester-on-the-Moors by Captain Rowley, undoubtedly received several hits, as did those at Carrington Moss, but so too did the intended targets.

"As a damage limitation exercise," declared Captain Rowley at a briefing to review its achievements a year later, "Operation Starfish has been a qualified success. Maybe this Modern Art rubbish has its uses after all…"

In truth it was difficult to be certain either way, for the frequency of raids by the *Luftwaffe* on Manchester steadily decreased, stopping almost completely until the V1 attack of Christmas Eve 1944, and this too was not repeated.

On one particular night in May 1941, George was stationed at Buckland Castle, a dozen miles to the east of Heaton Park, where one of the largest decoy sites had been erected, comprising a whole complex of dummy warehouses and factories, starfish fires, lights and lures. Manchester was in the middle of a series of renewed enemy attacks and George had been dispatched to observe how the decoys operated in a real situation, as opposed to the various tests and simulations that had been tried previously. Watching from a protective bunker sunk within the hillside overlooking the ruined castle, George scanned the skies with his binoculars. The site received a number of direct hits by enemy aircraft. The decoys were doing their job well.

Not long after the all clear had sounded, a little after four in the morning, George was just standing up, shaking out the stiffness from his body after several hours of being tightly cramped in a hunched, prone position, when he heard the unmistakeable drone of a *Junkers*. By this stage they were all of them experts in identifying the individual sounds of the different aircraft. He looked up in the noise's direction. The sky was faintly starting to lighten in the east. George could just make out the aeroplane's silhouette. It was headed directly for them. From the sputtering of its engines, it was clearly running out of fuel and the pilot, knowing that he had no chance of returning intact to Germany, had decided to empty the last of his bombs on Buckton Castle, on what he thought was a genuine industrial target. As it drew nearer, George could make out through his binoculars smoke issuing from the tail. They all dived for cover as the bomb was released, but it fell well short, harmlessly into a field about half a mile to the north of them, showering them with clods of grass and soil. Otherwise they were unhurt.

George continued to watch the *Junkers* as it continued to lose height, passing directly overhead. He could imagine the pilot struggling at the controls, trying to steer it towards a piece of open ground where he might crash land with just the possibility of escaping with injury rather than death, wrestling with the choice of whether he should instead, at the last possible moment, eject and attempt to parachute to earth. George tracked its descent for as long as he could, until he could see it no longer. A few moments later there was a brief, terrible silence, followed by a distant explosion. Plumes of black smoke rose above the trees just as the first birds started to sing.

Later George learned that the plane had limped its way to The Roaches, a prominent ridge of hills, where it had come to ground along the gritstone escarpment between Ramshaw Rocks and Hen Cloud on the edge of the Peak District, thirty miles to the south of where he now stood. The bodies of the pilot, observer, radio operator and gunner were all recovered at the scene. It joined the litany of the more than a hundred and thirty crash sites strewn across the Derbyshire hills.

When the War had ended George rode on his motor bike to Leek, from where he walked along the ridge towards the location of the site. It was a day wreathed in mist, reminding him of the flight with Lee from Farnham, when they too could so easily have lost themselves among these hidden peaks. The mist deadened all sound, save the occasional crow cawing into the wind. George continued to climb. The lack of visibility forced him to focus only on the few feet in front of him, so he could easily have missed them, the charred metal remains, which lay embedded in the land like bones awaiting discovery, before they decayed and sank completely from sight. He was lucky. Slipping on a tuft of grass, he put out a hand to steady himself on what he thought was a blackened shard of rock, only to realise when its sharpness split the skin on his fingers, that this was a small piece of metal from the aircraft, protruding from the hard packed earth, already a part of its history, its geology, which he felt compelled to mark. It was a place his father would have liked to bring him when he was a boy. It's important to honour the dead of both sides, he would have said. There's more that binds than separates us.

He took out a piece of rice paper he had brought with him and laid it across one of the larger pieces of metal, fixing it in place with a few loose stones. Then, with a soft pencil, he gently rubbed the back of the paper, until a palimpsest of the charred metal began to show through. There – he had it – something tangible to connect him with this place.

He cast his mind back to the day he had flown in the Avro Anson reconnaissance plane, gathering the images and information which led to the decision to place the decoy site at Buckton Castle in the first place, and which set in motion the train of events that saw him now, kneeling by the few scorched remains of wreckage from an aircraft whose demise he might have indirectly contributed to. On that particular day things had all seemed so clear to him, a barely discernible speck in the cerulean blue.

All of Manchester had lain before him, the shape of it,

like a body pulsing with life, the rivers and canals its veins and arteries, the roads and railways its muscle and bone, the mines and forges its beating heart, all united in the spirit of endeavour, the weight of work, each separate element joined to its neighbour, connected, not an extraneous screw or bolt, wheel or cog, anywhere that was not part of this mighty enterprise. At times they flew low enough for him to make out individual men, women and children teeming across its surface, from every country of the world, or so it seemed to him then, and he saw great strength in this diversity. It would cling on, hold fast, pull through. It would adapt and change, evolve and shift. A Manchester moth. But above all it, no matter what, it would survive. It would forge itself a future, one which George, looking down on it all, wanted to be a part of. He would record it, document it, photograph it, not as he was doing now, to hide it, conceal it, try to make it disappear, replicating it as an illusion of itself, a hall of mirrors whose reflections could not be trusted, but to celebrate it as it truly was, dynamic, difficult, complicated, real. As the Avro Anson rose another thousand feet, the city now appeared to resemble a many-headed hydra, a creature with lusts and appetites that would never be sated, its uncountable arms and legs constantly on the move, turning the soil, putting down roots, mining the earth for riches to be shared among all, a great leviathan, a writhing, surging unstoppable surge of rats, rising up to claim their birthright.

Lily lies awake.

The early morning light filters into her bedroom the morning after V.E. Night. A new reality dawns. She has been dreaming, she thinks, for five years. The no-time and never-where of war. She looks at her ATS Uniform hanging on the back of her wardrobe and decides she has no further use for it. Time for a fresh start. New rules for a new age. Time to begin making her own decisions.

She's already begun of course. Roland. She crossed that line two years ago and has run the gauntlet of taunts and disapproval ever since. Taboos are there to be broken, she thinks. You can't make an omelette without smashing eggs.

But her assignations with Roland have all been clandestine, waltzing in the wonder of why they're there. A secret, cloak-and-dagger affair, performed at night, in the shadows, away from prying eyes, like searchlights raking the skies for signs of the enemy.

She throws back the bed sheets, crosses to the window, pulls open the curtains. The sun streams in. It falls upon her grandfather's toy yacht, *The Tulip*, given pride of place on the narrow mantel above the fire place. She picks it up, runs her hand along the smooth, sleek lines of its painted wooden hull. The only thing connecting her to her lost, first family.

She has an idea. As instant as if it had sprung up overnight. Like immaculate conception. A night blooming cereus. The fabled moonflower. Which wilts in the dawn. She recalls again the film she saw at *The Scala*. Greer Garson finding homes for orphans in *Blossoms in the Dust*. Running the gauntlet of opposition and disapproval.

She will begin here. In Lapwing Lane. The house has plenty of room and she is sure George will not mind. She remembers one of Annie's favourite maxims. The quote from Deuteronomy embroidered onto the sampler, which hangs, framed, in the hallway downstairs.

That which was lost is found.

She'll begin this morning, make enquiries, set the wheels in motion, prepare the ground, before the idea can wilt.

Pearl gets married.

Lamarr is back on leave. Having liberated West Berlin, he returns to Manchester to liberate Pearl.

"I can't wait to show you Georgia," he says, "take you to Atlantic City, stroll along the boardwalk."

"Georgia," he sings, *Georgia*
A song of you
Comes as sweet and clear
As moonlight through the pines..."

Pearl disentangles herself from Lamarr's huge embrace.

"I can't leave Mrs Evelyn," she says. "She needs me."

"I need you too, honey," says Lamarr.

"You can live here," says Evelyn. "I've plenty of room."

Lamarr and Pearl stare open mouthed.

"You'll have to get married first of course," says

Evelyn, a twinkle in her still bright eyes.

"I'll need to find me a job," says Lamarr.

"You can have my job at Crossley's," says Pearl. "I want to start having babies."

"In that case," says Evelyn, "the sooner you two tie the knot, the better."

Less than six weeks later Pearl and Lamarr stand beneath the gilt wrought iron awning of Cheetham Hill Town Hall. Pevsner describes it as classically austere, a suitable setting for a wedding in post-war Austerity Britain, but one which is offset by the delicacy of its *porte cochère* and enlivened by Lamarr looking dashing in his G.I.'s uniform and Pearl with a red gardenia in her hair.

"That's as close to Georgia as I'm ever going to get," she laughs. Her fingers lovingly caress a simple, elegant string of pearls around her neck.

"A gift," says Evelyn, "for your name. Frank gave them to me for my twenty-first, I don't wear them any more. You look a picture in them."

Lily is there, throwing confetti. Jenny, too. And George, not yet demobilised, in his RAF jacket, taking photographs. In one of them Pearl is looking down and stroking her belly absent-mindedly.

Lamarr, when he sees this, laughs. "You already knew, didn't you?" he grins.

Pearl smiles back. "I reckon we made it to the altar just in time."

"Really? I don't recollect seeing no altar." His grin is getting wider.

"It's an expression."
"I don't see no shotgun neither."
"There was no shotgun."
"It's an expression."

In a different town hall, Chorlton-on-Medlock, less than three miles away, Delphine sits in the auditorium listening to the opening speeches of the 5th Pan-African Congress which, in this October of 1945, is taking place in Manchester.

The flags of Haiti, Ethiopia and Liberia fly from the town hall roof. Inside, delegates from more than ninety countries are gathered to share stories and exchange dreams. On the platform sits Jomo Kenyatta, Kwame Nkrumah and Haile Selassie.

After the opening ceremony and speeches of welcome, local hero Leonard 'Len' Benker Johnson is applauded to the stage. He is being symbolically honoured for his achievements, not only in boxing, in which he was consistently denied his right to be called a champion, but for his continuing community work in Moss Side after he stepped out of the ring for the last time less than a year after defeating Victor.

When the applause finally dies down, he is invited to say a few words.

"We are determined to be free," he says. "We want education. We want the right to earn a decent living, the right to express our thoughts and emotions, the right to adopt and create different forms of beauty."

Several of the delegates give Len a standing ovation,

Delphine among them. He is speaking for all who have experienced prejudice, or suffered discrimination, or have been singled out because of difference. She thinks of the deaf community, whose rights she has championed, whose needs she has campaigned for, whose voice she has demanded be heard for more than a quarter of a century.

And she remembers her mother, scratching her name in the dirt beside the Ship Canal.

Eve.

Looping fish and rabbits on sticks by the fading light of the moon to leave as offerings.

Carefully carrying hen's eggs in a makeshift nest of twig and straw stitched with moss and spiderweb, which Delphine has carried after her wherever she has lived, to whatever place she has called home. As dry and combustible as a tinder box, as delicate and fragile as a sparrow's wing bones.

She listens to the speakers in All Saints, at the Chorlton-on-Medlock Town Hall, one after another, extolling the virtues of working together towards a common goal, a common wealth, a word so much kinder than empire, some of them more strident than others, elder siblings ready to leave the nest, clamouring for independence. Delphine recognises in their voices the same impatience she hears from her students, who believe she has taught them all she can and who champ at the bit to be let off the reins, to go out into the world and make their own mistakes, as she herself had done at their age. She thinks back to her own mother, who, perhaps because she had been left to fend for herself from when she was so very young, a child still, had never tried to stop Delphine from ranging further and further from their camp by the river, and later their hut by the canal, confident that she would find her way as *she* had had to. Sooner or later we all become orphans, thinks Delphine. Better to be prepared than wait till we are abandoned, untested and alone. Fledglings need to stretch their wings early.

Delphine makes her way back home from the Pan-African Congress with a sense of cautious optimismm. She recalls the words of the boxer Len Johnson. We are determined to be free. Manchester seems a good place to begin that experiment, for she has always been an unruly child, the kind Delphine has always preferred as a teacher, those who ask awkward, challenging questions.

She ponders as she walks a decision she has to take. The University has offered her the Chair of the Audiology Department. It's a great honour and she's flattered to have been invited, but something is baulking her, holding her back from accepting, niggling the back of her mind, like a caught thread on a snag of barbed wire. It's not her age. She's fifty-five now but still feels full of energy. It's something else. Listening to the speakers in the Town Hall at All Saints has crystallised it for her.

The decision to appoint her to the Chair is not based on her abilities so much as her seniority. It's simply that she's next in line. It's her turn now. And that's not a good enough reason. The War has changed things irrevocably. Both sides claimed they were fighting for a better tomorrow. Well, thinks, Delphine, that tomorrow is here, today, and we must grasp it.

Mr Nkrumah had quoted Sherlock Holmes at the end of his speech to the delegates. From *His Last Bow*, Holmes's final case, something suitably English to remind the old country that her days as a colonial power were numbered, known to be one of Churchill's personal favourites.

"There's an east wind coming," he read, "such a wind as never blew on England yet. It will be cold and bitter, and a good many of us may wither before its blast. But it's God's own wind none the less, and a cleaner, better, stronger land will lie in the sunshine when the storm has cleared."

It was time to let the continent of Africa go free, he was implying. Time to let the children make their own mistakes. For in the end that's what good parents do.

Fanciful? Possibly, thinks Delphine. Hyperbolic? Certainly. But heartfelt nevertheless and not to be ignored. She walks down Oxford Road, past the University, on her way back to her flat on Upper Brook Street.

A crowd has gathered outside the Holy Name Church. Of course. It's Rag Week. Delphine had forgotten. An obstacle race has been laid out around Whitworth Park. A banner declaring *'The Race for Berlin'* is slung between two trees to mark the finish line. The competitors carry old car tyres around their waists, decorated to look like tanks, or spitfires. They wear exaggerated cardboard masks upon their heads and carry placards with their names written on them, in case any of the spectators should be in doubt about who they are meant to represent.

Patton, Monty, Zhukov.

Ike, Harris, Konev.

Patton and Monty, Ike and Harris have to take a much longer route than Zhukov or Konev, who proceed to shoot at each other with water pistols, until they all end up in a great heap, rolling about on top of each other in the dirt.

A different race, a pram race, is taking place up and down the street between Whitworth Park and the Museum. Inside each pram is a student dressed as an oversized baby, complete with dummy and rattle. Each of them wears a sign hung around their neck.

India. Palestine. Egypt. Singapore.

Rhodesia. Kenya. Burma. Malaya.

The prams are being pushed by students wearing striped pyjamas. They make Delphine think of concentration camps. Which she supposes is the point. The finish line turns out to be a large sand pit filled with mud, with *'Birth of a Nation'*, pasted around its perimeter. As each pram reaches the finish, the babies are tipped out into the pit, where they remain stuck, unable to get out. They proceed to throw mud at one another and any spectator foolish enough to venture too near.

Outside the Holy Name Church is a silent tableau. Three students, dressed as monkeys and wearing bowler hats, sit on the steps. Protruding from each hat is a small flag. Britain, Russia, the United States. The first covers his eyes, the second his ears, the third his mouth. See no evil, hear no evil, speak no evil. Behind them a figure dressed as the Grim Reaper holds above them a black umbrella, like a giant mushroom cloud, while congregations of homing pigeons are released from cages to fly out above the crowds to all parts of the city.

Delphine delights in their youthful irreverence. She may decide to call in on Charles when she gets back and tell him all about it. He will be outraged, and she will enjoy seeing him struggle to keep his temper.

She moves on, leaving the Rag stunts behind her. Behind the Infirmary an attachment of prisoners-of-war is working under a military guard to help with the reconstruction of the hospital, which is still ongoing after the damage incurred during the attacks of five years ago. She fumes with indignation. These men should all be repatriated, she believes. What right have we to keep them here? She knows there is much rebuilding that needs to be done. But not like this. It is shameful. No – she will not visit Charles this evening, for this is something else they will argue about, and she hasn't the stomach for it. Last week she received a letter from Esther, who, she has noted, has begun signing herself *Ishtar*, which contained a cutting from *The Manchester Guardian*, with an extract from a speech delivered by Harold Nicholson to the House of Commons underlined angrily in red.

"The repatriation of German and Italian prisoners of war should begin immediately. A ravaged Europe is looking for leadership. The Soviets may have the physical strength and resources, but it is Britain who has, by contrast, an enormous moral power. It is imperative that we practise what we preach. Our failure to deal fairly and decently with our prisoners is hypocrisy of the vilest and most damaging order. That we should treat human beings in this manner while proclaiming aloud our belief in the sanctity of human values, is more than wrong, it is blind and stupid."

She will go directly home instead, listen to some soothing Ravel piano music, *Le Tombeau de Couperin, Gaspard de la Nuit*, then write a reply to Esther and ask her about this sudden name change.

She will also write to the University. She has made a decision about the Chair of the Audiology Department. She will accept it. But on two conditions: one, that she gets to appoint her own Deputy, someone she can train up to take over from her when she herself retires in five years time, which she fully intends to do; and two, that the University appoints student representatives to its various sub-committees. We must listen to the voices of the young, she will argue, for it is for them that the University exists.

The War may be over but more change is coming – needed, she believes – and we're all of us, whether we like it or not, she thinks, orphans of the storm.

In 1853, twenty-five miles to the south of the city, in Holmes Chapel, the Reverend John Armistead went to the local workhouse, deposited a small sum of money, in return for which he secured the release of several orphaned children, whom he escorted to various families in his parish, who had volunteered to take them into their homes for a short period of time, until he could arrange longer term situations for each of them. This was the first recorded case of fostering anywhere in Britain.

Lily calls on some of Annie's former contacts in the Corporation and the various Charitable Committees. What's being done to house the children, she asks? Those who have lost their homes to the bombs. Those who have been evacuees and who are now returning with nowhere to come back to. Those who have become orphans.

She feels the Corporation must be stretched. There is a Children's Home at Ryecroft House in Worsley, she knows. It was opened by the Bishop of Manchester, she says. She remembers reading about it. But it is not yet ready. She understands there are plans to build more, but that will take time, and time is something these children don't have. There must be families here in the city willing to take in an extra mouth to feed, even with the strictures of rationing still in place. She herself, she explains, has room for eight children, and she is prepared to take them in immediately. There must be, she sympathises, some really desperate cases that are causing you a great deal of worry and concern.

Afterwards Alderman Hardcastle, who has accompanied Lily to the Town Hall, opens several doors for her, gets her to see the people who will make the various decisions, smiles.

"Well," he tells her, "you've got your late adoptive mother's skills of persuasion, and no mistake."

"She taught me well," says Lily. Listen, look and learn.

Lily fizzes with energy and zeal. She fills the house at Lapwing Lane with laughter and light.

Within a month she has her first full complement of eight blossoms from the dust, all girls, aged between four and seven, of various shades and colours, from different ports of origin, which she will plant and water, before they are potted on in more permanent soil. In each bedroom she hangs one of Annie's collagraphs of the spindle tree, in bud, in leaf, in flower. She is happy and sad to see each one go. But she knows their places will be filled with new seedlings.

Mancunians all.

Now she must turn her attention back to Roland.

Delphine watches the prisoners from her window.

There is one, she notices, who limps, who finds the unremitting grind of carting rubble to clear the site for rebuilding is taking its toll. One afternoon she sees him stumble and trip. A wheelbarrow of stone falls on top of him. Instinctively she rushes out to rescue him. A futile gesture for, by the time she has reached him, he has already been hauled back to his feet and ordered to carry on.

Delphine berates the guard. "This man is injured. He needs treatment. Is there not more suitable work can be found for him? Until he's repatriated?"

"I don't want to be repatriated," the man says suddenly.

Delphine regards him closely. She assumed everyone would wish to return home.

"I'm a mathematician. I want to stay here."

His English is perfect.

Delphine straightens herself and addresses the guard. "There is a doctor," she says, "who lives not fifty yards from here. Let me fetch him, so that he can diagnose this man's injury professionally and recommend a course of treatment."

"We have a doctor in the camp," says the guard.

"Indeed? And he declared him fit for work, did he?"

The guard looks away sheepishly. "He only comes in when he can."

Delphine turns back to the prisoner. "Don't move," she commands, "till I return with the doctor. I shall not be more than five minutes." She pauses briefly and asks, "What is your name?"

"Roland."

Later, when Charles has looked at him and dressed his foot and ankle, before moving away to have a private word with the guard, Roland speaks to Delphine in a low voice, which cracks with pain and emotion.

"I've met a woman," he says. "We love each other."

Afterwards Delphine invited Charles back to her flat to offer him a drink and thank him properly. He entered nervously, looking around. It had been several years since he last crossed this threshold.

"What did you say to the guard?" she demanded.

"You still waste no time in small talk, I see."

"I don't see the point."

Charles took a sip of his whisky to collect himself. "I told him that in my professional opinion the prisoner needed to be hospitalised. Immediately."

Delphine raised an eyebrow. "Can you still authorise that?"

"I may have retired," he replied somewhat huffily, "but I retain, I hope, a certain standing still among my former colleagues."

"Yes. I'm sure. And what did the guard say?"

"That he'd ask his Commanding Officer."

"Oh." Delphine was crestfallen. "That will delay things, surely?"

Charles shook his head. "The C/O used to drink at my club."

"Typical," Delphine tutted.

"I know you don't approve, but as you see, it can have its uses. He'll agree to my request that he be treated as a matter of extreme urgency."

"You make it sound extremely serious."

"It is. He may well lose the foot."

Delphine brought a hand to her mouth and sat down. Charles poured her a whisky and helped himself to a top-up. "Why the interest in this particular prisoner?"

"It's all prisoners," she said vehemently. "It's shameful that we haven't sent them home. The Americans did so as soon as the surrender was signed."

"The Americans," Charles scoffed, "do not have a country's infrastructure to rebuild like we do."

"That's beside the point."

They both paused and looked at one another. It had been some years since they had sparred like this.

"I'm sorry," she said. "Let's not quarrel. I just wanted to thank you, that's all. The man has formed an attachment, it seems, with a local girl."

"*Un amour de la commodité*," said Charles. "I expect it's a ruse."

"I don't believe it is. I was struck most forcibly by the sincerity of his emotion."

"How can you possibly know? You hardly spoke to him."

"Then let's put it down to woman's intuition, shall we?"

Charles let the matter drop. He knew when he was venturing into territory where he was on less solid ground.

The two of them sat silent for a few moments, each in their own separate, if parallel thoughts.

"So what happens next?" asked Delphine.

"With luck, I should be able to arrange to have him admitted tomorrow. For observation and assessment. Then we'll see."

Delphine stood, extending her hand. "Thank you," she said. "I am extremely grateful.

Charles stood too. He knew this was her signal for the evening to be over. He made his way down the stairs and along the corridor to his own flat in the same building. He opened the door and looked around. It struck him with an undeniable force just how sparely furnished, empty and unwelcoming his flat appeared after the cushions and flowers, pictures and ornaments, books and records at Delphine's. He closed the door behind him and stepped into his sterile sitting room without bothering to switch on the light.

And there, some hours later, he sits still.

He reaches back far into the darker recesses of his memory, those dusty corners of his brain he rarely allows himself to visit. He ventures even deeper, to a point where he needs a key to unlock and retrieve those moments he has hardly revisited in almost thirty years.

In his mind's eye his hand is visibly shaking. He inserts the key and tries to turn it. Stiff, after decades of non-use, he has to use all the force of his will to prise the rusty lock.

The door creaks open.

And there, sitting in the farthest corner of this secret chamber, is a figure with her back towards him.

Closing his eyes, so that he might fully enter this realm of his imagination, he steps inside. The floor beneath him makes the tiniest of groans, no more than if a mouse has tiptoed across it, but the figure, her senses acutely attuned to the slightest movement in the air, turns at once.

And Charles is lost.

He hears Ruth's voice, echoing down the years, a child's ball bouncing down a staircase, reverberating on every step, growing louder and louder, until she is all around him.

"Doubt thou the stars are fire;
Doubt that the sun doth move;
Doubt truth to be a liar;
But never doubt I love…"

He reels away, but whichever way he turns, she is

there before him, smiling radiantly, her trust in him unshakeable. It is that which has pained him most down the long years since, her faith and her courage, met only by his cowardice and betrayal. It will not leave him, like a dog that has captured a rat and will not let it go. It clamps its teeth around him and shakes him till his bones begin to rattle.

Each year, on 7th January, the day Galileo discovered and named the four largest of Jupiter's moons, the day they were to have married, he remembers her words.

"Let these moons be ours, my love. Let us both look at them each night between now and when we can be together always..."

Gannymede, Callisto, Europa, Io.
He has not looked at them since.
Tonight he believes he must.

He rises from the chair where he has been sitting for who knows how many hours. His knees unstiffen and creak. He crosses to the window where his rarely used telescope has been waiting patiently, primed and ready, mounted on its stand. He presses his eye to the ocular lens, tilts and pivots the tube in its cradle, adjusts the focus, widens the aperture. These long ago, practised movements come back to him now in a kind of muscle memory. He navigates his way around the night sky, seeking the familiar, something to anchor him, to tether him back through time. Orion strides reassuringly up the south-eastern quadrant. Above it glitters Aldebaran, vivid and orange, sixty-five million light years away. Above that, the *Pleiades*, whose dancing sisters cluster a further four hundred light years distant. And there, as he pans the telescope a degree or two towards due south, Jupiter awaits.

It is a perfect night for seeing the moons. Named for the lovers of Zeus, each in a differently coloured dress. Yellow Io. Red Europa. Blue Callisto. Silver Gannymede. Their pitiless clarity mocks Charles, who understands he must watch them till the sun begins to rise, but even then they will not fade. Just as Ruth does not.

Now that he has looked upon them once again, he knows he will watch them every night, until he can look no more.

Scanning the same night sky from an altogether very different telescope is Francis.

Twenty miles to the south of Upper Brook Street, Francis has been working in a voluntary capacity in a portable cabin on a field midway between Capesthorne and Goostrey in Cheshire, close to a nearby rise in the ground known locally as Jodrell Bank, which had been purchased from the Massey family, local farmers, by Manchester University's Botany Department. Nicknamed the Park Royal, the cabin, no longer required by the botanists, has been filled with former military hardware, including gun-laying radar under the supervision of the astrophysicist Bernard Lovell, with the purpose of investigating cosmic rays.

Lovell's principal field of research is the location, identification and recording of transient radio echoes. He intended to transfer the equipment to the University but electrical interference from the trams on Oxford Road prevented him from doing so. Consequently he put out a call for interested amateur astronomers and experienced radio communications operators to join him over at Jodrell Bank. Francis has answered that call. Having experience in both those areas, he quickly finds himself in much demand.

While Lovell's assistants, Alf Dean and Frank Foden, concentrate on observing meteor showers with the naked eye, Lovell himself attempts to record the same phenomena through the capture of their electromagnetic signals. Francis alternates between them.

In December 1945 they are able to confirm for the first time anywhere in the world that the *Geminids*, those same meteors spotted by Frances on V.E. Night, are the only ones whose origin is not a comet, but an asteroid. Encouraged by this success, Lovell acquires more redundant military equipment. A large searchlight is customised with a broadside array by the engineer John Clegg, using Yagi antennae, which deploys a series of directional dipole metal rods connected to a transmitter and receiver. Francis is familiar with these from his time with *Radio Aspidistra*. Through this searchlight telescope Lovell is able to observe for the first time ionisation, the process by which atoms acquire a negative or positive charge, actually occurring in the atmosphere.

Francis marvels at this rare glimpse into the workings of the universe, staring deep into the heart of its beginnings, the building blocks of life itself. He witnesses so many new, previously unseen or unrecorded events and feels himself quite at home travelling across these vast, unimaginable distances in space and time, while those which are so much closer to him remain a mystery.

Like George.

He received a letter from him recently in which he said he had been thinking about his future once he left the RAF, but he still did not know precisely when he would be stood down. They have seen so little of each other over the past five years that Francis wonders if they will ever be able to return to how things were between them. Time is passing. George is thirty-two now, while Francis is forty-seven. Less than the blink of an eye when he is scanning the skies, looking and listening so intently. He maps the constellations in ever more detail as new discoveries are made, while the texture of George's skin, whose every crevice he once knew intimately, could trace each contour blindfold, is now beginning to fade...

But it is the investigation of the radio waves emanating from the stars and planets which is now becoming his, and Lovell's, primary focus. Over the next two years the team builds what they call *The Transit*, the world's largest radio telescope, and the first to use parabolic zenith reflectors. Through it they discover white noise from the *Great Nebula* in *Andromeda*, the first definite detection of an extra-galactic radio source. They record the remains of the *Tycho Supernova* in the constellation of *Cassiopeia*. Radio frequency is now probing deeper into space than optical astronomy.

Decoding what it means proves another matter entirely. Francis spends hours listening for patterns among the ceaseless transmissions being received from other galaxies, while speaking on the telephone to George proves equally cryptic and inconclusive. Like Cassiopeia's daughter, who was chained to a rock out at sea, Francis waits for his hero to rescue him, but he has strayed so far out into space, he wonders now if he can ever be found and brought back home.

Roland is in the hospital.

Charles has arranged for him to be admitted. His successor as Head of Surgery, Dr Manfred Hart, speaks impeccable German, but in the case of Roland this will not be necessary, Charles assures him. He appears to speak better English than you or I. But it could prove helpful.

When Charles arrives mid morning, many former colleagues greet him warmly. It feels good to be walking these corridors again. He has not realised just how acutely he has missed it. His work, he realises with cruel self-loathing, has defined him. He is nothing without it.

He reaches the Surgical Ward where Dr Hart is already waiting for him. He shows Charles the X-rays. Together they study them closely.

"Whoever first set the broken ankle did an excellent job," remarks Charles.

"Particularly as it was done in the field. The patient informs me he fell from a tree after his parachute got entangled. An ARP Warden attended to him. She evidently had some first class nursing experience behind her."

"She?"

"The patient described her with glowing praise."

"But there's been extensive damage since."

"Being a POW can't have helped."

"Quite. So," asks Charles, "what are you proposing?"

Hart puts down the X-rays. "I see no alternative to amputation."

"I agree. The risk of a gangrenous infection spreading even further is otherwise too great."

"To put it bluntly, if we remove the foot, we can save the leg."

Charles nods. "There is a firm in Sheffield," he says. "Blatchford's. Do you know them?"

Hart shakes his head.

"They lead the field in prosthetics," says Charles. "Far superior to what we have in stock here. They use much more lightweight materials – aluminium, plastic. I'll give them a call if you like."

"Thank you, but no," says Hart. "I'll call them myself if you don't mind. When I know more details of what's required."

Charles nods. He knows when he is being told, however gently, to back off.

"I've not decided for certain if I'll proceed yet," continues Hart.

Charles raises an eyebrow.

"The paperwork. It's complicated. The patient being a prisoner."

"Perhaps that is something I might be able to assist with?" replies Charles tentatively.

Now it is Dr Hart's turn to raise an eyebrow.

"The Commanding Officer at the Camp is an

acquaintance of mine."

"Ah…" Hart responds in such a way as to leave Charles in no doubt that he understands no further comment is necessary. The Old Boys' Network. Instead he says, "Would you care to see the patient before you go?"

"Yes," says Charles. "Thank you." He knows when he is being dismissed, but he is reluctant to leave just yet.

"Along the corridor," says Hart. "I expect you can remember where."

"I believe I can," says Charles with a smile. He shakes Dr Hart's hand and makes his way towards the Ward.

He is about to step inside when he hears low voices talking urgently. One is the patient's, the other a female's. He assumes this must be the young woman mentioned by the patient the day before. A message must have been passed on to her of the prisoner's whereabouts and she has rushed here directly.

He hovers in the doorway, attempting to remain inconspicuous. He need not have worried. The two are oblivious of everything except each other. It is immediately clear to Charles that the young man spoke the truth last night when he declared that the two of them loved each other.

He watches them with a rare sense of privilege and awe. The young woman has her back to him. All he can see at first is the tousle of red hair that has been hastily pinned up in her hurry to be here. Something about the angle of her head is familiar to him.

He retreats from the doorway back into the corridor. He feels himself visibly shaking. He must somehow make sure of her identity without drawing attention to himself. He does not wish to speak to her directly in case she recognises him from when he treated her some fifteen years before. Surely she wouldn't? She was only sixteen at the time. But she might. And if she did, he might be tempted on this occasion to explain who he is, that he had been engaged to her mother, to somehow expiate the guilt he has carried all those years, especially since that terrible evening he had confessed to Delphine and she had been so outraged by his abandonment of the child after the promises he had made to Ruth. He could not submit Lily, if that indeed is who this young woman is, to such a shock, especially at a time like this.

He leans his back against the corridor wall and closes his eyes.

Dr Hart passes him. "Do you not wish to go in after all?" he enquires.

Charles does his best to collect himself. "He has a visitor," he explains. "I didn't wish to intrude."

"Ah yes," replies Hart, stroking his moustache, "one hears of such liaisons. She was quite desperate to see him."

Charles sees his opportunity. "Did she leave her name?"

Hart checks his chart. "Miss Lily Wright," he says. "Why the interest?"

"I believe she may once have been a patient of mine, that's all. Old habits, you know?"

"Well... I'm just going in. Do you want me to introduce you?"

"No, no, no. I shall leave both patient and visitor in

your capable hands. I do have a question, though, if I may?"

"By all means."

"The amputation – if you decide to go through with it – the fitting of the prosthetic and the subsequent rehabilitation, it will not be inexpensive, I take it?"

"Indeed it will not. We don't have this National Health Service Mr Bevan is urging upon us just yet. The final cost could exceed £100. Clearly the prisoner does not have such resources at his disposal, and the financial arrangements regarding the treatment of POWs remain haphazard, to say the least. The Government seems to have no clear plan or guidelines, and if we approach them, we're likely to be pushed from one department to another. The whole farce could take months before we get a definitive answer, and time is of the essence."

Charles rubs his chin abstractedly. "Yes. As you say. An impossible situation. What if I were able to source a donation? Might that expedite matters?"

Dr Hart, ever the pragmatist, seizes on the offer. "It most certainly would. If you could confirm that, I could operate tomorrow. It promises to be a most interesting procedure. You're welcome to scrub in and observe, if you like…"

"No, no, no. My days in theatre are over. But I can give you an assurance here and now that the money will be forthcoming as and when you require it."

"Thank you, Charles. I shall go and inform the patient and his 'friend' directly."

They shake hands, then go their separate ways. As Charles walks back along the corridors, there is a lightness in his step. He cannot recall when he last experienced such a feeling.

George has never forgotten the advice given to him by Mr Lowry when he first met him on the evening of *The Manchester Society of Modern Artists'* inaugural exhibition at the Blackfriars Gallery when he was just twelve years old, advice much repeated later when George was Lowry's student at *The Mechanics' Institute* – "find yourself a proper job".

It is partly this which keeps him in the RAF after the War has ended. He likes the camaraderie, the shared satisfaction of a job well done when each aircraft takes off cleanly and performs with ever-improving efficiency. It is not unlike the pleasure he felt when his 'tinkering' enabled a speedway bike to outpace all opposition and win its race, except that now the stakes are that much higher.

But when, twelve months after the Japanese have surrendered, the operation at Heaton Park is finally shut down and work begins to dismantle the camp completely, to erase it almost as if it had never been, George finds himself at a crossroads. Captain Rowley calls him into his office.

"I won't beat about the bush," he says. "You've done a damned fine job here during this last show."

"Thank you, sir."

He bats away George's gratitude. "Call it as I see it – that's always been my motto. Do you have plans for what you might do next?"

"Nothing definite, sir."

"Good. Thought not. Otherwise you'd have been off like a shot, no doubt."

"Sir."

"The fact is, I've been offered a new post myself. Head of Training at RAF Cranwell. I could do with someone like you as part of my team. Interested?"

"Cranwell, sir?"

"Yes, I know. Lincolnshire. Not the most attractive of propositions, but perfect for take-off and landing, what? Flat as a…"

"Plate, sir."

"*Altium altrix.*"

"Sir?"

"Written beneath the Cranwell badge. 'Nurture the winged'."

"A noble sentiment, sir."

"So? What's your answer?"

"Can I think about it, sir?"

"Oh." Rowley is clearly surprised. "Yes, I suppose. Let me know within the hour."

He immediately buries his head in the papers on his desk and George knows that he is being dismissed.

He doesn't need long to decide. He knows he isn't ready to leave Manchester. His grandmother's not getting any younger, and then there's Francis.

Francis.

The forced separation brought about by the War, even though in their case that has been less than a dozen miles, has left its mark. The opportunities to see one another have been few and far between. A distance greater than that between Heaton Park and Denton has grown between them. Lately Francis has grown fretful, peevish, demanding, and George has found himself volunteering for more additional shifts than he needed to, just so that he can postpone what he fears may be an unpleasant confrontation between them, when ultimatums may be given, stances and positions taken up, which might be difficult for either of them to step away from, especially Francis, who is more impulsive, less phlegmatic than George. Removing himself to Lincolnshire would only mean another postponement of a conversation that can't be put off any longer.

George informs Rowley that he has decided not to take up the offer at Cranwell. He cites his ageing grandmother as a reason, plus a desire to pick up the threads of his life before the War. Rowley sighs. He is clearly disappointed, which moves George more than he was prepared for, but he makes no attempt to try and change his mind, his temperament being such that once he recognises a situation has moved beyond what he can control, he immediately turns his attention to a contingency. He gets to his feet and shakes George by the hand.

"A word to the wise," he says, leaning in close, as if he doesn't want his next remark to be overheard, "watch out for those damned artists. A suspicious bunch, you never know what they're thinking. Stay well clear of 'em, that's my advice."

"Thank you, sir. I'll do my best."

Back on Civvy Street, in his ill-fitting demob suit, he heads straight for *The Mechanics' Institute* and offers his services as a teacher. They welcome him back with relief. The War has led to an inevitable shortage and in any case they remember him fondly. Even the increasingly taciturn Lowry recognises him, though he can't remember his name. He has all but withdrawn from the Manchester art scene these days. He still paints – obsessively so – but spends more and more of his time attending to his invalid mother, on whom he lavishes his unstinting adoration in the forlorn hope he may one day receive a modicum of approbation from her lips, which never comes. George agrees a contract which requires him to teach three full days and two additional evenings to both full and part time students. In addition to a salary the Institute offers him unlimited access to a dark room and a commitment to show exhibitions of his work.

It is an arrangement which suits George perfectly, allowing him the rest of the week to walk the streets in pursuit of suitable subject matter. Manchester and its environs will be his canvas. The collieries and canals, the factories and forges. The streets and squares. The pubs and legions, miners' welfares and working men's clubs. The dog tracks and football grounds. Weddings and Whit Walks, fairs and processions. The parks and playing fields. Above all, the people who inhabit all of these places. The men, the women, the children. Young, old; together, alone. Catholic and Jew, Baptist and Methodist, Hindu and Muslim, Sikh and Moravian. Irish, Italian, German and Russian. Chinese, Arabian, Bengali and Pole. Black, brown, yellow, white.

The restlessness, which threatened to overwhelm him after the bombing of the Printing Works and the death of his mother, could, he realises, so easily return, unless he guards against it. He knows he needs to be vigilant at all times. Work is the answer. Work, work, work. He will consume himself with it, so that he will allow himself no time to descend into the melancholy which so blighted his father's life after the last war.

He demands the same work ethic and commitment from his students. When drawing a still life, he brings in old engine parts, rusting bits of industrial machinery, which he insists his students first strip down and clean before they begin to draw them. You must know your subject intimately, he preaches, the nuts and bolts and guts and gristle of it, experience the weight of it in your hands. Only then will you be able to understand it and be able to draw it. He applies the same approach to life drawing, encouraging his students first to familiarise themselves with skeletal structure, muscle, bone and sinew. Skin is just a surface, he says, but what a surface, try to imagine the lifetime of experiences that have created this patina of years, this pocked and cratered landscape over which you must travel with your pencil.

Having sorted out his job, George turns his attention to where he will live. The house in Portugal Street is gone, for which he eventually receives, after months of correspondence and the inevitable filling in and sending off of multiple, complicated forms, a small amount of compensation from the War Commission. He has formally agreed that Lily can stay in the house in Lapwing Lane for as long as she wishes to, with an added clause that, should either of them decide to sell, they will split the proceeds between them. He has made it clear to her informally that he personally has no intention of selling it, that to all intents and purposes the house is hers. When she tells him, somewhat tentatively, about her plans for the *Blossoms in the Dust* project, he is delighted. He spends several weekends helping her to decorate bedrooms. He decides he will live in Salford, close to the Institute and, by chance one night at *The Queen's*, he learns from Cam that there is a flat available to rent in the same building as hers on Silk Street. He goes round the next day and it is exactly what he needs, a one bedroom flat with a small kitchen, bathroom and, what clinches it for him, a tiny box room which he can convert into an extra dark room. He moves in immediately.

Now, with all his ducks in a row, he is ready to face Francis.

He calls him on the telephone and suggests a day out, a picnic, the following Sunday. He knows how Francis enjoys a treat.

He arrives mid-morning outside the shop in Denton. Inevitably Francis is not ready. He is nervous. He fusses over what to wear, what to take. Eventually the two of them set off. Francis rides pillion on the back of George's new DOT Bradshaw and loops his arms around George's waist. When they are clear of houses and the risk of prying eyes, he allows himself the luxury of leaning in closer and pressing his face against George's back. The smell of the leather jacket, the cracked and crinkled, worn feel of it, is almost Proustian in its associative effect on him. A threat of tears pricks the back of his eyes.

"Are you all right?" asks George over his shoulder.

"Fine," says Francis. "It's the wind, that's all. Where

are we going?"

"It's a surprise," says George.

"Good surprise or bad surprise," says Francis.

"Good, I hope."

In half an hour Francis recognises the control tower of Barton Aerodrome.

"This was where we went on our very first trip together," he says, cautiously.

"Yes," says George. "Not much further now."

He heads off the main road into Raspberry Lane, deep into the heart of Chat Moss, down Cuthook Lane, then along the dirt tracks across the levees to Hephzibah, where George pulls into a wider patch of grass on the embankment.

The silence, after the roar of the motor cycle engine, hums in their ears.

"Thomas-a-Tattimus," says George.

"How many T's?" asks Francis.

"Two," says George. "There's only ever been two."

They look at one another, remembering.

"What are we doing?" asks Francis, fearfully. "This is not just Memory Lane, is it?"

"Let's just sit for a while," says George. "Get our bearings."

In the distance a bittern booms across the Moss. A grey heron lifts from further along the bank, its take off clumsy and awkward, before it rises in the sky with slow, strong wing beats. Close by a whitethroat chatters and churrs. Francis holds his breath. George waits till he is ready before he speaks. Not just yet.

He goes back to the bike, takes a thermos from one of

the panniers on the side, and pours them each a mug of strong tea. "It's only powdered milk, I'm afraid," he says, handing a mug to Francis, who sets it down beside him, saying nothing.

George takes a few sips of the scalding liquid, then tips the rest away. "Sorry," he says. "Disgusting."

Francis does not move.

The seconds squirm by. George sees a black and yellow striped caterpillar of the cinnabar moth feeding on a clump of ragwort by his feet. He allows it to crawl up onto his finger, which he brings close to his face and appears to study minutely, before releasing it back into the grass.

Francis can bear it no longer and snaps. "For God's sake, say what you've got to and have done with it."

George breathes deeply.

"I wanted to come here," he says, "because this is where it all began."

"And this is where it's all going to end, isn't it?"

"Please, Francis," says George very quietly. "Let me finish. I've been thinking about this for some time."

"That sounds ominous." He holds out his hands in a gesture of surrender. "Sorry."

"They say everyone has their 'Road to Damascus' moment, and this was mine. Even though I was only seventeen, I knew with absolute certainty that I loved you, and that I always would. I still do. That's not changed."

"What has then?"

George shakes his head. "In all the years since, I've never strayed from that. I've never been unfaithful. I've not even felt tempted. I know that's not been the case with you, Francis. No – please don't argue, I'm not criticising, just stating the facts. That's one of the differences between us. You've known who you were longer than I have. And I've always known that when you were with someone else, it didn't mean anything, that it was just a passion of the moment, and that what we had between us was altogether different, more substantial, that it would endure. And it has. It does. But…"

A clouded yellow butterfly alights on a tuft of white beak sedge below where they are sitting. It is quickly joined by another. George is silent, thinking back to when he saw a similar pair all those years ago in this very spot, while he waited for the ambulance to take Francis to a hospital called Hope.

"I've come to realise," he says, continuing once more, "that what I want is impossible. What I want, Francis, is to be married, like my parents were, like Victor and Winifred are, like Lily and Roland would like to be. You and me. Like any other normal couple. But we can't, can we? The law regards us as criminals, society as a whole doesn't accept us, so we have to hide away, meet in secret, pretend that we're just pals whenever we go out together. Oh I know that we have friends who know, good friends who understand. Christ, I'm pretty sure my mother knew but I could never have dared to mention it just in case she didn't, and I'm sick to death of pretending, Francis, that's the nub of it. We both of us spent the whole of the War engaged in deception of one kind or another, you with your faked news broadcasts and me with my decoy sites, trying to pull the wool over the eyes of the enemy, and in the end deception becomes an end in itself, you start to get less certain about what is and isn't real…"

"But the War's over now, George. Things are getting back to…"

"To what, Francis? Normal? And what exactly is normal? Are we normal?"

"God, I should hope not. You and I could never be anything like so dull as 'normal'. We're much more than that."

"But I want to be normal. I want this – us – to be so normal that it's not even remarked on."

As George is speaking, the two yellow butterflies are suddenly joined by a flock of perhaps thirty others, which descend in a cloud, fluttering around and between them, alighting fleetingly on their hands, their hair, before taking off again in a golden drift, until the whole of the Moss is alive with them, their fragile wings opening and closing like eyelids, blinking in the autumn sunlight.

The sight of them stops George and Francis in their tracks, lost in the wonder of it, each of them knowing they will probably never witness such a thing again. They sit, entranced. A whole minute stretches between them like a taut, invisible wire, which, if their senses were differently tuned, they might receive and hear their ultrasonic frequency and understand more of what was passing between them, filtering out the white extraneous noise to uncover that simple undiluted message.

Then, as if in response to the lifting of a conductor's unseen hand, the butterflies fountain into the air until only the original two are left, mating on the tip of the white beak sedge.

"I don't want to stop seeing you," says George. "But I want us both to stop regarding ourselves as a couple. Because we're not. We can't be. If you want to see other people, then do so with my blessing. If you find a new partner, then I'll be happy for you. I like the sex, Francis. I love it in fact. But I want it to lead somewhere. And it can't. So I'd rather manage without it. There. That's it. I've said what I needed to."

Francis doesn't reply. The cloud of butterflies reminded him of the *Aurora Borealis* he has been investigating with both the optical and radio telescopes at Jodrell Bank. Combining the two has enabled them to make new discoveries, to gain a deeper understanding of what is happening when the Northern Lights are putting on one of their firework displays.

"There are many things in space we just can't see," he says. "Like the air that we breathe. The atmosphere. We know it's a mixture of several gases, mostly nitrogen and oxygen, a little bit of hydrogen, with traces of helium and other even smaller compounds. But we can't see it. Not easily. Another thing we can't see is the earth's magnetic field. We've all played with a magnet and iron filings and seen the patterns they make. The lines closest together are where the magnetic field is strongest, the lines furthest apart where the field is weakest. The earth's magnet is deep inside the core. The field is strongest at the poles and weakest at the equator. Around the earth, in space, is plasma, made up of billions of charged particles – electrons and ions – we can't see these either. But they move in a distinctive way. They're guided and controlled by the earth's magnetic field. They travel along these field lines like wires, circling around them in a series of spirals. These are what fuel an aurora. These spirals accelerate into the upper atmosphere where they collide with gas atoms to give off light. And that's what we see. The light formed by these collisions, which are pushed around the sky by the power of the solar wind. Imagine a soap bubble. When you blow on it, it changes shape and you see different colours as it bends and twists. The build up of pressure from the solar wind creates an electrical voltage between the point where the atoms collide and the earth's magnetic poles, like a connection between the two terminals of a battery. That's what creates the aurora. Then the soap bubble bursts, and it disappears. Knowing all this doesn't make the Northern Lights any less spectacular or impressive, but it gives me hope, George, that one day we might be able to understand all of the invisible charges that are flowing between you and me right now. Who knows? We might even be able to explain the mysteries of the human heart."

"I'm not sure I'd want to understand that. It's better sometimes simply to be surprised and amazed."

"I agree, George. That's why I'll continue to live in hope, despite what you've said today, that maybe one day you'll change your mind and come back to me."

"I'm not leaving you, Francis. I just…"

"… want to be friends, I know. Let's not keep going round in circles."

Francis walks back to the DOT Bradshaw. "Luckily," he says, loosening the straps on the other pannier, "I brought something other than that disgusting tea." He pulls out a bottle of wine. "No glasses, I'm afraid. We'll just have to share and drink straight from the mouth."

By April of 1946 Atlee's Government finally bows to pressure from both home and abroad and begins the slow process of repatriating the German and Italian prisoners of war. Coinciding with this, it relaxes its rules concerning the supervision of prisoners who still remain. Officially they are to remain in the camps, but frequently they are now billeted out to families closer to where they have been assigned to carry out particular work programmes. In addition they are allowed to mingle unsupervised among the public at large, attending concerts, dances, even going to the cinema. This is not deemed a security risk since the prisoners have no access to official documents, such as passports or ID papers, without which they cannot proceed towards any form of permanent employment or citizenship. Mostly their only clothing is the army uniform they were captured in, so they are immediately recognisable. And although those assigned to work on the farms or building sites are paid, it is such a pittance, less than two shillings a week, that little by way of independence can be gained by that route either. The reality is that they must sweat it out, this protracted period of waiting, while the Government processes quite randomly the hundreds of thousands of prisoners of war awaiting release or repatriation.

Delphine continues to take a keen interest in Roland. She learns of the anonymous donation which enabled him to have his operation. She guesses this must have been

Charles, although she does not learn this from him directly. When she meets Lily, while Roland is learning to walk again, using his new lightweight prosthetic, and realises who she is, she is certain. Poor Charles, she thinks, imagining he can right a wrong with money. So typical of him. But at least he has had the good grace not to re-enter Lily's life in person at this late stage. That would have been an insensitivity too awful to contemplate. Perhaps he is finally acquiring some tact and understanding. She decides she will invite him for supper. She will not of course refer to the anonymous donation. Instead she will suggest that perhaps they might occasionally accompany one another to a lecture, or a concert, as they once used to, while making it abundantly clear to him that he should expect nothing more than social intercourse.

She uses her new found influence as the Chair of Audiology to enquire if technical assistance might be needed in the University Mathematics Department, who are, she learns, engaged in the development of what is hoped might become the world's first stored-programme computer. Citing national interest she arranges for Roland to join the team of engineers working under the project's leaders, Frederick Williams, Tom Kilburn and Geoff Tootill, to assist with the *minutiae* of installing the hardware. Permission is granted and Roland is accordingly billeted in Delphine's spare room in her flat on Upper Brook Street, a short walk away from the University which, after his rehabilitation is complete, Roland is able to undertake.

For the next two years, while he waits for his formal

release papers to be processed, he continues to work on the project. Williams, Kilburn and Tootill christen the computer the *Manchester Baby*, and on the 21st June 1948 the team runs its first successful programme. They ask her to provide the highest proper divisor of 2 to the power of 18 – 262,144 – a calculation they know will take a long time to run, and so prove Baby's reliability, by testing every integer from 2^{18} downwards. The programme, which Roland has helped to devise, consists of seventeen separate instructions and takes fifty-two minutes to run, before reaching the correct answer of 131,072.

The mood in the team is jubilant. When Roland arrives back at Delphine's late that evening, a letter is waiting for him. It confirms that his repatriation papers have come through. A perfect synchronicity.

Because Roland has no wish to be repatriated, there then follows a further period in which he must complete more forms, applying for permission to remain in Britain as a permanent resident, with the longer term goal of acquiring naturalised British citizenship. But this is not so daunting, now he is no longer a prisoner of war. There are procedures which have been clearly established. He simply has to go to the Town Hall in Albert Square, where he must wait in a series of queues at different desks, in different rooms, on different floors, where papers are shuffled, stamped and clipped together.

By September it is all complete.

With the necessary documentation now in place, Roland is able to apply for a permanent position at the University as part of the new team being put together by

Williams, Kilburn and Tootill to develop the *Manchester Mark 1*, a prototype for what they hope will become the world's first commercially available computer. They hire him on the spot.

With the security of residency status and a job, Roland feels emboldened at last to formally ask Lily to marry him.

"I thought you'd never ask," she says, smiling.

"I wanted everything to be in place first," he says.

"I know."

"I could have been deported."

"I'd have followed you."

"Yes, I believe you would. But I would not have wanted that for you. Manchester is where we met…"

"Five years to the day…"

"Is it really?"

Lily nods.

"Yes, I suppose it must be…"

They look at each other, remembering.

"And so," he continues, "Manchester is where we should stay."

"Yes," she says.

"Yes – what?" he replies, a little confused.

"Yes, I will marry you."

He sighs, a deep exhalation that seems to carry with it a release of everything that has led to this moment.

Ejecting from the burning *Messerschmitt*, floating down by parachute over Salford, searchlights criss-crossing the night sky, crashing through the canopy of trees, being rescued by the boy Richie, the agonising fall to the icy ground, the crunch of his ankle as he landed, the nurse with the white shawl on her head who dressed his wounds.

The drive by ambulance to Melland Camp, seeing Lily for the first time, her red hair tumbling over her shoulders, their fingers touching, interlaced between the wire mesh of the perimeter fence, her daily visits ever since.

Five years.

He takes her in his arms and kisses her deeply.

He feels her strength flow through him.

To have and to hold. From this day forward. For better, for worse. For richer, for poorer. In sickness and in health. For as long as we both shall live.

Lily and Roland were married the Saturday before Christmas at St Paul's Methodist Church on Wilmslow Road, Didsbury.

George gave Lily away. Fred Williams agreed to be Roland's best man. Francis was there, Winifred and Victor, Delphine – not Charles, who steadfastly chose to remain anonymous and not intrude upon what was quintessentially Lily's day – Pearl and Lamarr, who had two children already, Lamarr Junior and Candice, Evelyn, now in her 89th year, Jenny and Miss Riall, Tom Kilburn and Geoff Tootill from the University, and as many of Lily's 'Blossoms' as could be contacted. The four currently staying in Lapwing Lane acted as her bridesmaids, under Pearl's benevolent supervision.

All sat spellbound as Jenny sang, with Miss Riall accompanying her, Mendelssohn's *Hear My Prayer*.

"The enemy shouteth, the godless come fast
Iniquity, hatred, upon me they cast
The wicked oppress me, ah where shall I fly?
Perplexed and bewildered, O God hear my cry…"

Her voice soared up through the vaulted nave of Henry Hill Vale's Victorian Gothic chapel.

"O for the wings, for the wings of a dove
Far away, far away would I rove
In the wilderness build me a nest
And remain there for ever at rest…"

It rose past the lancet windows, the gleaming colonnades and marble columns with their carved capitals towards the painted barrel roof depicting flights of birds, where the notes hung miraculous and pure.

Afterwards there was a light tea in the school room at the back, principally for the children, who Pearl had promised to look after for the rest of the evening, while Roland and Lily went to a supper arranged for them by Francis at *The Queen's Hotel*. George led the way on his DOT Bradshaw, while Lily followed after on the old DOT RS, which she still had the use of, so they rode in convoy from Didsbury to Piccadilly, George and Francis, Lily and Roland, like knights riding out to the lists.

When they pulled up outside the hotel's stone steps, Luigi was waiting for them. He presented Lily with a bunch of December tulips. It was a special night for Luigi too, for after half a century at *The Queen's*, tonight was his last night, but he had insisted on no fuss. "Tonight is your night, *Signora*," he said to Lily, as he escorted her to her table. He continued to serve them personally throughout the evening, ensuring that glasses were never empty, and course followed course in swift succession. In true Italian style, *la torta* was ceremonially carried to their table, a sparkler fizzing and crackling from its centre, to the accompaniment of a *tarantella* from the restaurant's accordionist.

Lily could feel her face glowing and Roland, she saw, was beginning to show signs of becoming tired. She gently tapped George's ankle with her foot under the table.

"Well," he said, interpreting her immediately, "I think, Francis, you and I are what Luigi might call *di troppo*."

"*Assolutamente*," chipped in Luigi, who had been hovering close by in anticipation of this moment. "*Signor, signora,*" he said, addressing Roland and Lily, "*in questo modo, se per favore.* This way, if you please…"

He gently pulled back Lily's chair as she rose, then guided her and Roland out of the restaurant, into the foyer, and up the main staircase to the first floor bridal suite. He opened the door and gestured for them to enter.

"I hope that everything is as you would wish, but please do not hesitate to ring down if there's anything you need." Inside the room he indicated a bottle of champagne. "With the compliments of *The Queen's Hotel*. I wish you a most pleasant evening. *Buona notte.*"

With that, he inclined his head and withdrew from the room, closing the door behind him. Outside he permitted himself a small smile before making his way, for the last time, along his nightly round of all the hotel's corridors, luxuriating in the pleasure its hushed, carpeted corridors and polished mahogany surfaces always gave him. His final call would be the Lounge Bar. He wanted to be sure to catch the last half hour of Cam's show this evening.

Inside the bridal suite, Lily and Roland looked at one another. It was the first time they had been alone together all night.

"You look tired," said Lily. "If you just want to sleep…"

Roland blushed. "I don't think I'm quite that tired…"

Lily smiled. "I'm glad…"

They began to get undressed, quietly and without hurry. Lily watched Roland carefully remove his prosthesis, wincing slightly as he did so. Lily went over to him.

"Is it very sore?" she asked.

"A little."

He took out from his small case a bottle of lotion, which he began to apply to the stump.

"Here," said Lily. "Let me."

Roland instinctively drew back.

"It's all right," she said. "I want to. We're married now. We can do these little things for each other."

"Not so little," he said.

She took the lotion from him, squeezed some into the palm of her left hand and gently began to apply it to his leg. Roland closed his eyes and sighed. I must tell him, she thought. I must tell him everything. It's only fair that he knows…

When she began, he took her hand in his and said very quietly that there was nothing she needed to tell him. Whatever may have happened in the past was exactly that, in the past, over, *aus und vorbei*.

But it's not, she said, over for me, not until I've told you. I need to… let it leave me somehow, *ein für alle Mal*, once and for all.

Wenn du musst, he says. But come to bed first. Let me hold you while you tell me.

She turns out the light and lays her head upon his chest. She takes a deep breath and begins.

She tells him everything, from the night she leaves St Bridget's to the night George finds her in the rain at Angel Meadow. She tells him all about Globe Lane, about Godwit, Snipe and Crake, about finding Laura's diary, about her midnight escape. She tells him about sleeping under the railway arches by the foul smelling banks of the River Irk. She tells him about the Twins, and the things that they made her do. She tells him that if it had not been for George and Hubert and Annie she would probably be dead. She feels him physically shudder at these words. After a long time, when she feels she has told him everything and missed nothing out, she stops.

He strokes her hair.

Eventually he says, these men you describe, they are monsters, they would have destroyed you, but you have not allowed them to, you have such strength, Lily, such courage, you take my breath away.

Hold me, she says.

He turns her to face him, kisses away the tears on her cheeks, then pulls her close. Now I understand properly, I think, the reason for the song Jenny sang in the church.

Thank you, she says.

They make slow, very gentle, tender love.

At one point, in the middle of it, she looks at him very seriously and says, I may not be able to have children.

He tells her it doesn't matter.

I love you, she says.

I love you. *Ich liebe dich.*

Afterwards, when they have finished and Roland has fallen asleep across her, she holds him to her, feels the weight of him, begins to learn the map of him. She is too happy to sleep.

Lily lies awake.

Below them Cam is singing her final song for the night. The notes drift up to Lily and Roland above.

> *"Long ago and far away, I dreamed a dream one day*
> *And now, that dream is here beside me*
> *Long, the skies were overcast, but now the clouds have passed*
> *You're here at last*
>
> *Chills run up and down my spine, Aladdin's lamp is mine*
> *The dream I dreamed was not denied me*
> *Just one look and then I knew*
> *That all I longed for long ago was you…"*

TWO

On The Shoulders of Giants

4

March 1953

"Good evening, Ladies and Gentlemen. This is the BBC Light Programme, bringing you this week's edition of 'Friday Night Is Music Night', featuring the BBC Concert Orchestra conducted by Gilbert Vinter. Tonight's programme is being broadcast live from the BBC Radio Theatre in Hulme, Manchester and, given that we are currently in the month of March, we thought we'd begin with one – the March from 'Little Suite' by Trevor Duncan."

Mary had finished the washing up and was just settling down, as she liked to do every Friday evening, to listen to the music on the wireless, while she busied herself with whatever sewing needed to be done. Jabez sat opposite, reading his latest book from the local library, *The Carnegie* in Levenshulme, where he went each Saturday morning by bus to read the newspaper and select his next book. Since he'd retired from mining completely, only working now in Philips Park, he had more time to read, and he was enjoying it. Lately he'd been purposefully making his way through the Victorian classics – Mrs Gaskell, Dickens, George Elliot, Trollope, and now Hardy. Only Gracie of their children still lived at home, but she was hardly ever there, not since she had started at the University to study Archaeology the previous year.

When she wasn't in lectures, she was usually out with her friends.

On Fridays, while her parents listened to Gilbert Vinter on the wireless, Gracie met up with her fellow students in *The Kardomah*, a café on St Ann's Square, listening to jazz and taking part in heated political debate. Designed by Sir Misha Black to permit both public forums and private, more intimate conversations around tables in corners, it provided the perfect backdrop for Gracie's growing up. Here she learned to smoke *Sobranie* cigarettes and drink black coffee. More importantly it taught her to hone her views and stand her ground, especially against the young men, who liked to hold court there, regarding the women who went as little more than acolytes. Gracie made it quite clear from the start she had no intention of playing that particular role. She was headstrong, determined and popular, a force of nature, trailing whirlwinds in her wake, so that Mary and Jabez enjoyed these quiet oases of calm on Friday nights, listening to the BBC Concert Orchestra in companionable silence.

On this particular evening Jabez was nearing the end of Thomas Hardy's *Far From The Madding Crowd*. He would occasionally read a passage out loud, something which he thought Mary might enjoy.

"This is Gabriel Oak," he said, "reminding Bathsheba Everdine of what he had said to her all those years before, when they first met, when he proposed to her and she turned him down, now that they are happily married at last at the end. 'And at home by the fire, whenever you look up, there I shall be – and whenever I look up, there shall you be'. Remind you of anyone we know, love?"

Mary smiled distractedly. She was preoccupied in counting stitches. Harriet had recently informed them that she and Paul were expecting a baby. Mary had immediately embarked upon a major knitting campaign. After more than eight years of marriage, she had thought that they mustn't be able to have children, so when Harriet told her one Sunday afternoon after she and Paul had come over for their weekly visit, she was thrilled. Toby and Sandra already had two boys, with a third baby expected soon, but Sandra had her own mother to go to about such matters, and Toby had never been much of a talker, and so, before Harriet told her the news, she had resigned herself never to have those kinds of mother-daughter conversations.

"Have you chosen names yet?" she asked excitedly.

Harriet smiled fondly at her mother, knowing how involved she wanted to be. She would not disappoint her. "If it's a boy, John Mark, and if it's a girl Maria Magdalena."

Mary beamed. "After both sets of grandparents in each case." It was so typically thoughtful of Harriet and Paul.

"Very nice," she said, absent-mindedly answering Jabez's question. "Damn. I've dropped a stitch. I'll have to unpick this part and start again."

Jabez shook his head. "Sorry," he said. "I shan't interrupt again. Shall I make a brew?"

"Ta, love," said Mary. "That'd be grand…"

"To honour the fact that the world's first ever passenger

railway service commenced right here in Manchester, our next piece is that perennial favourite 'Puffin' Billy' composed by Edward White, played for us once again by the BBC Concert Orchestra under the baton of Gilbert Vinter…"

Back in *The Kardomah* Gracie was in full flow.

The boys, who were all Science or Engineering students, were goading her. "What's the point of Archaeology?" harangued one of them – Stephen, who was in his final year of Physics, and who Gracie quite fancied, not that she'd ever let on, he had far too high an opinion of himself already, but she did rather like the way his fair hair had a habit of flopping recalcitrantly over one eye as he spoke, so that he would toss his head in a cocky, provocative way, rather like a palomino stallion.

"What's the point?!" argued Gracie, rising to his bait against all her better intentions. She knew he was only trying to rile her, and he knew that she knew, but somehow she could never help herself. "You might as well say what's the point of History."

"I do," he said, throwing back his golden forelock. "Who cares about the past? It's dead and buried. It's the future that matters now."

"Oh. And I suppose you think only Science holds the key to that?"

"Naturally."

"I wouldn't call it natural."

"No? What would you call it then?"

"Myopic. Narrow."

"I prefer 'focused'."

"Limited."

"Limitless."

"Self-interested, self-seeking, self-serving."

"Ever heard of Darwin? Survival of the fittest. Adapt or die."

"And how did Darwin come up with this theory?"

"Observation."

"Precisely. Observation of how things had been in the past."

"So he could reject them, throw them in the rubbish bin. Like all those useless so-called 'artefacts' you spend hours digging up from sewer pipes and building sites."

"What would you know about it?"

"I went on a dig once."

"What for, if you don't see the point in them?"

"I wasn't so sure at the time."

"Why's that then? Blinded by science, were you?"

"By love, actually."

"Ooh!"

"I had a girl friend I wanted to impress. I was imagining some ancient Bronze Age hill fort, or some remote Saxon burial mound. Instead, it was a demolition site in Wigan. They were going to build a multi-storey car park where there'd once been a school which had been bombed by the *Luftwaffe* – I bet those kids were chuffed when they turned up for assembly the next morning…" He knelt down dramatically, placing his hands together in mock prayer, and began to sing. "*Now thank we all our God…*"

"*With heart and hands and voices…*" his cronies all

joined in.

"You don't believe in God," said Gracie.

"I might have done had I been one of those kids."

"How convenient."

"God helps those who help themselves."

" '*Destiny doesn't always come when it's convenient, or when you think it should*'."

"Where's that from?"

"Elementary, my dear Watson."

"Which of course Holmes never actually said."

"Though he did say 'elementary', I do believe."

"Which is what this conversation is rapidly in danger of becoming."

"Oh? Is it a conversation? I rather thought it was a monologue."

"Which it would be – if you didn't keep interrupting me."

"It seems I've found my vocation."

"A poor player who struts and frets her hour upon the stage…"

"And then is heard no more…?"

Stephen playfully mimed zipping his lips, then turning a key. "Now where was I?"

"A multi-storey car park."

"A demolition site. I don't know what your experience of being on a dig has been, Gracie, but I expected an air of quiet, painstaking concentration, almost scientific in its method …"

"High praise indeed."

"But I was quickly disabused of such romantic notions. Instead of delicately scraping away the layers of dirt and soil from a Viking buckle or Celtic amulet with a tiny brush, we were issued with a pick axe and instructed to hack away for all we were worth at concrete flagstones, shovel the debris into barrows, which we had to wheel up a series of precarious planks, and then tip onto a large ground sheet, where the more 'qualified' members of the team would sift through it for treasure. It was more akin to working on a chain gang."

"What was your crime?"

"Gullibility."

"How did you plead?"

"Guilty."

"And what was the sentence?"

"Six weeks hard labour. That was the amount of time the dig was given before construction work began on the car park. I only stuck it a week. Less."

"Why was that? Couldn't stand the pace?"

"I came to my senses."

"We must be thankful for small mercies."

"One became so terribly cynical."

"*Vous? Impossible, n'est-ce pas? Pourquoi, s'il vous plaît?*"

"Everything we unearthed assumed near mystical significance. 'Oh look,' they'd say as we showed them a shard of cheap blue and white Victorian crockery, 'it's a Roman pot'. I started to take the piss…"

"*Quelle surprise!*"

" 'An Elizabethan Coca Cola bottle,' I'd say, or 'a medieval cigarette packet'. And I never did get my leg over."

"The pain of a man thwarted in love."

"So I ask you again, 'What's the point of Archaeology'?"

"Do you really want an answer?"

"If you've got one to give me?"

"Buy me another coffee first."

"No sooner asked than granted."

"Then I shall gladly oblige."

She downed the espresso in a single swallow, looked around at Stephen and all of his cronies egging her on, longing for her to fall flat on her face, and grinned. She loved these Friday night duels, the cut and thrust, the rapier wit – or so she liked to think their repartee amounted to – and at last she had her moment in the spotlight, her chance to impress. She hoped she would find the right words.

"Gentlemen – you claim that only science can solve the problems that we face at present, that only science can shape the future, yet was it not one of your own, Sir Isaac Newton no less, who said – and I'm sure he wasn't the first – that if he had indeed been 'able to see a little further', he did so 'only on the shoulders of giants'? If you are to formulate your plans for our future, gentlemen, you need first to understand the journey you and your far more illustrious forefathers have travelled before you to get where we are today. While you look through your ever more powerful telescopes deeper and deeper into space, think of me, and others like me, who prefer to look through the other end of those telescopes, back into the mists of time, to unlock the secrets of the past. We are not so different, I think, for the light you seek from the stars in other galaxies, has that not been travelling for millions of years already before you see it for yourselves? In that way you too are studying the past, are you not? And those tiny shards of broken pots you delight in mocking so readily, which I seek like pinpricks of light, tiny stars glinting in the earth, they have such stories to tell us, of the hands of those who first used them, first made them, first passed them on for others to use. Just as you seek to penetrate the smallest of things – the atoms, electrons and protons – in order to understand the very heart of matter, so it is with us, who scrape the soil for fragments of the past, tiny scraps of memory which help us trace a narrative, find a through line, from there to here. We all of us, I believe, want to make our mark upon the land, leave something of ourselves behind, if only a footprint, to say we were here, we once walked this same stretch of earth that you do now. So gentlemen, aspiring Jet Morgans all, who desire to 'journey into space', is that impulse any different from our ancestors? You search for life on other planets, so that you do not feel lost, or abandoned, in the vast emptiness of the universe. These minute and insignificant archaeological artefacts we find, which you take such pleasure to scoff at, speak so eloquently of this same deep yearning not to be alone. My father is a gardener. When I was a child, he taught me an important lesson. Our dog unearthed some bones beneath our feet. I was frightened – I thought they might be my bones in the future – but he simply dug them back into the ground. Without these bones, he said, the flowers can't grow nearly so well in the future."

She took a deep breath. She looked around at all the faces bent in concentration, hanging on her every word, and exhaled loudly with relief. She'd done it. She leaned across the table, picked up Stephen's glass of beer and took a long, satisfying swig from it.

"The thing is," said Stephen, taking back the glass and looking into it with a frown, "I'm not sure I want to go where others have been before me."

Gracie wiped her mouth with the back of her hand and grinned.

"We interrupt this broadcast, ladies and gentlemen, to bring news of an accident, which has just taken place at Bradford Colliery, one mile to the east of Manchester's city centre. We have very little by way of facts at this stage. We understand the emergency services are already at the scene, and we will bring you more information as soon as we have it. In the meantime we continue with Malcolm Arnold's sombre but ultimately uplifting 'English Dances'…"

Mary and Jabez were already on their feet.

"Toby," said Mary, fumbling with her coat. "He's on 'lates' this week. We'd better go."

"Ay," said Jabez gravely. "There's a bus from the corner in ten minutes…"

At the surface in the main yard of the pit, the emergency siren was blaring incessantly. People dropped whatever they were doing and made straight for the winding sheds.

"What the devil's going on?" demanded an anxiously perspiring Howard Findlay, the Mine Manager.

"The winding gear at the head of Parker Shaft has snapped," replied Patrick Kinsella, the Site Foreman. "A fire broke out and melted the cable."

"How in God's name did that happen?"

"I don't know, Mr Findlay. Electrical fault maybe?"

"And the cages?"

"Both crashed, sir. All the way to the bottom. No one was inside at the time.

"Thank Christ for that."

"Yes, sir. I was just preparing to send it down to bring the men back up to the surface for the end of the late shift, when I first saw the flames, sir."

"How many?"

"Sir?"

"How many men are down there?"

Three hundred and fifty, sir."

Findlay whistled loudly. "You're sure?"

"Yes, sir. I have their tallies here, sir."

Each miner carried two brass identity tags. These were kept at the surface. Before a man could enter the cage to take him down to the coal face, he had to surrender one of these tags, these tallies, to the Site Foreman, who hung them on numbered hooks, and take the other down with him. When he returned to the surface at the end of his shift, he returned this tag to its twin. With this simple routine, the Foreman would know exactly which men had come back up and which were still down below. The tallies were also useful in cases of identification in accidents where bodies were not recovered, though no one liked to speak of this. There had not been an incident at Bradford Pit since 1924, when the tubs transporting miners back to the surface derailed, dislodging a pit prop, causing a crump, a roof collapse, killing three and injuring nine.

"And you're certain that no one was inside the cage when it crashed?"

"Absolutely."

"Thank heavens…"

"The thing is, sir…"

"Yes, Patrick…?"

"There's no way of bringing them back to the surface. The cables have completely sheared. It will take days to repair them. We dismantled the old railroad after the 1924 crump, and in any case Parker Shaft's been deepened since then, so the old route's been blocked off."

"Damn."

"And one of the cages still had coal inside it. It was shortly after it came back to the surface when the fire started, so that more than twelve long tons will have spilled out everywhere when the cage hit the bottom. There's no way of knowing how much damage might have been caused."

"So no way of sending men down to help them either?

"Not easily, sir."

The men for the next shift had already begun to assemble in the yard, as were many women – wives, daughters, sisters, mothers – who, like Mary and Jabez, had heard the announcement on the radio.

"How in hell did the BBC get wind of it so fast?" demanding Findlay angrily, looking hard at Kinsella.

"Someone must have heard the siren and put two and two together, sir."

"And, as usual, made five."

"Yes, sir."

The team of Surface Engineers had by now extinguished the worst of the fire. A harsh back-up light illuminated the yard, throwing enormous, eerie shadows on to the wire perimeter fence. The police, fire and ambulance services had all arrived, adding their own bells, horns, klaxons and whistles to the overall chaos and cacophony, the revolving lights on the tops of their vehicles heightening the already nightmarish quality of the scene.

"Henry?" called Patrick to one of the Surface Engineers. "What's the verdict?"

"Completely buggered. The fire's burnt right through the winding gear. There's no way of lowering anything down…"

"Or bringing anyone up?" interrupted Findlay.

"No, sir."

"Your initial diagnosis has proved correct, Kinsella."

"It's worse than that, sir," said Henry. "The force of the crash is bound to have brought some of the structure housing the machinery down with it. I wouldn't be surprised, even if we could get down there, that the men would be unable to make their way through."

"Shit," said Patrick.

"Kinsella," said Findlay, "we must remain calm. Families have started to arrive. We need to be able to let them know what we intend to do as quickly as possible."

"Yes, sir."

"Now – somebody, fetch me a map showing all of the different seams and shafts."

"How far back?" said Henry.

"As far back as you can."

A few moments later they spread out a much creased, much revised map before them on the ground, weighting down each corner with a lump of coal. Patrick was wearing his underground miner's safety helmet and switched on its light, which raked across the chart.

"There," said Henry. "is Parker Number Two Shaft, where the Koepe Winding Gear has snapped, and here is Number One Shaft, by which the coal is brought up to the surface. Both of these are now out of action. But here," he said, pointing to a smaller, narrower shaft, "is where we used to gain access to the Crombouke Mine, before we sank the deeper Roger Mine…"

"The one opened by King Amanullah in 1928?" asked Findlay.

"Precisely so, sir."

"We still use that as a downcast, to carry air down into the pit. It requires regular maintenance and there's a set of iron ladders, which descends right to the bottom."

"How deep does it go?"

"Nine hundred yards."

"Just over half a mile."

"Yes, sir."

"And how far above Roger Mine is Crombouke Mine?"

"Just over twenty-two yards."

"And is there a connecting route between them still?"

"Yes, sir. There has to be. Because of the need for

ventilation. It's one of the old worked out seams from when Parker Shaft was first sunk in 1908. It's narrow, sir."

"How narrow?"

"Six feet."

Findlay nodded. "It's wide enough."

"And steep."

"How steep?"

"One in two, but it's solid."

"And only for twenty-two yards?"

"Yes, sir."

"No more than a cricket pitch."

"No, sir. I reckon the men, unless any of them are injured – and there's no reason to believe any of them have been…"

"Let's hope not."

"… should manage that easily enough, and then it's simply a case of bringing them up the set of iron ladders in the ventilation shaft in single file."

"Single file?"

"Yes, sir. The ladders were installed for maintenance purposes only. Normally just a couple of us go down together, one after the other, to check there's nothing obstructing the flow of air."

"I see."

"The thing is, sir…"

"Yes?"

"These ladders have never taken more than two at a time. We don't know how they'll hold up under the weight of three hundred and fifty climbing them."

"A *series* of ladders, you say?"

"Yes. Every twenty-five feet or so, you have to transfer from one side of the shaft to the other."

Findlay considered the implications. Now that he had all the facts at his disposal he became decisive.

"We'll have to risk it. No more than five men to a ladder at any one time. Henry, you go down there straight away. Take someone with you."

"I'd like to go, sir," said Patrick.

"No, Kinsella, I need you here. This is going to be a long night. Inform the emergency services of our plan, while I go and speak to the families. Henry, as soon as you've climbed down the ventilator shaft, make your way from Crombouke to Roger, locate the men – they'll have assembled as near to Parker Shaft 2 as they're able to get – then explain what's to be done. You stay down there with them and guide them back to the ladders, while whoever you take down with you, instruct him to return at once to the surface to report back to us that the plan can work. Once the men have made their way to the old, worked out seam, you lead the way and appoint someone you can trust down there to organise the men into teams of five to follow you up."

"Vic Collins," said Patrick. "He's the most senior man down there."

"Very good. Now, Henry – on your way."

"What if this plan doesn't work, sir?" asked Patrick as Henry headed off in the direction of the ventilation shaft on the far side of the colliery workings.

"We think of another," replied the Manager grimly.

In little more than three quarters of an hour Henry and his colleague, Melvyn, had reached the men underground. Neither had ever descended the series of ladders in the ventilation shaft so quickly before. His assumption about the men's whereabouts proved immediately correct. They were all gathered close to the site of the cage fall, which, as also predicted, had brought down with it a large amount of rock, coal and other debris. There was no way through to Parker Shaft.

Victor had already taken charge of the situation down below. The others naturally looked up to him.

"Henry," he said, "I don't know when I've ever been happier to see anyone, tha's a sight for sore eyes and no mistake. I could kiss thee!"

"Is everyone accounted for?"

"Three hundred and fifty, all present and correct."

"No injuries?"

"None. We were a couple of hundred yards away, working down different off-shoots and insets, when we heard an almighty rumble. There was no warning, nothing. A great cloud of dust poured down t' tunnels along t' seam to t' face, showering us wi' a load of muck, but nothing worse. When it cleared, we made our way in t' direction o' t' noise, and here we all are still."

"Right." He turned to Melvyn. "You go straight back up and tell Kinsella and Mr Findlay that all the men are safe and sound and accounted for."

Without another word, Melvyn was off.

"I'm assuming, Henry, that if tha's managed to find a way to us, we can all use that same road to make it back up to t' top?"

"Follow me," said Henry.

When they reached the steep, worn path of the old worked-out seam leading up from the Roger Mine to Crombouke, Henry explained to Victor what was to happen, which Victor passed onto the men.

"We have to squeeze through here," he said. "It's narrow and it's steep, but it's short. Little more than a cricket pitch." He paused, scanning the men for a particular face. "Ian," he called out to one of the youngest lads among them. "You go first. Don't look so worried. I've seen thee shinnin' over t' wall at Maine Road to get in to see City wi'out payin', so don't look so frit. Tha' secret's safe with me – and every other bugger 'ere. Tha' can climb like a bloody monkey, so you show 'em 'ow it's done. Then t' rest of you, follow on behind. Tha' can 'old onto each other's shirt tails if need be. Once tha' makes it through, tha' comes out onto a bit of a platform. That means tha's reached t' ventilation shaft, which all of us are going to climb up. There's ladders leading all t' way to t' top. Henry'll lead the way. Only five at a time, mind." He glanced around once more until he saw who he was looking for. "Joe?"

"Yes, Father?"

"You go on behind Ian and make sure there's never more 'n five on a ladder at any one time."

"Right, Father."

"And whoever 'appens to be t' last of each set, make sure no bugger gets on tha' ladder till tha's stepped off it and transferred to t' next one. Got that, everyone?"

"Yes, Vic," they all shouted back.

"Good lads. Right – I'll keep at t' back, make sure

tha's all squeezed through t' cricket pitch, then I'll see thee up top."

The men greeted this with a roar. Ian, followed by Joe, made his way into the steep, narrow opening, and Victor chivvied the rest of them, one by one, till they were all safely through and finally it was his turn.

When he reached the platform himself, he could just make out a couple of stars glinting in the sky above the opening at the summit of the ventilation shaft, half a mile above where he was standing. They would be their guide, something to cling on to. Second star to the right and straight on till morning. He hoped to God no cloud would come and cover them up. The thought of being plunged into total darkness while they transferred from one ladder to the next all the way up to the top was not a pleasant prospect. They had their helmet lights of course, but these might be confusing, all throwing different kinds of shadows dancing at criss-cross angles all at the same time. Probably best to have just one light for each group of five, he thought. A steady, slow procession of men was making its way with careful, painstaking deliberateness, a silent column of ants, bound by a common purpose, climbing the ninety separate ladders towards the top.

"Good lad," said Victor to his son, straightening himself up. "Tha's done a grand job, keeping' everyone calm. Who's left?"

"Just us," said Joe, pointing.

Victor looked around. As well as himself and Joe, only three more remained – Derek Blundell, Toby Chadwick and Lamarr Young. He nodded.

"Let's get going then," he said.

He was just placing his right foot on the first rung the iron ladder, when Joe put a hand on his arm.

"Wait," he said. "Henry said we've not to start till he reaches the surface."

"How're we going to know when 'e's done that?"

"This." Joe held up a walkie-talkie. "Henry gave it to me just before he started. He's got one too. He said he'd contact us as soon as he got to the top, so we could confirm that everyone had made it through to the platform and started on the ladder. Just in case. So if there was some kind of problem, he could alert the emergency services."

Victor looked at the radio with a degree of scepticism. "Let's hope it works. They're not t' most reliable o' things when tha's underground."

"That's what Henry said, but he hoped they might just be able to maintain contact in a straight line between down here and up there."

"Let's hope he's right."

"Otherwise, he said, that if he didn't manage to get through, we're to wait till the five people ahead of us have climbed the first twenty ladders – he should definitely have made it to the top by then – and if we've not heard from him by then to just get going."

"Fair enough. Where've they got to?"

"They've just crossed onto the tenth ladder," said Toby, who was peering up into the shaft. "I've been counting."

"Another ten to go then. Are we good? Derek? Joe? Toby? Lamarr?"

They each nodded in turn.

"thirsty," said Victor. "Time for a quick
 before we go, I reckon."

 the top from his water bottle and passed
 ...ck, who was crouching beside him. "Are you
 ..., mate?"

"Summat in my eye, that's all."

"Coal dust, I expect."

"Ay."

They sipped. They waited.

The walkie-talkie in Joe's hand sputtered briefly into life, crackled, then went silent.

Up at the surface more than three hours had passed since Henry and Melvyn had first descended into the ventilator shaft, and an hour and a half since Melvyn had returned with the news that all the men were safe and well. But now, a further hour and a half later, with still no sign of the first of them emerging from the shaft into starlit yard, the waiting families were becoming increasingly anxious.

Mary and Jabez had found Toby's wife, Sandra, almost as soon as they arrived.

"Who's looking after the boys?" asked Mary.

"My mother," said Sandra. "She came as soon as she heard the news."

It wasn't long before Gracie arrived too. "Luckily Stephen had his car," she said, introducing him to her parents. His fair complexion looked even paler than usual as he shook Jabez's hand. "You don't have to stay," said Gracie to him.

He took off his coat and wrapped it around her

shoulders. "Of course I'll stay," he said.

Now, an hour later, they were all standing as near to the ventilation shaft as they were allowed, several hundred pairs of eyes all fixed on the same spot, from where the men would appear, over the iron stanchion on the rim, where the last of the ladders finished.

They had all lit candles, which they held before them, as they stood in silent vigil. Somebody began to sing.

> "*Lord of the oceans and the sky above*
> *Whose wondrous grace has blessed us from our birth*
> *Look with compassion, and with love*
> *On all who toil beneath the earth…*"

Gresford. The traditional Miner's Hymn.

> "*They spend their lives in dark, with danger fraught*
> *Remote from nature's beauties, far below*
> *Winning the coal, oft dearly bought*
> *To drive the wheel, the hearth make glow.*

One by one, others joined in…

> "*Now we remember miners who have died*
> *Trapped in the darkness of the earth's cold womb*
> *Brave men to free them, vainly tried*
> *Still their work-place remained their tomb…*"

… until they all were singing.

> "*O you who with such marvellous design*
> *The world and all that is within did make*

*The lofty mountain and the mine
Hear our prayer for pity's sake..."*

A lone cornet continued the lament. It was played by Derek's grandfather, Harold, Esther's brother, on the instrument that had been his father's, the notes tracing a line down the years, home and the world, hanging on the moonlit air.

As the final note faded slowly into silence, a shout went up from the waiting crowd.

"Look!"

It was Henry, emerging from the top of the ventilation shaft, followed in solemn turn by a seemingly endless procession of exhausted men.

A great roar surged through the waiting families, succeeded by a spontaneous round of prolonged, relieved applause. As each of the men climbed out of the shaft, stumbling bleary-eyed into the bright arc-lit yard, they handed their tallies to the waiting Patrick, before crossing the rope which had been erected to keep those waiting a safe distance from the accident scene to be reunited with their loved ones.

And still they came, tumbling out of the mine like rolled dice, some with a leap of joy, some barely able to take another step, and some with the air of all in a day's work.

Patrick counted them down. "One hundred... two hundred... three hundred... and ten... and twenty... and thirty... and forty... one... two... three... four... five..."

Then nothing.

The last ant had been counted.

"Five still not accounted for, Mr Findlay."

"Are you certain?"

"I have the tallies, sir."

"They couldn't have been misplaced?"

"Not possible, sir."

"Who are we waiting for?"

Patrick double-checked.

"Blundell – Derek, Collins – Joe and Victor, Chadwick, Toby, and Young – Lamarr."

A great cry went up from Pearl, waiting alone in the yard.

All who had been rescued had stayed, waiting to make sure that all their work mates had made it back. Now, small knots of those still waiting to be reunited with a husband, a son, a brother or a father, stood apart from the rest. Winifred and Martha, for once united in their anxiety and concern, stood side by side. Mary, Jabez, Sandra and Gracie huddled close together, with Stephen standing respectfully a few feet to one side. Harold, still holding his trumpet, had spotted his son, Alan, among the men due to have gone down on the next shift, who had pointed towards Maureen, Derek's fiancée, standing by herself not knowing what to do. She and Derek had only been engaged a month. They were saving up for a June wedding. She wasn't from a mining family – Derek had met her at a dance at the *Levenshulme Palais* – so she didn't know what she was meant to do.

"Come here, lass," said Harold. "Stand wi' me an' Alan. 'Appen 'e's been delayed, that's all. I'll wager 'e'll be along soon."

Maureen looked at these two men she scarcely knew,

who were soon to become family to her, with shining eyes, grateful for their strength and understanding. "Do you really think so?" she asked tremulously.

Harold placed a big arm around her thin shoulders.

Pearl was still crying, trying to get past the rope preventing her from getting closer. Melvyn guided her back into the yard, where Winifred beckoned her over towards where she and Martha were standing.

At the head of the ventilation shaft Mr Findlay called over to Henry.

"What do you think can have happened?"

"I can't say, sir. I radioed down to them as soon as I reached the top. They didn't respond but that was probably cos the reception's unreliable that far down. I'm sure they'd've set off anyway. They should've been here half an hour ago. I've looked down into t' shaft, but it's still too dark. I could make out nothing."

Findlay nodded, taking this in. "We'd best send someone down to investigate."

"I'm on my way, sir."

"You've already been down once. We need a fresher pair of legs."

"No, sir. I'm fine."

Findlay regarded Henry closely. "Are you sure, lad?"

"Yes, sir."

"On your way then."

Back on the platform, at the bottom of the shaft, half a mile below the surface, the five men looked at the silent walkie-talkie in frustration.

"I told you those things couldn't work this far down," said Victor grimly.

Toby shook it impotently.

"I reckon we just get going," said Joe. "The fact that we heard it, if only for a second, suggests to me that Henry's made it to t' top and that 'e wants us to get started now. All 'e'd 'ave wanted from us was confirmation that everyone else had set off, and he'll find that out soon enough once they all start climbing up out o' t' shaft after 'im."

"Ay," said Victor. "That makes sense. Let's not 'ang about any longer."

"I'll just radio up to tell them," said Toby. "You never know – we may not be able to 'ear *him*, but *'e* might be able to 'ear *us*."

Victor nodded. "Be sharp, though."

Toby pressed the button to speak. "Henry? I don't know if you can hear this but we're just setting off. See you at t' top." He flipped the switch back to see if he might receive a reply. Nothing. An unintelligible crackle. Then silence once more.

"Right," said Victor. "Toby – you lead off. Then you, Derek. Then you, Joe. Then Lamarr. Then I'll follow on behind."

At once Toby began to climb. Derek set off a little less certainly. He paused after just a couple of steps to rub his right eye, but a quiet word from Joe got him moving again.

"Go on then," said Victor to Lamarr, who at the last moment switched positions and placed himself behind Victor. "What the…?"

"It's OK, Champ," said Lamarr. "I'll be your nickelback."

"What the 'ell's that when it's at 'ome?"

"It's a position in American Football, Champ. Last line of defence. Usually a big guy. Like me."

Victor chuckled. "OK, Nickelback. Let's go."

As Victor and Lamarr each stepped onto the ladder, a shower of dust fell on them from above. Further up, Derek had to pause again to rub his eye. In the lead, Toby felt a sudden lurch. Looking up, he thought he saw the point where the top of the first ladder was fixed to the wall of the shaft loosen and sway, showering more dust upon them.

"Whoa!" he said, trying to regain his balance.

"What's going on?" called up Joe.

"I'm not sure," said Toby, "but we need to get a move on. If we can all reach the top of this first ladder, then go up in two smaller groups from then on."

With his next step the ladder began to come away from the wall altogether, tipping it away from the vertical, while his next, alarmingly, saw it start to topple backwards. The combined weight of Lamarr and Victor at the bottom was now in danger of pulling the whole edifice down.

Toby scrambled quickly to the top, transferring to the second ladder, then stretching down his hand to haul Derek up after him. The second the two of them stepped off the first ladder, it crashed back to the opposite wall of the shaft, leaning at a precarious forty-five degree angle. It was now temporarily wedged. Joe had to manoeuvre himself around from where he found himself – hanging underneath the ladder – to its top side, which he was then able to clamber up to join Toby and Derek. Below them, the force of the ladder's collision with the shaft wall had momentarily winded Victor, all the breath knocked out of him as his body hit the rock and his left hand let go of the rung it had been holding. For a brief moment he was left dangling, until Lamarr caught hold of him and pulled him back to the ladder.

"Take your time, Champ," he said. "How're you doin'?"

Victor finally managed to speak. "Like being in t' ring wi' Len Johnson again," he grinned.

"Just hang on in there, Champ," said Lamarr. "The bell ain't rung for Round Two yet."

For several seconds they all stayed exactly where they were. Toby, Derek and Joe standing at the base of the second ladder, looking down towards Victor and Lamarr hanging like three-toed sloths from underneath the first.

"The weight of all the other men climbing up before us must've weakened the structure," whispered Toby to Joe. He gingerly tested the second. "This feels solid enough," he said, "but just to be on the safe side, I think we should go up one at a time from now on."

"Agreed," said Joe, "but how are we going to get these two up first?"

"We need to make room for them. I'll take Derek up with me, while you reach down and help those two up."

"Right."

"What's going on?" said Derek. "There's summat the matter wi' my eyes."

"What do you mean?" asked Toby.

"I can't keep 'em from wobblin'. Everything's a blur. Except for what's right in front o' me. But if I try to look any further, I get dizzy."

"Have you had this before?"

"Once or twice," said Derek. "Not like this though."

"Does anything make it go?"

"If I nod my head up and down a bit and tilt my eyes upwards, it gets a little easier."

"Can you see the rungs on the ladder in front of you?"

"Yes."

"Well just focus on those. One step at a time. Do you think you can do that?"

Derek nodded.

"Good. What we're going to do is this. You and I are going to climb up to t' third ladder. So we can make space for Victor and Lamarr on this one. Understand?"

"Yes," said Derek.

"Just you and me," continued Toby. "You'll go first, and I'll keep right behind you, to make sure you don't slip. Then, once we know that Victor and Lamarr are safe, we'll carry on up to t' top, where we'll get somebody to look at those eyes of yours, while I tell Henry what the situation is down here. All right?"

Derek nodded again.

"Off we go."

Joe watched Toby guide Derek up the second ladder one rung at a time. It held. He now turned his attention back to his father and Lamarr, still clinging on to the underside of the first.

"Father?" he called. "Got your breath back yet?"

"Just about."

"Lamarr?"

"Uh-huh."

"Right. You both need to get over to t' other side o' t' ladder, then crawl as carefully as tha' can towards me. No sudden movements. We don't want to risk jerking that ladder any more than we have to."

Victor and Lamarr looked at each other.

"You first, Nickleback."

"No way, man. I'm your back up. But don't take too long about it. I don't think I can stay upside down like this for much longer."

Victor hooked his right leg over the top of the ladder, using the momentum to swing himself round in a single movement, so that, before he knew it, he was lying prone, facing up the ladder towards where Joe was waiting for him with an outstretched arm.

"Thatta boy," cheered Lamarr."

"Now you," said Victor.

Lamarr attempted to copy what Victor had done, but as he swung around, the extra force of his weight dislodged the base of the ladder from where it had wedged against the shaft wall, so that the ladder was now dangling free in mid air. Joe reached as far as he could towards Victor without stepping onto the ladder itself, which would have surely brought it crashing down to the bottom. He strained every muscle and sinew as he inched ever closer to his father's outstretched hand. Just as their fingertips touched, he called out for one final effort.

"Reach!"

Victor made a last agonising stretch, but the effort was too much, throwing him off balance. He missed Joe's hand and began to slide off the ladder. Lamarr threw out his hand in a desperate lunge, catching hold of Victor's ankle just as he fell. He held on for as long as he could, while Victor dangled helplessly in mid air, but the combined weight of the two of them dragged Lamarr from the ladder, and they both fell the remaining twenty feet to the bottom, where they landed in a heap.

Joe scrambled back to the base of the second ladder, his eyes wild with shock. Toby called down from where he and Derek had reached the start of the third.

Neither Victor nor Lamarr moved.

Eventually, after what felt like a lifetime to Joe, they began to stir.

"Father," he shouted.

It was Lamarr who answered.

"Just give me a second, will you?"

Joe waited again. He tried to make out what was happening in the darkness below. He switched the light on his helmet back on, but he could still make out little, except a few, blurred shadows and a pair of quiet, muffled voices.

In a few moments, Lamarr called back.

"Well… we're alive… I reckon I've bust a couple of ribs, sprained my ankle… but your dad… he's not in such great shape… hurt his back… not got much feeling in his legs… we're going to need some help down here…"

Toby climbed down to rejoin Joe just in time to hear what Lamarr had said.

"We've got to find a different way out of here," he said.

"I'm not leaving Father," said Joe.

"No. Of course not. And I can't leave Derek. He's only just holding it together."

"What're we going to do?"

A voice suddenly hailed them from above. "Ahoy there!" It was Henry. "I just passed Derek. He said I'd find you here. Oh..." He stopped short as he reached them, taking in the collapsed ladder, Victor and Lamarr on the ground below. "When you didn't show up top, we guessed something bad must have happened."

"I need to get down there," said Joe.

"Here," said Henry. "I came prepared." He took out a length of rope from the rucksack on his back. "I'll just secure it to the base of the second ladder so you can climb down."

While Joe was making his way slowly towards the bottom, holding tight to the rope, walking his feet down the wall of the shaft, Toby turned to Henry. "We need a new plan," he said. "Victor's in a bad way down there, and Lamarr's not much better. We can't get him back to the surface this way. I was thinking about the new tunnel to Stuart Street Power Station. Perhaps we could put Victor and Lamarr into one of the conveyors that transport coal there directly. If we could get to there from here, that is. I'd need to join Joe down there, and the two of us would somehow have to carry Victor, with Lamarr managing as best he can."

"Yes, that might work," agreed Henry. "It's t' quickest an' most direct route out of t' mine. But getting there won't be easy. It's five hundred yards higher up than we are down 'ere." Toby could see him rapidly trying to calculate the best way of reaching it. "How well do you know the mine?"

Toby thought for a moment. "Not bad," he said. "Victor knows it best."

"Keep 'im awake then. Tell 'im to guide you towards Livesey's New Shaft."

"Livesey's? I've never heard of it."

"I expect Victor knows it. It were sunk in 1854 and it were still in use before t' Great War, when Victor first started 'ere. It's only eighteen foot wide, but it's not that steep. The men used to walk up an' down it in th' old days. It connects to Forge Pit, and then to Little Pit, two of th' oldest in t' mine. We've kept 'em open in case we ever needed to evacuate t' new tunnel."

"It's a good job tha' did."

"Ay. It's a long way, mind. I've brought down some extra water bottles. Here – take 'em. You'll need 'em. And summat else too. In case you need owt stronger." He gave Toby a wink.

"Thanks, Henry. Look after Derek, won't you? He's got summat wrong wi' 'is eyes. He just needs someone wi' 'im, that's all."

"Don't worry, he'll be fine wi' me. I'll let all t' families know you're safe. I expect Mr Findlay'll arrange for a car to take 'em down to Stuart Street in relays to wait for thee there. Good luck."

They shook hands. Toby loaded the water bottles into the haversack on his back, then slowly lowered himself by the rope into the gloom below. Henry watched him till he could no longer distinguish him from the other shadows before climbing back up the second ladder to where Derek was waiting for him.

Toby made his way carefully down the shaft. Just as he was passing the point where the bottom of the first ladder had broken away from its moorings and was still hanging precariously in the air, like a forgotten Christmas tree decoration, something caught his eye glinting from the wall. He halted his progress, planted the soles of his boots firmly against the shaft wall, and pulled himself right up to the face with the rope.

There, protruding slightly from the hole left by the ladder's fixings, was a small silver coin. He delicately removed it with the thumb and forefinger of his left hand and brought it up close to inspect it further. It was covered in dirt, which he partially scraped away, to reveal the unmistakable head of a man garlanded with a wreath of laurel. An emperor. Fuck me, he thought. It's Roman. I must show this to our Gracie when I get out of here. And that thought gave him renewed hope. Gracie. His fearless sister. That she'd be out there, waiting for him, along with Sandra and his parents. And he knew, in that moment, they were going to make it.

Those still at the surface waited through the night, watched the stars fade and the sun rise. Mr Findlay did indeed arrange for them to be taken across to the power station at Stuart Street, not far from Philips Park. Stephen, who'd followed them there in his Triumph Vitesse, agreed to go and fetch Harriet, it being a Saturday morning. Mary had not wanted her to be standing all night, not now she was pregnant, but she worried she and Paul might make a wasted journey to the pit now that it had got light.

Harriet arrived with a thermos of hot coffee, which was shared around the dozen or so family members all still anxiously waiting for news.

The hours crawled by.

A few reporters, photographers, cameramen and broadcasters, who had alighted at the scene like vultures, drawn by the prospect of carrion, maintained a watchful distance.

Inside the power station, all was unusually quiet. The coal conveyor had emptied its last two hundred ton load before retreating back down into the darkness to await the hoped for arrival of Victor, Joe, Toby and Lamarr, to transport them back to the surface, once – if – they had reached the other end of the tunnel. All production had ceased in the meantime, and an unnatural calm had descended, at odds with the tension of all those waiting. The electric generator crackled and hummed above their heads.

Harold handed his cornet to Derek, who'd insisted he joined the wait for his friends, once Henry had safely escorted him back up the long series of ladders in the ventilation shaft to the surface. He took the cornet from his grandfather with a nod of recognition and began to play, a haunting, yearning refrain, almost as if he was trying to conjure the men out of the air with the notes that hung and danced upon the wind. From a pipe beside the tunnel four rats cautiously lifted their heads, eyes blinking in the unaccustomed light.

Toby put the Roman coin into his pocket. By the time he reached the bottom, Joe was trying to get his father to sit up.

"It's my back," he said weakly.

"Can you move your arms, waggle your fingers?"

He could.

"What about your legs?"

Nothing.

"Try again."

Victor shook his head.

Joe looked anxiously over his shoulder at Toby.

"Try flicking the side of his knees."

Joe nodded.

"Can you feel this, Father?" he asked.

Victor smiled. "Yes," he said. "Now take off my boots."

Joe unlaced one of them and gently pulled it off.

"Look," said Victor.

With a supreme effort of will, he just managed to flex his toes in a slightly upward direction.

"That's a good sign," said Joe, placing the foot back inside the boot.

"We need to get down through the cricket pitch and back to the main part of Roger Mine," said Toby. "Victor? Lamarr? Do you think you might be able to drag yourselves through it. It's too low and narrow for Joe and me to be able to carry you. Once we're down there, we'll figure out something better."

"Sure," said Lamarr and he immediately began to slide himself down on his back through the opening.

"Nothing ventured," said Victor. "If you two can get

me as far as th' entrance, I reckon I might just slide t' rest o' t' way."

Joe went on ahead, followed by Lamarr, then Victor, with Toby at the rear. Lamarr winced as he tumbled through, while Victor had to be pulled from in front and pushed from behind the whole twenty-two yards. When he emerged back onto the floor of the mine, he was ashen.

"This won't do," said Toby quietly to Joe, out of earshot of the other two. "You stay here, bind Lamarr's ankle as tightly as you can – use his shirt if you have to – then get Victor as comfortable as you can."

"What're you going to do?"

"Try and find a coal cart. There's no other way of moving them. Not the distance we've got to cover."

He came back a few minutes later with one of the small tubs they used for pushing heavier tools – jackhammers, drills, slicers, cutters – right up to the coal face, and for bringing the smaller bits of loose coal back. Taking great care they lifted and then very gently lowered Victor inside. Compared to the two hundredweight of coal the tub could carry, Victor was light to push.

"What about you, Lamarr?" asked Toby. "Can you manage to walk?"

"If I don't put no weight on the ankle, maybe lean on this old coal cart a while, I reckon I can."

Toby explained again what they were aiming to do.

Victor nodded. "I remember Livesey's," he said. "I pushed heavier tubs than this up there when I were younger, and I think I'll recognise a few short cuts along t' way." He was in considerable pain, they could tell, but he was damned if he was going to show it. He thought of that time in the ring with Len Johnson. Somehow he'd managed to keep going till the final bell. He'd do so again now.

They set off. Branching off from Roger Mine was an unnamed seam leading to the old Bradford Four Feet Mine.

"This used to be t' deepest seam when I started," said Victor. "Look out for t' bands o' shale an' fireclay in t' rock. They act as a guide. Just keep going up."

When they reached the first shale, they followed the narrower path to the left, which rose slightly more steeply than the one to the right.

"Three Quarters Mine," said Victor.

When the shale gave way to fireclay, they once again took the higher path.

"Charlotte Mine."

Half a mile further, they reached a second band of shale.

"Openshaw Mine."

This was the last of the Bradford Group, the network of mines sunk in the 19th century, which sat above the later, deeper Parker, Crombouke and Roger Mines. As they crossed from one seam to another, making their way slowly up towards the surface, they passed several tantalising, but encouraging, signs – old, abandoned workings, too narrow, too steep and too unstable for them to even contemplate attempting, but at the tops of which, if they craned their necks and looked up, distant pinpricks of light glinted and danced.

Toby fingered the Roman coin in his pocket. The higher they climbed, and the nearer to the surface they reached, the further back in time they stretched. It was humbling to think that people had been mining here since Roman times. The earliest record of the mine was a document recording its purchase, in 1610 during the reign of King James I, by one Thomas Charnock for £300. Toby knew this, because he'd seen a framed copy of it on the wall in Mr Findlay's office, when he'd been offered the chance of a management job, which he'd politely turned down. He preferred to be with his mates, underground, sharing the banter. Mr Findlay was all right, they had no complaints, but it would always be a case of 'us' against 'them', and Toby wanted to remain one of 'us'. Mr Findlay had shaken his hand and said he understood. He too had felt like that once upon a time, and if ever Toby might change his mind, his – Mr Findlay's – door would always be open. Toby had thanked him, and taken him up on his offer of a cigar. After all, why not? It was then that Mr Findlay had talked about the history of the pit.

"Where we're standing now," he had said, "used to be Bradford Manor. There are records of a pit being dug on the estate more than sixty feet deep as long ago as Tudor times. Just imagine, Toby. More than four hundred years of mining on this very spot…"

And Toby thought about it again, now, as they passed evidence of the lives of all those who had passed this way before them. Initials carved in the rock walls, and dates. John Seddon, 1740. Toby remembered a second framed document on the wall in Mr Findlay's office.

'I, Lord Mosley of Ancoats Hall, do lease to Mr John Seddon of Manchester, on this day, the 21st of October,

1740, the mines and veins, seams and beds of coal kannel to be found in the land around Bradford. In return Mr John Seddon does hereby agree to pay Lord Mosley the sum of £50 per annum for such coal as can be raised by ten hewers...'

Then more, later initials. EB, followed by the year, 1870.

Toby wondered if this might be the legendary Edward Bryan, whose story every miner who worked at Bradford knew from the moment he carried his first snap tin. Until that year, the small villages of Bradford, Clayton and Beswick provided all of the colliery's work force, when one day, it was said, Edward Bryan and his six sons arrived from Pendleton, having walked there to seek work. Only five miles but a whole world away back then. The local miners were so suspicious of these new, strange folk, that they refused to go down the pit for a day, until they'd had chance to have a proper look at them, thus initiating the first recorded strike. How times change, thought Toby with a smile, and for the better, looking back at Lamarr, who was still gamely keeping up with them as they continued to journey upwards through time.

"I don't know about you," said Toby, "but I could do with a breather."

"Going soft, are you?" wheezed Victor.

Lamarr merely gave him a playful cuff on the arm, before slumping down to the ground. He loosened the cloth around his ankle, which had swollen considerably. Joe shot Toby a look of concern, which Lamarr clocked.

"Don't worry, boys. I'll be OK." He took a sip of water. "I don't suppose anyone's got anything a bit stronger?"

"It just might be that today's your lucky day," laughed Toby, holding out the small hip flask that Henry had given him just before they'd parted company and waving it from side to side.

"That's just what I've been thinking ever since the cages crashed," grinned Lamarr. 'My lucky day'."

"Just take a swig an' pass it over," said Victor.

Joe re-tied Lamarr's bandage, while Toby carved their initials with a piece of coal into the rock face to join the centuries of others – JC, VC, TC, LY. After a few more minutes, they started up again.

They were now approaching Forge Pit and Little Pit. Sunk in the 19th century, during the height of the Industrial Revolution, these were the first of the deep mines, each penetrating several hundred yards below the surface. Underground railroads were constructed around the same time, connecting Bradford Colliery with other pits, in Ashton, Moston and Harpurhey, stretching for several miles below the surface, as the mine merged with its competitors to form Manchester Collieries Limited, a name it retained until nationalisation just a few years before, when it reverted to Bradford Colliery under the auspices of the National Coal Board.

They followed the railroad for almost an hour, until they finally reached a narrow opening on the left.

"This is it," said Victor, "Livesey's New Shaft. Dun't look so new now, does it?"

"Will we fit?" said Joe.

"Ay," said Victor. "This first part's a bit of a squeeze, but it opens up after that, an' levels off for a while too."

It took Joe and Toby the best part of a further half hour to manage to push the coal cart up the steep incline at the entrance to Livesey's. It was clearly difficult for Lamarr, who leant heavily on the cart to support himself, adding even extra weight for Toby and Joe to have to push. Eventually they made it and, as Victor had promised, the passageway widened and flattened a little at this point. They made slow but steady progress for another hour, but Victor was starting to become anxious.

"What is it, Father?" asked Joe.

"I think we might've missed our next turn," he said. "We should've reached it by now."

"What are we looking for?"

"It's another narrow gap, where Livesey's was linked to two horizon tunnels. One connecting to Ashton Moss Colliery, three an' a quarter miles away, t' other to Moston Pit two miles in th' opposite direction."

Lamarr groaned loudly. "There's no way I can walk that far, man."

"Tha' won't have to. These were all built to join everything up. We need to take t' tunnel to Moston for no more than a hundred yards or so, where we can turn into t' one we want."

"To Stuart Street Power Station?" said Toby.

"Ay," said Victor, "and that's nobbut half a mile all t' way to t' top. It passes straight under Mill Street and t' canal. Then we're there. But we've missed the turning into t' horizon tunnel, I'm sure of it."

"What should we do?" said Joe.

"We can't risk turning back, in case we 'aven't reached it yet. We've been walking for hours, it's easy to get confused."

"Tell you what," said Joe. "You all wait here. I'll run back t' way we've just come to see if I can find it."

"How far back will you go?"

"As far as the entrance to Livesey's. Then I'll come back. If I find it, then we'll all head for that. If not, we keep pressing on."

"Right," said Toby grimly. "Don't take too long."

"Look for t' shale," said Victor. "Shale'll show thee."

Joe ran off. He tried switching the light on his helmet back on, but the battery had died. In less than fifty yards, they could no longer see him. In another fifty after that, they could no longer hear him.

They waited. None of them spoke.

Finally, after what seemed an archaeological age, they began to hear his footsteps running back towards them.

"He's coming," said Toby, and they all audibly breathed out.

"You were right, Father," said Joe, excitedly catching his own breath. "We did miss it. I followed the shale. Just like you said. And I found it. A narrow opening."

"Will the cart fit through?" interrupted Toby.

"Ay," said Joe. "I reckon it will. And then it opens out into a wide, flat road."

They each gave a whoop of joy, then followed Joe back along the sloping shaft, Toby and Lamarr taking care not to let the cart run away from them. They quickly reached the gap. Joe was right. There was just enough room for the cart. Once they'd made it through, they stepped into a high, wide, cylindrical tunnel, stretching beyond sight in either direction.

"I see why they call 'em Horizon Tunnels," said Toby. "Which way do we take, Victor?"

"Left, lad. Always left."

They began to push the cart alongside the rails, which would normally convey the tons of coal between the different mines, when Lamarr stumbled and fell.

"Sorry, boys, but I'm done in. I don't reckon I can walk another step."

Joe looked down at his ankle, which had swollen to the size of a cricket ball. "He's right," he said to Toby, "and there isn't room inside t' coal cart for Lamarr as well as Victor."

Toby looked about him. Propped up against the wall on the opposite side of the rail track was a stack of offcuts from old railway sleepers. "Like I said before, Lamarr, it looks like this is your lucky day."

"I ain't in the mood for your jokes no more," he grunted. He was beginning to wish he'd not left the security of Crossley's five years ago, where he'd first worked after the War, to delve deep in these underground mines. The pay may have been worse and the banter nowhere near as quickfire, but at least he knew where he was each day, and the worst that could happen to him was a trapped finger in one of the lathes.

Toby and Joe selected a couple of the offcuts which roughly corresponded to the width of the cart and placed them across the top, towards the front edge.

"Victor," he said, "try and make sure tha's as far to t' back o' t' cart as tha' can." Victor painfully manoeuvred himself back a few inches. "Now Joe," continued Toby, "can you help to lift Lamarr so 'e can perch on top o' those sleepers at t' front, while I lean all my weight on to t' bar at t' back 'ere, to act as a counter balance. Then, as soon as Lamarr is secure, you come round to join me 'ere and, between us, we might just about manage to push the thing forward."

After a couple of unsuccessful attempts, when Lamarr threatened to tip the whole cart sideways, Joe eventually succeeded in getting him aboard.

"Right," said Toby. "Are we all set?"

"I feel like I'm driving a chariot," said Lamarr.

"Hold on tight," said Toby.

"Ay," muttered Victor. "Chocks away."

"Here we go."

Exerting what little strength they had left, Toby and Joe managed to move the cart forward. Once the wheels had started to turn, they were able to keep it moving more easily than they had feared. There were no thoughts now of transferring to one of the newer coal conveyors. They'd never be able to lift Victor and Lamarr a second time.

"How far to t' turning, Father?" asked Joe.

"A couple of hundred yards, that's all," said Victor. "Second turn to the left then straight on till morning."

"More likely afternoon by the time we make it," said Toby.

"D'you think so?" said Joe. "I've lost all track o' time down 'ere in t' dark. How long has it been?"

"Feels like years," replied Victor from inside the cart.

A few minutes later they reached the turning into the last tunnel, the one which led the final half mile directly into the Stuart Street Power Station. It was going to be a long, hard push. An unforgiving one-in-eight incline all the way. By now the lamps on all their helmets had given out, one by one, but in the distance, when they looked up, they could just make out the faintest glimmering of light, which marked their destination, a pale silver disc, no larger from where they stood than the Roman coin in Toby's pocket.

Joe and Toby pushed.

One yard at a time.

More and more often they had to pause, wait, while they got their breath back, had another small swallow of water, till their strength returned. Then they would set off again, each yard more difficult than the last.

Joe and Toby pushed once more.

Push, pause. Push, pause.

It was gruelling work, but it was a straight climb and, little by little, they slowly ground their way towards the silver disc at the tunnel's end, which imperceptibly grew larger and lighter with each painful step they took.

A sixpence. A shilling. A florin. A half crown.

They looked at each other and nodded. Yes. They were sure they would make it now. They leant their shoulders once more against the bar at the back of the cart and pushed again.

Now that they knew this, that they would, the four of them, reach the surface at last, a silence fell upon them, each giving themselves to their own private thoughts.

Lamarr gripped the sides of the sleepers on which he sat so hard that his knuckles were white through his blue-black skin. Victor had fallen into a troubled, rasping sleep. Joe looked down on him inside the cart, trying to wish away the time between now and when they could finally get him looked at by a doctor.

Toby marvelled at the construction of the tunnel through which they made their slow progress. The differently coloured striations of rock, the compressed pile upon pile of sediment, layer upon layer of history. Shale and fireclay, shale and fireclay. It seemed to him that not only were they moving from darkness back into light, but through time itself. Roman, Tudor, Jacobean.

Georgian, Victorian, Edwardian.

Right up to the present day, this moment, now, placing one foot in front of the other.

The found coin burned in his pocket.

The tunnel passed beneath the Ashton Canal, right under Mill Street. He found it hard to equate that directly over his head was the house in Philips Park he'd lived in as a child. Maybe it was the effect of the canal above him, maybe it was his imagination, or maybe a kind of delirium brought on by sheer fatigue, but the walls around him appeared to shimmer and ripple, like reflected water. They no longer seemed solid. It was as though he could see through them, past the layers of shale and fireclay. He saw the ghosts of men hewing the coal by hand. He saw them being hauled to the surface in wicker baskets. He saw different men, with picks and shovels, hacking at the seam. He saw whole armies of miners, crawling through tunnels on hands and knees. Each in turn stopped to look at him as he passed. They waved. They smiled. They raised their thumbs, they clapped their hands, urging them on. Thousands of them stamping their boots on the hard, packed earth. He felt their vibration rumbling beneath his own feet. The silver disc at the end of the tunnel grew larger. He sensed their hands on his back now, giving him and Joe the one last push they needed to make it. He heard their applause resounding through the rock, their roaring voices ringing in his ears. The silver disc exploded all around him as they broke through from darkness into light at last.

By the middle of Saturday afternoon, the crowd at the entrance to the Stuart Street Power Station had grown to more than two thousand as word had spread that this was where the last four survivors hoped to emerge from their ordeal underground.

Winifred and Martha had stood shoulder to shoulder for almost eighteen hours. Maureen had been clinging to Derek's side from the moment he'd been rescued and had vowed she would never leave it. Sandra's mother had brought the two children, Michael and Mildred, who played marbles in a corner of the yard, unaware of the day's significance. Sitting on the wall, her stomach somersaulting with a mixture of worry and morning sickness, which seemed to affect her in the afternoons and evenings too, Harriet watched the children play, wondering how Sandra was managing to appear so calm, while there was still no news of Toby. Paul stood beside her, his arm wrapped tightly round her shoulders. Pearl, who had hurried home to fetch Lamarr Junior, Candice and Dwight, and who had been keeping up a near non-stop running commentary ever since she'd come back, had finally grown silent, her eyes fixed on the opening to the tunnel. Mary and Jabez, living so close, had been back home more than once, and now Mary was handing round mugs of tea from a freshly refilled thermos.

A wedding car drove slowly by along Stuart Street, conveying a veiled bride and her proud father to St Jerome's Church, which provided a brief, but welcome diversion.

Gracie, despite the ache in her leg, would not sit down, and Stephen had long since given up trying to persuade her. She paced up and down, venturing ever closer to the tunnel's entrance, where now she stood, framed in the centre of its circular opening, peering deep into the darkness for any sign they might be on their way.

She heard them before she saw them.

The uneven, clinking, metallic roll of a coal cart trundling, unbalanced and heavy, along the compressed bed of gravelled shale between the rails in the tunnel.

She flung her arms into the air, hissing at everyone to be quiet. Instantly everyone was still. Even the children stopped their marbles. They waited. Nerves as taut as the overhead power lines. Gracie heard again the sound of the trundling coal cart.

"H-e-l-l-o…?" she called.

"Whoop-whoop-whoo…!" came a distant cry from within the tunnel.

"Whoop-whoop-whoo…!" echoed the thousands waiting outside the power station, who then burst into a spontaneous round of cheering and applause, which, back inside the tunnel, the four miners could feel as much as hear, like a wall of water engulfing them, and which continued right until the coal cart at last broke into the yard, Lamarr waving from the front like a charioteer. Joe and Toby slowly straightened themselves up from where they'd been bent over the metal bar at the back, blinking in the sunlight.

The church bells at St Jerome's began to peal as the wedding couple left the church.

Victor, hearing them as he woke, looked up at the others and managed a thin smile. "The end of the bout," he said. "I reckon we just about won on points."

5

October 1953

Low autumn clouds scudded across the Manchester sky. A light rain had begun to fall, gently pattering on the tarpaulin sheets erected on poles to protect the site. Dr Michael Neville, Head of the University's Archaeology Department, had been planning the dig for months. Permissions had been sought and granted from the various authorities, funds had been raised, his team had been assembled, and the initial heavy work of removing the top six feet of concrete and other layers from the site had been completed. Now the serious archaeology could begin.

The site lay in Castlefield, a square of land bounded by Liverpool Road to the north, Deansgate, the River Medlock and the Bridgewater Viaduct to the east, Cornbrook and the elevated railway to the south, and Potato Wharf, the River Irwell and the edge of Pomona Docks to the west.

It had long been known that the remains of a Roman fort were here, together with evidence of a Temple to Mithras. Several major artefacts had been found over the years, but no systematic mapping as yet had ever been undertaken to determine either the extent of the settlement, the way it must surely have evolved during the four and a half centuries of occupation, or the subsequent changes it must have undergone following withdrawal, when Manchester was not abandoned, but absorbed into the indigenous communities of the earlier Celtic tribes who still remained – the *Brigantes* and *Settanti*.

Dr Neville hoped to establish a timeline.

He gathered his team together for one final pep talk. They stood beneath the tarpaulin sheet, as the rain slanted in from the west, looking down at the rectangle of prepared ground waiting for them below. Two hundred yards by one hundred and twenty. Already marked up into rows of gridded squares, each to be allocated to an individual member of the team, to scrape and sieve every square inch of.

"Today is a most auspicious day," said Dr Neville, almost overcome with emotion after his many battles with the Corporation, the Ship Canal Company, the Port of Manchester, the British Waterways Authority and various private landlords and factory owners to reach this moment. "We stand, quite literally, on the brink of history. Below you, now that the layers of centuries have been removed, is the same earth trodden by our ancestors, the Romans and Celts. Soon each of you will be standing on that very soil. You all know your tasks and responsibilities. You have your kit bag of tools, trowels and brushes. If any of you unearths anything, raise your hand at once, blow your whistle, and stand away to one side. Either I, or my assistant, Angela, will be with you within seconds…" A woman in her forties, with long grey hair and thick pebble glasses, who clearly idolised Dr Neville, waved enthusiastically to the rest of the team. "We will then ascertain whether or not what you have uncovered is of value, ready to photograph it *in situ*, extract it if necessary, label it, annotate it in the dig's log, remove it to my tent over there, where it can be further studied. Any questions?"

There were none. The rain, if anything, had become heavier.

"Excellent. Now, before we begin, to mark the dig with due ceremony, I ask you all to raise the small beakers each of you has in front of you to drink a toast to our success. Angela?"

"Thank you, Dr Neville. It's a special kind of mead – that's beer mixed with a bit of honey." She raised her beaker. *"Sláintë!"* she proclaimed. "That's a Celtic word for 'success'. I thought it most appropriate."

"Sláintë!" they all shouted, in varying degrees of enthusiasm. A number of the team pulled a face as they tasted Angela's home brewed mead, but did their best to hide it, for everyone was excited at the prospect of the next six weeks that had been offered them as a window for the dig.

"Thank you, Angela," said Dr Neville. "So – good luck, everyone. To your posts."

Gracie, now in the final year of her degree, walked to her post with barely contained excitement. This was the first really serious dig she had been on, and she was the only undergraduate to have been selected.

She reached her allocated square, took the trowel out of her kit bag, knelt down, not noticing the rain, and began gently to dig.

Miraculously, within less than two minutes, she struck something solid. Using the techniques she'd been taught on various Field Study courses, she scraped away the soil until she reached the object her trowel had made initial contact with. It was bone. Almost certain it would prove to be animal, she scraped further. The bone was large. She scraped away more. There was no doubt now. This was human. An acromion. The shoulder. And it had been shattered by what must have been a heavy blow.

She stood up, as instructed, raised her hand and blew her whistle.

Dr Neville was by her side within seconds.

But as soon as he saw what Gracie had unearthed, he stopped abruptly, almost overbalancing in his haste.

"This is encouraging," he said. "There's a possibility there may be other bones close by. The last thing I want to do is risk any possible damage by adding my weight to the grid where you're standing, Gracie. So – what I want you to do is to keep digging and scraping very, very carefully, following my instructions as you go. Got that?"

"Yes, Dr Neville."

Breathlessly, she lowered herself back down, making sure her leg with the calliper stretched away from the grid. She began once more to scrape away the soil with her hands.

Nothing, in all the years that followed, or on any of the other digs she took part in, either as a member of the team, or as Director of her own unit, which is what she would become, ever compared with the visceral thrill of this first discovery. When her fingers touched the bone of another human, whose body had been laid in this very spot, more than one and a half millennia before, she felt that she was touching time itself, reaching deep inside a clock, to hold its stopped heart and make it tick once more. It was what she had been born to do.

Over the next several hours, the whole dig gathered round Gracie as she brushed away the particles of soil, speck by speck, atom by atom, to uncover bone after bone after bone, until the complete skeleton of a young man lay revealed before them. He appeared to have met a most violent death, with several of his bones smashed and broken, not by the ravages of time, but by a series of vicious attacks.

When she at last brought up the fractured skull, there was a collective gasp from the team. She placed it back in exactly the position she had found it. Just as she was about to stand up, thinking she had finished, the knee of her weaker leg, brushed against something just a few inches below the surface by the side of the skeleton.

Dr Neville held up his hand for silence once more. He looked at Gracie, as if to ask, "Can you continue for a little longer?" She nodded.

Carefully adjusting her position, so that her leg did not further disturb the soil where it had been resting, Gracie began again the painstaking process of digging and scraping.

It was a shield. Constructed of oak and lime, covered with leather, and strengthened with bronze. Crudely painted in the centre of the metal, almost worn away from its years in the ground, but unmistakable nevertheless, was the faded outline of a bee.

The next few hours were pandemonium.

Gracie was interviewed and photographed by dozens

of journalists, radio presenters and television reporters. At every turn she deferred respectfully to Dr Neville, who was able to describe in detail the nature and significance of the find, but it was Gracie they returned to again and again.

"How did it feel...?" they asked. "What did you think it was at first...?"

"What will you do next...?

"Just one more smile please for the camera..."

THE TIMES

Tuesday 6th October 1953

STUDENT MAKES SENSATIONAL FIND IN MANCHESTER DIG

Clear Evidence of Romano-British Settlement in Castlefield

Twenty year old University undergraduate Grace Chadwick of Philips Park, Manchester (pictured below) yesterday uncovered what may turn out to be the most important archaeological find in Britain since the discovery of the Sutton Hoo helmet....

*

The next morning Gracie got up early. She cycled to the newsagent's on Forge Lane to buy a copy of *The Times*.

"Someone's up with the lark," said Mrs Clark, the proprietor's wife. She was a tiny woman who had the disconcerting habit of peering at customers fiercely over the rim of her spectacles. But she always had a kind word for the children whenever they came in, never minding how long they lingered in deciding how they would spend their precious penny pocket money. With sweets from a farthing each, this required serious consideration, and Mrs Clark allowed them all the time they needed. She had especially fond memories of Gracie frowning furiously as she weighed up the pros and cons of pear drops as opposed to fruit gums.

Her husband, Mr Clark, was as large as she was small. He reminded the children of Mr Tubby Bear in Enid Blyton's Noddy books. Gracie had wondered, like they all did, whether, if he pressed his tummy, he might growl. As Gracie entered the shop, he was busy cutting the string from the bundles of newspapers which had just been delivered smartly with a pen knife

"Morning, Gracie," he said. "I suppose you'll be wanting a copy of every single paper?"

"No thank you," she laughed. "Just *The Times* please."

"You can have this for free," said Mr Clark, handing one over from behind the counter, "seeing how famous you are all of a sudden." He winked.

"Thank you very much."

"Don't let all this fame go to your head, mind."

The shop bell jingled as she closed its door behind her. Before cycling back, she opened the newspaper. There on page two was a photograph of her smiling and pointing to the skeleton in the ground, and another of her kneeling beside the shield. Underneath was a detailed account of how she'd made the finds, with learned quotes from Dr Neville, explaining their importance, and several further comments made by Gracie herself in answer to the journalist's questions. She quickly scanned the report, looking for one particular quote she hoped had been included.

It had.

There, at the bottom of the article, the journalist had asked, "What made you want to be an archaeologist, Gracie?"

Gracie had answered, "I'd like to say Maharajah the Elephant, whose skeleton my sister took me to see when I was just nine. But really the main reason why is all to do with my father, Mr Jabez Chadwick, Head Gardener at Philips Park. He taught me from an early age to pay close attention to what lies under our feet. If we're good to the earth, he said, the earth will be good to us."

She folded the newspaper back to its unopened state, popped it into the basket on the front of her bike, then pedalled quickly home.

"Hello, love," said Mary when she got back. "I thought you must've already left."

"No. I'm not needed at the dig till ten o'clock. It was such a lovely morning, I thought I'd just go for a quick cycle ride first."

"I don't know where you get all your energy from, Gracie," laughed Mary. "I feel worn out already."

"Where's Dad?"

"Out by the nursery, checking on the tulips."

"I'll just pop over and say hello," she said.

She stepped outside. Tag, their dog, was instantly at her side, jumping up, hoping she might have a stick to throw that he could fetch.

"Good boy," she said, bending down to fondle him behind his ears. "I've got a job for you," she said.

Tag barked happily. Gracie took the newspaper out of the basket, wrapped it in a piece of cellophane she'd taken from the kitchen earlier, and handed it to Tag, who held it carefully in his mouth.

"Now," she said, "go to Daddy."

Tag bounded off at once, while Gracie followed on behind. She saw her father greet the excited dog, who delivered the package safe and unharmed at his feet. She watched as Jabez picked it up, removed the sheet of cellophane from the newspaper, which he then proceeded to open. She saw him stop in his tracks, look up, then look back down again, as if he couldn't believe his eyes.

"Is this really you?" he said, shaking his head as she reached him a few moments later.

"The very same."

"And did you really find this shield and skeleton?"

"I did."

"On your first day?"

"In the first five minutes."

"I never doubted that you would."

He read the article to its end. "I reckon it was worth taking you to Central Library all those years ago."

"It was."

"You remember it then?"

"I do," she said. "*Wisdom is the principal thing.*"

"*Therefore get wisdom and with all thy getting, get understanding.*"

"*And she shall give to thine head an ornament of grace.*"

THREE

The Photograph

6

Sunday 8th May 1960

Sunday 8th May 1960
PHILIPS PARK, BESWICK

The Last Ever
TULIP SUNDAY

To Coincide with The Closure
Of the Park's Ponds & Boating Pools
This Popular Annual Event will End with a

DRAMATIC COLOURFUL DISPLAY

FREE ADMISSION
Gates Open at 8.00am

Welcome by Harold Lever, MP at 11.00am
Official Opening by **PAT PHOENIX**

Music is provided by Local Favourites
THE FOURTONES

FASHION SHOW
with *Gowns by Giulia*

REFRESHMENTS
kindly provided by the Levenshulme Women's Institute

All The Fun of the Fair!
SILCOCK'S TRAVELLING CIRCUS & FUNFAIR

**WALTZERS   FERRIS WHEEL   DODGEMS
ELEPHANT RIDES**

Special Fly Past by **THE BLACK ARROWS**

Gates Close: Sunset
For further information please contact Manchester Corporation
Committee for Public Walks, Gardens and Playgrounds

*

Jabez stepped out of the Keeper's Lodge in Philips Park just after dawn, as he did every Tulip Sunday. The times when he would stay out all night, patrolling the park with whichever dog he had at the time, were long gone. Not since 1932, when he and Mary, Harriet and Toby, had first moved into The Lodge, the year before Gracie was born. Now, twenty-eight years later, this was to be his last Tulip Sunday.

Jabez was sixty-five and due to retire. The Corporation had decided in 1959 to reorganise the way it managed the city's parks, but out of respect for Jabez and in recognition of his forty years of service, an employee of the Committee for Public Walks and Gardens since 1920, decided to wait until he retired before implementing the changes, which were radical and wholesale.

It had been decided that from now onwards none of the city's parks would retain their own individual keeper. Instead a small maintenance team would drive from park to park to cut the grass, clear the litter and report on any major repairs that needed carrying out. The Park Lodges would be shut and temporarily boarded up until they were either sold off or new uses could be found for them. Dressed up as cost-saving measures, in reality they reflected a general lack of interest in parks by the Corporation, which in turn had led to a gradual decline in their use by the public. Several were now neglected and overgrown, paddling pools clogged with dead leaves or strewn with broken glass, the swings and roundabouts removed or left to rust, bandstands either torn or fallen down. Many had become no go areas, especially after dark, the haunt of drunkards and gangs.

But not so Philips Park. Mary was adamant. "It's obvious," she'd say to anyone who cared to listen, "if a place is looked after properly, well maintained, clean and tidy, then the people using it are much more likely to treat it with respect too." Living on site meant that if any trouble ever did threaten to take place, Jabez was on the spot to nip it in the bud and deal with it before it got out of hand. He knew all the kids who hung out there anyway, had known their parents in all probability, and so they knew not to mess with him. The same went for Ted Albery, the local Bobby. Between them Ted and Jabez had the park covered.

But now the axe had fallen there too. Philips Park, the first ever public park to be opened in all of England, was to lose its keeper. Tomorrow the bulldozers would arrive to fill in the ornamental ponds and boating pools, remove the bandstand and board up the Lodge. Today's Tulip Sunday would be the park's last hurrah.

Mary was heartbroken, as well as angry. She'd set about packing up their things ready for when they had to leave with a fury that intimidated even Jabez. On the Saturday Toby and Paul had helped Jabez carry out all the furniture they were keeping, together with all the various smaller items, defiantly labelled in boxes, to a van Paul had arranged for them to borrow from the railway yard where he still worked behind Victoria Station, while Harriet and Sandra, with their respective children, came for a last look round.

Harriet, Toby and Paul remembered how they'd first moved in all those years ago, when they were the same age as their own children were now, marching behind Matteo's rag and bone cart, pulled by old Bombola, on whom they'd all had rides during the afternoon. Toby, ever the practical one, reminded them that Mum and Dad were not moving far, only to Rusholme, and to a house overlooking Platt Fields, where there'd be plenty of room for Rags, their latest dog, to run around, but if they were ever to get there, they'd best get a move on.

Jabez smiled when he overheard this. Toby was a chip off the old block, so very much like how he had been at that age. Taking everything in his stride, nothing bothered him for long. He'd followed Jabez into the pit at Bradford, and he'd helped with the Park since the end of the War at weekends and evenings. Before the Corporation had decided on these changes, Jabez had hoped that Toby would follow him as Head Keeper when he retired, and that he and Sandra would move in to the Lodge. But it was not to be and, like his father, Toby accepted it with a shrug. "There's nowt to be gained by moanin' over what can't be altered," he'd said. "Sandra, the kids and me, we're quite happy where we are, thanks very much." Where they were was a neat terraced house on Manipur Street in Beswick which, between them, Toby and Sandra kept immaculately. Toby also rented an allotment, on nearby Fairclough Street, where he grew enough vegetables to keep the family going for most of each year.

As Jabez stepped out of his front door that Sunday morning, P.C. Albery was just arriving, wheeling his bicycle up to the main gates on Mill Street.

"Morning, Jabez."

"Morning, Ted."

"All set then, are we?"

"I reckon so, Ted."

"No trouble overnight?"

"Nothing that woke me."

"Looks like the rain'll hold off."

"Let's hope so, Ted."

Neither of them referred to this being Jabez's last day.

"Two hours to opening time then," said Ted.

"Less three minutes," confirmed Jabez, checking against his grandfather's pocket watch, which he always carried with him on Tulip Sunday.

"I'll hold back the crowds till then," joked Ted, looking around at the completely empty roads.

"They'll come," said Jabez, "don't you worry. It'll be like the parting of the Red Sea once I open these gates."

"You might be right at that," laughed Ted, mounting his bike and cycling rather unsteadily away.

Jabez gave a low, sharp whistle and within seconds Rags was by his side. She was the last in a long line of dogs who'd worked with him here in the park. Meg, Peg, Tig, Tag, and now Rags. The last three all named by Gracie. There'd be no more after Rags. They'd take her with them to the house near Platt Fields, but after she'd gone, there wouldn't be another.

Together they walked briskly down the Carriage Drive, something of an anachronism now. Jabez could not remember the last time a carriage had been driven along it. Perhaps it was in 1941, when the cast iron Russian cannons, presented as a gift to the city of Manchester after the Crimean War, were ceremonially towed away by a team of cart horses to be melted for scrap as part of the War effort.

At the far end of the Drive, where there was an area of level ground that was sometimes laid out for a football pitch, several columns of thin blue smoke were rising up from the various small fires lit alongside the tents and trailers of Silcock's Travelling Fair, who'd been a regular feature of Tulip Sunday since the late 1920s. They would arrive the day before to set up, generating much excitement from the local teenagers, who would crowd round, eager for an early ride on the Waltzers or Dodgems before the Fair officially opened, and who would always be disappointed. One of Jabez's regular jobs was to enlist the help of the owners, Herbert and Jane Silcock, to prise the lads who ran the rides away from the local girls whose parents would have their guts for garters if they knew what their daughters had been getting up to.

Already the Fair was beginning to stir. Jabez noticed a dark-skinned young man with long hair leading a horse out of the small circular tent, which would later serve as the Big Top for the circus, over towards the back of the old Silcock Flyer, the Fair's original ride, old-fashioned and tame by today's standards, but a popular feature nevertheless. It was their signature attraction. The young man began to groom the horse. Steam rose from the animal's flanks in the early morning light. He appeared to be talking to the horse all the time, whispering in his ear, while the horse nodded its great head and pawed the ground with one of its hooves. Herbert Silcock saw Jabez watching them and came over.

"He's just joined us this year," he said quietly, so as not to disturb them. "He rides bareback in the circus. The things that boy can do on a horse need to be seen to be believed – standing on its back, swinging beneath its belly, somersaults, the lot. He's a real daredevil. But his real speciality is the way he gets the horse to dance. Equine Ballet – that's how we announce it in the ring. Poetry in Motion."

"I'll be sure to tell my grandchildren," said Jabez, impressed.

"What are their names?" said Herbert, "then I can let them in without a ticket."

"Thank you," said Jabez. "I appreciate that."

"Don't mention it. It's the least we can do for all the help you've given us over the years. We're very sorry to see you leaving us."

Jabez nodded. "Time and tide, Herbert. It catches up with all of us."

He shook Herbert's hand, then made his way past the ornamental ponds and boating pools, which he and Toby had spent the last week weeding and cleaning, so that they would look their best for the final time they would be used, before the Corporation came the following week to fill them in with concrete.

There were six pools in all, flowing one into another, all supplied by water issuing from a cast iron pipe from where the River Medlock had been culverted nearly a century before, after the Great Flood. Jabez wondered what would happen to this outflow when the concrete was poured in, whether the Corporation had taken this into account. The various departments were notorious for the way they didn't speak to one another. But that was no longer his concern. On this May morning, as the sun steadily climbed the sky, the ponds were already beginning to sparkle. Two were purely ornamental, with lily pads and irises. A third was populated by carp, some of them were more than twenty years old, the whole surface covered by a net to deter both birds and anglers. Next there were the two paddling pools. The largest would be set aside for the elephants when they arrived from Belle Vue, while the smaller would prove a magnet for the children if the day turned out to be as hot as was forecast. Finally there was the boating lake, where Mary would be in charge of organising races for the toy yachts, which was something she had started doing since the end of the War.

Leaving the ponds and pools behind, Jabez headed back along the Avenue of Black Poplars, from where he could view the tulips.

He and Toby had thought long and hard over the designs for this, their final display. Each year he would submit his ideas to the Committee for Parks & Gardens for their approval, which was always granted. This year, however, they had simply said, "As this is your last year, Jabez, we'll leave it entirely to you. I'm sure you won't let us down."

In the end it was Gracie who'd come up with the idea.

"Do you remember that day during the War," she'd said, "when you told me how the reason why the Park was so good for growing was because there were so many bones lying in the ground, from when the Great Flood washed out the graveyard that used to be here?"

"I do," said Jabez with a smile. "I remember it very well. It was the same day you went to see the skeleton of Maharajah, the elephant who'd walked from Edinburgh to Manchester, and you decided you wanted to be an archaeologist."

"That's right," laughed Gracie. "I think I had bones on the brain that day."

"You still do," joked Toby. "You should see her flat, Dad. It's full of all these weird things she digs up."

"So what's your idea?" said Jabez.

"Make the centrepiece entirely black and white. Fill all the paths and smaller beds with every colour that's possible, so that as the people wander through them they get completely dazzled, then really hit them hard with the contrast."

"But why black and white?" asked Toby, pulling a face.

"Shall you tell him, Dad, or shall I?" said Gracie with a grin.

"I think *you* should," said Jabez. "It's your idea."

"A bed of black tulips to represent the coal which lies under our feet, interspersed with thousands of white tulips to symbolise the bones of all those who've died, not just in the mines, but in factories, in wars, in accidents and plagues, who've given their lives to make Manchester what she is today, right from when she was first founded."

They all three sat silent, imagining what it might look like.

"Bloody 'ell, our Gracie," said Toby eventually, "you don't 'alf come out with some rubbish at times!"

Laughing, Gracie chased her brother round the kitchen table. Mary came in from outside to see what all the commotion was about. She and Jabez looked at one another, smiling. They were going to miss moments like this.

Toby allowed Gracie to capture him, then said, "But by 'eck, I reckon it'll look fantastic."

Now Jabez looked down on it from the Avenue of the Black Poplars. Toby had been right, it did look good, and Gracie's instincts were spot on. The whole display looked spectacularly dramatic and would certainly prove a talking point. Jabez doubted he'd ever put together a more memorable Tulip Sunday. Fitting, then, that it should be the last, for how would he have followed this next year?

Jabez checked his grandfather's pocket watch. A quarter to eight. Just fifteen minutes before he would be unlocking the park's gates. He began to set off back towards Mill Street when a thin, reedy voice hailed him from behind.

"I say, Jabez? Have you a moment?" It was Mr Pettigrew, former Chair of Manchester Corporation's Committee for Public Parks, Gardens & Playgrounds. Jabez waited for him to catch him up.

Mr Pettigrew was eighty now, but still elegantly dapper, sporting a Panama hat and a silver-topped walking cane. From the top pocket of his cream linen jacket, he produced a rather flamboyant spotted handkerchief, with which he mopped his brow.

"I see the weather gods have been kind to us yet again this Tulip Sunday?"

"Yes, sir. It looks that way."

"I'm so glad I caught you, Jabez, before we are trampled on by the crowds. I just wanted to say what a sad day this is. The Committee moves in ways I no longer recognise."

"I'm sure they think they're acting for the best, sir."

"I've no doubt, but I want you to know that had I still been a member, I'd have fought tooth and nail against it, all of it, especially the decision to turn you and Mrs Chadwick out of your home."

"Thank you, sir."

"You've done a magnificent job over the years. It has exceeded, I am certain, even the most ambitious dreams of the park's founder, Mr Philips."

"You're most kind, sir. I've enjoyed every minute of it. But I shan't miss it. I've had my time with it. I'm only sorry my son could not have taken it on after me, which is something I know he'd have done well in."

"Quite. He has other employment, I hope?"

"Yes, sir. At Bradford Colliery."

Mr Pettigrew nodded, then smiled. "I'm rather taken with your homage to the mine in your black and white central display."

"My daughter's idea, sir."

"The archaeologist?"

"I imagine she has always been something of a handful?"

"You could say that, sir."

"Well, she's certainly going to set some tongues

wagging today. Good for her."

"Thank you, sir."

"Anyway, I mustn't keep you. You must have a thousand things to attend to. I just wanted to thank you and…"

"Sir?"

Mr Pettigrew pulled out a small bag from his jacket side-pocket. "As a token of appreciation. My wife thought it might be something you'd like. To remember us by."

Jabez opened the bag. Inside was a green tie with a repeating pattern of red tulips running down it. He found he was extraordinarily moved by the gesture.

"Thank you, sir. Mrs Pettigrew is quite correct. I like it very much."

"Excellent. I shall tell her so. And look – there she is, waving her umbrella to try and attract my attention. Good day to you, Jabez." He extended his hand, which Jabez shook warmly. Before he finally took his leave, he pointed his walking cane towards the display of black and white tulips. "Bones and coal," he chuckled. "Clever girl…"

As the bells of St Jerome's Church finished striking eleven o'clock, a large crowd gathered around the bandstand for the official opening ceremony. The Besses o' th' Barn Brass Band finished their first selection of popular tunes and Mr Harold Lever, MP, took the microphone.

"Good morning, Ladies and Gentlemen, Boys and

Girls. For some reason it falls on me to open proceedings today. I can't imagine who thought that might be a good idea. The last Member of Parliament to do the honours here was back in 1922, the first Tulip Sunday after the end of the First World War, when Mr John Sutton was invited to say a few well chosen words. Either he spoke very badly, or it was decided that the good people of Manchester didn't want to listen to a politician berating them on a fine Sunday morning in May such as we are blessed with today, for there hasn't been another since. I suspect the latter, because, from what I've been able to find out, John Sutton made a fine speech that day. 'You all know me,' he kept saying – it was something of a catch phrase of his – and I'm hoping that you all know me here today. But for those of you who don't – 'You lucky people,' to quote another famous catch phrase – I'm Harold Lever and I've been proud to be the MP for this constituency since 1950. My brother, Leslie, is MP for Ardwick next door. Two years ago he was Lord Mayor of this fine city of ours, and he was standing where I am today to open the Tulip Sunday on that occasion. So – when I was approached to see if I would do it this year, I asked my brother for some tips. 'Keep it short,' is what he said. Good advice, no doubt. Unfortunately, I've always found it quite a challenge to do that, but I'll do my best. In Westminster I have something of a reputation for speaking at great length. 'That Harold Lever chap,' I overheard one toffee-nosed Tory say to his cronies one day, 'could talk for England'. 'No,' I replied, 'but I do intend to talk for Manchester.' And I will continue to do so, Ladies and Gentlemen, for as long as you carry on giving me your votes. You all know me, as John Sutton would have said, like most of you here I was born in Manchester but, like very many of you, my parents weren't. Mine came over from Lithuania. My father was a textile worker there, but was driven out by persecution. He arrived here with nothing, but he received such a welcome from everyone he met that he knew he'd found himself somewhere he could call home, where he could settle down and raise his children. Which he did. And that's what makes this city of ours so special – its kindness, its generosity, and its spirit of neighbourliness. 'Entertain the strangers at your gates,' says the Good Book, 'for that way you may also entertain angels.' Once I found myself speaking in Parliament for more than two hours on the subject of the coelacanth. For those of you who don't know what a coelacanth is, it's a very rare fish that people thought had been extinct for millions of years, until one was caught in a fisherman's net somewhere in the Indian Ocean. I talked and talked until the time being given for a particular Bill ran out, so it couldn't go to a vote. Which was a good thing, because it would have been a bad law. It would have put a tax on white fish, which in turn would have meant thousands of fish and chip shops having to close, and we'd none of us want that, would we? Afterwards, those same toffee-nosed Tories said that when I was talking about the coelacanth, I was really meaning Manchester, that it was a city whose time had been and gone. Manchester? Becoming extinct? I don't think so. 'Have you ever been there?' I asked them. And of course they hadn't. They'd never been farther north than Watford. So I had to educate them. Manchester is built on innovation, I told them. We have always embraced change. We're proud of our past, but we always look forward. Who built the Lancaster bombers that helped win the War? We did. Who first split the atom? We did. Who built the first computer? We did. And who was the first to spot Sputnik as it travelled across space from the world's biggest telescope at Jodrell Bank? We did. And while it may be sad that today marks the end of an era, with this being the last Tulip Sunday here in Philips Park for the foreseeable future, we have to remember that the Corporation isn't a bottomless pit when it comes to money. We've still got thousands of new homes that need to be built, and we see evidence of that in the skyscrapers sprouting up all around us, don't we? Those bright new towers of steel and glass, which rise up straight and tall, just like Jabez's tulips, and will once again put Manchester at the forefront of technology and change, a beacon of modernity. There've been times before when Tulip Sunday has had to be put on hold, to be temporarily set aside for other priorities, but it has always returned. Let us hope that it will not be too long before we are all gathered here again to celebrate its resurgence. And so, before I hand over to Pat to officially declare today's Tulip Sunday open, I call upon you all to give three Manchester cheers for Jabez Chadwick, Head Keeper here at Philips Park, whose last day this is, who has given the people of this city so much restorative pleasure and colour these past forty years. Hip, hip…"

"Hooray!"

"Hip, hip…"

"Hooray!"

"Hip, hip…"

"Hooray"

"Thank you. Now – it is my great pleasure to call upon Miss Pat Phoenix to officially open proceedings."

After prolonged applause, Pat stepped forward to the microphone.

"Thank you, Harold. I'm also tempted to say, 'You all know me,' but I'm not sure that you do. I can imagine some of you saying, 'Didn't she used to be Pat Phoenix?' Well, I did, and I still am. Like Harold, I too was born in Manchester, just down the road in Fallowfield. Some of you might have seen me in *Cup Tie Honeymoon* with Sandy Powell, which I'm proud to say was made at the Dickenson Road Film Studios in Rusholme, less than three miles away from where we're standing this morning. Sadly *Mancunian Films*, who ran the studios, is no more, but many of its fantastic technicians – its cameramen and sound recorders – have gone on to the newly opened Granada Television on Quay Street, where we can tailor-make programmes right here in the north for the people who live and work here, and then export them all over the world, so that even those MPs Harold mentioned, who've never been north of Watford, can watch them and learn summat about who we are and what it means to live in the greatest city on Earth. They say that when one door closes, another one opens. You may not have seen me on the big screen for a number of years, but pretty soon you'll be able to see me, and a whole cast of other great northern actors, on the small screen, in the comfort of your own front rooms, in a new programme that's being written and planned even as we speak. It's going to be set in a terraced street in Salford, with a pub at one end and a corner shop at t'other, full of people we all know and recognise, and soon the whole world will get to know and recognise them too. Watch out for it, it's going to be called *Florizel Street*, and it'll be on the telly around December time. Right. That's the commercial break over with. It now gives me great pleasure to declare the Tulip Sunday for 1960 open!"

As soon as Pat had finished speaking, Mr Willie Wood, the conductor of the Besses o' th' Barn Brass Band, raised his baton. At once the band launched into the piece which had won them The Belle Vue British Open the previous year. Composed by Eric Ball, it was called *The Undaunted*.

Esther had set off early. Being a Sunday, she had had to take three separate buses to make it to Philips Park from Patricroft, and even that had involved a walk of one and a half miles from Belle Vue.

Now she stood close by the bandstand waiting for Winifred. She had not been to Tulip Sunday since 1922, when she had taken her father, one of the last days he had enjoyed before he finally retreated so far back into his memories that nobody could reach him. Esther had found the prospect of a return visit to the Park the following year too painful to contemplate. The year after that the weather had been so poor it did not seem worth the effort involved in getting herself ready, and so the habit fell away. Then, in 1928, she had met Jaz and moved to

Patricroft and a whole new life.

But now circumstances had changed yet again. Jaz had died in the terrible winter of 1947, after which the light in Yasser's eyes had gone out, never to be rekindled. She had looked after him in his final years until he too had died ten years later. That had been three years ago, since when Sol had returned home from National Service in Aden, but he was not the boy he had been. Now he was sullen, morose, withdrawn. He was bitter and angry still that she had somehow not prevented him from going in the first place. But what could she have done? Lied about who he was? He'd only wanted to acknowledge his Yemeni heritage when it suited him, out of expediency. In every other respect he was as Mancunian as the boys he'd gone to school with. Now he had begun dating a Yemeni girl. Nadia. A nice girl, who Esther had met at Yasser's funeral. Sol thought she didn't know. They hardly spoke these days. He only saw Nadia on Friday evenings, something else he didn't know she knew, and so Sundays were terrible days, when he would just sit around and mope all day. He hated his job but did nothing to try and find a different one, a better one. He'd stopped drawing as well, or at least whenever she was around. That was something she hoped she didn't know about, that somehow he still drew in secret, for he had a real talent.

So, when Winifred had written and told her that this year's Tulip Sunday was going to be the last ever, and would she consider attending therefore, she had replied at once that yes, she would love to come. And here she was, waiting by the bandstand, wondering why Winifred was late.

She saw her eventually, hurrying along one of the many serpentine paths that wound themselves around the park, breathless and apologetic.

"I'm so sorry," she said. "It took longer to get Victor organised than it normally does, and I don't seem to have caught up with myself yet."

"How is Victor?" asked Esther.

"The same," said Winifred. "He never complains. I've parked him with some of his pals in the beer tent."

"Is that wise?" said Esther. Winifred had told her in the past about Victor's occasional descents.

"He'll be all right," said Winifred. "He doesn't drink so much these days, not since the accident. And anyway, Joe's there to keep an eye on him, just in case."

"It's good to see you again," said Esther. "How long has it been?"

"Too long," said Winifred. "Ten years?"

"Possibly more."

"Where does it go, eh?"

The two women held each other in a warm embrace.

"Let's walk," said Esther.

Winifred smiled. "That's what you said that last Tulip Sunday. 'Let's walk'."

"Did I? I don't remember."

"I was feeling sorry for myself. Still grieving over Arthur and thinking I was on the shelf."

"You'd just started at the Telephone Exchange."

Winifred laughed. "That feels a lifetime ago."

"It is. We've both taken directions neither of us could have predicted back then."

"You're right. But just a few minutes after we'd

parted, I found myself inside that Boxing Tent, and the next thing I knew I was spattered in blood and sweat and falling head over heels in love with the last man I'd've ever imagined."

"It's worked out well, though, hasn't it? In the end?"

"Yes," said Winifred, "it has. It's not all been a bed of roses, I can tell you."

"No, I don't imagine it has."

"But it's been... so unexpectedly exciting. After Arthur died I thought everything had come to a stop, that life would continue like that from then onwards, day after day the same, lonely and... pale – yes, that's it, pale. But then I met Victor and it was just like when Dorothy leaves the black and white of Kansas for the Technicolor of Oz. Nothing was ever the same again, and I never knew from one day to the next just what to expect. I've seen aspects of life I never thought I would – or should – not all of it very nice, but I wouldn't have missed a moment of it."

They had reached the corner of the park where Silcock's was swinging into action, the sound of the fairground organ mixed in with the squeals and screams of people on the Waltzers or the Ghost Train.

"It's just like this," she said, sweeping her arm around the coconut shies, rifle ranges, Ferris wheel and helter-skelter. "Roll up, roll up and take your choice. Stay on the kiddies' roundabout and just go round and round, or ride the roller coaster."

Esther nodded and smiled. "Good for you," she said. "Let's go on something, while we're here."

Winifred giggled. "Are you serious?"

"Aren't I always?" winked Esther.

"There isn't a roller coaster," said Winifred, looking around.

"Let's try that," said Esther, pointing towards Silcock's Flyer. She linked her arm through her friend's. "Let's see how high we can get."

"What will they think? Two women our age?"

"I don't care what people think," said Esther.

"No," said Winifred, looking at Esther's all white garb, "you never have."

While they were queuing up, she turned to Esther and said, "Come on – it's your turn now."

"For what?"

"To tell me all about you."

"There's not much to tell. I'm a widow."

"Widows don't usually wear white."

"Some Muslims do."

"Is that what you are?"

"Not formally, no. I've studied it and I practise some aspects of it, but I haven't gone through any sort of ceremony, if that's what you mean. Not yet anyway."

"But you might?"

"*Insh'allah*."

They strapped themselves into their seats on the Silcock Flyer. It slowly began to swing, like a pendulum, back and forth, higher and higher. Just when it was approaching its highest point and threatened to tip them both upside down, Winifred asked, "But doesn't it… you know…?"

"What?"

"Restrict your freedom? Stop you from doing what

you want?"

"Do I look restricted?" shouted Esther as they swung higher and higher. "I'm doing exactly what I want."

The Silcock's Flyer then plummeted them earthwards, their stomachs churning and somersaulting, as Esther and Winifred laughed and shrieked, their shouts and screams mingling with the rest of the crowds.

In another part of the park George was busy taking photographs.

In recent years he had forsaken his earlier method of introducing himself to potential subjects, obtaining their consent, then negotiating with them the pose and the setting, so that the sitter retained a measure of control and ownership in the finished photograph, in favour of a more candid *verité* approach. Now he preferred to shoot on the streets, or other public spaces – a football ground, a dog track, a park like today – and try to capture what he liked to refer to as 'authentic moments'. He'd been much influenced by the work of Robert Doisneau, Henri Cartier-Bresson and Bill Brandt. Following on from his early portraits of *'People at Work'*, as had featured in his first Nuts & Bolts exhibition, he'd wanted to emulate William Eugene Smith's photo-essays, spending time with a whole community, perhaps up to a year, to capture every aspect of its life, at work, at home, at play, eventually arriving at a point when the people who lived there came to forget he was even there, so that his camera would not in any way influence the way they allowed themselves to appear, a true 'fly-on-the-wall' account of how his subjects lived. His first thought had been to document the lives of the mining community around Bradford Colliery, but when he saw the photographs by Bill Brandt of miners in the north-east, he was disheartened. He could not hope to compare with those and anything he might produce would only be dismissed as derivative. He still cherished the idea of finding a voice that was distinctive and unique. And so instead he had turned to simply photographing what he saw when he went out 'on parade', as he called it, pounding the city's streets, watching, observing, trying to capture conjunctions of character and situation in ways that did not feel contrived, or did not in any way compromise the privacy of the individuals he photographed unaware. At first he felt that much of what he was recording was dull, ordinary, every day. Those heart-stopping, soaring flights of fancy – the couple kissing in a Paris street by Doisneau, the man leaping with an umbrella in front of the Eiffel Tower by Cartier-Bresson – had, he discovered, been either posed or doctored or both. This was disillusioning for George, even though he could not fail to appreciate their artistry and technique, capturing such apparent acts of spontaneity artificially. He remained steadfast and patient. Recalling his project with the spindle tree in Portugal Street, when he had taken exactly the same photograph from exactly the same position every single day for a year, the results of which were a poetic meditation on the duality of time, the subtle, unseen changes taking place over such a long period being represented by a series of images which had separately taken a fraction of a second to record, he decided, rather like a Bobby on his beat, to photograph the same set of streets near to his flat on Silk Street. People got to know him, just as they might the milkman or the postman, and so they began to trust him. To see him taking a photograph as he passed them on the way to work or the shops was no different from if he had been delivering a letter or a pint of milk on the doorstep. They no longer felt self-conscious, or posed in any way, they simply ignored him. In this way, George hoped, they were giving him implicit consent to include them in his images, lending them integrity and authenticity. Over the last ten years, he had been able to build up an encyclopaedic portfolio of literally thousands of pictures of these same streets, as the slums were cleared, bomb-damaged houses demolished, new tower blocks constructed. He photographed the city on the cusp of change. He captured a community trying to navigate their way with fortitude and dignity through this ever evolving landscape, picking their way round the mountains of rubble of what had once been their homes, some boarded up, some still lived in, the women walking through the dusk at twilight pushing prams, the jobless men loitering on corners waiting for the pubs to open after the betting shops had closed, the children transforming the bomb sites into playgrounds, cricket stumps chalked on back-alley walls, rope swings hung from lamp posts, hopscotch chalked on pavements. Teenage boys with James Dean quiffs cycling between lines of washing strung across the streets, girls with beehive hair dos and white stilettos linking arms for a night at the pictures. Children with cardboard boxes for space helmets planting home made flags on the dark side of the moon.

The last ever Tulip Sunday was too good an opportunity to miss therefore and he had been in the Park from the moment Jabez first unlocked the gates on Mill Street. He'd already taken several rolls of film juxtaposing the crowds of people circling the central display of black and white tulips against the backdrop of the winding gear of the headstocks at Bradford Pit and the statues of angels in the park's cemetery. Now, as the clock on St Jerome's struck one o'clock, he was hungry and thirsty and had naturally gravitated towards the Refreshment Tent, where he found Victor nursing the last few drops of a pint of mild.

"How do?" said Victor as he approached.

"Can I get you another one of those?" said George, pointing towards Victor's near empty glass.

"Best make it just a half. Win's meant to be here any minute, and she'll only fret."

"A half it is," said George.

"Cheers," said Victor a couple of minutes later. "Been having a good day?"

"Crowds," he said, gesturing back out towards the Park, "are my meat and drink. I can get lost in them, so that people don't notice me and, with a bit of luck, I manage to see something that might be of interest to others later."

"Slice of life," said Victor after draining half his glass.

"You could say that," said George.

"It were the opposite wi' me."

George looked at Victor quizzically.

"Crowds," explained Victor. "When I were in t' ring.

There were no place there for me to hide."

"But you liked that presumably?"

"Ay. When I won."

"Which you did mostly."

"Ay." He stared into his glass.

"Do you miss it?" asked George tentatively.

"No, lad. Not any more. But work I do miss." He pointed down to his legs lying limp below him in the wheel chair. "Summat to get up for in t' mornings. I'm neither use nor ornament these days."

"I'm sorry to hear that."

"Still – it's no use cryin' over what can't be 'elped."

They sat in silence. After a few moments Victor rallied. "Don't pay me no heed, lad, it's the beer talkin', not me. I'm not doin' so bad. I've been goin' back to t' gym, in Ardwick, the Boys' Club, where I started. Been doin' a bit of trainin' wi' t' young 'uns what're comin' through. They're all right, some o' them. Take Lily's friend Pearl's eldest – Lamarr Junior – 'e shows real promise. Quick hands, light on 'is feet. A bit skinny yet, but 'e'll fill out given time. They ask me what it were like, goin' into t' ring, wi' the lights overhead an' t' cameras flashin' and t' crowds all yellin' yer name, but I don't tell 'em. Boxing's no life. Stick to being an amateur, I say, that's the true sport of kings, before money taints it. Find yourself a proper job."

George chuckled. "That's what my great hero said to me when I was first wanting to be an artist."

"And did you take his advice?"

"I did. I teach. Like you."

Victor nodded appreciatively. "I hated school," he

said. "I used to play up my teachers summat rotten. I wish I'd paid more attention now."

"It's never too late."

"That's what Win says."

"She's right."

"Ay, she usually is." The two men laughed companionably. "But I reckon it's time to let today's young 'uns 'ave a chance, give summat back, like, you know?"

On the far side of the park, in the amphitheatre, a local pop group was tuning up.

"Hello, everybody. Testing one-two-three." The speakers whistled and hummed before emitting a loud scream of feedback.

"Turn it down," shouted several people in the crowd all at once.

"Sorry about that," said the singer, somewhat sheepishly. "Are we ready, lads?" he whispered over his shoulders to his mates. One of them said he thought they were, while another merely shrugged.

The guitarist stood by the microphone and began to speak. "Let's start again, shall we? I'm Graham Nash, the guitarist."

"I'm Alan Clarke, lead singer."

"I'm John 'Butch' Mepham on bass."

"I'm Joe Abrams, the drummer."

"And we," said the guitarist, "are *The Fourtones*. A one, two, a one-two-three-four...."

They then launched, not entirely together and not completely in tune, into a not particularly convincing version of a Buddy Holly song.

*"Every day things are getting closer
Coming faster like a roller coaster..."*

"Time to give the young a chance, eh Victor?" laughed George.

"Ay well, mebbe not this lot."

"Oh I don't know," said George, "they grow on you after a bit."

"Like fungus."

They listened for a while longer before Victor returned to his theme. "Ay, like I were sayin', when I'm in t' gym, tryin' to pass on to these young lads, like Lamarr Junior, little bits of advice here an' there, tips on 'ow to keep out o' trouble, you know, 'ow to avoid gettin' hurt, I get a real kick out of it."

"Ring craft."

"Ay – that's it exactly."

"I feel the same. My favourite classes are not with the full time students, the ones hoping to be artists themselves one day, but those that come to evening classes, straight after a hard day's work in a factory or an office. You can see them, shaking off the stresses and strains of whatever it is they've been doing all day, rolling up their sleeves and really getting down to it. They're hungry for instruction. They drink in everything you tell them. They're so eager to keep improving, it's a real privilege to be there with them, and you work extra hard so as not to let them down."

"I don't expect you do."

"I hope not. There's one lad, just started, reminds me a bit of the way you talk about young Lamarr, doesn't say much, but he's got this deep anger burning inside him, you can see it just in the way he looks at you, he's dying for you to give him a right bollocking, so he can get up, kick over a chair, then walk out, but it's all a front. Deep down he's really scared, you can see, that somehow, what he does all day, his dead end job – those are his words, not mine – is all there's ever going to be. But when he draws, he becomes an altogether different person. A kind of stillness settles on him. All the tension goes out of his body. Then, with just a few pencil lines, he conjures up a whole other world…"

"What kind o' things does he like to draw?"

"I don't think he knows yet. He was on National Service out in Aden. When he first joined the class, he showed me some drawings he'd done while he was out there. The desert, mountains, army jeeps, soldiers, young boys mostly, looking scared. They were wonderful. On one of the rare occasions when he actually said something, he told me he'd drawn them for his grandfather, who'd come from there, but since he'd died he didn't feel the same need. Then he just clammed up. Now, whatever it is I ask him to draw, he does it dutifully enough, but mostly he's just going through the motions. More often than not he tears it up before I can have a proper look at it. But one day, I hope, he'll discover who it is he's really drawing for."

"Himself," said Victor. "You can try an' please other people all you want, but in th' end you've got to be able to look yourself in t' mirror in t' mornings."

George nodded and drank the rest of his beer. "Here comes Winifred, look."

Winifred was hurrying towards them, looking red in the face.

"Always on t' last minute," chuckled Victor.

"Sorry I'm late," she said breathlessly, "but Esther and me got talking, you know how it is, then would you believe it, she insisted we went on the Silcock Flyer? Oh hello, George. Long time no see. How's tricks?"

"Oh, mustn't grumble. How's Francis?"

"Why don't you ask him yourself? He's about somewhere."

"I will."

"He needs taking out of himself. He's not been the same since... well, you know... He spends all his time fiddling around with whatever his new hobby happens to be. It's tape recorders at the moment. Ferrographs. You know what he's like. He can't sit still for five minutes."

"Yes," smiled George. "I know what he's like."

"Of course, the shop's closed now..."

"Is it? Since when?"

"Easter. I told him I wanted to stop – I'd been there thirty years – I wanted to spend more time with Victor, and Joe's kiddies. Well, he went into a kind of blind panic, you know how he gets. 'How am I going to manage without you?' he kept saying. 'You should have thought of that before,' I said. In the end he said he didn't have it in him to find a replacement, so he decided to close instead."

"I saw him around that time. He never said anything."

"Well, he wouldn't to you, would he? He'd want you to think everything was all hunky dory."

"Do you know where he is now?"

"Try the Marquee over by the main Carriage Drive. He said he might take a look at the Fashion Show there."

George nodded.

"Please don't tell me that's where *we're* going too?" groaned Victor.

"Relax, Victor," laughed Winifred. "I wouldn't inflict that on you. Come along, Finish your beer."

"Where are we going then?"

"Memory Lane, Victor, Memory Lane. Bye, George."

George watched them head down one of the serpentine paths towards the Boxing Tent, where an Amateur Boys Contest was about to start. George wondered whether Lamarr Junior might be taking part and whether he might go along too to take some photographs. No. Better try and find Francis, he felt. He picked up his camera and dived back into the crowds.

Further down the path Winifred leant down and whispered into Victor's ear as she pushed his chair. They had just reached a point where the path forked in two directions.

"I do believe," she said, "that I stood at this very spot back in 1922, having just finished talking to Esther, wondering which path I should take. I was so lonely and miserable, Victor. I heard a roar coming from a tent just down there." She paused while she pointed. "I thought, I wonder what's going on there. Just think, if I'd gone that way instead of this, we'd never have met, and we wouldn't be heading down this same path this afternoon. What are the odds, eh Victor? You're the betting man."

"A hundred to one," said Victor. "And even longer than that for us to stay together ever since."

"There've been a few bumps in the road, though, haven't there?"

"Ay, but that's what's made it interesting. Nobody wants a smooth ride, do they? That'd be boring."

"Is that right?"

"I reckon it is."

"Right then," she said, and she immediately took off, pushing Victor's chair as fast as she could, straight towards the Boxing Tent, causing the crowds walking along the path to dive to the sides for cover. "Who needs the Silcock's Flyer?" she roared.

"That's my girl," laughed Victor.

"That I am," laughed Winifred back.

Inside the Marquee along the main Carriage Drive, Giulia was busy putting the last minute touches to the designs for her Fashion Show to launch the opening of her new store on King Street in the centre of Manchester.

The cat walk was festooned with tulips, which Jabez had set aside especially for her, and she and Harriet had been up much of the previous night, arranging every last detail. The inside of the Marquee was made to look like an Italian street café, decked out with more green and red tulips in vases on white linen tablecloths. An area along the back of the Marquee had been screened off, where all of the dresses and outfits Giulia had selected for the show had been meticulously labelled and hung neatly in order, ready for when the models arrived.

They were here now, mostly fashion students from the recently opened Hollings College on Cromwell Range near Birchfields Park, affectionately known as the Toast Rack because of its distinctive shape, but the serene and ordered calm of the previous evening had given way to near panic and hysteria as the girls wrestled for their right clothes like they were at a jumble sale, more rugby scrum than fashion show.

Giulia clapped her hands and an immediate silence fell. The students were in complete awe of her and would have paraded up and down the catwalk naked if she'd asked them to. At this rate they might have to, she thought. Now they avoided her stern glare, shamefaced. Barely raising her voice above a whisper, she spoke. "We have just two hours to go, girls. That's more than enough time to rehearse and be ready for when we let the public in. But only if we all remain completely calm. Now, I want each of you to put the dress you are currently wearing back on its hanger and place it on the correct hook behind the screen. Every possible scenario has been anticipated and nothing can go wrong if you remain in your own individually allotted space back stage, if you allow the dressers to hand you the correct garment and help you in and out of each one, and if you all stay calm. *Capisci?*"

"Yes, Miss Giulia," they chorused.

"*Bene.* Then let us start again."

This time the rehearsal ran like clockwork, and at a quarter to two Giulia gave the signal to begin letting in the public, while the girls repaired their make up and got into their first costumes ready to begin.

There was a palpable buzz of anticipation as the audience, almost entirely female, arrived, eager to see

Giulia's latest designs.

In the last five years, after leaving *Mancunian Films* when they were forced to shut down, she had built up quite an exclusive following of devoted admirers, who, they declared, once they had worn just one of her garments, never wanted to wear clothes by anyone else. She became renowned for her simple, elegant lines and her dramatic, expert cutting. Up until this year she had only made to order, specially tailored items for individual customers, but now she was ready to branch out, making, as well, clothes which could be bought off the peg, by discerning young – and not so young – women with aspirations to be both modern and timeless, at affordable prices. Having saved assiduously she had managed to secure the lease on the perfect premises on fashionable King Street in the heart of the city. She had now embarked upon a series of Fashion Shows to announce its opening and attract new customers. This afternoon's at Tulip Sunday, was the first, the perfect venue, for there was a ready made captive audience of several hundred women all dressed up in their Sunday best, looking for something new to refresh their summer wardrobe.

The theme of the show was to be Italy. Not the Italy of Giulia's parents and grandparents, but the Italy of today. *La Dolce Vita, Roman Holiday, Bellissima.* Anita Ekberg, Gina Lollabrigida, Anna Magnani and, of course, Audrey Hepburn.

The show began playfully with one of the models, dressed in the matelot striped jersey, tight white trousers and jaunty cap associated with Hepburn, sitting astride a Vespa scooter in the centre of the catwalk to the backdrop of *Tu Vuo' Fa' L'Americano*, played on one of Francis's Ferrographs, which he had loaned her for the occasion. To further Italian café music – *Che Cossè L'Amor, Un Bacio a Mezzanotte* and *Petali e Mirto* – the show proceeded in two parts, first with day wear, followed by evening wear. The Hepburn look-alike model wheeled off the Vespa to be replaced by three different models, each wearing another classic from Roman Holiday, the mid-calf powder blue full, pleated skirt with the wide belt, tightly cinched in at the waist keeping a crisp, clean white blouse immaculately in place, set off by a vivid red neck scarf. The audience was transported, from Philips Park to the Trevi Fountain, so that by the time the show's final outfit made its appearance, a perfectly fitted black, sleeveless evening dress, worn with long matching gloves, the hand inside one of these decorously twirling a string of pearls, while the other glamorously sported a cigarette holder, the entire audience was on its feet, cheering. Giulia came on to take her own bow at the end, while the models handed out printed business cards with the name and address of the shop which was soon to be opening printed onto them.

Gowns by Giulia
King Street, Manchester

George arrived just as Giulia was taking her bow. She caught sight of him as he made his way around the edge of the Marquee and discreetly pointed toward a small table at one side and to the back of the cat walk, where Francis was sitting alongside a young man controlling the music. George made his way towards him while the applause continued. Francis saw him and froze. He whispered something in the ear of the young man, who nodded, then looked back towards George. Francis mouthed, "Outside," and wove his way to meet George, who intercepted him just outside the Marquee.

"I hoped you'd find me," he said.

"I saw Winifred. She said you might be here."

"Did you see the show?"

"Only the end."

"Pity. It was fabulous. Giulia is a genius. I want her to design all my gowns in future."

George smiled.

"Where've you been?" asked Francis, suddenly serious again. "I've missed you."

"Oh, you know, the usual. Working."

"My, but you're the busy bee these days, aren't you, darling? Can't you afford to take even one day off?"

"Yes. I'm sorry."

"Will you just look at all these crowds? It's impossible to hear oneself think."

"Winifred told me about the shop."

"Did she? Did she also tell you that she's irreplaceable?"

"Not in so many words."

"Well it's true. She is."

"What are you going to do instead?"

"You sound as if you care. Sorry. That was unnecessary. I know you do. Even if you don't come to see me any more."

"That's not true."

"Not enough then. I miss you, George. I turned sixty last year. There. I hadn't meant to say that. Suddenly I feel like I haven't any clothes on."

"What will you do?"

"When?"

"Tomorrow, next week, next year."

"I've no idea, George. I need a new adventure. When I followed those telegraph poles after I got off the ferry in Liverpool, I had no idea where they'd lead me. That was what was so exciting, the not knowing. They strode across the land like giants and I followed in their shadow. Now, when I gaze through a telescope, or listen to faint radio signals coming all the way from other galaxies to be picked up by the dishes at Jodrell Bank, I feel that just as the universe is expanding and we're able to reach further and further out into space, I'm getting smaller, diminishing, till I'm just a speck, smaller than that, nothing at all really."

"You'll never be nothing to me, Francis. Or to scores of other people who know you and love you."

"I went to the pictures the other week, *The Grosvenor*..." He paused to give George a knowing look. "I went with Julian..."

"Julian?"

"The boy in the Marquee working the music. Nice boy."

"What did you go to see?"

"I was coming to that. *The Incredible Shrinking Man.*" George smiled.

"Have you seen it?"

George shook his head.

"Julian thought it was all terribly funny. But I thought it quite profound, in a schmalzy 'B' movie kind of way. Oh yes, I know it's ridiculous, a radioactive cloud causes the hero who's been exposed to it to start shrinking. It's all rather jolly at first. First his clothes don't fit, then the next thing you know they're celebrities on the TV, till finally his wife has to put him in a doll's house. Soon he gets so small that he falls through a gap in the bath tub drain and has to fight a spider, which in comparison to him is the size of King Kong, with a pin for a sword. It's all very silly and I have to admit that the special effects are as cardboard as they come, but there's something quite metaphysical about it at the end, almost spiritual, as our hero continues to shrink, until he's no larger than a single atom. Afterwards Julian wanted to go to *The Queen's*, but I didn't feel like it. It's not the same since Cam died…"

"No. It's not."

"So I went straight home, but I couldn't stop thinking about it, so much so that I went again a couple of nights later. On my own. If anything, the ending got to me even more the second time. After he's vanquished the giant spider, he keeps on shrinking, till he's almost floating on the air, like thistledown, and we hear his voice-over as he drifts right out into space. 'I no longer had this terrible fear,' he said, 'only the sensation of instinct, of each movement, each thought, tuned to some great directing force. What was I to become? The infinitesimal or the infinite? But suddenly I knew they were really just two ends of the same concept. The unbelievably small and the unbelievably vast meeting in the same moment. And in that moment I knew the answer to the riddle of the universe. And I felt my body dwindling, melting, becoming nothing and, with it, my fears melted away too. It had to mean something. Which meant *I* had to mean something too. Yes – smaller than the smallest I meant something too. To God there is no zero'."

"But you don't believe in God, Francis."

"No, I don't. Which is why I can't understand why the ending of this stupid film affected me so much."

"We all of us want to feel that we matter, that we make some kind of mark on the land."

"And have we?"

"Who knows? All we can do is try. But this is gloomy talk, Francis. You sound like you think you're disappearing like that bloke in the film. But shrinking has never been your style. Larger than life and twice as ugly."

Francis laughed. "I'm sorry. I'm no good on my own. I get maudlin and sentimental. I need people with their feet on the ground, like you, or Winifred, to get me back on track." He took out a handkerchief and blew his nose.

"And which track is that, Francis? Now that you've shut the shop?"

Francis shrugged.

"If you want something that keeps your feet on the ground, why don't you sell television sets? I reckon everyone'll want one soon. Once this *Florizel Street* comes out..."

"But who would I get to manage it and do the accounts now that Winifred's retired? You know how hopeless I am at stuff like that. I should have done that years ago. I dabbled a bit, when the Queen's Coronation was broadcast, but my heart wasn't in it. No. That chapter's closed. But you're right. I do need to do something, instead of mouldering away feeling sorry for myself. It's not about the money, I've got more than enough these days, it's about maintaining contact with people."

"What kind of people, Francis? Whenever a customer came into the shop, you used to run away and hide, unless it was someone as much of a nerd as you."

"I know. You're right." He thought for a moment. "I have, I suppose, always got on rather well with artists..."

"Well then," said George, looking directly at his friend, "why not open a gallery? The city could do with one, especially one which focuses exclusively on contemporary work."

"I could exhibit you," Francis smiled.

"That's not what I meant," said George.

"I know it wasn't, but it's not a bad idea. And here's another – with your contacts at The Institute you know who's current. You could suggest people whose work I might show. We could meet, say, once a month to plan each season." Francis had become suddenly more animated, more like his familiar, enthusiastic self again. "That way I'd get to see you again."

George laughed. "I walked straight into that, didn't I?"

"You talk as though you think I had this planned all

along."

"I wouldn't put it past you."

"George," said Francis, placing his hand over his heart, "you cut me to the quick."

"Very well," said George, still laughing. "It's a deal."

Francis clapped his hands and burst into song. " *'With a song in my heart...'* "

"Be quiet, you fool."

" *'I behold your adorable face...'* "

George watched Francis make his way back towards Giulia's Marquee. He was practically skipping. Every few yards he performed a neat *cabriole*. Some people passing in the opposite direction applauded. In return he gave them the most flamboyant of bows.

From the amphitheatre across the other side of the park, *The Fourtones* began singing their final song.

"*Oh won't you stay
Just a little bit longer
Oh plea-ea-ea-ea-ease
Say you will, say you will…?*"

As Esther was walking away from the Fairground, her attention was caught by the sudden appearance of a freckled, skewbald filly racing out of the circus tent, apparently riderless. Only after galloping for some twenty-five yards or so did the horse show any sign of being under any sort of control, when a young man raised himself up from an unseen position on its far side, to sit astride it bareback, grip its flanks with his buckskinned legs and lean forward to whisper in its ear, whereupon he was able to bring it to an easy stop just a few paces in front of where Esther had been standing.

She raised her hands to her eyes to shield them from the sun, so that she might see the young man more clearly. He reared the horse up on its hind legs, a heroically romantic silhouette, pirouetting gracefully in a circle, before slowly trotting towards her. The young man had long hair beneath a broad brimmed black hat, trimmed with bird feathers, which he raised politely in her direction as he came level with her. His face was strongly sun tanned, as were his arms and bare chest. Around his neck he wore wooden beads strung on a thin cord of leather.

Esther felt her heart constricting her chest. Surely, it was not possible.

"Tommy…?" she called uncertainly, regretting that she'd done so the instant his name passed her lips.

The young man stopped, wheeled the skewbald filly round in a circle and slowly walked it back towards her.

"Yes?" he said.

The sun was now behind her, so she could see the young man's face quite clearly. The likeness was uncanny, but clearly this was a much younger man than the Tommy Thunder she remembered.

"I'm sorry," she said, feeling rather foolish. "I mistook you for somebody else."

"No," he said. "My name is Tommy."

"A coincidence," said Esther. She felt as though the ground beneath her had suddenly become unstable.

"Is everything all right?" said the young man.

"Yes, I… It was just a bit of a shock, that's all… Like seeing a ghost… Except I don't believe in them…"

"I do."

Neither the young man nor his horse moved a fraction. Esther found their stillness quite unnerving.

"What makes you say that?"

"My father. He said I look exactly like my grandfather, almost as if he'd been reborn in me."

Esther said nothing.

"He was called Tommy too. I'm named after him. He was good with horses, like I am. I don't just mean riding them. Sometimes… when I'm trying to teach her a new trick…" he gently ran his hand up and down the horse's neck, "I get the feeling that he's speaking to me, telling me what to do."

Esther paused before finally deciding to speak.

"I met him… your grandfather… a long time ago… twice. The second time was right here, in this park. Another Tulip Sunday. Nearly forty years ago. He was making bird masks for the children. He recognised me before he even saw me. From the way I walked, he said…"

The young man sat patiently upright on the horse's back, waiting for her to finish. The winding gear on the headstocks of Bradford Colliery just beyond the railings began to turn. A high-pitched hum filled the air, stretching out each word she spoke tautly on its wire.

"The first time I saw him was four years before… I'd fallen into a ditch and couldn't climb out… He appeared out of the shadows… Like a tree, or a rock… He rescued me… I'd broken my leg and he carried me back home…

I've never forgotten..."

"What was he like?"

Esther shook her head, as if the task of describing him was beyond her. "Like you," she said, "only older..."

"My father said he only saw him once, but he didn't remember... He was only a baby... His mother took him to the railway station at London Road... My grandfather was just going off to war... She ran along the platform, carrying my father in her arms... Just as the train was pulling out, she saw him in one of the carriages... She lifted my father high above her head... so that he might see him... know he was his... There was a hiss of steam... When it had cleared, the train had gone... Neither my father, nor my grandmother, ever saw him again..."

"What happened to them, your father and grandmother?"

"My grandmother died. Not long after I was born."

"And your mother?"

"She worked as a pit brow woman at Lumn's Lane. Near The Delph."

"That's hard work. I know that from personal experience. I didn't think women still did it."

"They do at Lumn's Lane. My father died in the war. My mother shortly after. I started down the pit myself when I was just fourteen. But I hated it. I couldn't breathe. I thought I'd die. Then one day the Fair came to Worsley. It stayed a week. I hung around at the back of the tents every night. On their last night I asked if I could join them. They asked me what I could do. I didn't know what to say. But then this filly," he said, taking hold of her mane in his fingers, "prodded me in the back with her muzzle, didn't you, my beauty? I'd never spent any time with horses but it was like I'd been around them always. I knew exactly what to do. Very slowly I climbed up onto her back and then stood up, without holding onto anything. I stretched my arms out wide…"

And as he has been describing this, he has re-enacted it, so that now he stands above her, high upon the horse's back.

"It was like someone was telling me what to do, whispering in my ear. Once I'd got my balance just perfect, I clicked my tongue, and she began to walk slowly forward…"

The horse took a few sure steps. Tommy extended his arms further, balancing on tiptoe.

"If I don't fall off, I thought, they'll let me go with them…"

The winding gear on the headstocks stopped turning. Esther could hear the crash of coal wagons shunting into one another. A low rumble boomed beneath the earth. Like thunder. The horse and the boy kept moving, his arms still stretched out wide, until they disappeared over the brow of the hill, which led down to the Fair's encampment. The sounds of Tulip Sunday slowly filtered back.

George had made his way down to the line of ornamental ponds and boating pools. It was hard to think that by the end of the following week these would all be drained and filled in with concrete, but today, for one last time, they were thronged with children and families. He slid down the slope towards the first and largest of the paddling pools, which for Tulip Sunday had been set aside for the two elephants on loan for the day from Belle Vue. When George skittered to a stop at the water's edge, both elephants were there, cooling off in the water. Their keepers were scrubbing them down with a long handled brush. At the side, inching forward as close as they dared was a knot of excited small boys. Among them George recognised Victor's grandsons Ray and Phil and Geoff, Harriet and Paul's son John Mark, Toby and Sandra's Mike, and Pearl and Lamarr's middle child Dwight, all of them dancing on their toes, unable to contain their excitement. George remembered how, once upon a time, he would have been among them. When he was just nine years old, he had been in this exact same spot, waiting on tenterhooks with the rest of them, wondering when the big moment would arrive.

He knew exactly what was coming. He got himself into position, squatted down low, and waited. There was no chance his presence would distract them or tempt them to play up for the camera. They were all far too excited to even register his presence, every ounce of their being focused on the elephant nearest to them.

The elephant swayed its enormous head from side to side, dipping its trunk into the water and spraying its back with it, which the keeper then spread along its sides with the long-handled brush. Then, almost casually, without warning, instead of spraying the water onto its back, the elephant appeared to become aware of the huddle of boys clinging onto each other just a few feet in front of it. It knew exactly what was expected of it, what role it had to play. It raised its trunk high above its head, trumpeted loudly, then sprayed the boys in a single jet propulsion.

The boys shrieked and leapt as one a few feet into the air, before landing in a bedraggled heap and running off to their respective parents, to shake themselves over them like soaked, bedraggled pups.

George had his picture. He caught them just as the water landed and their feet lifted off the ground. Like a many-headed hydra, each face registering its own unique expression of joy, fear, shock, delight. He even managed to capture individual droplets of water as they hung suspended directly above the boys' heads, arcing their way from the elephant's curled up trunk. In the bottom left corner of the image the keeper had lifted one hand away from his long handled brush and brought it towards his face, which was a grinning blur, an action echoed by that of a woman in the top right hand corner of the image who had lifted a gloved hand of her own up towards her face to cover her mouth, her eyes wide with an expression that was difficult to read, relieved to have avoided a wetting herself, or sharing vicariously the pleasure of the boys.

Later this would become one of George's most iconic photographs, which would first be exhibited in Francis's new gallery in Denton, before going on to appear universally in newspapers, books and magazines. But for now he was just pleased to have found himself in the right place at the right time, in Philips Park, on this Tulip Sunday afternoon, on the edge of Bradford Colliery, in the heart of the city of Manchester. He recalled that first essay he had handed in to Mr Vogts, his English teacher at Hulme's School, when he was just eleven, and he had written his address, concluding with: 'Manchester, England, Great Britain, Europe, The World, The Universe.' He slung his camera over his shoulder and smiled.

Less than a quarter of a mile further down the slope, in the last of the ponds, Mary glanced up towards the clock on St Jerome's Church just outside the park. Half past three. Just time for one more race. She stood up stiffly. She placed both hands in the small of her back, kneading the muscles gently to try and get some life back into them. She'd been supervising the children's boating pool all afternoon. It had become something of a tradition over the years, but she wasn't too sorry that this would be the last time. She was feeling more tired than she cared to admit and was looking forward to a cup of tea once the children had gathered up all their boats and gone back to their parents.

She clapped her hands together and called them all round. "Come on," she said, "chop chop. Place your boats in a line here by the steps and, when I give the word, all push them off together. Let's see which boat gets across to the other side first. Ready. Get set. Go."

The children launched their various boats, yachts, canoes and battleships all at once, excitedly shouting encouragement to their own particular craft. Quite soon, like a real boat race, it was impossible to tell which, if any, was winning, with most of them meandering becalmed somewhere in the middle. Some collided with others, while some capsized completely, until somehow they all managed to make it to the other side, sometimes with the aid of a judicious intervention from the long pole Mary had with her for the purpose. The race was judged a tie, and they were all jointly declared as winners, the prize for which was a sherbert lemon each that Mary had brought with her in a jar.

The children collected their boats and sweets and began to drift away until only one was left. A girl on the far side of the pool from where Mary was standing, who was still vainly trying to reach her boat, a wooden yacht, which was just beyond her grasp. Mary walked around the perimeter of the pool until she was beside the girl, who remained so entirely focused on throwing small pebbles towards the yacht in an attempt to change its direction back towards her that she did not notice Mary's arrival, until her shadow fell across the water beside her own much smaller one.

"It's no use," said the girl. "It's got a mind of its own."

"I think you're right," said Mary. "Would you like me to try and catch it for you?"

"Yes please," said the girl. "I'm worried that it might sail right to the far end, where there's a channel that takes it underground."

"Well, we don't want that, do we?" said Mary.

"No we don't," said the girl seriously.

A breeze had started to pick up. There were ripples spreading across the water, breaking up both their reflections. Mary stretched her pole towards the wooden yacht and manoeuvred it back to the edge, where she was able to pick it up.

She was just about to hand it back to the girl when something about it caught her eye. Written on the side of it was a name. Mary looked and read, then took out her spectacles from the pocket in the front of her skirt and read again.

T-u-l-i-p.

Mary froze. It was unmistakably the same boat she had handed over to Sister Clodagh at St Bridget's almost forty-five years before.

She turned to the girl who, up until this moment, she had not paid much attention to. "Where did you get this?" she asked, still holding on to it and examining it very gently.

"From my Mummy," she said.

Mary nodded. "It's a very beautiful boat, isn't it?"

"Yes," said the girl. "My Mummy said her Granddad made it for her."

Mary's mouth felt completely dry. Her fingers began to tingle. She looked more closely at the girl. She had a tangle of red hair, and on her left cheek, barely discernible but there nevertheless, the pale ghost of a strawberry mark.

"Is your Mummy about?" asked Mary, hardly daring to breathe.

"There," said the little girl, pointing along the path to where a woman was walking slowly towards them, her hand linked through the arm of a man who walked rather stiffly with the aid of a cane. Presumably the girl's father, thought Mary. Running alongside the couple, darting back and forth in every direction at once were two small boys, jumping up and down like over-excited puppies. The little girl waved and the woman hurried towards her, temporarily leaving her husband and the two boys to follow on behind her.

"Mummy," said the girl, "this kind lady rescued my boat."

"Did she, my little munchkin?" said the woman, stooping down to her daughter's eye level. She tried to pin up some of the recalcitrant strands of her red hair, but gave up after a few seconds. "Thank you," she said, turning her attention to Mary.

"You're welcome," said Mary. "Here. Don't forget the boat."

"No." The woman held Mary's gaze. "Do I know you?" she asked, drawing closer to her.

Mary swallowed hard. "You're Lily, aren't you?" she said at last.

"Yes, but… how did you know?"

"The boat," said Mary, her eyes welling with tears. "I… I knew your mother. I was with her when she… when you were born. This boat arrived from the Isle of Man earlier the same day…"

Mary felt that if she did not sit down her legs might give way beneath her. She moved towards a nearby bench facing out across the water. Lily sat beside her. Her daughter looked at Mary with a grave and solemn expression.

"You knew my mother?" said Lily, her voice barely a whisper.

Mary nodded. "Very well," she said.

"What... what was she like...?"

"She was the bravest woman I ever knew. Your daughter has a look of her. The hair..."

"Does she?" said Lily. "We named her after her. Didn't we, Ruth?" She extended her hand which her daughter took.

"It was the saddest day of my life having to leave you at St Bridget's... I want you to know... it was not my doing... Someone else..."

"My father...?"

Mary shook her head. "No... he wanted to be, but in the end, he wasn't brave enough... No... that's a story for another time."

Lily looked down, trying to take in the enormity of this chance meeting.

"I used to look for you," said Mary, "in the faces of children playing in the streets. And later in the young women I might pass or brush against in a crowd. I did see you once."

Lily looked back up.

"Here," said Mary, "in Philips Park. Another Tulip Sunday long ago, before we lived in The Lodge. There was a children's egg and spoon race."

Lily was hanging on Mary's every word.

"Our dog barked and it made you drop your egg, you'd been winning up till then, and it rolled towards me. I popped it back onto your spoon. I spoke to one of the Sisters afterwards, a very kind, warm lady..."

"Sister Clodagh..."

"And it put my mind at rest, knowing that you were being looked after."

Lily looked away again.

"I always hoped I might see you again, but I never did, till today…"

Lily cradled the wooden yacht in her arms, thinking of all the times she so very nearly became separated from it, and how, if she had been, she would never have met this woman who had known her mother.

"Ruth," said Mary, looking at the little girl, "do you know why your boat is called *'The Tulip'*?"

The girl shook her head.

"Because they were your Grandma's favourite flower. They used to grow wild in a wood near to where she lived. And when she was a little girl, not much older than you are now, she used to pick them and bring them home to give to her Daddy, who remembered, so that when he made this boat, he named it after them, as a present for your Mummy."

"And now it's mine."

"Yes."

They were now joined by the man with the cane and the two small boys.

"Is everything all right?" he asked, stooping to rub his ankle.

"Yes," said Lily. "This is Mary. Mary, this is my husband, Roland."

"Pleased to meet you," said Roland politely.

"Roland works for Ferranti's," said Lily, "making computers."

"Oh," said Mary, standing up again. "You'll have to talk to my youngest, Gracie, about that. She's an archaeologist. She tells me computers are going to change the way we do everything in the future."

"She's quite correct," said Roland animatedly, "even the way your daughter studies the past."

"Don't get him started," said Lily, laughing proudly, "or he'll never stop."

"And who are these two fine looking young men?" said Mary as the two small boys immediately hid themselves behind Lily's legs. "Are they your sons?"

"No," said Lily, smiling. "Ruth's ours, but these two scamps, Alec and Benji, we're fostering for a few weeks, until their adoption comes through."

"I thought about fostering," said Mary, "once upon a time, but we didn't have the room."

"How many children do you have?" asked Lily.

"Three," said Mary. "All grown up now, The eldest two married with kiddies of their own. You must meet them some time."

"I'd like to."

"We've a lot to catch up on."

"A lot, yes. I want to hear everything."

Mary nodded. "Listen," she said, "in a few minutes I've got to be somewhere else. My eldest daughter, Harriet, is organising a photograph, as a keepsake of our times here in the park. Family and friends. I'd like you to be in that photograph too please. All of you. Can you meet me on the Avenue of Black Poplars in half an hour? I'll look out for you. Then we can arrange to see each other again, when I'll be able to answer all of your questions." She held both of Lily's hands in her own.

"Yes," said Lily, "we'd love to, but we're meant to be meeting up with some other friends we came here with today."

"That's all right," called Mary. "Bring them too. The more, the merrier."

Lily watched her retreating figure hurrying up the slope, then looked back towards Roland, who gently caressed her left cheek. The pocket of emptiness which had always been there in the corner of her heart was slowly beginning to fill. She smiled.

"Come on," she said. "Let's find Pearl and Lamarr."

The photograph had been Harriet's idea.

"It's the end of a chapter," she'd said, "more than that, a whole era, and we ought to mark it."

"If you say so," Mary had replied distractedly. She was too busy sorting things into boxes for her to pay much attention to what her daughter was saying.

"It's not just about leaving here," Harriet continued. "It's the last ever Tulip Sunday. You can't just creep away like poor church mice."

"Right this minute that's exactly what I'd like to do," said Mary, sitting by a heap of clothes on the bed. "I just wish it was all over and done with. I can't think how we're ever going to fit everything into the new house. It's so much smaller. Not that I mind that. The house at Garibaldi Street was smaller still. But we didn't have so much stuff then."

"So get rid of some of it. Half of what's here's mine, Gracie's and Toby's anyway – well, not Toby's so much, he never hoarded things the way Gracie and I did, especially Gracie. Chuck the lot."

"You're welcome to take what's yours," said Mary.

"We already did when we moved out. Anything that's left I reckon's fair game for you to do with what you like. Bin or bonfire."

"I couldn't do that, Harriet. There are just too many memories. I mean – look at this."

She held up a child's drawing.

"I remember this," said Harriet, smiling. "It's the picture Gracie did of the skeleton of Maharajah…"

"The elephant that walked to Manchester?" Mary leant over to look at it more closely.

"It was a school trip to the Museum during the war," said Harriet.

"Yes. I remember."

"It's very good, isn't it?"

"It is… so you can see why I can't throw it out, can't you?" She took the drawing back from Harriet and placed it in the 'Keep' pile, which was so high it was threatening to topple over.

"I'm surprised Gracie didn't take it with her when she left to move into her flat. I'll ask her if you like."

"No, it's all right, love. I've got just the place for it in the new house."

"It's a lot quieter without our Gracie here, isn't it?"

"It is, love."

"Such a whirlwind."

"I know. But I miss it. I miss all of you, I really do. Your father and I just rattle around here half the time."

"That's why the move will be good for you."

"I'm still not sure about that. What your father's going to do with himself all day when he retires I've no idea."

"He'll find something."

"I hope so. I don't want him under my feet all day."

"He will, you'll see. He's always been very resourceful."

"He has, that's true. I expect he'll sort himself out. He's always liked going to the library. He'll have even more time for reading now."

"There you are then."

Mary looked around again helplessly at the various piles scattered on every possible surface. "That's if we ever get there. There's so much to do still, and we've only got another fortnight."

"We'll all help."

"I know you will, love."

"I've already told you. Paul's organising a van from the Yard. He and Toby will carry all the heavy stuff and drive it over to the new place. Then Sandra and I will supervise where everything goes. All you'll have to do is just arrive when it's all done."

"The life of Riley, eh?"

"Whoever *he* was."

Mary began half-heartedly to sort through one of the piles again. "I can't believe there won't be another Tulip Sunday. This would never have happened if Mr Pettigrew was still in charge."

"Well he's not," said Harriet briskly, "so we'll never know, will we? Which is why we've got to do something special to mark the occasion."

"What sort of something?"

"Why don't you just sit down while I make us a cup of tea, and I'll tell you all about it…"

When later Harriet suggested the photograph, Mary wasn't so sure.

"What if it rains?" she said.

"We'll find somewhere to shelter."

"What if no one turns up?"

"We'll just take a photo of you and Dad."

"Oh no – your father wouldn't like that. You know how he hates a fuss."

"I've already spoken to him about it."

"What did he say?"

"The same as you. 'What does your mother think'?"

"But we haven't got a camera."

"Don't worry about that. Giulia knows a photographer."

"Does she? I suppose she would. She probably knows dozens. Who is he?"

"Actually you know him as well."

"Do I?"

"Do you remember Wright's, the printers?"

"Yes. They used to print the posters for Tulip Sunday."

"Paul's Mum was best friends with Mrs Wright."

"Was she? Yes, I seem to remember Claudia mentioning her now I come to think."

"And Mrs Wright's son…"

"George, isn't it?"

"…is a photographer."

"Is he?"

"Quite a famous one. He's also a teacher."

"Like you?"

"No, Mum. Not like me. He lectures in a College."

"What did he say?"

"He thought it was a great idea."

"Did he? But if he's as famous as you say, how are we going to afford him?"

"He's not going to charge us. He wants to do it. As a gift. For you and Dad."

"Oh... It's going to happen then?"

"He suggests we all meet up on the Avenue of Black Poplars towards the end of the day."

"Yes. That makes sense."

"I'll let everyone know then."

"Yes, but..."

"What?"

"What am I going to wear? Everything will be all packed up."

Harriet laughed and put her arms around her mother, hugging her tight. "Something happy," she said.

The afternoon wore on. The Refreshment Tent was busy. Tired families converged there for a last cup of tea before getting ready to pack up and head for home.

Pearl, Lamarr and the children loitered outside.

"Can you just keep an eye on them while I go and spend a penny?" said Pearl.

"I'll join you," said Winifred, who was just arriving. "There's bound to be a queue, and we don't want to be crossing our legs for the photograph, do we?"

"You're right," replied Pearl. "I hadn't thought of that. I'd best take the kids along too."

Just then, Toby and Sandra, Joe and Beth, and Derek

and Maureen wandered up.

"How are you keeping?" asked Pearl, eyeing Maureen's swelling belly.

"Not too badly. I've stopped being sick now."

"That's something."

"I keep needing to pee all the time now, though."

"That's where we're just going," said Pearl.

"Now you've put it into my head, I'd better come with you."

"Me too," said Beth.

"And me," said Sandra.

They went off down the slope towards the Conveniences like a flock of geese, all talking at once.

It was suddenly very quiet in the Refreshment Tent.

Lamarr, Victor, Joe, Toby and Derek all watched their respective wives making their way down the slope with a shake of the head and a smile.

It was the first time since the accident, seven years before, that the five of them had been alone together, without anyone else. Realisation of that fact gradually dawned on them. They looked at each other slowly, in turn, remembering. None of them spoke. A whole minute passed. One by one they would recollect a particular moment, nod and smile, their eyes making contact. Derek took off the glasses he now wore, polished them on his jumper, tilting his eyes upwards as he did so, then put them back on. Lamarr rubbed his ankle. Joe moved to stand behind his father's chair. Victor patted the back of his son's hand. Toby took the Roman coin he always carried with him from his jacket pocket and rolled it between his fingers. The silence and the memory held them.

The mood was broken by the arrival of Ray, Joe's son, who stood soaking wet in the entrance to the tent.

"Mum says we've got to go for the photograph." He pointed down the slope to where Beth was waving and pointing to the watch on her wrist.

"Right-oh," said Joe. "Tell her we're just coming."

"Will do."

"Oi – wait a minute. What happened? Fell in the pond?"

"Nah," said Ray. "It were the elephant." Then he ran off.

Joe looked at the others. The moment between them had gone. They knew it would never be repeated.

"Kids, eh?" laughed Lamarr.

They all left the tent to join their wives and families before making their separate ways to the Avenue of Black Poplars.

Striding purposefully along the Avenue was Delphine.

In her younger days she had not been a regular user of public parks. Having grown up in the less tamed stretches of the Coroners Wood between the River Irwell and the Ship Canal and been allowed to roam more or less where she pleased around the Bob's Lane Ferry, parks had always felt rather manicured and constrained for her tastes. This was confirmed for her again after she first left home, for teacher training in Broughton Park, when she would regularly go on hikes in the Pennines, the Peaks and the Lakeland Fells with her girl friends from the

College. Taking part in the Mass Trespass on Kinder Scout back in 1932 had, for her, been a simple assertion of her right to roam where she pleased. But in more recent times, as her joints had stiffened and her stamina waned, she found she rather liked parks after all. She had come to recognise they were a necessary life blood for the city, an escape from factory smoke, foundry heat, colliery clatter and cotton mill dust, a chance for exhausted workers to snatch a little bit of cleaner air into closed and shuttered lungs, if only for a few hours on a Sunday afternoon.

Like today.

She appreciated the colour that the flowers brought, for all their municipal, regimented rows and straight lines, to otherwise dark and sunless streets. Within such parameters Jabez always managed a particularly impressive and creative display for Tulip Sunday, and this year was no exception. If anything he had surpassed himself. The riot of colour that festooned the park's many serpentine pathways offset perfectly the bold and dramatic statement made by the juxtaposition of black and white tulips along the Main Carriageway. She had not previously considered the political potential of flowers, but there was no mistaking the symbolism here. Coal and bones. Money and sacrifice. Profit and loss. She was sorry that this was to be the last, but she applauded the bold and provocative way in which it was making its final exit. She wondered what the future held for parks in Manchester. Philips Park had been the first such green space provided by a local authority anywhere in Britain. It would be a pity if this legacy was not to be preserved and improved upon.

Now that she had retired finally, having worked in the end until she reached seventy, she was looking for different causes to fill up her time. Perhaps Public Parks might be one of them. She had been invited to sit on the University's Board of Governors, a position she had accepted, and she would, she knew, remain in close contact with her former colleagues in the Audiology Department, just as she maintained links with *The Manchester Institute for the Deaf* for decades after she ceased to work for them. But she had perceived already, in the six months since she had finished teaching, that she had a lot of time on her hands with no shortage of energy to fill it. At the same time she had resisted the temptation to grasp at too many things immediately, for fear of making the wrong choices. Once she had committed herself to something, Delphine liked to see it through to its conclusion, and so caution was her current watchword. Whereas before, *carpe diem* had always been her motto, now it was more likely to be *cave*. One can never be too careful, she told herself. *Abundans cautela non nocet*. A little precaution does no harm. She would parcel out what precious time remained her judiciously. But walking in the fresh air of Manchester's public parks would certainly feature prominently.

She decided to take a short breather on a bench which became empty just when she had most need of it. Looking out across the park towards the ornamental ponds, she caught sight of Lily. She was deep in conversation with an older woman who appeared somewhat familiar, but whom she did not at first recognise. Then she remembered. This was Mary. The wife of Jabez, the Head Gardener, whom she had seen being presented to the crowds earlier in the afternoon. Mary had been standing proudly alongside him. Then she remembered something more. This was the same Mary who had wanted to look after Lily just after she was born, after Ruth had died, and who had been prevented from doing so by Charles's misplaced sense of propriety. Moral cowardice, she had accused him of when he first confessed the whole sad story to her... When was that? It must be almost thirty years ago, she realised. How the years have mellowed and softened all the players in that sorry tale. She had forgiven Charles the day he intervened to admit Roland into the Infirmary to see the specialist surgeon and have his foot amputated before the infection spread to the rest of his leg. It was that he had done so without in any way drawing attention to himself, without seeking any personal reward or satisfaction, or – and this was the clincher for Delphine – without letting himself known to Lily in some last ditch, vainglorious attempt to be embraced by her and so manufacture some pitiable happy ending for himself. He had, quite properly, made himself inconspicuous, recognised that this situation was no longer about him, or his needs, but what could be done for Roland, and thereby contribute to Lily's future happiness, a future in which he had no place, having twice forfeited that opportunity previously.

Unlike Delphine, Charles had not taken to retirement at all well. He had been unable to find a new place for himself in the world. Having solely defined himself by his work at the Infirmary and the reputation he had garnered through his achievements there, once he left, he became lost. He rarely went out. He wandered aimlessly around his flat, grew grumpier by the day, isolated himself from his former colleagues who, if they ever saw him by chance, would try to avoid having to engage in any kind of conversation with him beyond pleasantries, and resigned from his various clubs and societies. Delphine would drop in on him occasionally, mainly to check if he needed anything if she were going to the shops, but their socialising together had long ceased. To everything there is a season, she reflected, and a time to every purpose.

She noticed Lily and Mary speaking together in low, rapt voices, their heads bent towards each other. She saw the two of them embrace with great love and warmth, before Mary hurried on up the slope. She watched Lily sitting quietly alone for a moment afterwards, looking down at something she was holding in her lap, before her husband, daughter and two foster children rejoined her. She has learned who Mary is, Delphine realised. She has begun to understand the truth about her mother, and this elicited in Delphine more of an emotional response than she would have expected. She had grown fond of Lily over the past dozen years, since their paths had first crossed concerning Roland's citizenship and she had been able to set him on that first rung on his way towards becoming the accomplished and much sought-after computer engineer he had become today. Since losing her biological mother on the day she was born, Lily had latched onto a series of surrogates – Sister Clodagh, Annie Wright, Delphine herself for a time, and now, quite possibly, Mary, who had wanted to assume that role right from the beginning. She would tell Charles about this encounter the next time she saw him. It might bring him some much needed solace and comfort, she thought.

She stood up. The sun was dipping in the sky and she was starting to feel cold. She set off down the Avenue of Black Poplars, just as Lily, Roland and the children began making their way towards her. Lily's face was wreathed in happiness.

"Delphine," she cried, "the most wonderful thing's happened. Walk with me to the end while I tell you all about it. There's to be a photograph taken, for Jabez and Mary..." Delphine noted the way Lily's voice choked slightly as she spoke Mary's name. "Join us for it. There are bound to be people you know..."

Why not, thought Delphine? She looked at Lily, on the brink of a new chapter in her life, and thought back to that afternoon forty years ago when she herself was on the threshold of exciting change, about to begin at the University, and she had made her way by train to Bob's Lane Ferry, to visit her parents' cabin in the woods, only to find their bodies wrapped around each other in a final embrace. She had needed a friend back then, and he had materialised in the surprising shape of Francis, who now she saw skipping through the black and white tulips towards the large group of people who had gathered at the top of the Avenue for an unlikely photograph.

" *'Out of the ashes we rise'*," she thought.

By half past four George was setting up his tripod. He

had decided he would use a colour film, a medium he rarely chose, but which he thought would be more appropriate for the occasion.

"Nothing sad," Giulia had warned when she told him about it. "It's a celebration."

He had decided he would take it here, at the entrance to the Avenue of Black Poplars and use the trees to frame the composition. He placed a couple of the Park's benches in the middle of the path. His idea was to place Mary and Jabez in the centre, with their immediate family close beside them, the children sitting on the grass in front, and everyone else grouped behind. In the foreground would be as many of the brightly coloured tulips as he could fit in. He had arranged for Harriet to give everyone an individual tulip to hold as they arrived. The impression George was hoping for was for the people to look as though they had almost been planted there, as part of the display.

Gradually they began to arrive, converging on the spot George had chosen, from all corners of Philips Park.

Toby and Sandra, with their three children, Michael, Mildred and Martin.

Harriet and Paul, with their son John Mark. Paul had also brought his Uncle Matteo with him. Frailer now than he once was, but still bright-eyed and alert. "If only Bombola was still alive…" he said with a wink. "Who's Bombola?" asked John Mark. Paul smiled and shook his head, before tousling his son's hair.

Derek and Maureen. Derek in dark glasses, Maureen heavily pregnant, still clinging to Derek like glue, each gave a shy wave.

Winifred and Victor came next. Victor in his chair, pushed by Joe, followed closely by Joe's wife, Beth, and their three boys, Raymond, Philip and Geoffrey.

Alongside Winifred was Esther. Dressed in white from head to foot.

George, who had been watching them arrive through his viewfinder, looked up slowly. Could it really be the same...? He strolled across towards them, said hello to Winifred and Victor, then nervously approached Esther. "I'm not sure if I've got this right," he said, "but thirty years ago, I believe you were my Guardian Angel."

Esther looked at George curiously. "Explain," she said.

"It was on Chat Moss," said George. "My friend and I had come off my motor bike, trying to avoid a collision with a white heron. He broke his leg. You appeared – out of nowhere, it seemed – and set it for him, then went off to fetch an ambulance."

Esther smiled. "Yes, I remember now, though I wouldn't have recognised you. How is your friend?"

George looked around. "He made a complete recovery. He should be along here soon. I'll make sure he sees you."

Esther nodded. "I'm not hard to miss these days," she said, placing the white shawl over her head, and smiling.

Then came Pearl and Lamarr, in their usual flurry. Lamarr had his arm around Lamarr Junior who, with his boxing gloves looped around his neck, was shyly carrying a small trophy he had won earlier in the afternoon. Victor caught sight of him and gave him a thumbs up. Dwight was pestering his older brother to let him try on the boxing gloves. Lamarr Junior eventually relented and Dwight, refusing any offers of help, was focused on the difficult task of putting on the second glove using a mixture of his other gloved hand and his teeth, his brow puckered with concentration. Pearl, carrying her baby twin girls, Kendra and LaShawne, on one arm each, was at the same time trying to prise Candice from the posse of young boys she had trailing in her wake.

Behind them Lily, Roland, Ruth and the two foster boys, Alec and Benji, made their way towards the growing throng, accompanied by Delphine. Roland was tired. His leg was aching. "Not far now," said Lily. "We're almost there. Then we can sit down."

Mary had been looking out for them, ever since the first people had started to arrive and had been saving a space for them on the bench where she and Jabez had been asked to sit by George. She saw them and waved excitedly. "Look," she whispered to Jabez, "she's here. After all these years."

Lily sat down with her daughter, Ruth, cross-legged on the grass at her feet, holding the yacht her great-grandfather had made quietly on her lap.

Delphine caught sight of Esther, whom she had not seen for many years, and made a beeline straight for her. "Esther," she called. "Or should that be Ishtar now?"

Esther smiled. "Not here," she said. "They know me as Esther still here."

Mr and Mrs Pettigrew introduced themselves to George and asked where he would like them to stand, followed by dozens more, former work mates of Jabez, other gardeners and park keepers, a few councillors, all of whom George somehow managed to squeeze into the frame. The allotted time to take the photograph had come and gone, and George was beginning to get a little anxious about losing the light. He asked Harriet if she thought he should make a start.

"Not yet," she said. "Gracie's not here. She promised she would be. How long before it gets critical?"

George scanned the sky. "Another fifteen minutes," he said.

Harriet nodded and spoke to the assembled gathering in her best school teacher's voice, explaining that they were just waiting for one or two more people to arrive and thanking them for their patience.

The lull which followed Harriet's announcement was interrupted by the sound of Francis singing gaily unperturbed, as Giulia tugged on his arm.

"*Tiptoe through the tulips, in the garden, won't you pardon me…?*"

Giulia raised her eyes towards George, shrugging her shoulders helplessly, but the rest of the crowd, caught up in the rising euphoria, simply joined in the last line of the chorus, "*Tiptoe through the tulips with me,*" before bursting into spontaneous applause.

"Is that for me?" joked Gracie, pedalling her bicycle furiously with her good leg, seemingly out of control as she hurtled towards them, only to brake to a stop with an impressive three-sixty skid, throwing up shards of gravel and dust.

"Cool," said Dwight appreciatively.

"You're late," said Harriet.

"No, I'm not," she said. "I'm exactly on time."

The Fourtones had finished playing their set on the stage in the Amphitheatre more than half an hour ago, since when there had been a mixture of records and announcements issuing from the various public address speakers placed around the park.

"In just over two minutes," the latest of these now informed everyone, "we shall be having the moment we've all been waiting for, the climax to this year's Tulip Sunday, a fly-past by the RAF Black Arrows Aerobatic Display Team, under the command of Squadron Leader Roger Topp. Look out for them flying towards us from the direction of the colliery." A buzz of anticipation ran through the park. "But now, until they arrive, please enjoy the dulcet tones of the late Miss Chamomile Catch, the Manchester Songbird, in a recording of that classic song, *Here I'll Stay*, with music by Kurt Weill and lyrics by Alan Jay Lerner, requested especially for Jabez and Mary Chadwick, by all their friends, family and well-wishers."

George caught Francis's eye. This explained why he'd been on the last minute. The two of them nodded and smiled.

Just before Cam began to sing, George clapped his hands and asked everyone to look towards the camera. "Enjoy the music and smile," he said. "Harriet has asked me to thank you all on behalf of the whole family for agreeing to take part in making this special memory for their parents. Think of them as you listen and enjoy the colour of the tulips this one last time."

He set the timer switch on the camera for thirty seconds and then placed himself on the edge of the group, next to Francis.

"There's a far place I'm told
Where I'll find a field of gold
But here I'll stay with you

And they say there's an isle deep with clover
Where your heart wears a smile all day through

But I know well they're wrong
And I know where I belong
And here I'll stay with you

For that land is a sandy illusion
It's the theme of a dream gone astray
And the world others woo
I can find loving you
And here, I guess, I'll stay with you…"

Just as the final notes of the song had begun to fade, and the shutter on the camera had clicked for the last time, the Black Arrows tore across the sky in their signature diamond formation, leaving rainbow-coloured vapour trails painting patterns in their wake.

Everyone looked up and gasped in wonderment and joy. Later, when George was developing the finished print of the photograph to give to Mary and Jabez, he selected the final one, where they were all still looking towards the camera, smiling and united, framed by the black poplars, the Black Arrows just appearing above their heads, distant specks over the dark silhouette of the now stilled winding gear on the headstocks of Bradford Colliery.

Having performed their aerobatics, Squadron Leader Roger Tipp radioed the rest of his team to head back to base.

Flying over the mills, mines, factories and forges of Manchester, using the Ship Canal as his guide, one of the pilots looked down, recognising various landmarks with a smile. In his cockpit, Flight Lieutenant Richard Catch reached across to the upturned horse shoe propped up over the controls, which he always flew with, and tapped it three times, as he always did, once for his mother, once for his grandfather, and once for himself.

*

Mary introduces Lily to Harriet, whose face is wreathed in smiles. Harriet takes Lily across to Paul, to Toby, to Gracie. She watches them engage in easy, unforced conversation. She looks down at the tulip she is still holding from the photograph and conjures up a memory she has not allowed herself to revisit since the day Ruth died. She wonders if at last the time has come to take it out, dust it down, and hold it up before her once again, shake it, like a child's snow globe, watch and wait till the flakes all settle…

"I had a dream last night, Mary," said Ruth. "I dreamed that a great cloud hung above us, filled with a

isonous gas, which killed every living thing, , flowers, trees, so that the whole of the earth was like the battlefields of Europe, a grey ocean of mud, devoid of colour, in which we all struggled to keep upright, floundering and drowning. Most of the buildings were flattened too, from the bombardment of the guns and the explosions of the shells, but a few were still standing, and those people who had managed to reach these last few survived, until the gas had cleared and the guns were silent. You and I were among them, Mary, and as we stumbled through the wreckage, pockets of rats nosed in and out of the shell holes. We came across a patch of ground where a small flower grew, stunted but bravely pushing through from deep underground."

*

The day draws to a close.

The crowds slowly depart. The tents and marquees lie empty, their flaps all neatly tied up. Contractors will arrive tomorrow to take them down and cart them away. The final few stragglers are gradually leaving the park. A hot and harassed family are the last to leave, Mum pushing a pram with the baby grizzling inside, another child reluctantly holding her hand, struggling to keep hold of her balloon, and Dad with a small boy on his shoulders bawling loudly, a dog pulling hard on its lead, still in pursuit of fresh, new scents.

Jabez sees them safely out, then locks the park gates behind them. He pockets the keys, conscious that this is an action he will not be doing again. He and Mary stand hand in hand by the railings, looking back at the Lodge, which has been their home for the last thirty-one years. It has a sad and somewhat forlorn air, with all of the curtains removed and sheets of hardboard nailed up from the inside to deter any unwonted prying, while the Corporation decides what's to be done with the building. One thing's for certain: there won't be another park keeper and his family living there. Tomorrow a council official will unlock the gates, as part of what will become his daily round of parks across the city.

Mary is remembering the day they moved in, all their possessions piled on the back of Matteo's rag and bone cart, pulled along by old Bombola, the children taking it in turns to ride upon his uncomplaining back. Now the children have once again assisted them to move. Not that they're children any more, sighs Mary. Grown ups now, all of them, with children of their own. By now they will have unpacked all the boxes, put the furniture in place, hung the curtains and – knowing Toby – put up a vase of fresh flowers in every room.

"It's been a good place," says Mary at last.

"Ay, lass. It has, that," says Jabez.

"I wish we didn't have to go."

"Now then, Mary," says Jabez, putting an arm around her shoulders, "there's nowt to be gained by crying."

"No, love, I know, but still…"

"You know what I always say?"

"I do, but I reckon you're going to say it anyway."

"When one door closes, another one opens."

"Yes, I suppose."

"We're luckier than most. We've both still got our

health. I may be retiring, but I'm not dead yet."

Mary is silent. Finally she turns away and says, "I shan't be coming back here again. Not even for a visit."

"No need to, love. We've Platt Fields just down the road from our new place. Pastures new and all that."

"Though I reckon I'll come back to the cemetery each year. On the anniversary of Ruth's death."

"To lay some tulips?"

Mary nods. "Maybe Lily will come with me."

"Let's take a last look at the Avenue of Black Poplars before we go, shall we?"

"Yes, please."

They skirt round the boundary of the park towards the railings on the corner of Mill Street and Stuart Street, at the junction of which is a small gap just wide enough for them to squeeze through. They pick their way carefully through the undergrowth till they reach the clump of pines. The patch of wild tulips, which has now spread to cover an area of more than a hundred yards by fifty, lies before them, its colours caught by the rays of the evening sun, just beginning to dip below the level of the trees.

"We created this," says Jabez, "from that very first bunch you threw down in anger on the day we met.

"Gracie was conceived here," remembers Mary fondly and smiles.

"That's better," says Jabez. "Come on, let's be catching our bus."

Three quarters of an hour later they are walking down Albion Road, a quiet *cul de sac* of red brick terraced houses bordering Platt Fields, not far from the bandstand there, about a quarter of a mile from the junction of Wilmslow Road with Dickenson Road, along the course of the old Nico Ditch.

Jabez takes the key from his jacket pocket and opens the front door. "Come on then, lass," he says, holding out his arms.

"You're not thinking of carrying me across the threshold, are you?"

"A tradition's a tradition."

"Don't be so soft. You'll do yourself a mischief."

But before she can say anything more, he has swept her up in his arms and staggered into the hallway, where they both collapse in a heap on the floor, laughing.

"You daft beggar," she says.

"I'll put the kettle on, shall I?" he says, picking himself up.

Mary looks around.

"Harriet and Toby have done a wonderful job. Everything's just as it should be."

Jabez brings in the tea. Mary is looking out of the window at the front, where there's a spindle tree just coming into blossom.

"I'd forgotten about this tree," she says, leaning into Jabez.

"I'll just go and check upstairs," says Jabez. "I'll be down again in a tick."

Mary listens to the creak of the stairs as he climbs, one of the many new sounds that she will have to learn.

"They've only half-finished putting up the curtains on the landing," calls Jabez. "They must've been interrupted and then forgotten. I'll just fetch the step ladders and do the rest while I'm here."

Just then Mary notices a middle-aged couple walking past the window. She hears them talking but can't make out what they are saying. In the next moment they're knocking on their front door.

"Just a minute," she calls out. She walks slowly and rather painfully down the hall. It's been a long day and she's suddenly very tired. She can feel the joints in her hips aching. When she opens the door, the couple are standing on the step waiting for her.

"Good evening," says the man, holding out his hand in greeting and smiling broadly, "we are your new neighbours." Mary shakes it automatically and smiles back.

"Good evening."

"Pardon us for intruding on you like this," says the woman, throwing her husband an exasperated look. "But we know how exceedingly busy you must be, so we thought we would just save you some time by preparing you a little something for your supper." She thrusts a dish of lamb curry into Mary's hands.

"Thank you," she says, somewhat taken aback. "That's so kind of you."

"It's nothing," says the woman with a wave of her left hand, her right hand pulling the scarf which had slipped back over her head. "You can give us the dish back any time. No hurry."

"No," says the man, his smile still beaming, "no hurry."

"Would you like to come in?" asks Mary, standing

back and gesturing for them to step inside.

"Thank you," says the man, but just as he is about to enter, his wife tugs his sleeve and pulls him back.

"No, no, no. We know you must have a thousand and one things to do, isn't it? We mustn't take up any more of your time."

"Mr. and Mrs. Agrewal Singh," says the man, as they are beginning to back away from the house. "We are most happy to meet you."

"Mr. and Mrs. Chadwick. But please call me Mary. Everybody does."

The woman steps forward once more. "Urja," she says, then indicates her husband. "Ramesh."

By this time Jabez has joined them on the step.

"Jabez," says Mary, "this is Urja and Ramesh. They've brought us some supper. Look?"

"Pleased to meet you," says Jabez, smiling. "Thank you."

"It's nothing," says Urja once more.

Ramesh offers his hand to Jabez. "Welcome to Manchester."

Ornaments of Grace continues with Book 6
Laurel, vol 1: Kettle

Dramatis Personae

(in order of appearance)

CAPITALS = Major Character; **Bold** = Significant Character;
Plain = appears once or twice

FRANCIS, Hall & Singer Optics
Lord Haw Haw
Alvar Lidell, BBC Newsreader
JABEZ CHADWICK, Head Keeper of Philips Park
Dru, leader of the settlement of Manceinion
Bron, Dru's woman
Pard, Bron's son
Wem, Bron's daughter
Eä, Cora's man
Cora's baby
Moire, a Pict woman
Dr Garfield Williams, Dean of Manchester
Survivor of The Beehive pub
Child with doll
MARY, Jabez's wife
DELPHINE, an audiologist at Manchester University
PAUL LOCKHART, Claudia's son
WINIFRED HOLT, manager of Hall & Optics
Martha, Victor's ex-wife
VICTOR COLLINS, a miner and ex-boxer
JOE, Victor's son
ANNIE WRIGHT, George's mother
LILY, an orphan, Annie's adoptive daughter
Evelyn, Annie's mother-in-law
Pearl, Lily's friend
RICHARD CATCH, Cam's son
Mack, boy in Buile Hill Park
Maisie, Mack's sister
Ian, Mack's friend
CATCH, a blacksmith, Richie's grandfather

CAM, a night club singer, Richie's mother
Roland, German pilot rescued by Richie
ESTHER, an ARP Warden
Home Guard Officer
Home Guard Corporal
CLAUDIA, a night school teacher in Ancoats
Matteo, Claudia's brother
Father Fracassi, a priest in Manchester's Little Italy
GIULIA, Claudia's daughter
HARRIET, Jabez and Mary's daughter, a teacher
Rt Hon. Colonel Victor Cazalet MP
John Jagger MP, Manchester Central
Journalist, Manchester Evening Chronicle
Lamarr Young, a G.I., later a miner, married to Pearl
Mags, a prostitute at Melland Camp
Sefton Delmer, Radio Aspidistra
Der Chef, fictitious Prussian Officer
Vicky, the Sailor's Sweetheart
Brigadier Gambier Perry, Head of Naval Intelligence Communications
GEORGE WRIGHT, a photographer
Squadron Leader Captain Peter Rowley, George's C/O
Roland Penrose, surrealist, decoy artist
Julian Trevelyan, surrealist, decoy artist
Hugh Catt, zoologist
Hugh Casson, architect
Geoffrey Barkas, film maker
Jasper Maskelyne, stage magician
Lee Miller, Penrose's wife, photographer
Dr Manfred Hart, surgeon, Manchester Royal Infirmary
Lamarr Jnr, Pearl & Lamarr's son
Candice, Pearl & Lamarr's daughter
Sandra, Toby's wife
Stephen, physics student, Gracie's friend at university
Howard Findlay, Mine Manager
Patrick Kinsella, Site Foreman
Henry, surface engineer

TOBY, Jabez and Mary's son, a miner
Derek, Esther's great nephew, a miner
Melvyn, surface engineer
Ian, a young miner
Maureen, Derek's fiancée, later wife
Alan, Derek's father
Harold, Derek's grandfather, Esther's brother
Michael & Mildred, Toby & Sandra's two children
Dr Michael Neville, archaeologist
Angela, Neville's assistant
Mr Clark, newsagent
Mrs Clark, newsagent's wife
Harold Lever, MP
Pat Phoenix, actress
The Fourtones, local pop group
PC Ted Albery, local Bobby
Herbert Silcock, owner of Silcock's Travelling Fair
Julian, a friend of Francis
Tommy, Tommy Thunder's grandson
Ray, Phil, Geoff, Victor's grandsons
John Mark, Harriet and Paul's son
Dwight, Pearl and Lamarr's middle child
Urja & Ramesh Agrewal Singh, Jabez and Mary's new neighbours

The following are mentioned by name:

[Firefighters]
[Pict warriors]
[Brigantes tribesfolk]
[Area Team Co-ordinator]
[Gun crews]
[Royal Engineers]
[Wedding Party, Manley Arms]
[George Formby Jnr]
[Old couple on mattress]
[Four priests at St Augustine's]

[Medical Superintendent, Manchester Royal Infirmary]
[Surgeons performing operations by candlelight]
[Grammar School boys bearing stretchers]
[Rescue Team, Gorton]
[Carollers, Manchester Cathedral]
[Ancoats Excelsior Perseverance Brass Band]
[Burne-Jones]
[Peter Marron, Head Groundman Old Trafford Cricket Ground]
[Elsie Carlisle, singer]
[Sandy Powell, comedic actor]
[Two babies born in the Blitz]
[Homeless families outside bombed out houses]
[Child with doll's mother]
[Screaming man]
[Lecturer at University]
[Claudia's Superior at Ancoats Reading Room]
[Survivors on Portugal Street with tea and blankets]
[Young Constable on Lapwing Lane]
[Children playing in Buile Hill Park]
[Jim, Mack's older brother in RAF]
[Sir Thomas Bayley Potter, 1st Mayor of Manchester]
[Frances Hodgson Burnett]
[Rommel]
[Registrar, Denton Town Hall]
[Postman in Little Italy]
[Lieutenant-Governor Isle of Man]
[D.G. Seex, Chairman Regional Advisory Committee Alien Internment]
[Constanzia, Matteo's wife]
[Father Brown]
[G.K. Chesterton]
[Students in Claudia's evening classes]
[Internees on board SS Arandora Star]
[Chief Officer Frederick Brown, SS Arandora Star]
[Captain Moulton, SS Arandora Star]
[Sgt Norman Price, survivor SS Arandora Star]
[Signor Francesco Testa, teacher at St Michael's School]
[Ronald Moss, Minister for Information]
[Henry Marshall, Bishop of Salford]
[Osbert Peake Under Secretary for the Home Office]
[Penny Wilkinson, Gracie's clever class mate]
[Dance Band from The Savoy]

[Betty Hutton]
[John Lund, screen actor]
[Wardrobe mistresses and assistants, Dickenson Road Film Studios]
[Organist at St Jerome's]
[Audie Murphy]
[Italian internees in Australia]
[Giancarlo, Filippo, Franco, friends of Matteo]
[Sailor on ship bringing Matteo home]
[German POW's after El Alamein]
[Lieutenant-General McCreery, X Corps]
[Italian Partisans]
[Italian Blackshirts]
[Gustav Klimt]
[Plotters in Ops Room]
[Men & Women at Levenshulme Palais]
[Bing Crosby]
[Dorothy Lamour]
[Bob Hope]
[Greer Garson]
[Walter Pidgeon]
[Joan Crawford]
[WRVS Nurse, Dukinfield]
[Lily's ATS Supervisor]
[Caroline, an ATS Girl]
[Italian & German POWs, Melland Camp]
[Prostitutes outside Melland Camp]
[Women at Levenshulme Market]
[Victor Foto, Hasselbad's of Sweden]
[Rudolf Hess]
[William J. Donovan, Head of US Co-ordination of Information]
[President Roosevelet]
[David Bowes-Lyon, Queen Elizabeth's brother]
[Escaped former U-Boat Radio Operator]
[Captain Mole]
[Captain Mole's wife]
[Captain Mole's 1st Officer]
[Torpedo Officer Hans Braun]
[Captain Wolfgang Weiner & Crew]
[Sceptical BBC Boffin]
[Himmler]
[Studio Announcer, Crowborough]

[Don Quixote]
[Miro]
[Kokoschka]
[Picasso]
[Man Ray]
[Stalin]
[Gilbert & Sullivan]
[André Breton]
[Salvador Dali]
[Stanley Holloway]
[Cole Porter]
[Flight Engineer, Farnham Castle]
[Robert Louis Stevenson]
[Pevsner]
[Jomo Kenyatta]
[[Kwame Nkrumah]
[Haille Selassie]
[Crowds watching Rag stunts on Oxford Road]
[Students wearing masks of Patton, Montgomery, Zhukov, Eisenhower, Bomber Harris, Konev]
[Students dressed as babies in Pram Race]
[Students as three brass monkeys]
[Student as Death]
[Harold Nicholson MP]
[Ravel]
[Couperin]
[Reverend John Armistead, Holmes Chapel 1853]
[Bishop of Manchester, 1945]
[POW Guard]
[Guard's C/O]
[Galileo]
[Bernard Lovell, Jodrell Bank]
[Alf Dean, Lovell's assistant]
[Frank Foden, Lovell's assistant]
[John Clegg, engineer]
[Blatchford's, Sheffield, makers of prosthetics]
[Anuerin Bevan]
[Giancarlo, Filippo, Franco, friends of Matteo]
[Sailor on ship bringing Matteo home]
[German POW's after El Alamein]
[Lieutenant-General McCreery, X Corps]

[Italian Partisans]
[Italian Blackshirts]
[Gustav Klimt]
[Plotters in Ops Room]
[Men & Women at Levenshulme Palais]
[Bing Crosby]
[Dorothy Lamour]
[Bob Hope]
[Greer Garson]
[Walter Pidgeon]
[Joan Crawford]
[WRVS Nurse, Dukinfield]
[Lily's ATS Supervisor]
[Caroline, an ATS Girl]
[Italian & German POWs, Melland Camp]
[Prostitutes outside Melland Camp]
[Women at Levenshulme Market]
[Victor Foto, Hasselbad's of Sweden]
[Rudolf Hess]
[William J. Donovan, Head of US Co-ordination of Information]
[President Roosevelet]
[David Bowes-Lyon, Queen Elizabeth's brother]
[Escaped former U-Boat Radio Operator]
[Captain Mole]
[Captain Mole's wife]
[Captain Mole's 1st Officer]
[Torpedo Officer Hans Braun]
[Captain Wolfgang Weiner & Crew]
[Sceptical BBC Boffin]
[Himmler]
[Studio Announcer, Crowborough]
[Don Quixote]
[Miro]
[Kokoschka]
[Picasso]
[Man Ray]
[Stalin]
[Gilbert & Sullivan]
[André Breton]
[Salvador Dali]
[Stanley Holloway]

[Cole Porter]
[Flight Engineer, Farnham Castle]
[Robert Louis Stevenson]
[Pevsner]
[Jomo Kenyatta]
[[Kwame Nkrumah]
[Haille Selassie]
[Crowds watching Rag stunts on Oxford Road]
[Students wearing masks of Patton, Montgomery, Zhukov, Eisenhower, Bomber Harris, Konev]
[Students dressed as babies in Pram Race]
[Students as three brass monkeys]
[Student as Death]
[Harold Nicholson MP]
[Ravel]
[Couperin]
[Reverend John Armistead, Holmes Chapel 1853]
[Clement Atlee]
[Frederick Williams, mathematician]
[Tom Kilburn, mathematician]
[Geoff Tootill, mathematician]
[Felix Mendelssohn, composer]
[BBC Radio Light Programme Announcer]
[Gilbert Vinter, conductor BBC Concert Orchestra]
[Trevor Duncan, composer]
[Misha Black, designer of The Kardomah]
[Thomas Hardy]
[Edward White, composer]
[Charles Darwin]
[Stephen's ex-girl friend in Wigan]
[Students in The Kardomah]
[Malcolm Arnold]
[Miners, Bradford Colliery]
[Surface Engineers]
[Henry, surface engineer]
[Sandra's mother]
[Trapped miners' families waiting at surface]
[Reporters, broadcasters, photographers, cameramen waiting at surface]
[King James I]
[Thomas Charnock, original owner of Bradford Colliery]

[Sir Oswald Mosley, owner of Ancoats Hall, 1740]
[Mr John Seddon, renter of Bradford Colliery, 1740]
[Edward Bryan, 1870, miner from Pendleton]
[Ghosts of former miners]
[Crowd waiting at Stuart Street Power Station]
[Wedding Couple in car coming back from St Jerome's Church]
[Members of Dr Neville's archaeological team]
[Journalists, radio & TV reporters interviewing Gracie]
[Enid Blyton]
[Besses o'th' Barn Brass Band]
[Mr Willie Wood, conductor]
[Leslie Lever MP, former Lord Mayor of Manchester]
[Toffee-nosed Tory]
[Mr Lever, Harold & Leslie's father from Lithuania]
[Eric Ball]
[Robert Doisneau]
[Henri Cartier-Bresson]
[Bill Brandt]
[William Eugene Smith]
[Men, women and children in George's photographs]
[Fashion Students, Hollings College]
[Anita Ekberg]
[Gina Lollabrigida]
[Anna Magnani]
[Audrey Hepburn]
[Tommy's mother, father and grandmother]
[Elephant Keeper 1960]
[Elegant Woman with Gloves, photographed by George]
[Children sailing toy boats in Philips Park]
[Gardeners, park keepers, councillors, former colleagues of Jabez]
[Alan Jay Lerner]
[Squadron Leader Roger Tipp, Black Arrows]
[Black Arrows]
[Tired mother, father and small child with a balloon]

Acknowledgements
(for Ornaments of Grace as a whole)

Writing is usually considered to be a solitary practice, but I have always found the act of creativity to be a collaborative one, and that has again been true for me in putting together the sequence of novels which comprise *Ornaments of Grace*. I have been fortunate to have been supported by so many people along the way, and I would like to take this opportunity of thanking them all, with apologies for any I may have unwittingly omitted.

First of all I would like to thank Ian Hopkinson, Larysa Bolton, Tony Lees and other staff members of Manchester's Central Reference Library, who could not have been more helpful and encouraging. That is where the original spark for the novels was lit and it has been such a treasure trove of fascinating information ever since. I would like to thank Jane Parry, the Neighbourhood Engagement & Delivery Officer for the Archives & Local History Dept of Manchester Library Services for her support in enabling me to use individual reproductions of the remarkable Manchester Murals by Ford Madox Brown, which can be viewed in the Great Hall of Manchester Town Hall. They are exceptional images and I recommend you going to see them if you are ever in the vicinity. I would also like to thank the staff of other libraries and museums in Manchester, namely the John Rylands Library, Manchester University Library, the Manchester Museum, the People's History Museum and also Salford's Working Class Movement Library, where Lynette Cawthra was especially helpful, as was Aude Nguyen Duc at The Manchester Literary & Philosophical Society, the much-loved Lit& Phil, the first and oldest such society anywhere in the world, 238 years young and still going strong.

In addition to these wonderful institutions, I have many individuals to thank also. Barbara Derbyshire from the Moravian Settlement in Fairfield has been particularly patient and generous with her time in telling me so much of the community's inspiring history. No less inspiring has been Lauren Murphy, founder of the Bradford Pit Project, which is a most moving collection of anecdotes, memories, reminiscences, artefacts and original art works dedicated to the lives of people connected with Bradford Colliery. You can find out more about their work at: www.bradfordpit.com. Martin Gittins freely shared some of his encyclopaedic knowledge of the part the River Irwell has played in Manchester's story, for which I have been especially grateful.

I should also like to thank John and Anne Horne for insights into historical medical practice; their daughter, Ella, for inducting me into the mysteries of chemical titration, which, if I have subsequently got it wrong, is my fault not hers; Tony Smith for his deep first hand understanding of spinning and weaving; Sarah Lawrie for inducting me so enthusiastically into the Manchester music scene of the 1980s, which happened just after I left the city so I missed it; Sylvia Tiffin for her previous research into Manchester's lost theatres, and Brian Hesketh for his specialist knowledge in a range of such diverse topics as hot air balloons, how to make a crystal radio set, old maps, the intricacies of a police constable's notebook and preparing reports for a coroner's inquest.

Throughout this intensive period of writing and research, I have been greatly buoyed up by the keen support and interest of many friends, most notably Theresa Beattie, Laïla Diallo, Viv Gordon, Phil King, Rowena Price, Gavin Stride, Chris Waters, and Irene Willis. Thank you to you all. In addition, Sue & Rob Yockney have been extraordinarily helpful in more ways than I can mention. Their advice on so many matters, both artistic and practical, has been beyond measure.

A number of individuals have very kindly – and bravely – offered to read early drafts of the novels: Bill Bailey, Rachel Burn, Lucy Cash, Chris & Julie Phillips. Their responses have been positive, constructive, illuminating and encouraging, particularly when highlighting those passages which needed closer attention from me, which I have tried my best to address. Thank you.

I would also like to pay a special tribute to my friend Andrew Pastor, who has endured months and months of fortnightly coffee sessions during which he has listened so keenly and with such forbearance to the various difficulties I may have been experiencing at the time. He invariably came up with the perfect comment or idea, which then enabled me to see more clearly a way out of whatever tangle I happened to have found myself in. He also suggested several avenues of further research I might undertake to navigate towards the next bend in one of the three rivers, all of which have been just what were needed. These books could not have finally seen the light of day without his irreplaceable input.

Finally I would like to thank my wife, Amanda, for her endless patience, encouragement and love. These books are dedicated to her and to our son, Tim.

Biography

Chris grew up in Manchester and currently lives in West Dorset, after brief periods in Nottinghamshire, Devon and Brighton. Over the years he has managed to reinvent himself several times – from florist's delivery van driver to Punch & Judy man, drama teacher, theatre director, community arts co-ordinator, creative producer, to his recent role as writer and dramaturg for choreographers and dance companies.

Between 2003 and 2009 Chris was Director of Dance and Theatre for *Take Art*, the arts development agency for Somerset, and between 2009 and 2013 he enjoyed two stints as Creative Producer with South East Dance leading on their Associate Artists programme, followed by a year similarly supporting South Asian dance artists for *Akademi* in London. From 2011 to 2017 he was Creative Producer for the Bonnie Bird Choreography Fund.

Chris has worked for many years as a writer and theatre director, most notably with New Perspectives in Nottinghamshire and Farnham Maltings in Surrey under the artistic direction of Gavin Stride, with whom Chris has been a frequent collaborator.

Directing credits include: three Community Plays for the Colway Theatre Trust – *The Western Women* (co-director with Ann Jellicoe), *Crackling Angels* (co-director with Jon Oram), and *The King's Shilling*; for New Perspectives – *It's A Wonderful Life* (co-director with Gavin Stride), *The Railway Children* (both adapted by Mary Elliott Nelson); for Farnham Maltings – *The Titfield Thunderbolt, Miracle on 34th Street* and *How To Build A Rocket* (all co-directed with Gavin Stride); for Oxfordshire Touring Theatre Company – *Bowled A Googly* by Kevin Dyer; for Flax 303 – *The Rain Has Voices* by Shiona Morton, and for Strike A Light *I Am Joan* and *Prescribed*, both written by Viv Gordon and co-directed with Tom Roden, and *The Book of Jo* as dramaturg.

Theatre writing credits include: *Firestarter, Trying To Get Back Home, Heroes* – a trilogy of plays for young people in partnership with Nottinghamshire & Northamptonshire Fire Services; *You Are Harry Kipper & I Claim My Five Pounds, It's Not Just The Jewels, Bogus* and *One of Us* (the last co-written with Gavin Stride) all for New Perspectives; *The Birdman* for Blunderbus; for Farnham Maltings *How To Build A Rocket* (as assistant to Gavin Stride), and *Time to Remember* (an outdoor commemoration of the centenary of the first ever Two Minutes Silence); *When King Gogo Met The Chameleon* and *Africarmen* for Tavaziva Dance, and most recently *All the Ghosts Walk with Us* (conceived and performed with Laïla Diallo and Phil King) for ICIA, Bath University and Bristol Old Vic Ferment Festival, (2016-17); *Posting to Iraq* (performed by Sarah Lawrie with music by Tom Johnson for the inaugural Women & War Festival in London 2016), and *Tree House* (with music by Sarah Moody, which toured southern England in autumn 2016). In 2018 Chris was commissioned to write the text for *In Our Time*, a film to celebrate the 40th Anniversary of the opening of The Brewhouse Theatre in Taunton, Somerset.

Between 2016 and 2019 Chris collaborated with fellow poet Chris Waters and Jazz saxophonist Rob Yockney to develop two touring programmes of poetry, music, photography and film: *Home Movies* and *Que Pasa?*

Chris regularly works with choreographers and dance artists, offering dramaturgical support and business advice. These have included among others: Alex Whitley, All Play, Ankur Bahl, Antonia Grove, Anusha Subramanyam, Archana Ballal, Ballet Boyz, Ben Duke, Ben Wright, Charlie Morrissey,

Crystal Zillwood, Darkin Ensemble, Divya Kasturi, Dog Kennel Hill, f.a.b. the detonators, Fionn Barr Factory, Heather Walrond, Hetain Patel, Influx, Jane Mason, Joan Clevillé, Kali Chandrasegaram, Kamala Devam, Karla Shacklock, Khavita Kaur, Laïla Diallo, Lîla Dance, Lisa May Thomas, Liz Lea, Lost Dog, Lucy Cash, Luke Brown, Marisa Zanotti, Mark Bruce, Mean Feet Dance, Nicola Conibère, Niki McCretton, Nilima Devi, Pretty Good Girl, Probe, Rachael Mossom, Richard Chappell, Rosemary Lee, Sadhana Dance, Seeta Patel, Shane Shambhu, Shobana Jeyasingh, Showmi Das, State of Emergency, Stop Gap, Subathra Subramaniam, Tavaziva Dance, Tom Sapsford, Theo Clinkard, Urja Desai Thakore, Vidya Thirunarayan, Viv Gordon, Yael Flexer, Yorke Dance Project (including the Cohan Collective) and Zoielogic.

Chris is married to Amanda Fogg, a former dance practitioner working principally with people with Parkinson's.

Printed in Great Britain
by Amazon